More praise for *A Conspiracy of Paper*

"A tale of eighteenth-century finance, murder, and religion that is a remarkable debut and a thoroughly satisfying novel."
—ARTHUR GOLDEN
Author of *Memoirs of a Geisha*

"An old-fashioned detective story, with London's teeming streets and taverns as its backdrop. . . . An artfully constructed potboiler: the sort of thing that would make a good 'Mystery!' series on PBS."
—*The New Yorker*

"*A Conspiracy of Paper* is exciting, intelligent, and witty—a rare combination in historical novels. It is rich in intriguing detail and peopled with fascinating characters. Recommended enthusiastically."
—JOHN JAKES
Author of *American Dreams*

"A well-researched and highly entertaining historical mystery . . . [A] tale of financial skullduggery and multiple murder . . . Conveyed in vivid extended scenes characterized by crisp dialogue and a keen sense of the ways in which character reveals itself . . . The very model of a modern historical mystery."
—*Kirkus Reviews* (starred review)

"Terrific . . . Set in a vividly realized eighteenth-century London . . . Although a financial boom fueled by a new economy or a personal struggle with ethnic identity may seem awfully contemporary, Liss keeps us firmly in another time. . . . The book crackles with period detail, yet the immense research never shows. . . . One can only hope that Liss isn't finished with Benjamin Weaver."
—*Booklist*

A
CONSPIRACY
OF PAPER

A Novel

David Liss

Ballantine Books
New York

A Conspiracy
of Paper

ONE

FOR SOME YEARS NOW, the gentlemen of the book trade have pressed me in the most urgent fashion to commit my memoirs to paper; for, these men have argued, there are many who would gladly pay a few shillings to learn of the true and surprising adventures of my life. While it has been my practice to dismiss this idea with a casual wave of the hand, I cannot claim to have never seriously thought on it, for I have often been the first to congratulate myself on having seen and experienced so much, and many times have I gladly shared my stories with good company around a cleared dinner table. Nevertheless, there is a difference between tales told over a late-night bottle of claret and a book that any man anywhere can pick up and examine. Certainly I have taken pleasure from the idea of recounting my history, but I have also recognized that to publish would be a ticklish endeavor—the names and specifics of my adventures would touch nearly on so many people still living that any such book would be actionable to say the least. Yet the idea has intrigued—even plagued—me, no doubt due to the vanity that breeds within all men's breasts, and perhaps within mine more than most. I have therefore decided to write this book as I see fit. If the gentlemen of Grub Street wish to dash out names of obscure connections, then they may do so. For my part, I shall retain the manuscript so that there can be some true record of these events, if not for this age, then for posterity.

I have been at some pains to decide how to begin, for I have seen many things of interest to the general public. Shall I begin like the novelists, with my birth, or like the poets, in the midst of the action? Perhaps neither. I think I shall begin my tale with the day—now more than thirty-five years ago—when I met William Balfour, for it is the matter regarding his father's death that brought me some small measure of success and recognition with the public. Until now, however, few men have known the whole truth behind that affair.

Mr. Balfour first called on me late one morning in October of 1719, a year of much turmoil upon this island—the nation lived in constant fear of the French and their support for the heir to the deposed King James, whose Jacobitical followers threatened continually to retake the British monarchy. Our German King was but four years upon the throne, and the power struggles within his ministry created a feeling of chaos throughout the capital. All the newspapers decried the burden of the nation's debt, which they said could never be paid, but that debt showed no sign of decreasing. This era was one of exuberance as well as turmoil, doom, and possibility. It was a fine time for a man whose livelihood depended upon crime and confusion.

Matters of national politics held little interest for me, however, and the only debt I cared for was my own. And the day I begin my tale I had even more pressing cares than my precarious finances. I had been long awake, but only recently out of bed and dressed, when my landlady, Mrs. Garrison, informed me that there was a Christian gentleman below who wished to see me. My good landlady always felt the need to specify that it was a *Christian* gentleman come to visit, though in the months I had resided with her, no Jew but myself had ever entered her premises.

That morning I found myself disordered and in no condition to receive visitors, let alone strangers, so I asked Mrs. Garrison to send him away, but in her intrepid manner—for Mrs. Garrison was a stalwart creature—she returned, informing me that the gentleman's business was urgent. "He says it relates to a murder," she told me in the same dull tone she used to announce increases in my rent. Her pallid and beveined face hardened to show her displeasure. "That's what he said—*murder*—plain as anything. I cannot say it pleases me, Mr. Weaver, to have men come to my house talking of *murder*."

I could not fully comprehend why, if the word was so distasteful to her ears, she should pronounce it quite so loudly within the halls, but I saw my task was to comfort her. "I quite understand, madam. The gentleman surely said 'mercer' and not 'murder,' " I lied, "for I am engaged in a concern of textiles at this moment. Please send him up."

The word *murder* had caught my attention as well as Mrs. Garrison's. Having been involved in a murder of sorts not twelve hours earlier, I thought this matter might concern me indeed. This Balfour would certainly be a scavenger of some kind—the sort of desperate *renegado* with which London seethed, a creature who combed the dank and filthy streets near the river, hunting for anything he might pawn, including information. No doubt he had heard something of the unfortunate adventure with which I had met and had come to ask me to pay for his silence. I knew well how to dispose of a man of this stripe. Not with money, certainly, for to give a rascal any silver at all was to encourage him to return for more. No, I had found that in these cases violence usually did my business. I would think of something bloodless—something that would not attract Mrs. Garrison's attention when I escorted the blackguard out. A woman with no taste for the talk of murder under her roof should hardly countenance an act of mutilation paraded down her staircase.

I took a moment to order my receiving room, as I called it. I took two rooms of Mrs. Garrison, one private, the other in which I conducted my business. Like many businessmen—for so I fancied myself, even then—I had been used to order my affairs in a local coffeehouse, but the delicate nature of my work had made such public venues unacceptable to the men I served. Instead, I had set up a room with several comfortable chairs, a table around which to sit, and a handsome set of shelves that I used to store wine and cheese rather than the books for which they were designed. Mrs. Garrison had done the decorating, and while she had given the room an inappropriately cheery tone with its pinkish-white paint and light blue curtains, I found that a few swords and martial prints about the walls helped to add a sufficiently manly corrective.

I took pride in these rooms being so very proper, for the genteel tone put the gentlemen who came to seek my services at ease. My trade frequently involved the unsavory, and gentlemen, I had learned, preferred the illusion that they dealt in simple business—nothing more.

I should like to add, though I risk accusations of vanity, I took pride in my own appearance as well. I had escaped my years as a pugilist with few of the badges that gave fellow-veterans of the ring the appearance of ruffians—missing eyes, mashed noses, or suchlike disfigurements—and had no more to show for my beatings than some small scars about my face and a nose that bore only the mild bumps and jagged edges that come with several breakings. Indeed, I fancied myself a well-enough-looking man, and I made a point of always dressing neatly, if modestly. I wore upon my body only clean shirts, and none of my coats and waistcoats were more than a year old. Nevertheless, I was none of your sprightly popinjays who wore the latest bright colors and frills; a man of my trade always prefers simple fashions that draw to himself no particular attention.

I seated myself at my large oaken writing desk, which faced the door. I used this desk when I ordered my affairs, but I had discovered that it served to make clear my authority. I thus picked up a pen and contorted the muscles in my face to resemble something like a man both busy and irritated.

When Mrs. Garrison showed this visitor in, however, I was at pains to conceal my surprise. William Balfour was no prig—as we called thieves in those days—but a gentleman of fine dress and appearance. He was perhaps five years younger than myself: I gauged him at two- or three-and-twenty. He was a tall, gaunt, stooped man with something of a sunken look on a wide, handsome face that was only slightly marred by the scars of smallpox. He wore a wig of the first quality, but it showed its age and wear in its stains and a dingy sallow color poorly hidden by powder. Similarly, his clothes bore the signs of fine tailoring, but they looked a bit overused, covered with the dust of road and panic and cheap lodgings. His waistcoat in particular, once laced with fine silver stuff, was now tattered and threadbare. There was, too, something in his eyes. I could not tell if it was suspicion or fatigue or defeat, and he observed me with a skepticism to which I was all too accustomed. Most men who walk through that door, you understand, had a look prepared for me—scorn, doubt, superiority. A few even had admiration. Men of this last category had seen me in my prime as a pugilist, and their love of sport overcame their embarrassment at seeking the aid of a Jew who meddled in other men's unpleasantries. This Balfour looked at me as neither Jew nor pugilist, but as something else—something of no consequence whatsoever, almost as though I were the servant who should take him to the man he sought.

"Sir," I said, standing up as Mrs. Garrison closed the door behind her. I gave Balfour a short bow, which he returned with a wooden resignation. After offering him a seat before my desk, I returned to my chair and informed him I awaited his commands.

He hesitated before stating his business, taking a moment to study my features—I should say gawk at my features, for he regarded me as more spectacle than man. His eye roamed with clear disapproval at my face and clothing (though both were cleaner and neater than his own), and squinted at my hair; for, unlike a proper gentleman, I wore no peruke, and instead pulled my locks back in the style of a tie-periwig.

"You, I presume, are Benjamin Weaver," he began at last in a voice that cracked with uncertainty. He hardly noticed my nod of acknowledgment. "I come on a serious matter. I am not pleased to be forced to seek your peculiar skills, but I require the assistance that only a man such as yourself can provide." He shifted uneasily in his chair, and I wondered if Mr. Balfour was not what he claimed—if he were perhaps a man of a much lower order than he affected, masquerading as a gentleman. There was, after all, the *murder* he had spoken of to Mrs. Garrison, but I now could not but wonder if the murder he mentioned was the one that so plagued my own thoughts.

"I hope I am able to be of some assistance to you," I said, with practiced civility. I laid down my pen and cocked my head slightly to show him that I put my full attention at his disposal.

His hands shook distractingly while he studied his fingernails with unconvincing indifference. "Yes, it is an unpleasant business, so I am sure you are quite equal to the task."

I offered him a brief bow from my chair and told him he was too kind or some other like platitude, but he hardly noticed what I said. Despite his attempts to perform a sort of fashionable lassitude, he appeared for all the world like a man on the brink of choking, as though his collar tightened about his throat. He bit his lip. He looked about the room, eyes darting here and there.

"Sir," I said, "you will forgive me if I note that you appear a little discomposed. Can I offer you a glass of port?"

My words all but slapped him in the face, and he collected himself once again to the posture of an insouciant buck. "I must imagine that there are less presumptuous ways for you to inquire into a gentleman's distresses. Nevertheless, I shall take a drink of whatever quality you have upon you."

It was not out of deference that I allowed Balfour to insult me freely. Once I had established myself in my trade, it took no great amount of time to learn that men of birth or standing had a profound need to demonstrate their superiority—not to the man they hired to meddle in their private business, but to the business itself. I could not take Balfour's freedoms personally, for they were not directed at me. I also knew that once I had effectively served such a man, the memory of his discourteous behavior often inspired him to pay promptly and to recommend my skills to his acquaintances. I therefore tossed off Mr. Balfour's insults as a bear tosses off the dogs sent to bait it in Hockley-in-the-Hole. I poured his wine and returned to my desk.

He took a sip. "I am not discomposed," he assured me. If the quality of my drink pleasantly surprised my guest, as I expected it should, he thought this fact not worth mentioning. "I am certainly tired from a poor night's rest, and indeed"—he paused to look at me pointedly—"I am in mourning for my father, who died not two months ago."

I offered my apologies and then startled myself by telling him that I too had recently lost a father.

Balfour astonished me in return by telling me that he knew of my father's death. "Your father, sir, and my own were acquaintances. They did business together, you know, at times when my father had the need to call on a man of your father's . . . sort."

I would like to believe that I showed no surprise, but I doubt it was so. My given name is not Weaver, but Lienzo. Few men were familiar with my true name, so I could not have anticipated that this man would know the identity of my father. I could not guess what else Balfour knew of me, but I asked no questions. I only nodded slowly.

I was now thoroughly confused as to what this man wanted, for it was perfectly plain that he had not come regarding my unfortunate affair of the previous night. As I mulled over my many uncertainties, it occurred to me that I vaguely recalled Balfour's father. I remembered hearing my father speak of him—he had said only good things of the man, for they had been closer, I think, than simple acquaintances, though to call them friends would have been exaggerating the possibilities of their interaction. I remembered Balfour's father, where I might have forgotten the numerous other men with whom my own father did business, for it was unusual for him to have been on such familiar terms with a Christian gentleman. I had not recalled, however, my father's association with this man when I read in the papers of Michael Balfour's self-murder. He had been a wealthy merchant, and, like many men of business who took risks, he had suffered drastic financial reversals. His particular reversals had been severe; he had lost more than everything on a series of bad ventures, and unable to face his creditors with his insolvency, or his family with the shame of his ruin, he had hanged himself in his stables. This act he had committed not twenty-four hours before my father's own death.

"Is it then through your father that you learned of my services?" I asked Balfour. It was an irrelevant question—at least to Mr. Balfour's concerns. I wished to know if my father had spoken of me—indeed if he had spoken approvingly of me—to his colleagues and business associates. Much to my own astonishment, I felt myself hoping that Balfour had knowledge that my father had, in some way, respected the life I had made for myself.

Balfour quickly disabused me of these fictions. "The recommendation comes not so directly. I had certainly heard your name in the past—in the same connotation, you understand, as one hears of ropedancers and raree-shows and that sort of thing—but recently I found myself in a coffeehouse, when I heard a gentleman mention your name. A friend of his, a Sir Owen Nettleton, had engaged you in a matter of business and believed you to be competent—a rating of sufficient merit in this age. I then conceived of the idea that your services might be of some use to me."

I often marveled that London, for so enormous a city, is sometimes astonishingly small. Among countless thousands, these kinds of interactions occur almost daily, for men of like nature and like concerns congregated inevitably at the same clubs and taverns and coffeehouses and tea gardens. I had indeed served Sir Owen Nettleton, and his concerns very much occupied my thoughts that morning, but I shall discuss more of him below.

Balfour finished his port with a mighty gulp and looked straight into my eyes with an intensity that suggested a mustering of forces. "Mr. Weaver, I shall be direct with you. My father, sir, was murdered. I believe by the same person or persons who murdered your father."

I could not even think how to react. My father had been killed, certainly, but not murdered, some two months earlier—a drunken coachman had run him down as he crossed Threadneedle Street. The business had been shrouded with a kind of uncertainty. How reckless had the coachman been? Had my father stepped blindly in his way? Could it have been avoided? All answerless questions, the magistrate determined. The coachman, while negligent, had acted without malicious intention, and could have had no reason to want to do harm to my father. The same act perpetrated against an earl or a Parliamentarian might have earned the coachman, at the very least, seven years of transportation to the colonies, but the careless trampling of a Jewish stock-jobber was hardly a matter over which to unfurl the full majesty of the law. The magistrate released the coachman with a stern warning, and that had proved the legal end of the matter.

At that time I had not spoken to my father for close to ten years. I knew nearly nothing of his affairs, and it had hardly occurred to me that his death might have been anything as horrid as murder. This thought had, however, occurred to my father's kinsman, my Uncle Miguel, who had written to inform me of his suspicions. I blush to own I rewarded his efforts to seek my opinion with only a formal reply in which I dismissed his ideas as nonsensical. I did so in part because I did not wish to involve myself with my family and in part because I knew that my uncle, for reasons that eluded me, had loved my father and could not accept the senselessness of so random a death. Yet now, once again, I was confronted with the suggestion that my father had been the victim of a malicious crime, and once again I found that my self-imposed exile from my family made me wish to disbelieve it.

I forced my face to conform to the rigid angles of impartiality. "My father's death was an unfortunate accident." Balfour knew more about my family than I knew about his, and I saw that as a disadvantage, so, already in an agitated state of mind, I proceeded at the slowest of paces. "And if I may be so indelicate, the papers reported your father's death as something other than murder."

Balfour held up his hand, as though the idea of self-murder might be ordered away. "I know what the papers reported," he snapped, spittle flying from his mouth, "and I know what the coroner said, yet I promise you something is amiss here. At the time of my father's death, his estate was revealed to be quite broken, yet only weeks before he told me himself that he had been profiting in his speculation, taking advantage of the fluctuation in the markets caused by the rivalries between the Bank of England and the South Sea Company. I had no desire to see him meddling in the affairs of 'Change Alley, buying and selling stocks in the manner of—well, in the manner of your people, Weaver—but he believed there were ample opportunities for a man who kept his wits about him. So how can it be that his finances were so"—he paused briefly to choose his terms—"ill ordered. Do you think it any coincidence that both our fathers, very rich men of acquaintance, should have died suddenly and mysteriously within the span of a single day, and my father's holdings reveal themselves to be in chaos?"

As he spoke, Balfour's face revealed no small number of passions: indignity, disgust, discomfort, even, I believe, shame. I thought it passing strange that a man out to expose so terrible a crime displayed no attitudes of outrage.

The claims he made, however, sparked within me an agitation, which I sought to contain by setting my mind to the facts before me. "What you present does not offer any kind of evidence of murder," I said after a moment. "I cannot see how you have reached this conclusion."

"My father's death was made to look like self-murder so that a villain or villains could take his money with impunity," he pronounced, as though he unveiled a discovery of natural philosophy.

"You believe his estate to have been robbed, and your father to have been murdered to hide this robbery?"

"In a word, sir, yes. That is what I believe." Balfour's features settled, for a brief moment, into a look of languid contentment. Then he eyed his empty wineglass with nervous longing. I obliged him by refilling.

I paced about the room, despite the distracting ache of an old wound in my leg—a wound that had ended my days as a pugilist. "What is the connection between these deaths, then, sir? My father's estate is solvent."

"But is anything missing? Do you even know, sir?"

I did not, so I ignored what I considered a presumptuous question. "It is in your best interest that I be blunt. Your father has died recently, under terrible conditions, and unable to leave a legacy. You have grown up with the expectation of wealth and privilege, with every reason to believe you would live a gentleman's life of ease. Now you find your dreams dashed, and you look for ways to believe it is not so."

Balfour reddened dramatically. I suspect he was unused to challenges, particularly challenges from men such as myself. "I resent your words, Weaver. My family may be under disabilities at this moment, but you would do well to remember that I am a gentleman born."

"As I am," I said, looking directly into his reddish eyes. It was a harsh blow. His family was an upstart, and he knew it. He had earned that most ambiguous title of *gentleman* through his father's aggressive dealings as a tobacco merchant, not through the majesty of his bloodlines. Indeed, I recalled that old Balfour had made a bit of a stir among the more established tobacco merchants by angering the men he hired to unload his vessels.

Dock laborers have, by custom, always been given scant wages, and they have evened out their earnings through a kind of quiet redistribution of the goods they handle. For vessels carrying tobacco, the process is known as "socking"; the laborers merely plunge their hands into the bales of tobacco, sock away as much as they can hold and then resell it on their own. True enough it was a kind of sanctioned theft, but years ago tobacco merchants had realized that their porters were helping themselves to the cargo despite any measures meant to prevent them, so they simply cut the wages and looked the other way.

Old Balfour, however, had taken the unhappy step of hiring men to inspect the workers and make sure no one socked his goods, but he refused to raise wages proportionately. The laborers had grown violent—smashing open several bales of sot weed and boldly liberating their contents. Old Balfour only relented once his brother merchants convinced him that to pursue this mad course was to risk riot and destruction of all their trades.

That this merchant's son should assert that his was an old family was patently absurd—it was not even an old *trading* family. And while in those days there was, as there is now, something decidedly English about a wealthy merchant, it was a relatively new and uncertain assertion that the son of such a man could claim the status of *gentleman*. My declaration that our families were of a piece sent him into a kind of fit. He blinked as though trying to dispel a vision, and twitched irritably until he regained himself.

"I think it no coincidence that my father's killers made his death appear self-murder, for it makes all ashamed to discuss it. But I am not ashamed. You think me now penniless, and you think I come to you begging for your help like a pauper, but you know nothing of me. I shall pay you twenty pounds to look into this matter for one week." He paused so I might have time to reflect on so large a sum. "That I should have to pay you anything to uncover the truth behind your own father's murder is the more shame for you, but I cannot answer for your sentiments."

I studied his face, looking for signs of I'm not sure what—deceit, self-doubt, fear? I saw only an anxious determination. I no longer questioned that he was who he claimed to be. He was an unpleasant man; I knew that I disliked him immensely, and I was certain that he felt no love for me, yet I could not deny my interest in what he claimed about my father's death.

"Mr. Balfour, did anyone see what you claim to be this falsification of self-murder?"

He waved his hands in the air to demonstrate the foolishness of my question. "I do not know that anyone did."

I pressed on. "Have you heard talk, sir?"

He stared at me in astonishment, as though I had spoken gibberish. "From whom would I? Do you think me the sort to correspond with men who would talk of such things?"

I sighed. "Then I am confused. How can I find the man who committed a crime if you have no witnesses and no contacts? Into what, precisely, am I to look?"

"I do not know your business, Weaver. It seems to me that you are being damnably obtuse. You have brought men to justice before—how you have done it then, you are to do it now."

I attempted a polite, and I admit, condescending smile. "When I have brought men to justice in the past, sir, it has been in instances wherein someone knew the villain's identity, and the task lay before me to locate him. Or perhaps there has been a crime in which the scoundrel is unknown, but witnesses saw that he had some very distinctive features—let us say a scar above his right eye and a missing thumb. With information of this nature, I can ask questions of the sort of people who might know this man and thus learn his name, his habits, and finally his whereabouts. But if the first step is your belief, what is the second step? Who are the right people to inquire of next?"

"I am shocked to hear of your methods, Weaver." He paused for a moment, perhaps to drive home his distaste. "I cannot tell you of second steps nor of which rascals are appropriate for you to speak with regarding my father's murder. Your business is your own, but I should think you would consider the matter of sufficient interest to take of me twenty pounds."

I was silent for some time. I wanted nothing so much as to send the man away, for I had always been willing to go considerable lengths to avoid contact with my family. Yet twenty pounds was no small amount to me, and while I dreaded the terrible day of reckoning, I knew I needed some external force to push me toward reestablishing contact with those whom I had long neglected. And there was more: though I could not then have explained why, the idea of looking into a matter so opaque intrigued me, for it occurred to me that Balfour, despite the bluster with which he presented his notions, was right. Had there been a crime committed, it seemed only reasonable that it could be uncovered, and I liked the thought of what a success in an inquiry of this nature could do for my reputation.

"I expect soon another visitor," I said at last. "And I am very busy." He started to speak, but I would not let him. "I shall look into this matter, Mr. Balfour. How could I not? But I have not the time to look into this matter right away. If your father has been killed, then there must be some reason why. If it is theft, we must know more details of the theft. I wish you to go inquire as nearly as you can into his matters. Speak to his friends, relatives, employees, and whomever else you think might perhaps harbor some of the same suspicions. Let me know where I can find you, and in a few days' time I shall call on you."

"For what shall I pay you, Weaver, if I am to do your work for you?"

My smile this time was less benign. "You are, of course, right. When I am at liberty, I shall speak to your father's family, friends, and employees. That they do not dismiss me, I shall be certain to tell them that you have sent me to ask questions of them. You might wish to inform them in advance to expect a Jew by the name of Weaver to inquire closely into family matters."

"I cannot have you bothering these people," he stammered. "Gad, to have you asking questions of my mother . . ."

"Then perhaps, as I suggested, you would like to look into this yourself."

Balfour stood up, performing gentlemanly composure. "I see you are a clever maneuverer. I shall make some discreet inquiries. But I expect to hear from you shortly."

I neither spoke nor moved, but Balfour took no notice, and within an instant he was gone from my rooms. For some time I remained motionless. I thought on what had transpired and what it might mean, and then I reached for the bottle of port.

Two

M Y BUSINESS IN those days was new—I had not quite two years' experience and I still struggled to learn the secrets of my trade. I had fought my last pitched battle as a pugilist some five years earlier, when I was not more than three-and-twenty. After that line of work had come to so violent a conclusion, I had found various means of maintaining a livelihood, or perhaps I should say of surviving. Of most of these vocations I am not proud, but they taught me much that later proved useful. I was some time employed upon a cutter making the run between the south of England and France, but this ship, as my perceptive readers will guess, was not of His Majesty's navy. After our captain's arrest on charges of smuggling, I drifted from place to place, and even, I blush to own, took up the life of a housebreaker, and then a gentleman of the highway. Pursuits of this nature, while exciting, are rarely profitable, and one grows weary of seeing a friend with the noose around his neck. So I made vows and promises, and I returned to London to seek some sort of honest living.

It is a shame that I did not anticipate the pugilists of today who, like the famous Jack Broughton, in their retirement open fighting academies to train the young bucks that would take their place. Broughton has indeed been ingenious enough to construct a piece of apparel he calls mufflers— a kind of voluptuous padding for the fist. I have seen these things, and I suspect to be hit by a man wearing these gloves is quite like not being hit at all.

I was much less clever than Broughton, and had no ideas of such ambitions, but I did have a few ill-gotten pounds in my pocket, and I besought a partner with whom to open an alehouse or some business of that nature. It was at this time, walking to my lodgings late in the night, that I had the good fortune to offer assistance to an old fellow besieged by a band of wealthy young bucks. These aristocratic ruffians, known as they were in those days as Mohocks—a name that gave insult to the honorable savages of the Americas—loved nothing more than to roam the London streets, tormenting those poorer than themselves by hacking away at their limbs, cutting off ears or noses, rolling old ladies down hills, and even, if rarely, reveling in the most permanent crime of murder.

I had read of these arrogant puppies and had longed for an opportunity to inflict some of their violence back upon them, so I know not if it was my hatred for the privilege these men thought belonged to them, or the kindly concern I felt for an old victim, that brought me into the fray. I can only say that when I saw the scene before me, I acted without hesitation.

Four Mohocks, dressed in satin and lace finery, and wearing the masks of Italian revelers, gathered around an elderly fellow who had crumpled upon the street and sat like a grotesque sort of child with his legs folded. His wig had been removed and cast aside, and a thin stream of blood trickled down from a gash upon his head. The Mohocks tittered, and one made a slurred joke in Latin, which brought the others to uproarious hilarity.

"Now," one of them said to the old man, "you must make the choice yourself." He drew his hangar and sliced through the air with the practiced ease of a sword-master before thrusting the point of the weapon in the man's face. "Do you wish to lose an ear or the tip of your nose? Make up your mind soon, or you'll get both prizes for your efforts."

For a moment there was no sound but this besieged man's gasping breaths and the trickle of city filth running down the kennel ditch in the center of the street.

The break in my leg that ended my career in the ring left me without the endurance of a pugilist, but I was still more than equal to the task of a short-lived street brawl. The Mohocks were too drunk with cruelty, and wine as well, to notice my presence, so I rushed to the victim's assistance, immediately dispatching one of the bucks with a fierce blow to the back of his neck. Before his companions even knew that I had entered the fray, I had grabbed a second villain and thrown him headfirst against the wall—a maneuver that left him unfit for further mischief.

The old man, whom I had believed to be as helpless as a woman, saw the odds suddenly evened, and roused himself to a more manful posture, taking a sharp swing at the assailant who had threatened him with the hangar, knocking the long and elegant blade from his hand and sending it clattering into the darkness. I now matched fists with one of the two men who remained in the battle, while my companion, who must have drawn power from his indignation, took a few mighty blows upon his face but bravely withstood the pain. Blood flowed freely from a fresh cut above his left eye, yet he proved a spirited warrior and remained in the game long enough that a parish watchman, lantern raised, appeared at the end of the street. The Mohocks, spotting this guardian, chose to discontinue their sport, and the two upright villains gathered their fallen comrades and hobbled off to tend their wounds and invent stories that might account for their bruises.

As the watchman neared, I approached my fellow-battler, and held his shoulders to steady him. Through tired eyes, made hazy with blood and perspiration, he stared hard and then offered me an exuberant grin. "Benjamin Weaver," he spouted. "The Lion of Judah! Why, I never thought I'd see you fight again. And certainly not at this proximity."

"Nor did I plan to," I said, catching my breath. "But I am glad to have been of some service to a man in distress."

"Gladder than you know," he assured me, "for I should be damned for a servant of Satan himself if I did not reward your valor as it deserves. Give me your hand, sir." This unfortunate now introduced himself as Hosea Bohun, and begged that I come to see him the next day that he might do me some small service to show his gratitude. By that time the watchman had reached us—a scraggly fellow, hardly fit for his duties. Having lost the assailants, the watchman thought it a very fine idea to carry the victims to the Compter as punishment for being out upon the street after curfew, but Mr. Bohun made liberal application of the names of his friends, including the Lord Mayor, and sent the watchman on his way.

The next day I discovered that I had been lucky enough to give vital aid to an opulently wealthy East India merchant, and at Mr. Bohun's splendid town house, this grateful man rewarded me with a sum no smaller than a hundred pounds, and a promise to be of service to me if he ever had occasion. And indeed he was of service to me, for the story of how he had been set upon by Mohocks, and how he had been lucky enough to battle them with Benjamin Weaver by his side, made its way into the papers.

Soon thereafter I had visits from other men—some genteel, some poor, but all with offers to pay me for my skills. One gentleman planned a trip to his country estate, and he wished me to ride along to protect him and his goods from highwaymen. Another man was a shopkeeper whose premises had regularly been set upon by rascals; he wished me to spend some time in his shop and await the villains, whom I would recompense for their tricks. Yet another wished me to collect a debt of an elusive fellow who had successfully dodged the bailiffs for more than a year's time. Perhaps the most significant request—one that again landed my name in the papers—was from an impoverished woman whose only daughter, not twelve years of age, had been attacked in the most scandalous manner by a sailor. There had been witnesses to the attack, but this woman could neither find them nor learn the whereabouts of the sailor himself. I soon discovered that it was only a small matter to ask questions, to listen to the talkative talk, and to follow trails left by unthinking culprits. This sailor, as my readers may know, was convicted of a rape, and I myself had the pleasure of seeing him hang at Tyburn.

And so began my work as protector, guardian, bailiff, constable-for-hire, and thief-taker. It was this last duty that I had found most lucrative, for by bringing felons to justice I received not only the reward of my hirer but also the considerable forty-pound reward of the state as well. Three or four such bounties over the course of a year amounted to a handsome wage for a man of my station.

I say with some pride that I quickly built a reputation for honesty, for it is well known that thief-takers are in general the most wretched of villains who care not for the guilt or innocence of the poor sod they drag before the magistrate, only for the reward that comes of conviction. When I set up my trade, I let it be known that I would have nothing to do with thief-takers' tricks, and I concerned myself only with capturing villains and with recovering lost goods. I did so not only to avoid running afoul of the law, but so there might be a man that a victim of theft could trust.

To my misfortune, employment as a thief-taker had become scarce at the time I begin my story, for a notorious villain named Jonathan Wild had begun to make a name for himself as Thief-Taker General. Wild appeared to work magic for the countless victims of robberies about London, for he could discover the whereabouts of nearly every thief in the city, and he could recover almost any stolen item. As we know now, and as many of us knew at the time, Jonathan Wild could do all of these things because there was hardly a prig in London who was not in his employ. When a man discovered an article had been stolen, he frequently found it more convenient to pay the same thieves to return the item than to hire a man such as myself who could offer no guarantees of retrieval. Wild never made guarantees, for he posed as a concerned citizen merely offering to help, but I had rarely heard that he failed to recover a stolen item. According to the custom, his victims placed notices in the *Daily Courant* announcing the items they wished recovered. It took no long amount of time for the victim to receive word of Mr. Wild, who would explain that he believed he might be of service if the good gentleman or lady would only be willing to offer the thief half or three-quarters of the value of the stolen item. It was no fair deal, but a fairer one than having to replace the property, so in this way the citizens of London retrieved their lost goods and praised the man who stole them. Wild, in turn, received far more money for his booty than he ever could have hoped for had he fenced it or attempted to resell it himself. He had grown so rich upon this scheme that it was said that he had agents in nearly every town of note in England and that he owned smuggling ships that sailed constantly from these shores to France and Holland and back again, loaded with contraband.

Despite his great success, there were always those who knew Wild for what he was and would do no business with him. Sir Owen Nettleton was such a gentleman; he had come to me with a request only two days before my encounter with Mr. Balfour. Sir Owen was an engaging man, and I took an enormous liking to him immediately. He appeared in my receiving room, proud and jovial, slightly fat and slightly drunk. Some men were ashamed to come see me in my neighborhood—perhaps because Covent Garden was too unfashionable, perhaps because they did not wish publicly to enter the home of a Jew, but Sir Owen was nothing if not open and nothing if not conspicuous. With his unmistakable gold-and-turquoise coach left standing directly in front of Mrs. Garrison's house, he walked in, boldly prepared to give his name to anyone who might request it.

He was near forty, I think, but his clothing and spirit gave him a look of a man at least ten years his junior. He was naught but gay colors and silver thread and fancy embroidery, and his jolly face looked all the more wide and ruddy under the enormous canopy of his perfectly white full-bottom wig. Sitting comfortably in the chair before me, he talked of the gossip of the town and drank the better part of a bottle of Madeira before he even hinted that he had any business with me. Finally, he set down his glass and walked over to the window just behind my chair and peered at the street below. Standing so close to me as he was, I grew lightheaded in the fog of his liberal application of civet perfume.

"It is a fine Sunday afternoon for October, do you not think so? A fine Sunday afternoon."

"It is a fine afternoon," I agreed, by now somewhat eager for Sir Owen to come to his point.

"So fine an afternoon it is," he explained, "that I cannot tell you of my business indoors. We want fresh air, Mr. Weaver, and sunshine, I should think. Let us take a turn about St. James's."

I found his proposal perfectly agreeable, so we headed downstairs, where we subjected ourselves to the baldly curious stares of my land-lady and three of her equally corpulent and bitter friends who sat hunched around a card table, playing at piquet for small stakes. Mrs. Gar-rison's mouth surely dropped as she saw me enter Sir Owen's handsome equipage.

Now, I have lived in London almost all of my life, and I have many times witnessed the spectacle of St. James's Park on a glorious Sunday afternoon, but owing in no small part to the social estrangement that comes with being a Jew of limited means, I had never thought I should someday participate in it. Yet there I was, strolling by the side of a fash-ionable baronet, feeling the sun full on my face as I made my way about the park along with countless fashionable ladies and gentlemen. I flatter myself that I was not swept away by the vivacity of it all, but it was a daz-zling entertainment to witness the bowing and the curtsying, the display of the latest coat styles and hair fashions, of wigs and ribbons and silks and hoops. I think that Sir Owen may have been the perfect man to initi-ate me into this world, for he knew a fair portion of gentlemen and ladies, and he doled out and received his share of bows, but he had not so many acquaintances as to make taking a step impossible. So we strolled among the *beau monde*, the fragile warmth of the dying summer upon us, and Sir Owen told me of his difficulties.

"Weaver," he began as we walked along, "I am not a man to hide his feelings. I shall tell you straight away that I like your looks. You strike me as a man I can trust."

I smiled inwardly at his manner of expressing himself. "I shall in every way attempt to be worthy of that trust."

Sir Owen stopped and glared at my face, moving his head from side to side as he inspected my features. "Yes, I like your looks, Weaver. You dress like a man of sense, and you conduct yourself like a man of sense, too. I might not even know you to be a Jew, though I suppose your nose is perhaps a bit larger than an Englishman would strictly permit—but what of it?"

I resumed our perambulation, hoping movement would bring Sir Owen to a more relevant topic of conversation.

"And you're a game-enough-looking spark," he continued. "I would wager you are a man who likes his pleasures. I can assure you I am. I shall be bold with you. I like gambling, and I like whores. I like whores very much, sir."

Pressed on by his spirit, I said, "And do they like you, Sir Owen?"

For an instant I feared I had offended him, but he burst into a laugh as thick as a dish of chocolate. "They like my money tremendously, Mr. Weaver. I can assure you of that. They like it as much as the masters of the gaming houses. For all men—and women too—like money. I like money," he droned, losing his thoughts as a group of pretty young ladies crossed our path, all a-giggle over a broken parasol.

"As you like whores," I offered in assistance.

He snapped his fingers. "Quite right. Whores. Yes, well my fondness for whores has gotten me into a bit of trouble, I'm afraid." He paused to laugh at a joke he thought of. "But I don't need a surgeon. Not that kind of trouble. Not this time. You see, I had an amorous encounter last night with a whore not content to be a simple whore, not content to earn an honest living for an honest tumble. It seems I took upon myself a bit too much wine, and this little jade took upon herself every possession I had." Sir Owen cut short his narrative to bow deeply to an excessively painted lady who displayed an elaborate dress of greens and yellows and wore her hair piled high, after the Hanoverian style. She took some small notice of the baronet, and continued on her way. Sir Owen then proceeded to explain to me that he had been lured into taking a walk with the whore after, as it happens, he had been weakened with spirits, which he had been encouraged to drink far beyond even his considerable measure. When he awoke in an alleyway, his coat, watch, shoes, sword, purse, and pocketbook had been taken. "I'm not a man who carries a grudge," he assured me. "I am willing to let her keep all—but I must have my pocketbook back. It has much in it that is of value to me—and to me only. It is very important that I retrieve it, and that I do so as soon as possible."

I thought about this for a moment. "Do you know this whore's name or where I might find her?"

He grinned. "When I was a young man, the parish vicar always told me that being a whoremonger would be my undoing, but this is precisely where being a whoremonger has done me service. I know her name, indeed, for I have seen her going about her trade, if before last night I have not had the displeasure of knowing her, shall we say, intimately. I think perhaps in her way of whoring, men seldom return for more. Her name is Kate Cole, and I've seen her many a time at an alehouse called the Barrel and Bale. I believe she takes a room there, but I am not certain."

I nodded. I'd never heard of this whore, but there were thousands of her trade in London. Even a man of Sir Owen's enthusiasm could not expect to know them all. "I shall find your Kate Cole for you, then."

He proceeded to describe her looks to me in great detail—giving me more information than I should necessarily require to find a woman in a full state of dress. "I trust," he then said, lowering his voice, "that I need not discuss discretion with you at any great length. Surely a man in your position understands the needs of a man in my position."

I told him I understood perfectly, though I wondered why he should choose to parade about the park with me if he desired secrecy.

Sir Owen surprised me by guessing my thoughts. "I do not mind that the world knows I've been to see you, or even that I've been to see you for your help in recovering stolen goods. But I would prefer that you say no more. It is none of the world's business what I have had stolen or how I lost it."

"I agree entirely," I told him with a reassuring nod. "I think you will find all men I have dealt with will attest to my discretion."

"Splendid. If men wish to speculate what it is I do with you, let them," he said haughtily. "If they profane my name, they will certainly answer for it, for there's not a man in London who would dare offer me insult. I am, I assure you, no mean swordsman," he told me as he theatrically gripped the handle of his hanger, "and I've spent more than a few dawns at Hyde Park defending my honor."

"I take your meaning," I told him, although I did not. Did he mean to boast or to offer a warning? "I do have a further question," I proceeded. "Sir Owen, may I ask why you do not seek out Mr. Jonathan Wild, for he is the man most sought in the matter of stolen goods." And he would no doubt be far more likely to return the goods with all haste, I added silently, for this whore was almost certainly in his employ, along with so many of London's thieving whores.

"Wild is a thief," he said in a measured voice, "and everyone in London knows it—at least they know it if they are not fools. A man like you—I am certain you know it. I believe this whore to be in his stable of thieves, and I'll be damned to hell for eternity, sir, before I pay money for what is rightfully mine to the very scoundrel who took it of me in the first place. I tell you, I know not how London considers him a public servant, when he is nothing but a mountebank whose elaborate tricks have left him rich and the city fleeced." His face had by now turned a deep ruddy color. Conscious that he had grown overly warm, he took a moment to compose himself. "Tell me," he said more coolly, "what should you ask for the recovery of a pocketbook?"

"Have you any banknotes within it?" I inquired.

"Yes. I think about two hundred and fifty pounds."

"My fee, Sir Owen, is usually one guinea for an item such as a pocketbook and then 10 percent of the value of the notes. I shall round it off to an even twenty-five pounds."

"That is certainly what Wild would charge as well, and I shall have none of it. I'll pay you twice as much as Wild would ask, for I want my money to land in an honest man's hands. You will find this whore for me, and return to me my pocketbook and its contents, and I shall pay you fifty pounds. What say you, sir? Surely a pugilist like yourself is not afraid to cross Wild's path?"

I felt an exuberance at the thought of so enormous a fee, for like almost everyone else in London, and indeed the nation itself, I maintained some uncomfortable debts. And like the Earl of Stanhope, our First Lord of the Treasury, I had grown considerably skilled at paying off a creditor here and there that I might avoid ruin and still maintain myself in a fashion I could not, in the strictest sense, afford. Fifty pounds would make an enormous impact on my little share of ready money, but even if the thought of so much money made me giddy, I showed Sir Owen only my cool determination. "I delight in crossing Wild's path," I promised him. Though Wild and I had met only once, our competition was a vigorous one, and I enjoyed nothing more than tracking down the goods his men stole. I made it my policy, when possible, to avoid impeaching thieves in Wild's employ, for their master had no similar scruples, and my mercy toward these prigs had earned me some little gratitude.

Sir Owen smiled broadly. "I like a man of your spirit," he said, and then grabbed my hand with a wrenching vigor.

I smiled as I governed my hand's retreat from Sir Owen's enthusiastic grip. "I shall make every effort to retrieve your possession with all aste and contact you the moment I have any news to report."

Sir Owen stepped to the side of the path to let a handsome colle   n of young couples pass us. "I like you, Weaver," he said. "I have never   en a bigot in matters of religion, and now I can see why. What s   ifies whether or not a man eats pork? Get me my pocketbook, and I s   ll say you are as good a man as any and better than most."

I sensed that I had been dismissed, so I bowed to Sir Owen and allowed him to walk over to a group of gentlemen of his acquaintance. I turned to make my way home, fired by a fierce determination to resolve Sir Owen's matter as quickly and as efficiently as I might. I had such confidence in my skills that I considered his pocketbook as already in my possession. In my sanguine mood, such as I was, I could not have known that the business would erupt so dangerously.

THREE

I
T SHOULD HAVE BEEN a simple matter. I dressed the part of a gentleman—ostentatious coat and sword, overflowing wig, gleaming silver buckles upon my shoes. I had learned to appear the perfect gentleman when, in my less scrupulous days, I had spent some time traveling about the country working as what we called a *spruce prig*. I would present myself to a landlord like a gentleman, rent a furnished lodging with no more security than my appearance, and then proceed to clean the place of everything of value. Now, with more honorable motives, my task was to imitate a man of means in the service of undoing theft, and this task called for a particular sort of gentleman. I therefore put some padding about my midsection, making myself look more inclined to fat than muscle. Knowing that the evening would call for drunkenness, and that drunkenness was indeed the enemy, I fortified myself as best I could. I first took down as much cream as I might hold, for it would help to absorb the spirits I drank. Next I gargled with wine, and spilled some about my clothing, giving myself the scent of a man who required little more to render him senseless. Having thus prepared myself, I hired a hackney to take me to the alehouse, sat myself down in a well-lit spot, and boisterously called out for wine.

The Barrel and Bale was what one might expect of such places in the more colorful parts of town. It was near the river, close by the Temple Bar, but its patrons were mainly porters and journeymen, sprinkled with a few Templars looking for relief from their studies of the law. I stood out in this place, but I was not conspicuous. They had seen my type before—indeed, they had seen my type in Sir Owen. So with few eyes upon me, save those who wondered how they might become better acquainted with the contents of my purse, I sat at my table and watched the mixture of life circulate. The alehouse was full, but not packed as such places can get. The smell of filthy bodies and cheap perfumes and thick, choking tobacco made a man labor for each breath. I heard no music but that of the shrill laughter of women and the shouts of men and the unmistakable clatter of dice upon the tabletops. A wounded soldier insisted on standing upon his chair every quarter hour and howling forth a bawdy song about a one-legged Spanish whore. He bellowed with little regard for tune until his friends dragged him down, and, in the jovial manner of such men, beat him until he was quiet.

My refined readers may only know of these places from reports they have read, but I had traveled through suchlike dark havens many times before, and I had little difficulty disregarding the turmoil around me. I had a mind for business, and as the baronet had given me a description of the woman I sought, I scanned the room repeatedly, trying hard to appear a drunk in search of company. I tried too hard, I think, for I had to turn several women of Kate Cole's profession away. A man such as I was, who looked well-moneyed and, if I may be so bold, was far more attractive in person than the more usual patron come in search of companionship, could always depend upon finding favor among the ladies.

The one I sought, according to Sir Owen, was not more than nineteen, she had bright red hair, a fair and freckled complexion, and a prominent mole upon the bridge of her nose. Finally I saw her sit down at a table and engage in a conversation with a vicious buck who, by his look, could have served himself well in the ring. He was a tall, wide, muscular piece of flesh, with a face misshapen into an immutable scowl. I could see that the back of his hand revealed the mark of a branding, so I knew he had run afoul of the law at least once in his life—no doubt on a matter of theft, but I should have been surprised if that had been the only crime to his credit.

I could not guess the whore's connection to this ruffian, and I feared she might be bespoken for the night. But I thought it unlikely that a woman like that would allow a gentleman with a purse to be long disappointed, so with a variety of looks and smiles I made it plain that I had a liking for her, and I hoped that any business she might have with this fellow could be dispatched quickly.

My wishes were gratified. In less than a quarter of an hour, the ruffian stood up and left the premises, and I began to stare hard at Kate, looking at her in the most uncivilized and lascivious way imaginable. She was not shy of my meaning and lost no time removing herself to my table, where she sat down very close to me. Placing a hand upon my leg she leaned forward and whispered, allowing her breath to caress my ear, that she should like a glass of wine.

My enthusiasm was genuine, though not the kind she would have anticipated, and affecting a great drunkenness, I called for a bottle of the sour piss the Barrel and Bale was proud to serve.

Up close I could see that Kate was a woman not without charms for gentlemen who are so inclined, but she had the kind of hard, hollow look of the street about her, and that was always for me enough to tame my more lickerish passions. I had no amorous feelings for women I could not trust with my purse should I doze off. Moreover, Kate was badly in need of a washing, and her dress, while tight about her pleasing shape, was soiled with the leavings of customers gone by. The once-ivory muslin was now yellowish brown, and her plain tan stomacher had grown so filthy as to almost want delousing.

"You are a very pretty lass," I told her, slurring my words enough to allow her to believe I had already had more than my fill of spirits. "I could not help but notice you, my dear,"

"And what didcha notice?" she asked me coyly.

I confess that I had a bit of the libertine about me in my younger years, and even in this matter of business, I could not resist the temptation to win over this woman. It was a great weakness of mine, I suppose. So many of my friends enjoyed conquering only women they found charming, but I felt some need that women should find *me* charming.

"What did I notice about you?" I repeated back to her. "I noticed the redness of your lips, the whiteness of your throat, and the delicate curve of your chin"—I reached out and rested my hand against the side of her face—"and the marvelous line of your cheekbones. You look to me like a glorious and sensual angel in an Italian painting."

Kate squinted at me. "Most gen'men say they likes me arse."

"You were sitting upon it when I noticed you," I explained.

Satisfied, Kate laughed and returned to her drink.

I joined her, gulping my wine, and allowed Kate to encourage me to drink more. Even when I drank in great quantities I rarely lost my head to spirits, but the cream in my stomach safeguarded me well. To my dismay, it had begun to turn sour, and it took some concentration to keep this unfortunate mixture of liquids in its place. I gritted my teeth together and disregarded my unease, acting the drunken fool, shouting, stumbling upon my words, and once, falling over in my chair.

"Ya get full of wine easy, don'cha, me big man," she said with a smile of irregular teeth. "What ya need is a good walk, yer do. Clear your 'ead. And if we 'appen to find ourselves a quiet spot, what's wrong with that, eh?" She gave my upper arm a good squeeze and then paused briefly to consider the resistance of muscle where she had anticipated a more pliable kind of flesh.

After fumbling through my purse to pay the reckoning, all the while making sure that Kate could see that there were many more coins to be had, I walked with her into the October night. It had grown cool with nightfall, and pulling her close to me, I let Kate lead me through a winding maze of London back alleys. I understood that she sought to disorient me, and though I was far less cloudy with wine than she believed, she had me all but entirely confused within a few minutes, for she knew well the dark and labyrinthine streets. I could only be certain that we stayed near the river and walked in the direction of Puddle Dock.

It was late and quite dark, and close to the river as we were it should have been dangerous for us to walk in that way. A strong wind blew the fetid Thames stench into my face. Kate clung to me for warmth as much as to entice me on in a direction she knew no sober gentleman with any valuables about him would willingly venture. Even a man skilled in the art of self-defense avoids any excursion into the dark streets upon the river, for in a time when gangs of violent thieves, a dozen or more strong, freely roamed the city, a man could offer himself or his companion but little protection. A young woman with a staggering gentleman upon her arm must have appeared a delicious target; I could only assume that the scurrying we heard around us bespoke footpads and prigs who knew Kate and understood what she was about, for there were surely others out who crept close enough to inspect us, but they always walked away, and sometimes with a laugh. Once a group of linkboys surrounded us, attempting to aggravate Kate into agreeing to pay one of them to light our way, but she had an acquaintance with these urchins and dismissed them with a few affable quips.

Finally she took me down an alley until we were almost at the dead end and in near-total darkness. We were perhaps ten yards in from the entrance and only a few feet away from the end. The alley was narrow and gave of the cool of the surrounding stones; the ground below us was wet and foul odors drifted up from the puddles of putrid water and the moldering garbage that littered the ground. We discovered a wooden crate set against the wall almost for our convenience, and I could scarce believe that in this part of town an item that might fetch at least a few pence would not be salvaged and sold within minutes of its abandonment. Indeed, I should not have believed it, but more concerned with Kate, I dismissed my curiosity almost at once.

"No one'll bother us 'ere," she said. "We can get some privacy."

I followed silently, her willing partner in the lusty adventure. I must say that I little understand those gentlemen who take pleasure in a hurried dalliance in a damp alley or under a musty bridge. Yet, were men to forswear such outdoor delights, I believe that half the whores of London would be forced to turn to the workhouses.

I sat down upon the crate and let my head fall to the side. Kate stooped down and offered me a kiss just to the side of my lips. She was a clever one, for she wanted to learn if my intoxication overpowered my desire. If I had pulled her closer and directed the kiss, she would know I had at least some of my wits about me yet.

I did not move.

"You're not planning on falling asleep before we get to know one another better, are ya?" she asked, hoping I would do just that. She knew her business, Kate Cole. Some thieving whores would have made their move at that instant, but she stood quietly, watching me for a good five minutes, letting me, as she believed, fall into a deeper, more certain sleep until she was sure my repose would be uninterrupted. She then knelt before me and began unbuttoning my coat, her fingers nimbly reaching for the fob of my watch. Kate had a great talent, I noted with hesitant admiration, for she too had been drinking wine, but the spirits affected her not at all; her fingers dexterously danced about my middle, and I knew that if I did not act with haste I would be forced to demand the return of my watch along with Sir Owen's pocketbook.

With a rapid and violent burst that I had calculated to both shock and unbalance Kate, I arose, knocking her down into the filth of the alley. She fell backward, as I had intended, and she only kept herself entirely off the ground by holding herself up with her arms behind her. Her position was to my advantage, for she could make no moves quickly. I, meanwhile, removed an imposing pocket pistol I was certain always to have about me and pointed it directly toward her. "You'll excuse the ruse, madam," I said. "I can assure you your charms are not lost on me, but I've come on another gentleman's business."

"You bastardly gullion," she breathed. Even in the dark, I could see her eyes shifting as she calculated. Who was I? What was my business? How might she gain the advantage?

I held the pistol in my steady hand. My face bespoke calm and determination. Whores and thieves tended not to respect authority or law or even danger, but they respected terror, and nothing filled street filth with terror so rapidly as an enemy who displayed a mastery of his passions. "This need not become more than a simple matter," I said in an even tone. "Let me explain our business. Last night you met a gentleman and had an adventure much like the one you were planning with me. You took a number of his goods, and he wants them back. Give me this man's property and I shall leave you unharmed. He knows who you are, but he won't swear out an arrest on you should you cooperate."

If Kate felt terror, she did not show it. She sucked on her bottom lip like a pouting child. "An' what if I say you was a liar and I weren't near no one like a gentleman last night? Then what?"

"Then," I said calmly, "I'll beat you until you're bloody and unconscious, search your room until I find what I am looking for, and when you wake up you'll find yourself in Newgate prison with nothing to look forward to but the next hanging day. You see, you are in a bit of a situation, my dear. Why not be helpful so I may proceed with my business?"

I hope my reader recognizes that I had no desire to harm this woman, for I never choose to inflict violence upon that sex. I have, however, few scruples about the threat of violence, and with the more delicate sensibilities of the female constitution, threats are generally all that I require.

Not so in this instance. "I should help so you can proceed with your business, I should?" she repeated with a wicked smile. "Your business is getting yourself dead, and I'll help with that'n plenty."

It was at that moment I realized that I had underestimated Kate Cole's operation, for the sound behind me was that of a pair of heavy boots moving forward from the shadows. In an instant I knew that Kate did not work alone, and that at least some of the footsteps I had heard belonged to her partner. This operation was one they used to call the buttock and twang: a whore would lure a drunken victim to a secluded place, and if the wine failed to do the business, the twang completed the task. I, though armed, found myself at a severe disadvantage, for I did not dare turn my back on Kate, but I had to turn, and turn quickly, to face my as-yet-unseen adversary.

Taking one step onto the wooden crate, and grabbing a crevice in the wall, I leapt over the still supine Kate, and pivoted quickly, pistol pointed forward. What I saw was the ruffian from the Barrel and Bale, rushing for me with a sword thrust outward. My back was against the wall, and I had no room to maneuver. Had I nothing in my hand, my first choice would have been to draw my hangar and take the man in fair competition, for I flattered myself that I was a skilled swordsman and that I would be able to disarm the fellow without loss of life. But there was no time to drop my firearm and draw my blade, and regretting that I had to take these extreme measures, I pulled back the hammer of my pistol and fired into the oncoming shape. There was the loud crack, a momentary flash, and a burning sensation upon my hand, blackened now by the powder. For an instant I thought the gun had misfired, but then I saw the ruffian stop, as a steady dark stain spread across his threadbare shirt. He fell to his knees, his hands covering the wound, and in a matter of seconds he fell backward, and his head hit the dirt hard.

Dropping the warm piece into my pocket, I squatted down and grabbed Kate, who had already begun to flex her face muscles to let out a shriek. I clasped my hand over her mouth to prevent this outburst and held her as still as I could, for she struggled violently against my grasp.

I felt nothing but rage at that moment. Black, violent, seething rage that nearly incapacitated me. I had no love for killing my fellow-men, and I despised Kate for having forced me to fire the pistol. I had taken life only twice before—both times when I had sailed on a smuggling ship and we had been attacked by French pirates—and both times had left me with a kind of intangible anger for the man I had killed, for forcing me, as he did, to kill him.

With my hand squeezed tight upon her face, feeling her writhe, feeling her hot breath upon my palm, I was nearly overwhelmed with the seductive urge to twist hard, to break her neck, to make the difficulties she had caused me disappear in the dark of this alleyway. Perhaps my reader will be shocked that I write these words. If so, the shock is that I write the words, not that I felt the impulse, for we are all driven by our passions, and our task is to know when to submit to them and when to resist. At that moment I knew that I wanted to hurt this whore, but I also knew that I had just killed a man and that I was in great danger. No danger, however, excused me from carrying out the task Sir Owen had hired me to perform. I had to calm Kate, to make her cooperate that I might finish my business and escape this misadventure without finding myself before the magistrate's court.

"Now," I said, trying hard to keep my voice as calm as it had been before, "if you promise me you won't call out, I'll take my hand from your mouth. I won't hurt you; you have the word of a gentleman. Will you listen to what I have to say?"

She stopped squirming and feebly nodded her head. I slowly took away my hand and looked at her face, ashen with terror, streaked now with gunpowder I had smeared upon her.

"You killed Jemmy," she whispered, through lips grown stiff with terror.

I let my eyes flash to the lifeless mass beside me. "I didn't have much choice."

"What do you want of me?" she whispered. A tear began to roll down her cheek.

My passions dissipated somewhat at this unexpected display of tenderness. "You know what I want. I want that gentleman's goods. Have you got them?"

She bobbed her head incoherently. "I tell you, I don't know who you mean," she whimpered. "I got some things in me room—just take 'em if that's what you want." After a few more questions I learned that what goods she had were in her room above the Barrel and Bale. I was concerned to hear that, for with a dead man on my hands, I had no wish to return there, but I saw that I had little choice if I were to retrieve Sir Owen's pocketbook.

"Now listen to me," I said. "We are going to your room and we are going to get what I am looking for. If you act as though anything is wrong, if I even suspect you are considering playing me ill, I shall not hesitate to bring you to the magistrate's office and tell him precisely what happened. Your friend was shot while you tried to rob me, and you'll hang for it. I do not wish to pursue that course, but I shall have that pocketbook and I shall have it whether you live or you die, whether you are free or in prison. I know you understand me."

Kate nodded suddenly and sharply, as though the act of agreement was a torture best completed quickly. That we might not attract attention, I removed my handkerchief, which I now moistened with Kate's tears and used to wipe the gunpowder from her face. My own gentle impulse disturbed me, so I pulled her to her feet, and, with my hand clasped hard about her arm, she led me back to the Barrel and Bale. I had been concerned that we would encounter Kate's friends as we returned to the alehouse, but the prigs must have heard the report of my pistol and fled into their dark holes and kennel gutters for the nonce. No one chose to be upon the streets when the constables came looking for a blackguard upon whom to blame the murder.

It was a long walk—silent, jerky, and tense. Upon our return, the Barrel and Bale was now sufficiently filled with merrymakers that our entrance and ascent up the stairs appeared, as nearly as I could ascertain, to go by unnoticed. I entered her room cautiously, not wanting to be duped again, I saw nothing but a rough, straw-stuffed mattress, some broken furniture, and a hoard of stolen goods.

I struck a pair of cheap tapers and then barred the door. Kate let out a whimper, and only half aware that I spoke, I muttered to her again that she had nothing to fear as, in the flickering light of the candles, I cast my eyes about the room for anything that might be Sir Owen's.

With a quivering hand she pointed to a pile of items in the corner. "Take what you're looking for," she said quietly. "Take it and be damned."

Kate had been a busy girl. Here were wigs and coats and the buckles of belts and shoes. There were purses—I presumed already emptied of their gold and silver—and handkerchiefs and swords and rolls of linen. There were even three volumes of the writings of the Earl of Shaftesbury, which I suspected Kate had not looked into. She had enough here that, could she but sell it, she might acquire a neat little fortune. I presumed that though she might work for Wild, she was not quite willing to hand over all her stolen loot, but fearful of placing these goods in the hands of Wild's fences, she had no safe place to unload her booty. Such was Wild's power—those who did not work for him had no way to sell their merchandise and thus gained little for their pains. Kate was certainly stuck with a collection of goods that, while valuable, were all but useless to her.

I searched through the booty carefully, for I had to keep my eye upon Kate as I proceeded, but I finally saw a handsomely bound leather pocketbook protruding from under an ostentatious periwig. I took a step back and instructed Kate to hand it to me. A quick inspection revealed that this was indeed Sir Owen's book. With a sigh of relief I pocketed this prize and told her I was satisfied and that she might keep the rest.

Now I found myself facing the very troubling dilemma of what to do about Kate. I knew it a risk to leave her where she was, for I could not doubt that her taskmaster, Mr. Jonathan Wild, would force her to tell him what had happened, and I did not want her to reveal anything that could be traced, no matter with how much difficulty, back to Sir Owen. He had requested privacy, and I aimed to give it to him. It occurred to me that I could report what had happened to a magistrate—Kate would be taken for theft, I would in all likelihood be acquitted of any blame, and I should receive a reward for her conviction as well. The difficulty with this ma-neuver lay in that I had promised Kate I should do no such thing. Besides, Kate knew too much of my purpose for me to believe that any inquiry into this incident would not lead back to Sir Owen. Furthermore, had I been a Christian gentleman in a similar situation, I could have approached a judicial bench with the certainty that a judge would look with approba-tion upon my necessary killing of a felon. I could by no means be certain that a judge would think more highly of a thief-taker of the tribe of He-brews than he would of a robber. What I required was that Kate depart on her own, without speaking to anyone—particularly Jonathan Wild. I could not suppose that Jemmy was well loved nor that he would be missed. Should Kate disappear for even a few weeks it would be sufficient to gen-erate a protective coat of apathy should the matter ever thereafter be discussed.

I therefore attempted to convince Kate that taking a holiday was in her best interest. "I suggest you collect your things and depart quietly. Tell no one what has happened. If you do tell, I shall inform the magistrates what I know and see you hang for certain. I fear that your only chance for safety is to leave London for a while."

"But if I leave," she whispered, "they'll think I killed Jemmy sure."

"So they might," I said, "but they'll have to catch you to do anything about it, and you'll be long gone. And those who think you've killed Jemmy will soon forget that there ever was such a man. I fear, Kate, that if you don't leave London, you will be hanged." I meant it to sound more like a threat than a prediction.

Kate had gathered some strength, and she produced a rather dazzling volley of curses that I should be ashamed to expose to my reader. I let her vomit forth her indignation, standing impassively until she collapsed into a defeated slouch. "All right then, you miserable sod."

I again smiled, hoping to impress upon her the cold implacability of my intent. I hoped to impress it upon myself as well, for I was in no way confident Kate would behave as I instructed. With nothing more to say then, I calmly left the room and descended down the stairs into the chaos of the Barrel and Bale's yeasty stench. Dazed, shaking, and fingering the rough leather of Sir Owen's book in my pocket, I forced my way through the crowd and left the tavern. Once outside, I hoped to feel some satisfaction at having completed my task, but no satisfaction came. I could not shed the memory of this villain Jemmy as he lay in the alley, dead of my hand. I huddled my arms against myself as I fought the growing conviction that his death could not but have a dreadful impact upon my life.

FOUR

I EXPERIENCED A wide mixture of feelings the next day as I awaited Sir Owen's arrival. I was gratified that I had been able to retrieve his pocketbook so rapidly, but I was also apprehensive about Jemmy's death. I replayed that instant a hundred times in my mind, wondering if I had missed an opportunity to extricate myself from my danger without taking a life. I could not see that I had acted too quickly or too rashly, but I remained shaken and in no small way concerned.

I continued to doubt my decision to let Kate walk free, for were my name to be drawn into the matter too long after the incident, my hesitation to come forward should certainly appear as guilt. It was not yet too late for me to tell my tale to the magistrate if I wished. I had spent time as an outlaw and I had lived among outlaws—I did not choose to turn a woman over to hanging simply because I believed it the most expedient path.

You can see then, reader, why Mr. Balfour's pronouncement that my father had been murdered left me so vulnerable, for the events of the previous night had certainly heightened my sensibilities. It took near an hour after Balfour's departure for me to calm myself, and just as my feelings had begun to settle, Mrs. Garrison showed in Sir Owen. I had contacted him early that morning to let him know the pocketbook was in my possession, and when he arrived he strolled in with unbridled jollity. Approaching my desk, from whence I stood to greet the baronet, he clapped me heartily on the arm as if I were one of his gaming partners.

"This is good news, Weaver," he said, bouncing himself happily upon the balls of his feet. "Good news, indeed. These shall be the best fifty pounds I have ever spent."

I unlocked the desk drawer, removed the pocketbook, and held it out to him. He grabbed it as I have seen tigers on display in Smithfield snatch their daily meat. Indeed, I thought there was something like hunger as he unclasped the leather strip that bound the book and began to thumb anxiously through the loose pieces of paper contained therein. I sat down, trying to appear as though I did something other than peer at the book's contents. Sir Owen had been injudicious to carry the book about him—I spotted the banknotes he had spoken of; had Jemmy or Kate known what they were, they surely would have used them as cash, but Sir Owen took no pleasure at their safe return. As the baronet neared a complete review of the contents of the book, he grew increasingly apprehensive, turning pages with greater urgency. The look of exuberance left his wide face, and only the outline of his jolly countenance remained upon his now-ashen features.

"It's not here," he muttered, starting again from the front of the book. He turned the pages so rapidly I should have been surprised had he found anything at all. I do not even think he still looked; panic now drove him to continue turning the leaves. "Not here," he said again. "Not here at all."

I had no idea what it was he could not find, but I felt a pressing concern. I had presumed that once the baronet left my rooms he would have his book upon him, and the matter would be closed. That no longer appeared to be the case. "What is missing, Sir Owen?"

He froze for a moment and then confronted me with a cold glare. I had been so used to seeing the baronet cheerful and merry that I had not considered that, like all men, he could know his share of rage. The severity of his gaze told me that he suspected me of taking whatever it was that he missed. In truth, I had not even looked through his book but to determine that it was indeed his. I admit that if the evening had not ended in violence, I would surely have been tempted to examine the contents more closely, and I might even have given in to the temptation, but the taint of blood upon my hands inspired me to remain sinless in all other respects.

Yet, as Sir Owen studied me, I felt myself awash in guilt—the guilt that only the innocent feel when under close scrutiny. It is an inexplicable thing. I have been guilty of many things in my life, and when confronted

I always faced my accusers with calm assurance. Now, under Sir Owen's condemnatory gaze, I colored and grew anxious. The book, after all, had been my responsibility. Had I dropped something? Had I not been sufficiently diligent in searching Kate's room? My mind examined every possible avenue of failure.

It was this senseless guilt he responded to. Sir Owen's eyes narrowed. He stood up so as to raise himself to an intimidating height. "Do you seek to trifle with me, sir?" he asked in a low growl. I could smell his sour breath from where I sat.

I felt the muscles in my face shift from aimless guilt to burning indignation. Now that the accusation had been uttered, I arose to a more defiant stance. I realized, however, that my reputation would not be served by any visible display of anger, so, calming myself, I met Sir Owen's accusation directly. "Sir, you said you came on the recommendations of many gentlemen. I defy you to find one who would impute that I had deceived him in any way, under any conditions. Do you wish to give me the lie?"

I must say with all humility that, though no longer in my prime and certainly no longer the man I had been when I fought in the ring, I cut an imposing figure. Sir Owen shrank from me. He took a step back, and lowered his eyes. He did not, apparently, wish to give me the lie at all. "I am sorry, Mr. Weaver. It is only that there is something yet missing. Something to me more valuable than all the information and banknotes in this book." He sat back down. "Perhaps it is my own doing. I should have made certain you knew to look for it." He lowered his face into his cupped hands.

"What is this thing that you have lost?" I asked in a gentler tone. Sir Owen had softened—almost broken—and I considered it prudent I soften as well.

He looked up, despondence inscribed upon his once-jovial features. "It is a bundle of papers, sir." He cleared his throat and attempted to regain his calm. "Papers of a personal nature."

I began to understand the situation more clearly. "Is there anything else missing, Sir Owen?"

"Nothing of importance." He shook his head slowly. "Nothing I can see."

"And would someone inspecting your book know these papers were valuable to you?"

"Someone would who knew enough of me. And such a man would know how much I would value their return." He thought for a moment. "But there are several pages, and this person would have to read everything. And, as I say, this person would have to know much of my private life."

"Yet," I mused aloud, "surely anyone literate enough to know the value of a packet of private letters would know the value of the banknotes yet in your book. Are any of your banknotes missing?"

"I think not. No."

"It seems to me unlikely that the papers have been intentionally taken," I reasoned. "For who would steal the papers and then neglect these notes? Is it possible that these papers might have fallen out? That they might not have been clasped securely within the book?"

Sir Owen reflected upon this observation for a moment. His face was suddenly creased with lines, and his eyes were bloodshot. "It is *possible*," he said. "I cannot say for certain how rough things became with the whore, you know. And once my goods were in her possession, she may not have known to be careful. They *might* have fallen out, certainly."

"But you think it unlikely?"

"Mr. Weaver, I must have these papers returned." Sir Owen crossed his legs and then crossed them back the other way. "I shall give you an additional fifty pounds to retrieve them. One hundred pounds if you can do so within twenty-four hours."

I had ample use for the money, but I saw now a greater opportunity for service. If I could remedy Sir Owen's matter, I knew, he would not be illiberal in his praise of me thereafter. "You offered me before fifty pounds for the return of your pocketbook and its contents. I have not yet fulfilled the contract. I shall find these papers, sir, and ask nothing more of you."

Sir Owen brightened a little. "Did you, by any chance, inspect the area around which the book had been stashed, or among my other belongings?"

"Sir, there was no time. I am afraid my encounter with the woman went somewhat shakily." I proceeded to inform Sir Owen of the previous evening's adventure. This confession was unguarded, but I felt the need to secure the baronet's trust. And I knew that he understood his implication in this matter quite clearly, for I could not be brought forward for punishment without exposing Sir Owen's secret. He listened to my story with grave concentration. "Gad," he breathed. "This is a serious dilemma. You know that this whore must never speak. She must not be permitted to drag you into a trial, and you must not drag my name into it. You understand that such a thing cannot happen." His voice rose with increasing levels of panic. "I cannot allow that such a thing could ever happen."

"Of course," I said, as if soothing a child. "You have made it clear that your privacy is of the utmost importance, and I shall treat it as such. In the meantime, I believe I have imparted unto Kate the importance of keeping silent and leaving London. There is little to fear on that head." I overstated the case, but it was important that I resolve the baronet's anxieties. There would be ample time to manage Kate Cole should she prove unruly. "We must concentrate now on finding your property. If these papers have fallen out of your book, or happened to be among any other possessions, then they are still among Kate's goods now, wherever that may be."

Sir Owen let out an exasperated sigh, and seeing him to be in need, I stood up to gather for him some refreshment. "Might I pour you some wine?"

He looked flushed. "I fear wine will not do the business, sir. Have you any gin?"

I had not. I knew too well the insidiousness of gin from the unfortunates with whom my trade brought me into almost daily contact. Cheap, flavorless, and potent, it ravaged both the minds and bodies of countless thousands in London, and I ill-trusted my indulgent nature with so powerful a poison. Instead, I offered Sir Owen a dram of a Scottish liquor that my friend Elias Gordon had brought me back from his native land upon his last visit. Sir Owen sniffed the dram glass with hesitant curiosity, squinting at the liquor's sharp, malty odor. Absently nodding as I warned him of the drink's great strength, he proceeded to probe it with his tongue. What he found excited his curiosity, and he then swallowed the contents with a mighty gulp. "Wretched," he said after screwing his face into a look of both disgust and a kind of surprised enjoyment. "The Scots are certainly animals. But it does the business." He helped himself to another glass.

I took my seat again and studied Sir Owen carefully, attempting to gauge his mood. His agitation thickened the room like summer humidity, and I wished to comfort him, though I knew not how. I could not imagine the nature of these documents, but I assumed the baronet feared some knowledge contained therein falling into the wrong hands. "Sir," I began hesitantly, "I wish to retrieve your private papers. I do not think all is lost. I have many contacts in London; I can find Kate Cole, and she can bring me the documents. But," I said slowly, "I must be able to recognize this packet when I see it. I must be able to tell I have your papers, sir. And that I have all of them."

He nodded. "I see that I am exposed before you, Mr. Weaver. My own foolishness, many times over, has put me in this situation, and now I must rectify it. So be it." He straightened himself into a posture of fortitude. "I shall have to trust you."

"I assure you that I shall never reveal your secrets."

He smiled as to show his faith in me. "Do you, Mr. Weaver, trouble yourself with the matters of fashionable life—marriages and those sorts of affairs?"

I shook my head. "I fear my business does not leave me the time for pursuits of that nature."

"Then you will not have heard that in two months I am to be married to the only daughter of Godfrey Decker, the brewer. Decker is a rich man, and his daughter comes with a considerable portion, but I care nothing for the wealth. It is a love match."

I awkwardly offered a sympathetic nod. I wished to avoid any appearance of cynicism, but while I considered Sir Owen to be a man of many feelings, I was not convinced tender love was among them.

"There has been some talk," he continued, "for it is scarce a year since my late wife, Anne, passed on. You must not think that I was, or still am, unaffected by her loss. I loved her very dearly, but mine is a susceptible heart, and in the loneliness that comes with a widower's state, Sarah Decker has brought me much contentment and happiness. Yet the passing of my wife is no simple matter, sir, for she died of a disease that she contracted of me." He paused for a deep breath and then turned away. "A disease that I, in turn, contracted of an amour."

"I understand," I said after a moment, wanting to fill in the silence but feeling foolish for having said anything at all. Sir Owen would hardly be the first fashionable gentleman in London to have clapped his own wife. I shall not understand why so many men refuse to take the trouble of procuring the armor of sheep intestines to guard against Cupid's most pernicious arrows.

"I had always responded so well to the treatments the surgeons offered, but the disease proved too much for Anne's delicate constitution. Perhaps because she knew not what she had and waited too long to seek help."

I had no skills to find the right words and I could only wait for him to continue.

"I fully intend to reform my behavior once married to Sarah," Sir Owen continued. He sniffled a little and I thought I saw something vaguely tearlike in his eye. "I am a changed man. The papers that are missing testify to that. It is a series of letters, Mr. Weaver, between me and my dear, lost Anne, in which I express in damningly unambiguous terms the nature of my transgression and a spirited and sentimental desire to reform. A reader of these letters would quickly discern the nature of her disease and the nature of its contraction. I have tried very hard to conceal this information from Sarah, who is a virtuous young woman of exceptional delicacy. Should she learn of the contents of these letters, I fear she would sever our connection. And if some unscrupulous villain were to learn of the contents, he would have me at a terrifying disadvantage." He poured himself another dram of the Scottish liquor. "I can only hope the letters remain sealed. I kept them about me wrapped in a yellow ribbon, with a wax seal bearing the imprint of a cracked shilling. A broken seal I should see as the worst news in the world." He lifted the glass and swallowed hard.

"I cannot risk these letters falling in with a man like Wild. He should rake me over the coals before returning to me what is mine. But your reputation precedes you, sir. I believe you to be the only man in London who has both the knowledge and the integrity to retrieve what I have lost."

I bowed at Sir Owen. "As it is a matter of delicacy, you are certainly right to come to me rather than to have gone to Wild."

"You see why I am very much in your power."

"As I am in yours," I returned. "For you know of my involvement in a man's death. We are thus beholden to each other, and neither man may fear the indiscretion of the other."

He brightened considerably at this observation, and I must confess that I was no longer horrified that the matter was not yet concluded. I even felt somewhat relieved. Had I returned the pocketbook and its contents been intact, then the matter would have been resolved. I would have had to wait to learn if there would be any consequences of Jemmy's death. Sir Owen's missing letters gave me license to involve myself in the matter once more. I could not say if this involvement would prove to my benefit, but by taking action I would feel less powerless.

"I shall begin my search for these letters immediately," I told Sir Owen, "and this search shall be my first priority until they are recovered. If I have any news, sir, any news at all, I shall not hesitate to send it to you."

Sir Owen rolled the glass between his hands. "Thank you, Weaver. I flatter myself that I shall see my letters soon. You do understand, sir, that if you must ask questions of any of these scoundrels, you should make no reference to what these papers contain."

"Of course."

"My happiness, you see, is in your hands." He turned to my window and stared outward. "Sarah is such a lovely woman. So very delicate."

"I am sure you are a most fortunate man." My words sounded to me hollow platitudes.

After making certain there was nothing else of use Sir Owen could tell me, I showed him out and began to formulate a plan of action. I decided the most effective course would be to visit some of the unpleasant institutions I knew of, in which the dark engineers of the underworld convened to discuss their business and unburden their minds in fellowship. Such a place was a gin shop on Little Warner Street, near Hockley-in-the-Hole—a place equally repulsive to the senses of smell and sight, for it was so close to that fetid sewer known as the Fleet Ditch that it was not uncommon for the entire place to be flooded with the sickening scent of kennel and waste. This gin house had no proper name, and the sign above it was merely a faded image of two horses drawing a cart—a remnant of a previous shop. Among its patrons, the house was known as Bawdy Moll's, for its proprietress was an affectionate and buxom woman whose onset of middle years she combated with an excess of concupiscence and a minimum of attire.

I entered Bawdy Moll's in the early afternoon; the place was then far less inhabited than in the busy nighttime hours, when impoverished men sought refuge from their lives in pints of gin sold for almost nothing. A penny or two was enough to transport the most miserable of sods to a painless realm of drunken oblivion. In the afternoon, however, the shop served a more sporadic sort—perhaps the petty thief or pickpocket seeking refuge from a job turned sour, the beggar who had chosen to surrender his pennies for drink rather than food, or the out-of-work laborer who preferred to face a senseless stupor rather than a heartless London that would care not a whit for his starvation.

There were also the visitors who came each Monday and Thursday to see the bullbaiting. On other days one could find a variety of different exhibits to be seen in Hockley-in-the-Hole. In my younger years, I had been one of them, for before I had taken to fighting exclusively with my fists, I had been part of a troupe of sword-fighters who demonstrated for paying crowds the noble art of self-defense. Such things are no longer seen today, but as a young man I had marched about the city amidst a troop of fighters clad in our poor and tattered estimation of military uniforms, drums a-beating, while boys passed around handbills detailing the thrills of our shows. During my days sword-fighting at a ramshackle outdoor theater near Oxford Street, I would risk life and limb with another man as we demonstrated our daring skill with our swords, each of us trying to best his opponent without doing him any serious harm. Despite our efforts to spare one another, I was usually bloodied and covered with cuts by the end of a performance, and I have many a scar upon my body to testify to these exploits. When the theatrical manager asked me if I wished to earn my bread by fighting with fists only, I confess I was delighted at the prospect of so painless an employment.

I suppose I was prone to reminisce about those awful times, but the gin house quickly reminded me of what life engendered in that part of town. Bawdy Moll's had few windows, for her patrons had no wish to see the world around them, and they had less of a wish for the world outside to look in. I braced myself against the stink as I saw Bawdy Moll, who stood behind the counter talking excitely with a haggard-looking cutpurse whose name I knew but whose acquaintance I had never sought. They both hovered over a pile of papers that from where I stood I recognized as tickets for the illegal lottery that Moll, like so many tavern-owners in that part of the city, ran from her place of business. The drawings were always biased, rigged, and small, and the revenue from them added handsomely to Moll's purse.

Moll wore her hair high, in a grotesque parody of the ladies' fashion. Her dress opened wide at the neck to reveal an ample if withered bosom, and the paint upon her face bespoke a woman who believed these artificial and conspicuous colorings had power not to deceive but to blind, for her skin put me in mind of bark ready to drop from the tree. Grotesque as she was, Moll was well loved, and she frequently provided me with valuable news of back streets and thieves' dens.

Upon my entrance the cutpurse looked up from his conversation with Moll and scowled. I heard the words "Weaver the Jew," but I could discern no more. It was often hard for me to ascertain my status among such men. I had friends within the armies of prigs, but I had enemies too—and I knew that their master, Jonathan Wild, encouraged no fellowship between their ranks and me. I assumed this man to be a fellow who took Wild's advice to heart, for as I approached Moll he finished hard his pint of gin—throwing back a quantity that should have caused a healthy man to lose his senses—and stalked into the dark shadows of the gin house where there were always piles of straw for the poor and the desperate to crawl into and sleep off their poison.

"Ben Weaver," Moll called out as I approached, as always speaking more loudly than she needed. "A glass of wine for ya, then, me 'andsome spark?" Moll knew enough that I would not partake of gin, and I accepted with good humor a glass of her vinegary wine, of which I sipped only enough to be polite.

"Good day to you, Moll," I said as she rubbed my arm with a leathery hand, her sausage-like fingers clinging absently to me. There was no getting what one wanted from this woman without indulging her need to feel desirable. "I trust your pleasant company keeps your business healthy?"

"Aye, business is brisk. A penny a glass is a small business, it is, but counting the coins is a fine enough occupation, I reckon." She gently pulled at the tie of my hair. "How many of them would it take to buy yer company, I wonder?"

"Not many," I said with a smile that would have been unconvincing in a better-lit room, "but I find I have little time at the moment."

"Yer always a busy man, Ben. Ye must make time for yer pleasures."

"My business *is* my pleasure, Moll. You know that."

"That's right unnatural," she assured me with a coo.

"What news," I responded, as though it were the perfectly correct response to her amorous oglings, "have you heard upon the street?"

I cannot claim to be astonished that the first news upon her lips was of Jemmy's death, for word of a murder spread like the French pox in London's dark quarters. " 'E was shot dead, 'e was. You knew 'im?"

"I met him but briefly," I told her.

" 'E wasn't much, I reckon, but 'e 'ardly deserved to be shot like a dog, such as 'e was. Like a dog." She scratched her head. " 'E wasn't much smarter'n a dog, though, was 'e? And vicious too, with a taste for young girls—young, I say—whether they would or no. Now that I think on it, gettin' 'imself shot down was just the thing for a bastard like 'im." She shrugged at her own observation.

"Who shot him?" I asked, keeping my voice steady.

" 'Is 'ore," she leaned forward and spoke in what I can only describe as a shouting whisper. "Kate Cole's 'er name. Jemmy and Kate kept a buttock an' twang together, but if anyone was to shoot anyone I would have thought 'e'd 'ave done 'er in, not t'other way, for she 'ad a few other coves what she kept, and she even spent a night or two with Wild 'imself."

"She was Wild's whore?"

"Well, who ain't? I won't say I 'aven't 'ad a tumble with the great man meself, but Jemmy was a man quick with his anger, and if Wild's to keep his prigs in line he oughtn't to make them want to kill 'em. All's the more wonder that 'e done what 'e done."

"And what has he done?" I asked.

"Why 'e's 'peached 'er, 'e 'as. Wild turned 'is own 'ore in. Now I've seen 'im do it many a time and often with a prig what 'e couldn't trust no more, but to 'peach a woman what you've swived not a week before shows a lack of"—she fumbled for a word—"manners, I should think. Now the poor lass is sittin' in Newgate. How long before she gets what all women get there, I wonder? All those men there, looking for distraction. I got it sure enough in my day."

My innards writhed as I listened to Moll's cackling speculations, for if Kate had been arrested she would have no reason not to speak of my involvement. It was true that though she had no idea who I was, she did know what I had been after, and if she had only the slightest grain of cunning she would know that the goods I had sought were the key to her surviving the next hanging day.

"What does Kate have to say about all this?"

"I should 'ardly know." Though I could see little humor in the question, Moll burst into an uproarious laugh that sounded to me like a seagull's cry. "I suppose ye better go down to Newgate and ask 'er yerself what opinion she has of the matter."

Such was my intention. So, doing my best to conceal my panic before Moll, I made some small chat with her for a little while, pretended to seek information on a house broken into, and then made my first convenient escape.

FIVE

I COULD MUSTER no considerable surprise to learn that Jonathan Wild
had 'peached Kate, for profiting from the conviction of his own creatures
was no small part of the key to his fortune. It was said that he held a book
with the name of every felon in his employ, keeping count of numbers as
though he were a merchant or a trader as much as a thief. When he believed one of his prigs to be withholding goods, he put a cross next to the
name, indicating that it was time to hand the poor sod over to the courts.
Once the prig was hanged, Wild put a second cross next to his name, and
so the thieves of London now held the expression of *double-crossing* as one
and the same with betrayal.

Long before I'd turned to thief-taking Wild had been plying his trade
from the Blue Boar Tavern in Little Old Bailey, making a name for himself
by impeaching highwaymen like James Footman, a renowned villain of
his day, and by breaking up the robbery gang of the most notorious Obadiah Lemon. He brought these blackguards to justice as he later did his
own blackguards, by betraying their trust and leading them to believe he
was one of their brotherhood—for indeed he was, and how were the likes
of Obadiah Lemon to know that a fellow-thief would suddenly appoint
himself magistrate? I believe that even in the early days of Wild's power,
most everyone suspected what this man was, but crime had grown so
rampant, with armed gangs of men prowling the streets like hungry dogs,
and old ladies and pensioners fearing to step outside lest they be brutally
knocked down, that all who lived in the metropolis wished for a hero, and
Wild proved flamboyant and ruthless enough to announce himself to be

precisely that. His name was in every paper and upon all lips. He had become the Thief-Taker General.

I had only been in my current trade for three months before I met Wild, but in a way it is strange that it took as long as all that. London, after all, is a city in which any man of a particular business or interest is destined to meet all others of a like mind in a surprisingly short period of time. My friends may prove his enemies, but we shall all know each other soon enough.

If it took me some months to meet Wild, I had seen him about the city many times. We all had, for Wild made it his business to be visible, showing up at fairs and the Lord Mayor's Show and market days, riding horseback with his men in attendance, directing them to seize pickpockets as though he were in command of some tiny army. I suppose that if we in London had some sort of body devoted to apprehending criminals, what the French call a *police*, a man like Wild could never have come to power, but Englishmen are far too quick to feel the squeeze upon their liberties, and I seriously doubt if we shall ever see a *police* on this island. Wild took advantage of this need for regulation, and I fully admit when I would see him astride his horse, handsomely dressed, pointing this way and that with his ornate walking stick, it was all I could do but to admire him.

By the time Wild and I met face-to-face, he had moved over to the tavern called the Cooper's Arms, where he set up his "Office for the Recovery of Lost and Stolen Property." It is with some shame that I recount the story of my meeting with Wild, for it is a story of my weakness. My new business of thief-taking had been flourishing—largely, I suspect, owing to luck more than skill, but my luck began to run thin when I set out to serve a rich merchant whose shop had been broken open and robbed of a half-dozen ledger books. Before they grew brazen, Wild's prigs preferred the theft of ledgers and pocketbooks and other items of value only to their owners, for if such thefts went to trial, goods without an estimable intrinsic value could not command a hanging penalty.

Much like my new acquaintance Sir Owen, this merchant sought my services because he understood Wild's game and refused to pay him to return what he had taken in the first place. Unlike Sir Owen, he was unwilling to give me double Wild's fee, and proposed one pound per book, which I gladly accepted, for I earnestly desired the chance to beat my competitor at his own game.

I knew well the sort of coves who would take down ledger books, and I toured the gin houses and taverns and inns, seeking out men I thought might have the goods. It was at this time, however, that Wild had begun to discover the joys of 'peaching his own prigs, and with three of his army dangling at the last hanging day, the men I spoke to all kept themselves cautiously silent—none of them wishing to incur Wild's displeasure.

I spent a full week asking questions and pressing upon weaker men, but I found no sign of the books I sought. I then bethought myself of a plan that, I now blush to own, struck me as ingenious. I would go to Wild's Lost Property Office at the Cooper's Arms and pay for the return of the books. Even if I made no profit of this transaction, I could hand over the property to my merchant and he would speak to others of how I could find goods taken by Wild's men. Why I thought I could retrieve other articles in the future when I could not retrieve these now, I cannot say.

Thus, on a hot June afternoon, I entered Wild's abode, this dark tavern smelling of mold and spirits. The great man sat at a table in the center of his room, surrounded by his minions, who fairly treated him as though he were an Arabian sultan. Wild was a man of a stocky nature—he had a broad face with a sharp nose and protruding chin and eyes that glistened like a harlequin's. Dressed as he was, like a man of mode, in his yellow-and-red coat and neat little wig propped beneath a hat cocked just so, he looked to me like a farcical character in a Congreve comedy, but I saw right away that his frivolity was not to be taken at face value. I do not say that he played at gayness, for that would be misleading, but he had a look about him that said that, even in the midst of celebration, he might be thinking of what mischief he could perform upon the man who poured his wine.

When I entered he was in the midst of a celebration indeed; I had heard upon the streets that Wild had just that morning 'peached a gang of a half-dozen buffers—thieves that steal horses, slaughter them, and sell their skins—and he was in a jolly mood at the prospect of collecting forty pounds' bounty a head. The moment I stepped inside I saw three villains swig down full mugs of ale. A drunken fool paraded around the room, abusing a fiddle most appallingly, but the lickerish audience stomped and danced to the music for all its chaos.

Hanging over Wild was his favorite wench, Elizabeth Mann, along with a dozen or so of his lieutenants. Among these was a miserable sod called Abraham Mendes, Wild's most trusted soldier, and, I am shamed to say, a Jew of my own neighborhood. Mendes and I had attended the same small school as boys, and I had even maintained a cautious sort of friendship with this menacing lad who was, even by my standards, violent and dangerous. I had often seen him in the company of Wild, but I had not spoken to him since I was perhaps twelve years old, and he had been exiled from our school for attempting to blind the instructor with a Torah pointer. Now he was a game-enough-looking buck—hardened by ill fortune; his face, which bore the twisted and misshapen look of a man who had been in the thick of more fights than even I had, was now a grizzly cast of vile apathy.

When I walked in, Mendes glanced over and met my gaze, as though I had arrived late for an appointed meeting. Without changing his expression, he leaned forward and whispered into Wild's ear. The thief-taker nodded, and then slapped his hand hard upon the table like a judge banging his gavel; the fiddle ceased, the revelers stopped dead, and a tense silence descended. "We cannot allow our good cheer to hinder business," Wild announced. "The Lost Property Office remains open."

The wench and the bulk of his prigs disappeared in an instant, melting quietly into the back rooms. Only Mendes remained, standing quietly behind his master like a demonic statue.

Wild rose to his feet and took a few steps forward, perhaps exaggerating his famous limp. There were those who claimed that Wild falsified his lameness, perhaps to make the world think him less dangerous, but I did not believe it. I too had suffered a leg injury, and I knew the difference between a true limp and a false one.

"Please come have a seat." He gestured toward a chair at his table. "You will excuse my companions' merrymaking, but we have had a successful morning, Mr. Weaver."

The sound of my own name struck my ears like a blow, and I wanted nothing so much as to flee. I had been fool enough to think that I might retrieve these ledger books anonymously, that Wild should never recognize me. I could not now swallow my pride and tell him what I wanted. I would be laughed at throughout the town. Yet it was too late to retreat, and I stepped forward, slowly lowering myself into a chair while he did the same.

I said nothing.

Wild smiled as unctuously as a shopkeeper. "Would you care for some refreshment?"

I still said nothing. I could think of nothing to say, and so I hoped he would find my silence menacing.

"Mr. Weaver, I cannot help you if you will not state the nature of your business. Have you lost some property?" He waved his hands in the air as though attempting to summon such examples as came to mind. "Some . . . ledger books, perhaps?"

I felt like a child who had been caught in an act of mischief. It was no surprise that Wild knew what I sought; the only surprise was that I hadn't anticipated it. I had been making inquiries and threats of his men for the past week, and I should not have expected him to be ignorant of a man who sought to impose on his hold of the thief-taking trade.

I could not leave, and I could not ask for his help. My only option, and it was one that in the past had brought upon my head as much success as injury, was bravado. "I know you have the ledgers," I said. "I want them."

Wild pretended not to hear my threat. "It has reached my attention that you have been making inquiries about town, and I believe it is *possible* that I may be able to locate these books for you. As you are certainly aware, I take no money for my services here at the Lost Property Office, but I may have to offer the person who finds himself in possession of the items some small consideration. I am certain one pound per book should suffice."

I wished most heartily to beat his false look of complaisance into the tabletop, but I knew this was not the place for violence. Mendes had the instincts of an animal—he narrowed his eyes and flared his nostrils, as though smelling my thoughts, and he thrust forth his chest as a sign of warning.

Turning to face Wild, I held myself erect in my seat and met his sparkling gaze with my own tired and certainly dull eyes. "I do not seek to play your little games, sir. The men of your gang have taken the books. If you do not give them to me, you may be sure I shall employ the law to have you answer for it."

Mendes took a step forward, but Wild shook his head. "The law, you say? What fear have I of the law? I am the law's servant, Mr. Weaver, and all of London applauds me. Have you some evidence connecting me to this theft? Are there witnesses who will name me? The law, indeed! There was a time when I thought you might offer me some game, but now I see that your talk is but a bubble."

"You ought not to underestimate me," I said, hoping my tone would give my words credit. I wanted nothing more than to be gone, for in this game of words he surely had the advantage.

"Oh," he said, laughing, "I never underestimate anyone. That is my secret, you know. I think I value your talents quite as I ought. Tell me, what do you expect to earn for yourself this year? You might catch yourself two or three bounties and the odd pound here and there. That shall bring you one hundred pounds? One hundred and fifty? If you would like to come work for me, Weaver, I shall pay you two hundred pounds per annum."

I stood and leaned forward only slightly that I might hover over the great man as I spoke. From the corner of my eye I saw Mendes offer some vague gesture of warning, but could not bother myself with him. I knew that he would not touch me without his master's permission. "I scorn your offer," I told Wild. Mendes stepped from behind Wild's chair, and so, to demonstrate this scorn, I turned my back upon him and departed as slowly as I might, that no one could say I ran from the encounter. I believe that I made the most dignified exit possible from so shameful an errand.

I had hoped to have nothing more to do with Wild for some time, but the next day he honored me with his mockery by sending me the ledger books I sought, accompanied by a note saying only, "My compliments." I returned the books to their grateful owner, and he announced to all the world that Benjamin Weaver had retrieved goods stolen by Wild.

It was a bitter moment for me—one that I have tried hard to forget— but I do not flatter myself too much when I say that Jonathan Wild came to regret this gesture of contempt.

MY HISTORY WITH Wild had taught me that he was assuredly dangerous, but that he was quite capable of tripping upon the belief of his own power. Earlier that year, Wild had emerged unscathed from a felony prosecution that had threatened to expose his villainous schemes and utterly undo him, and only recently he had recovered entirely of a disease so severe that the papers had announced his imminent demise. These narrow escapes, I had been told, had not taught Wild that he, too, was subject to the misfortunes of humanity, but rather the lesson he learned was that he was impervious to attack from either man or nature.

I did not for a moment suppose that Wild knew he did me harm by impeaching Kate Cole, but I could take no chances that he would learn the truth. Wild had betrayed her for his own gain, set her up for the double cross, and I believed my only choice now was to make her my creature.

After returning home from Bawdy Moll's, I once again donned the attire of a wigged gentleman, and made my way to Newgate prison, where Kate was housed. My business had taken me to Newgate many times before, and I had no intention of plunging any deeper into the heart of the beast than necessary. No place on earth bears more resemblance to the Christian notion of hell than does this pit of rotted, wretched bodies, stripped of even the remnants of dignity. I only hoped for Kate's sake that she had converted Sir Owen's remaining goods to cash that she might afford more than common lodgings in the prison. In Newgate, unless she shielded herself from the vile rabble, what little honor she might possess would find itself under merciless assault.

As I approached, I saw from a distance that a crowd had gathered, and I quickly realized that a man stood pilloried in the courtyard. A few dozen onlookers had gathered to cheer his misery and to pelt him with rotted eggs and fruit, and occasionally something much harder, for the poor unfortunate bled from several deep wounds about his head, and one of his eyes looked swollen and black and perhaps quite ruined. A sign above him read that he had been charged with Jacobitical sedition, a crime that could unleash the most hateful violence from the crowd. Many a man so charged and punished failed to emerge alive from three days in the pillories. As I hurried past, a ruffian in the crowd hurled an apple with murderous force, shouting, "This'n's from King George, you papist bastard." I cannot say if this man had any real loyalties to our King, but the delight for such a man was in the throwing. The apple landed high and burst on the pillory above the prisoner's head, raining rotted fruit upon him. A few oyster women roamed the courtyard, crying their goods, and the men and women of the crowd devoured their oysters as they looked on merrily at this man whom they tortured, perhaps to death.

I took no pleasure from the spectacle, and pushed on, passing through the terrible prison gate, where I found a warder and instructed him of my business. He was an imposing fellow of average height but of more than average thickness. His arms were of twice the circumference mine had ever been, and he folded them boldly before me to indicate that he should not move without my *touching* him—that is to say, offering him some compensation for his time. Like all those who worked in the prison, from the governor himself down to the lowest turnkey, this man had paid a healthy sum in order to obtain his post, and he needed to exploit his power as best he could in order to earn back his investment. I therefore touched him for a few shillings, and he led me to the Common Side of the prison, where he expected he should be able to find Kate. "I remember her," he said with a leer that spread like the Thames tide across his broad, stupid face. "She was new, and she didn't have no money. Find her by her hollering, I reckon."

What can I write of Newgate prison that my reader has not read already? Shall I describe the stench of rotted bodies—some alive, and some long dead—of human waste, of sweat and filth and of fear, which has its own scent, I assure you. Shall I write of the conditions, not fit for any creature that bears the name *human*? As I followed the warder through these dark halls, I, who had seen so much and thought myself so immune to the sights of misery in this world, averted my eyes from the spent and sickly bodies visible through the bars. Fettered to the cold stone walls, they lay in their own feces, their bodies a-crawl with all manner of vermin. Turning my head away accomplished little, for the sounds of their groans and their pleadings echoed through the ancient stones of that dungeon. I should like to believe, reader, that it is only the most dangerous and violent criminals who endure these tortures, but you and I know that is not the case. I have learned of pickpockets—pickpockets, I say—who have been chained and left to die, swallowed alive by rats and lice, because of a lack of money to procure their easement. I have heard of men acquitted of all charges who have rotted to death for want of their discharge fees. Better to hang, I thought, than to remain in this place.

I followed the warder through this worst of abodes and we climbed the stairs to the women's ward of the Common Side. Perhaps my reader believes that there the female prisoners are protected from the molestation of the stronger sex, but in Newgate there can be no protection without money. Silver can procure nearly anything, including the right to hunt among the weak and defenseless women. When we entered the ward, we saw such bestial predators slink off into the shadows.

The warder called out Kate's name. It took but a few moments for her to appear, not of her own volition, but shoved forward by fellow prisoners who, out of the maliciousness bred in prison, denied her the right to hide herself.

I confess I felt remorse as I looked upon her. She was not the comely, if well-used, girl I had seen the night before, but a beaten and bloody waif. Her clothes had been torn and soiled, and she smelled strongly of urine. Filth of some sort was streaked across her face and in her hair, and she had open and bleeding wounds stretching from her forehead to her chin. Her legs were shackled in irons, an unnecessary precaution for a woman like Kate, but she had no doubt been unable to afford their removal. Women such as you know, reader, would find themselves reduced to unstoppable tears or perhaps even rendered insensible by the treatment Kate received in her first few hours at Newgate, but her misfortunes only made her stony and remote. Perhaps it was not her first time in the great prison, and perhaps it was not the first time she had been used so ill.

I whispered to the warder to remove her chains. I would pay for her easement when the sight of my silver would not cause either of us a problem. He nodded and crouched down to unlock the irons; Kate neither thanked him nor acknowledged in any way that her state had changed.

I required a private audience, and for an additional shilling the warder provided me with a closet, illuminated only by a tiny slit of a window. After indulging himself in a knowing grin, he closed the door and bade me holler if I required assistance. It was an overcast day, and once inside it was hard to see in the dingy room, but I required not much light for my purposes. The only furniture, I was hardly surprised to note, was a narrow bed covered with a tattered blanket and a family of rats that scurried away as we entered.

I hardly knew enough of her to speculate how the interview would proceed—I knew not if she would fight or cower. She sat quietly upon the bed and looked down, neither asking nor expecting anything of me. "Well, Kate," I said, forcing an ironic smile, lost upon her in the dusky cell. "You've landed yourself in a bit of a situation, haven't you?"

"I won't 'ang for something I didn't do." She so struggled to master her voice, I thought her jaw might snap from the pressure. She looked me full in the face. I could not mistake that she meant to challenge me. "Ah, Christ," she muttered, "ah, Jemmy."

"I am sorry for what happened to Jemmy," I told her softly.

She shook her head. "Jemmy," she muttered. Her head sunk low, almost to her lap. "Well, 'e won't be 'itting me no more, least. Or making me 'oard that what we can't sell to no one without Wild finding out. This is all 'is fault, I reckon." She suddenly looked up and met my eye. "And yer fault too. And I won't 'ang for what I didn't do."

"No," I said. "You won't hang, Kate, if we strike a bargain. I shall see to it. I cannot guarantee you will not be transported—but perhaps seven years in the colonies will help you to recover from the misfortunes of your life, as well as to escape the clutches of an unforgiving benefactor such as Mr. Wild." She started at the sound of his name. "This is what I shall do for you, Kate. I shall give you money enough to keep yourself away from the common sort while you stay here. Further, I shall use my influence with the magistracy to make sure that if you are convicted you are not sentenced to hang. I shall do what I can to see you acquitted—I don't want Wild to earn any money from your misfortune—but I can only promise you that you will not hang. Do you understand?"

"Aye," she said, her lips turning in a hint of an ironic smile. "I understand yer afraid I'll tell them about yer." She used the ends of her hair to wipe blood and filth from her forehead.

"No, I'm not, Kate. For you don't know my name and you don't know who I am. Further, were I to be brought forward, I would be forced to tell the court the truth—that I killed Jemmy while he tried to rob me—while he tried to rob me with your help. I can keep you alive if you cooperate with me, but if you force my hand you will hang. You are angry to be sure. You have been betrayed by Wild; I understand that. But if you want to stay alive, you had better listen to what I tell you. I know you do not like me—you see me as the reason that you are here, but you must understand that I am the only person who is able to help you presently."

"Why should ya 'elp me?" She did not look up, but her voice was steady and demanding.

"Not out of kindness, I assure you. Because it is in my best interest to do so." I kept my voice calm as I spoke to her. She saw I had a little power—enough to bribe the guard. For a woman in Kate's position, having a few pounds in one's purse and a mighty wig upon one's head was no great distance from influence with the courts. It was all a lie, of course. I had no influence, but I had to do everything in my power to keep her quiet. In return I would help as best I could, and make her believe that my influence would be enough. "Do not think you can harm me, Kate. You can make my life more complicated—no more. In exchange for promising to avoid these complications, I shall promise to keep you alive, and if I can, to have you declared innocent of this murder."

The look about her face did not change, but I now had her attention. She stared at me for many minutes before speaking. "What do ya want of me?"

I had accomplished *something*, for she now showed at least that she was willing to listen to me. "Two things only. First, that you do not mention me in any way. I care not what you tell the court—but you are not to mention that a gentleman did this thing. Jemmy was a dangerous man with many enemies far more likely than you to shoot him. For all I care, you can hint that there was a rivalry with Jemmy and Wild—that should prove a just recompense for his treachery. But you must not mention me nor your own knowledge of this accident. Do you understand, Kate? There is no evidence to support a conviction. Tell the court you know nothing, and the evidence will work for you—the facts will do you more service than your words ever could."

"Why should I trust you or the court?" she asked. "They 'ang them they want and free them they want. With Wild sayin' I done it, I'll never live to see Christmas 'less I plead my belly." I wondered if she was indeed pregnant, or if she simply intended to plead her belly, as so many women did, to grant them a few extra months of life.

"You overestimate Wild's influence," I said, finding no alternative than to lie boldly, "and you underestimate mine. You can see I am a gentleman and that I have powerful friends who are gentlemen. Do you understand what I have been telling you? If you admit to being there, to seeing what you saw, you will be admitting to a capital crime—if not the crime for which you are sitting here. If you are quiet, you cannot be convicted. Do you want to live?"

"Of course I want to live," she said bitterly. "Don't ask me foolish questions."

"Then you will do as I tell you."

She eyed me boldly. "Give me any reason to doubt ya, any reason at all, I'll tell what I know, and the devil take the consequences. That's why I want ya should tell me yer name."

"My name," I repeated.

"Aye. Tell me yer name, or I don't do what yer ask."

"My name," I said, attempting to think of some lie I might easily remember. "My name is William Balfour." Perhaps I should have picked a name with even more distance from myself, but it was the first thing that came to mind. Besides, I thought, any confusion I might dump on Balfour was no less than the pompous fellow deserved.

Kate studied me. "I know a William Balfour, and yer not 'im. A niggardly gentleman what used to come see me. But I reckon there might be more'n one of such a name."

Indeed there might be, I silently agreed, wondering if the Balfour she knew was the Balfour who had hired my services. But I could not worry myself about which whores a man like Balfour visited. "There is another, more important matter that we must attend to. As you know, I came to you to retrieve a friend's goods. There was something in particular that he believed to be in his pocketbook, but that was not in there. Did you take anything from that book, Kate?"

She shrugged. "I don't remember 'im. One drunken fool's the same as the next."

I sighed. "Where do you keep the goods you take?"

"Some Wild's got—but most of the things I stashed before I went to tell him 'bout Jemmy."

"What do you have stored now?"

"Wigs, watches . . ." She trailed off, as though forgetting of what she had been speaking.

I sighed. If Wild had the letters then I would have to tell Sir Owen that precisely what he wished to avoid had come to pass. "You know of no papers? A packet of letters, bound with a yellow ribbon, sealed with wax?"

"Oh, aye, the papers." She nodded, strangely pleased with herself. "Quilt Arnold's got those, 'e does. 'E thinks they're worth somethin'. 'E saw 'em and said they must be some gentleman's love letters—all smelling pretty and nice—and that such a gentleman would want 'em back, 'e said."

I tried to disguise my relief. "Who is Quilt Arnold, and where might I find him?"

Quilt Arnold, it turned out, had been Jemmy's competition for Kate's affections before Jemmy had met with his unfortunate rendezvous with my ball of lead. He frequented an alehouse at the sign of the Laughing Negro located in Aldwych, near the river. She ran a similar buttock-and-twang scheme with Arnold there, but the pickings had been slimmer for the patronage had been poorer: mainly sailors and porters and others who could be taken for a few shillings at most. Kate had sent Arnold word after I'd put a hole in Jemmy, and he promised he would take care of her, although mainly what he did was load himself up with as much of Kate's booty as he could carry and then advise her to talk to Wild.

"Have you any notion," I asked Kate, "what exactly Quilt Arnold thinks these letters worth?"

"Oh, I reckon 'e expects to get ten or twenty pound, 'e does."

I feared that this business was turning less and less profitable. I was loath to hand over twenty pounds to this blackguard, but I had no choice but to regain these letters. "Do you know where he keeps them?" If I could burgle the letters, I thought, rather than negotiate for them, I might save myself some time, money, and danger. Such was not to be the case.

" 'E said 'e would keep 'em 'pon 'im," Kate told me, "for 'e said 'e knew that someone would be comin' for 'em sooner or later. They wasn't safe nowhere else, 'e said."

This information certainly narrowed my options. If this Arnold had a notion of what was in the letters, it could be quite bad for Sir Owen. They need not have the proof to spread damaging rumors, particularly if this Sarah Decker he intended to marry was as delicate as Sir Owen claimed.

I went over with her what she had told me and then handed her a purse with five pounds in it, enough for her to eat, drink, and clothe herself in relative comfort until her trial.

Once I left her cell I would have to make arrangements for her lodgings. In order for her to cooperate with me, Kate would have to be made comfortable, and that meant moving her to the Press Yard—no inexpensive place, I can assure you, as it was the most desirable section of the prison. There the inmates could enjoy relatively spacious and clean rooms, walk about unmolested in the open air of the courtyard, and be waited on by turnkeys who had more in common with tavern publicans than jailers. Anything could be procured for silver in the Press Yard. While the drink was weak and sometimes stale, it was better than the foul water of the Common Side. And if the food was overpriced and bland, it proved far superior to the slop the poorer prisoners endured, often so crawling with maggots as to be nearly inedible.

The price of these accommodations would injure me severely: twenty pounds to gain Kate entrance to the Press Yard, and another eleven shillings a week for her rent. After the money I would have to pay this villain Arnold, and the several bribes that had already lightened my purse, I saw no possibility that Sir Owen's remarkable fee of fifty pounds should so much as cover my expenses. A matter I had believed should be simple and lucrative was now to cost me an amount that would reckon in the shillings if not the pounds. Parting with so large a sum to house Kate made me miserable, but I could not see that I had a choice. I would pay as required for her silence.

"I shall come back to make sure you are well," I told her, though it was a lie, just as my assurance that she would not hang was a lie. I expected the evidence would acquit her, though I knew not to what lengths Jonathan Wild would go to procure witnesses for a prosecution. Nevertheless, I could not make myself Kate Cole's protector, so I left Newgate prison hoping, in the weeks ahead, to think of her as little as possible.

Six

RATHER THAN RETURN HOME I went immediately to the vicinity of Bloomsbury Square, where my friend Elias Gordon took a lodging he could ill afford on Gilbert Street. I was younger in those days, and required little in the way of assistance, but at times when I could not adequately serve one of my patrons without some aid, I was accustomed to calling on Elias, a Scottish surgeon and a trusted friend. I met Elias after my last fight, when I had so permanently damaged my leg. It had been during my third pitched battle with Guido Gabrianelli, that Italian whom I had beaten twice before and whose beatings had earned me so much notoriety.

Gabrianelli had come from Padua, where he was known as the Human Mallet or some other such rot uttered in his native and effeminate tongue. I had boxed against foreign men before; Mr. Habakkuk Yardley, who arranged my fights, loved a match against foreigners, for Englishmen gladly paid forth their shillings to see one of their countrymen—or even a Jew they could pretend was a true Englishman—fight a Frenchified dandy. There was something rather leveling about the conflicts of fists— Jews became Englishmen and all foreigners became Frenchmen.

This Human Mallet Gabrianelli arrived in England, and without so much as inquiring of me or Mr. Yardley about arranging a pitched battle, he proceeded to publish the most infuriating notice in the *Daily Advertiser:*

> It has come to my attention that there is a Boxer on this island
> who is credited with the strength of a Samson—one *Benjamin*

Weaver, who calls himself the *Lion of Judah*. But if he claims he can
beat me, I call him the *Liar of Judah*. In my native *Italy* no one
dares fight me, for I break every opponent's jaw with my fist. Let
us see if this *Weaver* has the courage to match his strength with
mine. Standing ready and at his service, I am

> Guido Gabrianelli, the Human Mallet

My fellow-fighters and I were astonished at the belligerence of this foreigner. It was no uncommon thing for boxers to take out provoking notices in this paper, but one usually waited until a conflict had produced a
grudge—to begin a relationship with a grudge was a very preposterous
thing. But Mr. Yardley saw that there was silver in Gabrianelli's absurdity,
and that these flamboyant boasts should draw us a pretty crowd. So while
he made arrangements with this worthy, I replied in kind, taking out my
own advertisement, which Mr. Yardley had advised me to make as provoking as I could.

Let *Mr. Gabrianelli*, this fighter from *Italy*, be aware that I am ready
and eager to box with him at a moment's notice. I do not doubt
the veracity of his claims that in his native land he breaks every
opponent's jaw with his fist, but *Mr. Gabrianelli* ought to be
advised that here he will be fighting men of grit, and I have reason
to doubt that he could break a *Briton's* jaw with an anvil. Should
Mr. Gabrianelli be reckless enough to agree to the challenge he has
proposed, I heartily hope all natives of this Island will attend to
see what happens to foreigners who come to these shores to make
idle boasts to,

> Ben. Weaver

This fight became the talk of the votaries of the art of pugilism, and it
proved to be better attended than we had dared to hope, bursting to its
very capacity Mr. Yardley's theatre in Southwark. Indeed, the take at the
door was in excess of one hundred and fifty pounds, of which Yardley took
a third and the fighters each a third.

Gabrianelli arrived looking like a game-enough boxer. I had seen this
man once before, and that at a distance, as he paraded about town in his
silly red suit, dandified with stuff and ribbons, and from the look of him I

thought any Briton at all should be able to fell the Italian with no greater weapon than his breath. Now, stripped as we both were to naught but our breeches, stockings, and pumps, I could see he was a man of some muscle. More than that, he had a frighteningly bestial quality about him, for beneath his freshly shaved head, his back and chest were matted with thick black hair like an ape of Africa. The crowd, too, had been expecting a silly fop who knew not enough to remove his wig for the match, and many stared in mute amazement at this shaggy creature as he lumbered back and forth along his end of the ring, flexing the muscles of his chest and arms.

My concerns, at least for this fight, proved groundless. Once the battle began, Gabrianelli lashed out with a powerful blow to my chin. It came quite suddenly, and it hurt tremendously, I admit, but I made a show of demonstrating to the cheering crowds that my jaw was not broken. I turned my back to my opponent and slapped my own face lightly on either side, which gesture awarded me an uproarious cheer.

Gabrianelli attempted to sneak up behind me, to take advantage of my antics. I knew my behavior was dangerous, but it pleased the crowd, and thus it pleased Mr. Yardley, who was never ungenerous with bonuses for his best fighters, just as he was merciless to his fighters who lost too often. In any event, I ducked just in time to evade a powerful blow of this Human Mallet, and taking advantage of my crouched position, I lashed out with a right fist pointed directly to his gut, cutting upward just as I made contact, in the hopes of lifting him into the air.

I succeeded. It is no idle boast that I sent him reeling backward, as though blown by a great gust of wind, until his feet met the railing of the ring, and he tripped over, falling onto an eager gathering of spectators, who joined in the fun by beating him down until he grew quite intertwined with the thicket of legs. The crowd was now wild, and I raised my hands in victory, even as I taunted Gabrianelli to return to the ring. He lay motionless for only a second, and then he stirred, rising to his feet, his mouth agape with confusion. When he turned to look upon me, I saw that his face, along with much of his bald head, had turned a blinding crimson, and he began waving a fist about him in a challenging manner, shouting something in his own whimsical language.

Mr. Yardley, a notorious fighter in his own day, now grown fat and jolly, called to me from below, "I think he's challenging you, Ben."

"Challenging me to what?" I inquired with some difficulty, for my jaw had already grown sore from the blow it had taken. "This is a boxing ring. What more of a challenge could he desire?"

As it happened, he wished to challenge me to a duel of blades. It seemed that in Italy, one never strikes an opponent in the stomach. It is considered unmanly. There, I suppose, they simply strike one another in the face all day—making it no surprise that these jaws of theirs shatter so routinely. Gabrianelli believed that I had committed an outrage and re- fused to step into the ring again with a man who knew no honor. I was thus declared a winner, and Mr. Yardley narrowly averted a riot, for the crowd began to murmur with rage that they had paid a shilling to see only three punches thrown. By announcing that their admission fee had paid for them to witness proof of the strength of the Briton over the foreigner, Yardley saved his neck and our proceeds.

My reputation only grew as a result of this match, and while I contin- ued to fight, and quite frequently win, all about the city—in Smithfield, Moorfields, St. George's Fair Grounds, as well as Yardley's theatre at Southwark—Gabrianelli crawled off to lick his wounds and to learn that in England boxing is more than just an endless volley of jaw-pummeling. After spending some months sparring in the British fashion, he sent me another challenge, which I happily answered. Gabrianelli had improved his skills, but I found him still weak about the middle section. He struck me in the jaw. I returned in the stomach. He launched another peg to my face, and I to his middle. This continued, almost monotonously, for a quarter of an hour, until out of pure spite I aimed a blow as hard as I could to his chin, sending him down on his back. I ran over, ready to serve him more of the same, though I could not believe that his jaw had taken any more punishment than had my hand, for Gabrianelli had a solid chin, and it hurt far less to punch him about the middle. Further blows, fortunately, were not called for, for he lay still, his arms high above his head, his legs curled up like a baby's. It was a position from which he did not stir for a full half an hour.

When Yardley and I received our third challenge of Gabrianelli, we lit- tle thought to accept it. It was unclear that the crowd would pay to see me beat this man a third time, but while we hesitated, Gabrianelli assaulted us with insulting advertisements almost daily, first calling me *coward* and *buffoon*. I laughed these insults off, but when he changed his tack to call- ing me *a coward from an island of cowards* and a *British buffoon, the most laughable kind of buffoon in the world*, Yardley believed these insults should produce a sufficient interest in the match. Indeed, the crowds did turn out for this third fight. I had grown overconfident of my abilities to defeat this man, which was foolish of me, for I knew Gabrianelli to have some true skill; I had tasted myself the power of his blows. But I believed too strongly in my own previous victories, and the bets placed on the fight echoed my confidence, for the odds that I should lose were placed at twenty to one.

My opponent had trained for this fight. I later learned that he had spent hours allowing men to strike him in the stomach, hoping to build an endurance. Now, when I began, as I had before, with a frenzied assault upon his middle, he manfully withstood my blows. He continued with his own strategy of pummeling me about my face, and I, with an equally masculine resolve, withstood his best. We beat each other fiercely for the better part of an hour until my naked skin glistened with sweat and his black hair clumped in ugly tangles about his body. This fight lasted so long that I believe the crowd began to grow restless, for by the end we circled one another listlessly, as though underwater, aiming blows, or slowly avoiding them.

It was then that he hit me. It was a marvelous and artful punch, one I did not believe him to have in reserve. He aimed directly at my jaw, and in my weariness I did not see it coming. Or rather, I did see it coming, but I could not quite remember what to do about a punch aimed full to my face. I watched it sail toward me like some demon bird, until he struck me hard upon my chin. I remember thinking, as a hot, obscuring whiteness clouded my vision, and I lost all sense of balance, that I should be the object of unceasing ridicule if my jaw should indeed be broken. My concern was misplaced, for my jaw survived the day with only a severe swelling, but the force of Gabrianelli's blow knocked me backward and quite out of the ring in a mirror image of our first match.

I cannot easily describe what I felt—confusion, horror, shame, and a kind of focused agony so intense that I could not even tell if it was pain at all or something entirely new to my experience. At first I could not quite locate its source, but as my vision cleared, I noted with the kind of calm acceptance that sometimes befalls the victims of misfortune that my left leg lay at the most damnable angle. Upon flying from the ring, my right foot had caught upon the very edge of the stage, and I landed hard upon my left shin, which broke in two separate places.

As the shock of the moment wore off, my torment, the likes of which I hope never to know again, rendered me insensible, and I must rely on Elias's account of what happened next.

Then a complete stranger to me, Elias Gordon had chosen, in a gambler's panic, to bet a hundred pounds against the favored fighter. When I landed against the ground in a twisted heap, he had jumped up and shouted "Two thousand pounds!" at the very top of his voice. I do not believe he had ever been in possession of so massive a sum before, and overwhelmed with the possibilities that my misfortune had provided for him, he arranged with Mr. Yardley that he should tend to me himself at no charge. My supposed friend, Yardley, was agreeable, for Elias expressed some concern over the injury. The break was serious enough that he considered my life to hang in the balance for the next few days, and should I live, he doubted that I should ever walk again, and fully dismissed the idea that I should ever fight again. Like all medical men, Elias perhaps exaggerated the dangers of my condition, so if matters turned out badly his predictions would prove accurate, and if I recovered he should appear a miracle worker. Mr. Yardley listened to Elias's evaluation and pronounced that it was all one to him and that he had no regard for ruined fighters; I never saw the man again but when he came to deliver my share of the proceeds.

Elias, however, made my recovery his only concern; he stayed with me in my rooms almost every night the first week, to make certain my fever did not carry me off. It was a testament to his skills as a surgeon that I can even walk at all, for most men to suffer damage of this severity can move about only with the aid of crutches or must bear the indignity and torment of amputation. As I lay under his care, growing fond of this whimsical Scotsman, I confess I felt the greatest envy of him. My livelihood had been wrested from me, and here was a man gifted at his craft who had procured enough money that he could set himself up in the proper style and never want for bread again.

Elias, unfortunately, like my new acquaintance, Sir Owen, had a taste for the pleasures of the town—he also had a bit of poetry in him. Just a bit, I say, as anyone who had read his volume of verse, *The Poetical Surgeon*, would agree.

Elias never explained to me how he spent that money—no doubt he had squandered it in endless and unmemorable bouts of whoring, gaming, and poetic composition—but after I recovered from my injury, and spent my darker years away from London, I returned and called upon my old friend to find him as jolly as ever, dressed in the fashionable style and following after the amusements of the town—but for all his gaiety, he was entirely penniless.

Elias was something of a fop, I suppose, but a thoughtful one—if the thinking fop is no contradiction of terms. I knew him to be a surgeon of uncommon skill, but he was none the most devoted to his art. Had he spent as much time pursuing surgery as he did women, I believe he might have been the first name in fashionable society, but his love of his craft could not compete with his love of his pleasure. Elias was friends with every bawd, whore, and merrymaker in town. Whores, I suspect, liked me because I was pleasant and courteous, and perhaps because they found my Hebrew physiognomy entertaining. They liked Elias, however, because he spent all of his money among them and therefore he was an honored guest in every bawdy house in London.

This dissolute manner of living left him happy but short of ready money. Consequently, he was always eager to offer me assistance for a few pounds thrown in his direction.

In light of Elias's lax attention to his surgical arts, I was surprised to learn he was about the town assisting a patient when I called on him, so I cooled my heels in the parlor of Mrs. Henry, his landlady. She was a delightful widow; once, I suspect, quite pretty, but now, past thirty-five, she was in the autumn of her beauty. Yet she had charms aplenty to keep me occupied in a parlor, and as I had often detected a fondness she harbored for me, there was no small amount of gratification in passing the time with her.

"Have you some particular business today?" Mrs. Henry asked me as we sat together. She stared bluntly at my head.

I had all but forgotten that I wore a wig. I should have forgotten entirely, but for the unusual warmth of this autumn afternoon. "I had need to appear the great gentleman for a matter of business in which I am currently engaged," I explained.

"I should very much like to hear more of it," she told me, as her servant wheeled in the tea things. I found Mrs. Henry to have a most complete service. Tea had not yet reached its stature of domestic necessity, but Mrs. Henry was enamored of the drink, and her tray held a variety of charming china. The drink she poured was a strong blend that she told me had been sent by a brother who was in the East India trade.

"I am employed upon a complicated if uninteresting affair," I told her evasively, while gently indicating that I wanted none of the sugar she was poised to drop into my tea.

"Do Hebrews not eat sugar?" she asked me with a genuine curiosity.

"As much as anyone, in the abstract," I told her. "This Hebrew too much enjoys the taste of tea to have it compromised by a cloying sweetness."

She squinted in confusion, but she handed me the dish just the same. "Can you tell me about this employment?"

"I'm afraid not, madam. I am operating under strict confidentiality at present. Perhaps when the matters are resolved I may be able to inform you—omitting proper names, you understand."

She leaned forward. "You must learn so much in your line of work that others do not know."

"You make it seem far more interesting than it is, I assure you. I suspect a woman in your position to have more knowledge of the doings of the town than ever I could."

"Then should you ever require information, I hope you will not hesitate to ask it of me."

I thanked her for her kindness just as Elias appeared, to Mrs. Henry's evident disappointment. He entered the room wearing a scarlet waistcoat, with a royal-blue frilled shirt beneath. His wig was over-large, almost a relic of fashion since past—a bit spotty in places and excessively powdered. It draped onto his angular face, which, like the rest of his body, was thin and marked by sharp and unexpected protrusions of his skeleton. Elias's trousers had an obvious tear above the left knee, and though they were similar enough to attract no undue attention, I could not help but notice that his shoes were not of precisely the same color. Yet my friend walked in with the dignity of a returned conqueror and the self-assured stance of a favored courtier of Charles II's day.

"It is so very warm outside, Mrs. Henry," he said to his landlady, waving an indigo-colored handkerchief at her. "Lady Kentworth nearly fainted, though I took scarcely a thimbleful of blood from her. She has the most delicate constitution, you know. Hardly prepared for this kind of weather in October." Elias had been marching toward Mrs. Henry, no doubt prepared to pay her in gossip what he could not afford her in rent, but he saw me offer him a slight smile from my tattered but comfortable armchair. "Oh," he said, as though I were a debt collector. "Weaver."

"Have I reached you at a bad time, Elias?"

Remembering himself, he forced a smile. "Not at all. Merely a bit out of sorts from this dreadful heat. You must be, as well. Shall I bleed you?" he asked, recovering from his momentary confusion by displaying the kind of impish grin he reserved for the moments he wished to harass me with either railleries or requests for ready money.

Elias thought my refusal to undergo phlebotomy was perhaps the most entertaining thing he knew of, and he jibed at me constantly. "By all means, bleed me," I said. "And perhaps you would like to remove my organs for me and place them in a box. Where they will be safe."

"You mock modern medicine," Elias noted as he strolled across the room and seated himself, "But your mockery does not lessen the value of my surgical skills." He turned to Mrs. Henry. "Perhaps some tea, madam."

Mrs. Henry flushed and then stood, holding her body unnaturally erect. She smoothed out her skirts. "You expect many honors, Mr. Gordon, for a man who has not honored me with the rent this quarter. You may pour it yourself," she said as she left the room.

Upon her departure, I asked Elias how long he had been bedding his landlady.

He took a seat across from me and removed a snuffbox, taking a delicate pinch. "Is it so obvious, then?" He turned to inspect a painting upon the wall, that I might not witness his embarrassment. Elias always preferred that I should think of him as successful with only the most beautiful young ladies of the town. Mrs. Henry was still handsome, but hardly the sort with whom Elias wished to be identified.

"I have never heard of a landlady refusing to pour tea for a tenant upon any other grounds," I explained. "I assure you, Elias, I have myself negotiated rent in a similar fashion."

"Gad!" he nearly snorted snuff about the room. "Not that virago with whom you now rent, I hope."

I laughed. "No, I cannot say that I have had the honor of sharing an intimacy with Mrs. Garrison. Do you think it worth a try?"

"I have heard you Hebrews to be lascivious," Elias said, "but I have never seen any evidence that you lacked judgment."

"Nor have I with you," I told him, hoping to make him feel at ease with my discovery.

He set aside his snuffbox and arose to pour himself a dish of tea. "Well, it's been a pleasant arrangement, you know. She's not a terribly demanding mistress, and the money I save in rent is useful."

"Elias," I said, "these private matters are always fascinating, and I should very much like to hear about your amorous conquest of all the landladies in London, but I have come upon business."

He returned to his chair and took a cautious sip of the hot drink. "A very bewigged business, I see. What occupies your thoughts, Weaver— your overly phlegmatic, in want of being bled, thoughts?"

"Quite a bit, in fact. I have a complicated matter to attend to, and a ticklish one to set aside before I can address it." Feeling invigorated by Mrs. Henry's excellent tea, I took the time to tell Elias not only of my unexpected encounter with Balfour but also of my troubles in retrieving Sir Owen's pocketbook. I felt perfectly at ease confiding in Elias, for though he loved gossip more than any man I knew, he had never betrayed a confidence when I had asked for his silence.

"I am not at all surprised to learn that Sir Owen Nettleton should find his life complicated by whores and the French pox," Elias assured me with a smug twitch of his eyebrows.

"You know him, then?"

"I know the principals in fashionable life as well as any man in this metropolis. Besides," he added with the practiced look of the sly rogue, "who do you think it is that has treated Sir Owen each time he finds himself clapped?"

"What can you tell me of him?"

Elias shrugged. "No more than you might imagine. He holds a large and prosperous estate in Yorkshire, but his revenue in rent is no match for the costs of his pleasures. He's a notorious bawd and a womanizer—an exceptionally vigorous one, even by my standards. I shouldn't be surprised if he had tried every whore in town."

"He takes no small pride in his prolific dealings with the ladies of the street."

"These men of wealth must do something to fill up their time. Now, who is this jade who took his things? I wish to know what goods your little misadventure has taken out of circulation."

I gave him her name.

"Kate Cole!" he exclaimed. "Why, I've tasted of her wares—no poor wares are they, either. You've gone and ruined a perfectly good whore, Weaver."

"Am I the only man in London not to have swived this Kate Cole?" I gasped.

"Well, I should not think it too late," Elias said with a grin. "She must owe you something if you've purchased for her a room in the Press Yard. You could buy tumbles for a year on what a month in the Press Yard will cost you."

I opened my mouth in order to change the topic, but Elias, as he often did, took command of the conversation. "This matter of Balfour, now *that* is interesting. I can only imagine your disorder when you heard him speak so of your father's death. You will certainly contact your uncle now."

Elias knew of my estrangement from my family, and indeed he had often urged me to approach my uncle. He, too, had spent several years in the displeasure of his father. Elias had been in attendance at Saint Andrews University when his father had learned of malicious, if entirely accurate, accounts of my friend's many debaucheries. This knowledge had produced a rupture between Elias and his family, and rather than continuing in studies that would have led to a career as a physician, Elias was forced to leave and take up as a surgeon—without burdening himself by attending to the usual seven years of apprenticeship. After many years of no communication, Elias had managed to resolve the difficulties with his family, if not entirely, then at least to the point where he received a quarterly remittance. This arrangement seemed to me to be to everyone's advantage, for Elias's older brother, to whom the family estate should descend, was a sickly fellow, and the family patriarch wished to at least be on amicable terms with Elias should fate decree that he become the scion. I could easily relate to Elias's difficulties as a younger son, for my elder brother, José, had always appeared to my father to be destined for greatness, while I, the bearer of the congenital defect of having been born four years after him, had been made to feel like an expendable appendage.

I recounted for Elias the details of my conversation with Balfour, and my friend became less interested in mending for me the rupture with my family than in learning more about what Balfour believed to be the true story of these deaths. "I must say, Weaver, that this inquiry is indeed unusual. How will you find a murderer whom no one has seen or even believes exists?"

"I do not know that I can. But I must look to Kate Cole first, I think."

"Kate Cole is devilish less intriguing, I assure you, than your phantom murderer. But you are right—we must attend to these letters, and that shall certainly give me time to think on how we are to proceed with finding this killer."

"I say, Elias, you are an enthusiastic sort. Balfour is hardly paying me so much that I shall be able to share excessively with you."

"You wound me, sir. You think it is only money I am after. I find the challenge stimulating, you know. But I assume your wealthy baronet shall be able to reward me more generously than your impoverished parvenu."

"My wealthy baronet has so far proved himself generous." I now had Elias's attention, and explained to him that I was in a bit of a bind and required him to play a role for me.

"It sounds shockingly exciting," he said, his eyes sparkling at the thought of this adventure.

"Oh, I hope not too exciting."

I had concocted a delightfully simple plan to retrieve Sir Owen's letters of this prig Arnold. I would enter the Laughing Negro dressed as a porter. Kate Cole had no doubt spoken to Arnold of a muscular gentleman, and I did not want to complicate things by having him suspect me to be the man who killed Jemmy. Elias, whom no one would accuse of being overly muscled, would enter and speak to Arnold, explaining that he was the owner of the letters. I had authorized him to give up to twenty pounds for their return, though he was to start with five pounds, for I still clung to some small hope that this business of the pocketbook would not run me into debt. If I could profit but a few pounds, and Sir Owen, in turn, was to speak well of me in public, then I would have good reason to consider my efforts well expended.

I had advised Elias that when dealing with this thief he was not to use Sir Owen's name—for there was a good chance that he had not read the letters, or at least not read them all the way through. I was sure Sir Owen's contrition and his widow's sentiments were too dull for a common thief. In any event, even if he knew the letters were not Elias's, I could not imagine him refusing the coin on a matter of principle.

I arrived at the Laughing Negro near seven in the evening. I easily spotted a man with coppery whiskers and bristly hair several shades darker than his beard. One eye was a cold and penetrating blue, the other lay dead in his skull. This was the man Kate had described to me. He sat at a table with four other men, each as dangerous in appearance and as foul in grooming habits as he. They were a miserable and drunken lot, grimly rolling a few dice back and forth across the table at one another. I paid for a pint of yeasty ale and sat as nearly behind him as I could, selecting a spot from which I could best observe Arnold and his companions without appearing to do so.

Elias came in precisely as I told him. His fanciful attire—all bright reds and yellows—rendered him the object of the room's attention, and the scrutiny instantly made him uneasy. I judged his discomfort a useful thing, however, for a gentleman in such a place should be uneasy. I had withheld from him Kate Cole's description of Arnold that he might have no expectations of the man. He thus inquired of the counterman, who pointed him to the fellow we sought.

Elias slowly walked over to the table, time and again putting his hand on his hangar and then removing it. I was careful not to watch him too closely, not wanting to risk any eye contact between the two of us. He approached Arnold and stood before him. "Are you, sir, one Quilt Arnold?" he asked in the loud, declamatory voice of a stage-play hero.

These men let out a round of guffaws before Arnold looked up, unable to fathom what this peacock could want with him. "Aye," he said, making no effort to hide his amusement. "I'm Arnold, me lud. What of it?"

"Yes," Elias said in a voice that bespoke his apprehension. "I am told by a woman called Kate Cole that you have something of mine. A packet of letters bound with a yellow ribbon."

Arnold raised one bushy eyebrow. "She tell you this before or after she gone to Newgate?"

"Have you the letters or no?"

The rogue showed him a large, yellow grin. "That's your business, is it, me lud? Well now, since it's your goods upon me, I'm glad to tell ye I got 'em," he said, patting his jacket. "I got 'em right 'ere. You'll be wantin' them, then. Is that right?"

Elias straightened his posture. "That's right."

Arnold had none of Elias's desire to transact the business rapidly. He patted his jacket again. He whispered something in the ear of one of his friends and then laughed a ghastly dry laugh for a full minute. Finally he turned back to Elias. "Ye don't mind that I blew some snot in 'em, do ye?"

Elias shook his head, doing his best to appear calm, and perhaps even irritated. "Mr. Arnold, I'm sure your life is uneventful enough that you feel the need to prolong this transaction, but I have business elsewhere. Now I want the letters back, and I shall give you twenty pounds for them."

I winced, and I was sure Elias inwardly did the same. He had misspoken, and if Arnold wished to haggle, there was no money with which to do it. Were I to stand up and offer Elias extra coin, of which I had little upon me, he would know the business was more complicated than it appeared, and he might withhold in the hope of more money yet.

"Any man who'd be willing to pay twenty pounds for a few pieces of paper," he said, leaning back in his chair and extending his legs, "would be willing to pay fifty. Since they belong to ye, if you see what I mean."

Elias surprised me with his courage, for Arnold was an imposing-looking villain. "No sir," he said. "I do not see what you mean. I come not to haggle with you. I shall give you twenty pounds for those letters or snot rags is all they will be to you."

Arnold thought about this for a moment. "You know what, me lud, I don't think a gentleman like yourself would come to a shithouse like this and talk to a shitten prig like me for a few folds of paper wrapped in a dainty if they was only worth twenty pounds. How about ye stop talkin' to me like I'm some whore what ye can swive and throw a few shillings at. Give me fifty pounds. And then maybe—maybe I say, because it depends on me mood—maybe I'll give ye the shitten papers. And then again maybe I won't. So when ye give me my money, me lud, be polite about it."

Elias had blanched with terror, and a filigree of blue veins now bulged at his temples. Arnold was unpredictable, and there was no telling how far he would push his antics. I understood then that there was no answer for it—I had no choice but to step in. Pushing my chair aside I stood and approached him. "Excuse me," I said. "I could not help but overhear what you were saying to this gentleman, and I wonder if you are aware of this?" And with a rapidity that astonished even myself, I removed from my belt a dagger, grabbed Arnold's left hand, which I pressed down to the table, and jabbed the dagger down hard, slicing through his hand and landing deep in the soft wood beneath.

Arnold let out a howl, but I quickly clamped a hand down over his mouth and removed a second dagger from my boot, which I held to his face.

I glanced hurriedly about the room, taking in as much information as I could in but a fleeting instant. The barkeeper looked over at me as he wiped down a glass. A few of the men about the Laughing Negro looked on. They cared only so much as the show intrigued them. I had no worry that a kindly stranger would rise to defend this brigand, but I had been concerned about his companions. Arnold's friends, however, made no moves. They sat stiffly, glancing at one another, exchanging looks of be-fuddlement while they tried to decide, no doubt, if should they wait to see what happened or if they should depart. I could tell from the way they pushed their bodies back into their chairs that they had no wish to inter-fere. Such were the friends men like Arnold made.

Elias had taken a step backward. He looked so pale one might think *he* had been stabbed. His limbs trembled noticeably, but he attempted to hold himself straight and present the demeanor of a dangerous buck. Al-though Elias had not the temperament for the situation in which we found ourselves, I knew I could trust him to acquit himself honorably.

I looked back to the table. There was less blood than I would have thought, for the blade itself stemmed the tide. A thick pool did begin to ap-pear around the blade after a moment, and trickled down upon the filthy table. I shifted slightly, so the issue of Arnold's veins would not drip upon my boots, and I pressed down hard as I moved, feeling the heat of Arnold's gasping breath upon my hand. Grabbing his face tighter, I waved my dag-ger before his good eye. "You are in pain, and I understand that, but I have no more patience for this. You will reach into your pocket with your one good hand and remove the papers we seek. This gentleman here will give you twenty pounds, just as promised. If you do anything else, if your friends make any moves, I shall not kill you, but I shall carve out your good eye and turn you to a beggar. Now you can give us what we want and receive a sizable profit for it, or you can lose everything you have in this world."

Arnold's friends exchanged glances once again. They now had hope that their friend would, notwithstanding the unpleasantness of the transaction, earn his twenty pounds.

With his good hand, Arnold tried to reach into his pocket, but he had to stretch across his body and by the way he twisted his face the pain must have been horrific. Finally, against the weight of my hand, he slammed his teeth together and grabbed a purse from his pocket, and in a jerky and ag-onized motion, threw it upon the table.

I told Elias to look inside, and he did, taking out the packet of letters. They were as Sir Owen had described—a thick bundle bound with a yel-low ribbon and sealed with a wax imprint. I had him hand them to me, and I quickly counted that there were four separate packets, each a half-inch or more thick. Even in the flurry of the moment, I could not but smile to think what a prolix correspondent the libertine baronet turned out to be.

I placed the bundle in my pocket and told Elias to hold down Arnold's hand as I pulled out my dagger. Now the blood began to flow with an unchecked burst. Arnold slipped from my grasp and dropped to the floor, uttering low, growling noises.

"Give him the money," I said to Elias.

I could see the way he thought behind his shifting gray eyes. *Why?*

"Give him the money," I said again. "That was the bargain."

There must have been something about the way I spoke that ended the argument, for Elias sighed, agonized about letting go of the twenty pounds unnecessarily, and dropped the purse upon the table. Each of Arnold's companions reached forward to grab it.

Elias looked ready to make a running escape, but I shook my head at him. There was no need to run. Arnold lay defeated, and no one would trouble us. I considered drinking an ale before I left to show my contempt, but I had no one to gratify but myself, and the drink was not to my liking. Instead I smiled with grim satisfaction and held the door for Elias as we departed.

SEVEN

THE MORNING FOUND ME refreshingly calm. I was pleased to have retrieved Sir Owen's documents, and I felt tolerably confident that the business of Jemmy's death would pass without any serious harm. Hard upon noon, Mrs. Garrison announced that Sir Owen was below to see me, and when the baronet entered my rooms he could not have shown more pleasure in my success. He clutched his letters from my hand and pressed them to his bosom. He sat down and then immediately stood up again and paced about the room. He asked for a drink and then asked for another one, having forgotten about the first.

Sir Owen insisted upon paying me a bonus, and after some formal protests, I accepted reimbursement for the expenses I had met in my dealings with Kate and Arnold. This gesture was a generous one, for it doubled his original fee and it significantly improved my little stock of money. Sir Owen then convinced me to join him for a meal that he should pay for, so he would not have to collect the letters, as he said, without having shown some measure of the fellowship his gratitude bred within him. I attended him to a local ordinary, and ate and drank heartily, and I remained with Sir Owen until near two o'clock in the afternoon, when he said he had appointments to keep. Before we parted, however, he shocked me by asking me to join him next Tuesday evening at his club.

"It is no formal affair, I assure you," he said, reading the astonishment on my face. "I thought it might be of some advantage to a man in your position to have occasion to introduce yourself to some gentlemen."

"I would be delighted to attend," I told him in earnestness. "And I would hold myself in your debt for your generosity."

Sir Owen cleared his throat and shifted in his seat. "You, shall we say, understand that I am in no way proposing you for membership." His voice trailed off.

"I quite understand," I cut in quickly, wishing to defuse his embarrassment. "I am, as you have surely surmised, anxious to meet gentlemen who may someday have need of a man such as myself. And a recommendation from you is a powerful thing."

Pleased with my understanding, Sir Owen gave me a friendly clap upon the back and thanked me again for my effort to retrieve his papers. Then, after a protracted farewell, he made his retreat.

With a satisfied stomach and a head full of good wine, I thought to myself that it was time to discharge my duties. I therefore took a hackney to Mr. Balfour's lodgings off Bishopsgate to see what, if anything, he had learned from his inquiries into what his father's family knew of that death. I hoped he would have learned nothing. I hoped he would have concluded the fruitlessness of his search and discharged me from this affair with an unblemished conscience.

I found Balfour in a respectable set of rooms in a respectable home, but he sat in his parlor as though it fit too snug upon him. He held himself unnaturally erect in his chair, as if afraid to recline. He wore almost precisely the same suit of clothing that I had seen upon him the previous day, though he had made some effort to clean the cloth of some lint and remove the more conspicuous stains.

I stood before him, my hat tucked under my arm. He stared at me. He crossed his legs. I expected him to offer me a chair, but he studied me with an expression that could have been either anxiety or boredom. "Next time you wish to speak to me," he said with a slow and deliberate tone, "please inform me in advance. We shall establish a meeting place more appropriate than my own residence."

"As you wish," I replied with a broad smile, meant to irritate him, for I found Balfour's penniless superiority filled me with both anger and contempt. "But as I am here, I shall make myself comfortable." I noticed a decanter of wine on the mantel, and still warm from my luncheon with Sir Owen, I thought a bit of wine was just the thing. "Would you care for some?" I asked, as I poured for myself.

"You are insufferable," he snapped. "This is my home, sir!" His hands clutched at a newspaper that rested in his lap.

I took a seat and slowly sipped the wine, an inferior claret. It was not undrinkable but it tasted sour in comparison with the fine drink Sir Owen had provided. I suspect that my host saw the signs of my displeasure, for he moved to open his mouth. I thought it best to avoid what I was sure would be an expression of his ungrounded pomposity, so I began rapidly. "Mr. Balfour, you have hired my services, but I am not a servant. After all, we have a mutual interest in the inquiry you wish to set me upon. Now, shall we discuss the particulars of this situation?"

Balfour glowered at me for a moment and decided that impassivity was his best option. "Very well. I am afraid you will have to do the work your-self, which is, I expect, why I am paying you. I have spoken to my father's chief clerk, and he has informed me that my suspicions are not un-founded. He claims the estate was much poorer at my father's death than he, the clerk, had any reason to suspect."

"Indeed," I noted coolly.

"As I believe I mentioned, my father had profited somewhat from the late rivalry between the Bank of England and the South Sea Company—all that fluctuation of stock prices. He spent his time down in 'Change Alley, with the Jews and other foreigners, buying this stock and selling that."

"And some of these stocks are missing?"

He shrugged as though I had just rudely changed the subject. "I know nothing of the details. I have no head for things such as finance, but in light of the profits he made from these dealings, his accounts are inexpli-cable. According to the clerk, you understand."

"I see. Can you tell me what else you learned?"

"Is that not enough? What I have learned is that a financial person be-lieves my father's death suspicious. What more do you require?"

"Nothing," I said, "to make me wish to look into this matter further." I had spoken this before I had realized it to be true. Now, as I sat across from Balfour, sipping his poor wine, I realized the course upon which I found myself. I would certainly have to learn more of my own father's dealings, and to do so I would need to talk with my uncle. After my years of wan-dering, this jackanapes Balfour would be the man to send me home.

Pushing this idea from my mind, I pressed on with Balfour. "I fear I require much more if I am to unearth anything that might help you to recover your estate. Your mother is still living, is she not? I believe you mentioned her last time we spoke."

Balfour reddened, I thought inexplicably. "I say, sir! You ask unaccountably impertinent questions. What is my mother to you?"

"I suspect your mother may know something that could be of use. I really do not understand why you must make everything difficult. Do you wish my help or no?"

"Certainly I wish your . . . services. That is why I have put you in my employ. That does not give you license to go about asking me questions about my mother, who would be utterly horrified to learn that men such as you even exist, let alone that you speak of her. My mother, sir, knows nothing of these matters. There is no point in talking to her."

"Did your father have any other relatives—a brother perhaps, an uncle—with whom he dealt in business?"

Balfour continued to sigh with exasperation, but he answered the question. "No. No one."

"And you can think of nothing else that might be of use to me? Something to help me find how to begin my inquiry?"

"If I could think of anything, would I not tell you? You drive me to distraction with your endless questions."

"Very well. Then you only need let me know the name of your father's clerk and where I might find him."

Balfour's jaw went slack. He knew something that he refused to tell me. No, he knew many things that he refused to tell me. And I suspect he knew I saw through the façade of family pride and detected his screen of blustering. But he did not back down from it. "I have told you what he knows," Balfour said stiffly. "You have no need to talk with him."

"Mr. Balfour, you are being difficult. Where may I find this clerk?"

"You may not. You see, he is now employed in my mother's service, and my mother and I, since you insist upon knowing, are not upon the best of terms. She would not appreciate my meddling in her business."

"But surely she has much to gain from these inquiries."

"No, she has not. My mother had a jointure of separate property settled upon her. She was to inherit none of my father's wealth, and his death has not affected her at all, except to free her from a marriage that was broken in all but law. She and I had been upon poor terms for a very long time, for in the matters of my parents' disagreements, I took my father's side. Now I wish to arrange a . . . rapprochement with her, and I do not choose to antagonize her by looking into this business. I handled this clerk so that he would not know the nature of my inquiries. I do not believe you could do the same."

"I assure you I can. Give me his name, sir. I shall in return promise you that I shall not approach him at your mother's home."

Balfour screwed up his face to launch another protest, but he soon thought better of it. "Oh, very well. His name is Reginald d'Arblay, and if you really must speak to him you will find him, sooner or later, at Jonathan's Coffeehouse in 'Change Alley. He wishes to become a stock-jobber in his own right, so he spends his time in a stock-jobbing coffeehouse—I suppose in the hopes of having his foreskin removed. It is not all he will have removed, I should wager."

I sat silent for a few minutes, taking all of this in. "Very well, sir." I stood up and finished my wine in a long swallow. "I shall let you know when I have anything to report."

"Do not forget what I told you about calling on me here," he said. "I have a reputation to uphold, you know."

I COULD SEE THAT Balfour's mother would be of no use to me, but I wondered for how long I would respect Balfour's desire for me to avoid his father's clerk, d'Arblay. Not long, but I did not wish to call upon such a man unprepared. It was time, I knew, to do what I should have done years before, what I had so often both wished for and dreaded. This matter gave me the excuse I had long required, and the wine I had drunk gave me the courage I had long wanted. So I found myself walking briskly toward Wapping, where my uncle Miguel kept his warehouse.

I last had seen my uncle at my father's funeral, when I had stood, with a few dozen others, representing the family and members of the Dukes Place enclave, staring mutely beside the open grave, my coat offering little protection from the unexpected cold and wind and ceaseless drizzle of rain. My uncle, my father's only brother, had done little to make me feel welcome in my return. He acknowledged me only now and again, when he looked up from the prayer book that he hunched over to keep dry, in order to cast suspicious glances in my direction, as though I might, if given the opportunity, pick the other mourners' pockets and disappear into the fog. I could not help but wonder if my uncle resented that I had not returned home three years earlier, upon the death of his son, my cousin Aaron. I had been at that time still riding upon the highway, as the saying goes, and had not even learned of Aaron's death until some many months later. In all candor, I am not sure I would have returned even if I had heard; Aaron and I had not much liked each other as boys, for he had been a weak, timid, and sneaking sort, and I admit I had been little able to resist bullying him. He had always hated me for a monster while I hated him for a coward. When we grew older and I recognized that it was time to manage my rougher tendencies more carefully, I had made the effort to mend our friendship, but Aaron only walked away from me when I spoke to him in private, or mocked me for my lack of learning when we spoke in public. When I learned that he had been sent away to the East to become a trader in the Levant, I was glad to be rid of him. I could, nevertheless, feel sorrow for my uncle, who lost his only son when a trading vessel capsized in a storm and Aaron was swallowed by the ocean forever.

If my uncle treated me as an unavoidable interloper at my father's funeral, I must confess that I did little to convince him to see me otherwise. I found myself angry then at having to spend time with these people; I resented my father for having died, as his death had placed me in an uncomfortable state. It came as no surprise to me that my father left his estate to my older brother, José, and I was not disappointed he chose to do so, yet the knowledge that everyone at the funeral believed me bitter vexed me. I cast my eyes about me nervously as the mourners prayed dutifully in Hebrew and conversed in Portuguese, both of which I pretended to have forgotten, though I was alarmed to realize how much I had forgotten indeed; these languages sounded often like alien tongues made familiar but not intelligible through frequent exposure.

Now, as I went to see my uncle, I again felt like an interloper who should be stared at with suspicion and unease. All my efforts to calm my spirits—my pronouncements to myself that I went to visit Miguel Lienzo upon business, that I, as the initiator of this exchange, held the power to terminate it at will—failed to make me forget how little I welcomed this visit.

I had not been to the warehouse in many years—not since I was a young man running errands for the family. It was a largish affair—a storing house near the river, used both for the Portuguese wine that my uncle imported and the British woolens that he exported. He also maintained a less legal trade in French cambrics and other textiles, goods that had become the victims of the mutual embargoes with our enemies across the Channel; for there has ever been a great gulf between the hatred of the French engendered by politics and the desire for French goods inspired by fashion. Let the papers and Parliamentarians decry the dangers of the French military; ladies and gentlemen still clamored to buy French attire.

When I entered my uncle's warehouse, I was overwhelmed by the rich smell of wool, which made me feel damp and tight in the chest. This was an enormous, high-ceilinged place, alive with activity, for I had the ill fortune to arrive while a customs inspector went about his business. Brawny laborers hauled boxes or piled them up, packed or unpacked at the inspector's pleasure. Clerks ran about with ledgers in hand, attempting to keep a record of what was moved and to where.

I tensed with a boxer's preparedness when I saw my uncle at the other end of the room, metal bar in hand, ripping open crates for a fat, misshapen, pockmarked toady whose income depended upon finding violations and accepting bribes from violators. The look on his face told me that he had encountered neither. My uncle had always been a cautious man. Like my father, he believed that it would not take much for the Jews to be expelled from England as they had been from so many other countries—indeed, as they had been from England long ago. He therefore obeyed laws where he could and disobeyed carefully when he could not. It took no ordinary inspector to locate his contraband.

I stood watching him, admiring his poise and the respect he commanded. At my father's funeral, Uncle Miguel had looked not much older than I remembered. His hair had begun to turn a speckled color, his close-cut beard had grayed almost entirely, and the lines upon his face bespoke his near fifty years, but there was still youth in his eye and an energy in his motions. He had hardly taken his turn in the ring, but he was a fit man of sinewy muscle, and he indulged himself in well-tailored clothing that showed his shape to advantage. He shied away from the French fashions he surreptitiously imported, but his clothes were of the finest cloth, immaculately clean, and dark in color so as to recall the sober fashions of the Amsterdam business world in which he had come of age.

As I stood there, a darkish man of some middle years approached me with an obvious caution. I could see he was a Jew, but clean-shaven and dressed much as an English tradesman might have been—boots, sturdy linen pants and shirt, a protective but not decorative topcoat. He wore no peruke, and his real hair, like my own, was pulled back to resemble a tie-periwig. As I looked at this man, English in dress and manner, but Jewish in face—at least recognizably so to other Jews—I wondered if this was how I appeared to the Englishmen around me: unassumingly dressed, properly groomed, and for all that, quite alien.

"Can I be of some service?" this man asked me with a practiced smile. He paused and looked at me again. "Good Lord. Strike me dead if it is not Benjamin Lienzo."

I recognized the man then as Joseph Delgato, a longtime assistant to my uncle. He had been employed in my uncle's trade since I was but a boy. "I did not at first know you, Joseph." I held myself nervously as a long moment of uncomfortable silence passed between us. There was much that we both thought, but I think we separately concluded that there was little to be said. I grabbed his hand warmly. "You look well."

"And you too. I am glad you are come home. It is a terrible thing about your father, sir. A terrible thing."

"Yes. Thank you." I wondered if he thought that I had been reconciled with my family since the funeral. He appeared confused, but I suspected he merely considered himself to be excluded from private family matters.

"Mr. Lienzo will be done soon. The customs man has grown weary of trying to catch your uncle in an infraction of the law, so he now settles for the performance of an inspection, to be followed, naturally, with a polite acceptance of a bribe."

"Why must he be bribed if he has found no violation?"

Joseph smiled. "There is as much feigning and dodging in the world of trade as there is in the world of fighting," he told me, pleased with himself for having honored me with a pugilistic reference. "Were we not to offer him a token of our respect, shall we say, he would surely invent an infraction, and that would be far more troublesome and costly for us than a simple bribe. For then we would need to involve lawyers and judges and Parliamentarians and the Common Council, and all other manner of bodies you can think of. It is prudent to pay him. This way he becomes our employee rather than our persecutor."

I nodded and watched my uncle hand the inspector a small purse. The inspector bowed and walked off with a contented look upon his face. And well he should have been content. My uncle, I later learned, gave him twenty pounds, far more than he could have received of any native-born businessman in my uncle's trade—at least one who had not been caught with contraband. Their fear of prosecution made Jews useful to such men.

When finished with the inspector, my uncle turned in my direction and recognized me with what I took to be agreeable surprise—as though a visit to the warehouse was a recreation I engaged in regularly. He strolled over to me and shook my hand warmly, in the manner he would a friend with whom he was on regular terms.

"Uncle," I said simply, for I wished this encounter to be upon business alone.

My uncle was not an easily startled man, so I considered it something of an accomplishment that he arched one eyebrow as he turned to me. "Benjamin," he said, nodding, quickly regaining his composure. It was more a look of satisfaction, as though I had proved him right by appearing before him. I saw he wished to measure me, to determine what I did there before he chose how to react to my presence. I smiled briefly, hoping to put him at his ease, but his expression changed not at all.

"If I trouble you at an awkward time, I can call on another occasion."

"I think that no time can be less awkward than another for such a meeting," he answered after a moment. "Let us retire to my closet that we may talk in private."

My uncle led us to a comfortable room with an impressive oaken desk and a few hard wooden chairs, softened with pillows upon the seat. There was a bookshelf lined not with poetry, or works of antiquity, or religious books, but with ledgers, atlases, price guides, and records. This was the room in which my uncle conducted the greatest share of his official business, a business that had served him well since he and my father had come to the country some thirty years earlier.

After ordering his servant to prepare us tea, he settled into his desk chair. "I can only assume you have not come out of family feeling, and there is some crisis that brings you here. No matter, I suppose. Your father once said to me that, should you return for any reason, he would listen to you and weigh your words carefully and fairly."

We were both silent. My father had never said any such thing to me. Of course, I had never given him a chance, yet it did not sound like the father I remembered, the man who always demanded to know why I was not as studious or dedicated or clever as my brother José. I recalled that once when I was eleven years old I ran home, fairly trembling with excitement, my stockings torn and my face smeared with mud. It was a Sunday—a market day for the Jews at Petticoat Lane—and my father vaguely supervised while the servants put away the goods they had purchased, for my father was a man who wished every servant in the house to know that they might, at any time, be subject to scrutiny. I ran into the kitchen of the house we rented on Cree Church Lane, and I all but collided with my father, who stopped my progress by placing a hand upon each shoulder. But this was no gentle gesture; he looked down upon me with his most unflinching gaze. He appeared something comical, I was beginning to realize, beneath his absurdly large, fleece-white, full-bottom wig, which only emphasized the growth of black beard that began to sprout within three hours of his taking a shave from his barber. "What has happened to you?" he demanded.

It occurred to me, with a certain amount of indignation, that as I looked rather ruffled, he might inquire if I was hurt or no, but pride squelched indignation as I recalled the victory still fresh in my mind.

I had been wandering from stall to stall in the crowded market, for Sunday was the busiest shopping day for the Jewish community, and the best merchants were out to peddle their foods and clothes and all manner of goods. The air was thick with the smells of roasted meats and freshly baked pastries and the stench of London that drifted east to our neighborhood. I had no particular needs at the market, but I had a few pence in my pocket, and a quick hand beside, and I only sought an opportunity to spend my coin or grab something tasty and disappear into the crowd.

I'd been eyeing a pile of jellies that were too deep within the stall to filch, and I had not yet decided if they looked delicious enough for me to surrender my precious coins. I had all but determined to buy a dozen of the sweetmeats when I heard the raucous cry of boys forcing their way through the crowd. I had seen their kind before—little rogues who liked to push the Jews about because they knew the Jews dared not push them back. They were not a villainous lot, these boys of perhaps thirteen years, sons of shopkeepers or tradesmen by their look—they took no delight in torturing their victims, only in creating mayhem and avoiding punishment. They barreled through the crowd, pushing down this man here, or knocking over that table of wares there. Such antics filled me with rage, not because of the mischief itself, for I had been guilty of much the same and far worse in my day, but because no one dared give these fellows the whipping they deserved and, though I should not have known how to express this notion then, because they made me yearn to be an Englishman and a Jew no longer.

They moved in my general direction, and I stared hard, hoping to catch their attention even as everyone about me continued with their purchases, attempting to make the boys disappear by ignoring them. They grew close to me, shouting and laughing, and plucking sweetmeats from stalls and daring anyone to stop them. They stood perhaps fifteen feet away from me, when, backing off from a stall where he had knocked over a display of pewter candlesticks, the tallest of the boys slammed hard into Mrs. Cantas, a neighbor and the mother of a friend of mine. This lady, a stout woman of late-middle years, her arms full of cabbages and carrots, fell to the ground, her vegetables scattering like dice. The fair-haired boy who had slammed into her spun around, already in mid-laugh, but stopped in something like shame when he saw the spectacle before him. He might have been a troublesome fellow, but he had not yet reached the stage of maliciousness wherein he could attack women and feel no remorse. He paused for an instant, some sort of regret creeping along his face, which, streaked though it was with dirt, still revealed a base coloring of milky whiteness.

He might have apologized; he might even have recruited his fellows to help collect the scattered purchases, but Mrs. Cantas, red-faced with rage, let out a spew of the most insulting epithets I've ever heard escape from the mouth of any female but the most callous of jades. She formed these insults in our Portuguese dialect, so the boy and his companions merely stared, not knowing how to respond while their victim shouted in what to them was an incomprehensible gibberish. I, for one, silently praised Mrs. Cantas for at least having the courage to say her piece, if only in a language these fellows could not understand. And her piece was most colorful, and I listened with only vague amusement until she called the boy a "whoreson of one-legged poxy slut, a stinking rascal who needs to push about women because his own uncircumcised manhood might be taken for the shriveled parts of a female monkey."

Without even meaning to, I burst out in a laugh, and I saw I was not the only one. Around me men, and women too, stood laughing, stunned into amusement at the hyperbole of this lady's rage. The fair-haired boy's milky face had become crimson with anger and humiliation, for he stood laughed at by a crowd of Jews for an insult he had not even understood.

"I damn you for a bitch," he shouted at Mrs. Cantas in the tremulous voice of an agitated boy who wishes to be taken for a man, "and I spit upon your gypsy curse." And, indeed, he did spit upon her, directly into her face.

I am ashamed that no one but myself moved to give this urchin the pummeling he deserved, but the crowd only looked on in shock, and Mrs. Cantas, who had invigorated herself with her insults, now appeared to me on the precipice of tears. For my part, I had been raised to show a much greater deference to women, and for whatever reason, this lesson was one that I had taken to heart while so many others had received only my contempt—perhaps because my own mother had died when I was but an infant, so other folks' mothers held a special place in my heart.

I cannot even now explain my reasoning, only describe my actions: I struck this boy. It was a clumsy, poorly planned blow. My hand clenched into a fist, I raised it above my head and pounded downward, pummeling his face as though with a hammer. They boy fell to the ground, only for an instant, and then picked himself up and ran off, his friends following closely in tow.

I expected the crowd to cheer for me, Mrs. Cantas to proclaim me her savior, but I saw only that I had caused embarrassment and confusion. My actions had not been those of a protector, but of a troublemaker. Mrs. Cantas nervously pushed herself to her feet, but avoided my gaze. Around me I confronted the backs of those I had known all my life—shopkeepers crept back into their stalls, their patrons moved hurriedly away. All tried to forget what they had seen and to hope that their forgetfulness would make others forget as well and that my violence would not bring upon us an Inquisition here in England.

I would not have my joy so easily sabotaged, however. I ran home, hoping that someone in our house would hear the story and praise me as I thought I deserved. As my father was the first person I saw, he was the first to hear the tale, though the version I gave him showed a certain lack of narrative imagination.

"I was down at the market," I said in a panting voice, "and a nasty, ugly boy spat upon Mrs. Cantas. So I beat him," I proclaimed. I broke away from my father's grip and swung my fist through the air by way of illustration. "I felled him with one blow!"

My father hit me hard in the face.

He made no habit of hitting me, and I fully admit I was the sort of boy who wanted hitting from time to time. This was the hardest he had ever stuck me—indeed, it was, at that time, the hardest I had ever been struck; he hit me with the back of his hand, curled almost into a fist, aiming, I believed, to hit bone with the bulky ring he wore upon his third finger. The blow had come unexpectedly, lashing out like a serpent, and the force of it reverberated through my jaw and down my spine, until my limbs felt light and tingly.

I suppose he was scared; my father hated trouble and hated anything that might draw attention to our community in Dukes Place. Sometimes, in the hopes of making me more of a man, or rather more of his sort of man, he invited me to join with him and his guests for their after-dinner bottle; there he always talked of remaining invisible, of avoiding trouble, of angering no one. This blow of his—I knew what it was about. My father saw everything in patterns, everything as woven together—one act always engendered a hundred others. He feared I should make a habit of beating upon Christian boys. He feared my rashness should bring the plague of hatred down upon the Jews. He feared a gathering momentum that began with my violence against this one boy—a momentum that would lead to persecution and torment and destruction.

His expression changed not at all. He stood there, his features twisted into a mask of unease and fear, and perhaps disappointment that I had not dropped to the ground. His eyes fixed suspiciously upon the red welt he had left upon my face—as though I had somehow falsified the evidence of his violence. "That is what it is to be hit," he said. "It is a feeling you would be wise to avoid."

My pride had fled, but my indignation remained—and I remembered thinking, *It's not so very terrible.*

It was a moment that I think anticipated my career in the ring, for it was in fact more than simply not that bad—there was a strange kind of pleasure in it. It was the pleasure of endurance, of knowing that I had been able to take the pain without dropping, without flinching, without weeping. It was the pleasure of knowing I could endure another blow, and another after that—perhaps enough blows to make my father too weary to strike again. It was on that day that I first began to think of my father as weak.

But my uncle was a different sort of man—his smuggling trade had taught him more subtlety than my father ever understood. He had advised patience to my father; he always argued that I should find my own path, that my father should not demand that I be like my brother. As I sat in my uncle's warehouse, it occurred to me that I owed him something for the understanding he had always advocated on my behalf, even if the well of understanding had now run dry.

It seemed like a quarter of an hour that we sat there, saying nothing, but I suppose the time was only a few seconds. At last my uncle spoke, softening his tone, hoping, perhaps, to spare me embarrassment. "Do you need money?"

"No, Uncle." I was anxious to disabuse him of the idea that I had come a-begging. "I am here, in a way, upon business of the family. You told me once that you believed my father had been murdered. I want to know why you think so."

I now had his attention. He was no longer contorting himself, attempting to find the correct attitude with which to face the wayward nephew returned. He now stared at me hard, trying to determine for himself why I had come to him with this question. "Have you learned something, Benjamin?"

"No, nothing of that sort." Skipping over any superfluous details, I told him about Balfour and his suspicions.

He shook his head. "Your uncle tells you your father has been murdered, and you ignore him. A complete stranger tells you the same thing and now you believe it?" In his agitation, my uncle's Portuguese accent grew more pronounced.

"Please, Uncle. I have come for information. To find out if my father was murdered. Does it matter why?"

"Of course it matters. This is your family. I have not seen you since Samuel's funeral, and not for ten years before that." I sighed and began to speak, but my uncle saw that I grew impatient and anxious, and he censured himself. "But," he said, "that is the past and this is now. And if you want to do something good for our family, that is the important thing. So, yes, Benjamin, I suspect your father was murdered. I told the constable as much, and I also told the magistrate. I also wrote many letters—to men I know in Parliament, men who owe me money, I might add. All say the same—that the man who killed your father is a wretch, but there is no law to punish an accidental death, even if we can prove that the accident was due to carelessness or drunkenness. Samuel's death is but an unfortunate mishap to them. And I, for thinking otherwise, am an excitable Jew."

"What is it that makes you believe he was murdered?"

"I am not certain that he was murdered, but it is something that I suspect. Samuel was a man who made many enemies simply because of his trade. He bought and sold stocks—and as many people lost money of him as made it. I don't have to tell you how much the English hate stock-jobbers. They depend on them to make their money, but they hate them. Is it just a coincidence that someone runs him down in the street? And that Balfour, with whom he had dealings, should die as he did? Perhaps, but I would like to know for certain."

I hesitated before asking my next question. "What does José say to this?"

"If you want to know what your brother has to say," my uncle replied tartly, "maybe you should write to him. You know he came to London shortly after Samuel's funeral—he dropped everything and sailed for England as soon as he heard. You knew he would, and you did nothing to seek him out."

"Uncle," I began. I wished to say that José had not sought me either, but the words sounded childish to me—and also disingenuous, for I had made a point of not being home when he had been in town so if he had called on me I could have avoided him.

"Why do you hide from your own family, Benjamin? What happened with you and Samuel is long past. He would have forgiven you if you but gave him the chance."

I misbelieved that, but I said nothing.

"This distance you have is about nothing, it stems from nothing. Now your father is dead, and you can never reconcile with him, but it is not too late to reconcile with your family and with your people."

I thought on this for some time—I know not how long. Perhaps my father *had* changed since I had last known him. Perhaps the cold tyrant I remembered was as much a product of my fancy as my experience. I could not say, but my uncle's words stung me; they made me feel like an irresponsible wretch who had brought misery to his family. All these years I had always thought of myself as the one who suffered. I chose to separate myself from wealth and influence. Now I began to understand how my uncle saw my self-imposed exile—to him my absence had been senseless and selfish and had hurt my family more than I had ever hurt myself.

"You are much older now, yes? Maybe you regret some of the things you did in your youth. Now you have grown into a respectable man. You remind me even a little of my own son, Aaron."

I said nothing, for I wished neither to insult my uncle nor speak ill of the dead, but I hoped most earnestly that I in no way resembled my cousin. "I shall need to know the name of the coachman who ran down

Father," I said, returning the discourse to business. "And I would like to know if there was anyone in particular you knew to be Father's enemy. Maybe someone who had threatened him. Will you do this for me?"

"I shall do this, Benjamin. In part I shall do it for you."

"Is there anything else that struck you as important? Any link you can see between my father's death and Balfour's? Balfour's son believes there may be some connection with the dealings of Exchange Alley, and these financial matters are far beyond my understanding."

Uncle Miguel looked around. "This is no place to discuss concerns of family. It is no place to talk of the dead, and it is no place to order affairs of so private a nature. Come to my home tonight for dinner. Come at half past five. You will dine with your family, and after we shall talk."

"Uncle, perhaps that is not the best way."

He leaned forward. "It is the only way," he said. "If you want my help, you come and have dinner."

"You would risk letting your brother's killer go free if I refuse?"

"There is no risk," he said. "I have told you what you need to do, and you will do it. Protests only waste our time. I shall see you at half past five."

I left the warehouse astonished at what had happened. I was to dine with my family, and I anticipated this evening with a healthy quantity of dread.

EIGHT

I ARRIVED NEAR ENOUGH on time at my uncle's home on Broad Court in the parish of St. James, Dukes Place. In the year 1719, foreign Jews were still not permitted to own property in London, so my uncle rented a pleasant house in the heart of the Jewish neighborhood, only a brief distance from the Bevis Marks synagogue. His house was three stories; I cannot recall how many rooms, but it was well-proportioned for a man living with a wife and a single dependent and hardly more than a handful of servants. Still, my uncle often worked at home, as my father had, and he enjoyed entertaining guests.

Unlike many Jews who moved to Dukes Place and then left when they made their fortune—relocating to the more fashionable neighborhoods to the west—my uncle chose to remain behind to share his lot with the poorer members of his nation. It is true that the eastern parts of the city are none the most pleasant, for London's prevailing winds blow every foul stench of a foul-smelling metropolis right to his doorway, but despite the odor and the poverty and the isolation of Dukes Place, my uncle would not think of relocating. "I am a Portuguese Jew, born in Amsterdam and moved to London," Uncle Miguel told me when I was a boy. "I have no desire to move again."

As I walked toward the door it occurred to me that it was Friday night, the beginning of the Jewish Sabbath, and that my uncle had tricked me into attending a Sabbath meal. Memories of my childhood bombarded me—the warm odor of freshly baked egg bread, the din of conversation. Sabbath meals had always been held at my uncle and aunt's house, for the

Sabbath was, by tradition, a family occasion, and where I lived was less a family than a household. Every Friday before sundown we would walk from our house on Cree Church Lane to my uncle's place, where we would share prayers and food with his family and whatever friends he had invited. My uncle would always talk to my brother and me as though we were adults, a habit I found both confusing and gratifying. My aunt would slip us jellies or little cakes before dinner. These meals were one of the few rituals from my childhood that I thought on with any fondness, and I felt a fleeting rage toward my uncle for exposing me to these memories once more.

Even after I had knocked upon the door I thought of running away, of abandoning my plans and my inquiry and Mr. Balfour and the idea that my father had been murdered. *Let him stay dead,* I nearly muttered aloud, but despite the urge to flee, I remained fast.

Isaac, a short and stooped curmudgeon who had been my uncle's servant since I was but a boy, met me at the door. Nearing, I suppose, sixty or more, he appeared to me in good health and as close to good spirits as he was capable. "Had you come but a few moments later," he said by way of greeting me, whom he had not seen in a decade, "Mr. Lienzo would have had to answer the door himself." Isaac had always been particularly nice about matters of religion, and he refused to work on the Sabbath, as Jewish law dictates. As my uncle refused to work as well, he could hardly resent the same adherence to the law in a servant.

This house brought upon me a flood of ancient memories, for I had spent untold hours here as a child. Most of the furnishings were precisely as I recalled—the blues and reds of the Persian rug, the ornate woodwork of the stairway, the austere portraits of my grandparents upon the wall. More than the appearance, the scents recalled the Sabbaths of my childhood—stewed meats and boiled raisins and the sweet aromas of cinnamon and ginger.

In the parlor I was greeted by my uncle, who sat alone with a paper. It looked to be one of the publications that specialized in the dealings of government issues and stocks in 'Change Alley. Upon my entrance he set it aside. "Benjamin," he said as he rose from his seat, "I am so glad you came. Yes, it is a very good thing to have you here."

"You tricked me, Uncle," I said. "You did not tell me it was a Sabbath meal for which you invited me."

"I tricked you?" He grinned. "Did I hide from you the day of the week?

You ascribe to me more wile than I have—though I should be glad to be as clever as you say."

My retort was cut off by the entrance of my aunt, followed by a beautiful woman of perhaps one- or two-and-twenty. Aunt Sophia was an attractive older woman, a little inclined to be fat, and a bit silly in her manner. Her social interactions were almost exclusively with other Jewish immigrants, and she had never learned to speak English very well. Like my uncle, she wore clothing that spoke of her time among the Dutch. Her dress was of a thin black woolen, high in the neck and long in the sleeve, and her hair was piled up, pointing to a small, white bonnet upon her crown, so as to remind me of women in Dutch paintings of the last century.

She clasped my shoulders with her arms and asked me questions in halting English, which I answered in equally halting Portuguese. I astonished myself at the happiness I took in seeing her. She was a kind woman, and she looked at me with no judgment—I saw only her pleasure at having me in her home. She was, in fact, just as I remembered her.

"And this," my uncle said at last, placing his arm around the beautiful woman, "is your cousin Miriam."

The term *cousin* I knew was somewhat formal, for Miriam was my late cousin Aaron's widow. I knew little of her or their marriage, for Aaron had wedded her after I had left home, upon the return from his first voyage to the Levant, but London is not so large that one does not hear stories. She had been my uncle's ward, her own parents having died before she was fifteen, leaving her a handsome fortune. She had married Aaron by the time she was seventeen and been widowed of him by the time she was nineteen. Now, still in the bloom of her youth, and presumably possessed of a fortune, she remained within her father-in-law's household.

Miriam had a Jewess's coloring—olive skin, black hair, which she let dangle down in ringlets like a fashionable London lady, and rich green eyes. Her dress, too—a gown of sea green with yellow petticoats—bespoke a particular attention to the styles of the town. I could not help but think of this lovely woman, who came complete with her own fortune, as somehow trapped in my uncle's house, only wanting a rescuer. Though I came with no fortune of my own, I suspected hers might prove sufficient for the two of us, and I almost laughed as I considered that I, a Jew, should wish to play Lorenzo to her Jessica.

I bowed deeply. "Cousin," I said, feeling worldly and dashing. I was the wayward cousin returned, and I hoped that she might find me fascinating.

"I have heard much of you, sir," she said, with a smile that showed white and healthy teeth.

"You honor me, madam."

"We are in England, not France, Benjamin," my uncle said. "You may omit the formalities."

That I had no clever response was fortunately hid by a knock at the door. "The sun," my uncle said, "is too far set for Isaac to answer that." He and my aunt walked forth to greet his visitors.

"Do we expect others?" I asked Miriam, pleased with the early opportunity for conversation.

"Yes," she said with a scowl that for a moment I thought directed at me. She circled around the sofa upon which I sat and gracefully lowered herself into a well-cushioned armchair across from me. "Do you know Nathan Adelman?" Her displeasure, I saw, belonged to another.

I nodded. "I know *of* him, certainly. An impressive dinner guest." Adelman had come to England from Hamburg to join King George's court five years earlier, in 1714. He, as my father had been, was one of the handful of Jews allowed to hold the title of licensed broker upon the Exchange; he was also a powerful merchant with ties to the East and West Indies, the Levant, and, surreptitiously, to the South Sea Company and even to Whitehall itself. Rumor held that he was the Prince of Wales's unofficial adviser in all matters financial. I knew no more of him but that the displeasure so evident upon Miriam's face suggested she took no delight in his company.

When he walked into the room, the situation unfolded itself. He offered an optimistic, almost exuberant smile at Miriam, who was near thirty years his junior. Adelman looked only slightly younger than my uncle— he was a short, plump, handsomely dressed man, clean-shaven, attired in a full, black bob-wig and looked for all the world as much an English gentleman as anyone in a respectable London coffeehouse. It was only his voice that gave him away. Like my uncle, he had clearly worked hard to eliminate much of his accent—though in his case, having a touch of the German in his speech offered perhaps some advantage in a court with a German king. It was well-known that King George's first priority was his German principality, Hanover, and Adelman's first priority was King George's son. This dedication to the Prince left Adelman in a ticklish situation, for at the time the Prince and the King were feuding, and Adelman therefore lacked the King's ear, which he was said to have in the past possessed.

Miriam offered him a disaffected nod, while I arose and bowed deeply upon my introduction. By the time I sat again I understood that it did not take a man trained in uncovering secrets to read the relationships before me. Adelman wished to marry Miriam, and Miriam had no desire to marry Adelman. I could not even venture a guess as to how my uncle felt about this courtship.

After a few moments of polite conversation concerning the weather and the political situation in France, a knock at the door produced our final dinner guest. My uncle disappeared briefly and then returned, one hand pressed in a friendly fashion to the back of Noah Sarmento, a clerk who worked within my uncle's warehouse. This was a very young man with a polite but severe countenance. He was clean-shaven, wore a small, tight wig, and though his clothes were not of poor quality, they were of nondescript grays and browns and of equally bland tailoring.

"Certainly you know Mr. Adelman," my uncle began.

Sarmento bowed. "I have had the pleasure many times," he said with a cheer that seemed ill-suited to his features, "though not so many as I should like." Sarmento's smile rested as naturally upon his face as an admiral's uniform upon a monkey. This image is perhaps a false one, however, for to liken Sarmento to a monkey would be to suggest there was something playful and mischievous about him. Nothing could be more false. He was as dour a man as I had ever met, and though I know many philosophers argue against the science of physiognomy, here was one man whose very character could be read in the pinched and unwelcoming shape of his face.

Adelman returned a shallow bow as my uncle introduced me in such a way as to avoid the mention of my assumed name. "This is my nephew Benjamin, son of my late brother."

Sarmento nodded only briefly before he abandoned contact with me. "Mrs. Lienzo," he said, bowing in her direction. "It is a pleasure to see you once more."

Miriam nodded, half-closed her eyes, and looked away.

"Tell me," Sarmento began to address Adelman, "what news in South Sea House? The coffeehouses are all a-flutter to see what shall happen next."

Adelman smiled politely. "Come sir. You know that my relationship with the South Sea Company is purely informal."

"Ha!" Sarmento slapped his thigh. I could not see if he did so with pleasure or to spur himself on. "I hear the Company makes not a move without consulting you."

"You do me too much honor," Adelman assured him.

I valued this discourse only because Miriam and I exchanged quick glances to express our mutual lack of interest. We soon moved to the dining room, where I continued to find the conversation awkward and halting. My uncle several times pressured me to say the prayers traditionally uttered with Sabbath dinner, but I pretended forgetfulness of what had been so ingrained upon me as a child. In truth, I felt an odd inclination to participate, but I was unsure that the prayers I remembered were the correct ones, and I did not wish to err before my cousin. I did not say as much, but I suggested that I thought of blessings upon food as so much superstition. When my uncle uttered these prayers, however, I felt the tug of something—memory or loss, perhaps—and I took a strange pleasure in the sound of the Hebrew words. There had been no prayer in my house when I grew up; my father sent my brother and me to study the laws of our people at the Jewish school because that was what men did, and we attended the synagogue because my father had found it easier to go than to explain why he did not.

I looked about the room to see how the others responded to the blessings. I thought it odd that Sarmento, who had demonstrated a clear admiration for Miriam before, could hardly allow his gaze to waver from Adelman. "Tell me, Mr. Adelman," Sarmento began once my uncle finished with the prayers, "will the recent threats of a Jacobite uprising affect the sale of government issues?"

"I'm sure I have nothing to say that is not said throughout the coffeehouses," Adelman demurred. "Upheaval always promotes fluctuation in the prices of the funds. But without such fluctuation, there could be no market, so the Jacobites do us some small favor, I suppose. But that, as I say, is but common knowledge."

"There could be nothing common about your opinions," Sarmento pressed on. "I should so much like to hear them."

"Indeed, I believe you," Adelman said with a laugh, "but I wonder if our friends who do not spend their time in 'Change Alley are as curious as you." He bowed his head at Miriam.

"Perhaps I might make an appointment to meet with you then at another point."

"You may call on me at any time," Adelman responded, although with such little warmth that he should have frightened off all but the most determined of sycophants. "I am often to be found at Jonathan's Coffeehouse, and you may always send a message there knowing I shall receive it."

"If we may not talk about the funds, then let us talk of the amusements of the town!" Sarmento cried, with a loudness I suppose he meant as enthusiasm. "What say you, Mrs. Lienzo?"

"I should think that my cousin can speak more to that topic," Miriam said quietly, carefully avoiding my gaze as she did so. "I am told he knows something of London amusements."

I knew not how to take her comment, but I could detect no insult. I could only be sure that Sarmento had asked Miriam a question and she had deferred to me. I rose to the challenge, feeling that I now had the opportunity to impress her. I spoke only of what I had heard of the new theatrical season, and I gave my opinion on a variety of players and performances from the previous year. Sarmento proceeded to seize upon each of my points, using them to launch some discourse of his own on ideas about acting or plays and such. This popinjay would never dare to insult me in public, but here, at my uncle's dinner table, he made no effort to hide his contempt for me; I could hardly embarrass my uncle by challenging his puppy. Instead I pretended not to understand his looks and gestures, and silently hoped I should have the opportunity to meet him elsewhere.

It was a tradition in my uncle's household that, with the servants dismissed, the resident ladies would serve the meal on the Sabbath. And so it was, and to my delight I observed that Miriam seemed particular about both avoiding Sarmento and Adelman—leaving those gentlemen for my Aunt Sophia—and to seeking me out when delivering her bowls of soup or plates of cardamom-scented lamb. I looked forward to each new course, that I might bask in her proximity: the rustle of her skirts, the scent of her lemony perfume, and such tantalizing hints of her bosoms as her bodice offered. Indeed, the third and final time she served me she caught my eyes indulging in such pleasures, and she trapped my gaze within her own. In an instant I braced myself, for London ladies know of only two responses to a gaze such as mine, and I knew not if I would receive the hard scowl of chastisement, or the equally disappointing lascivious smirk. I cannot adequately describe my confused pleasure when Miriam declined to pursue either of these courses, and only offered me a smile of knowing amusement, as though the joy I took in her nearness was a secret we both shared.

After the meal, in the best English fashion, we four gentlemen retired to a private chamber with a bottle of wine. Adelman, on several occasions, attempted to discuss affairs of business with my uncle, who made it clear that he would not talk of these things on the Sabbath. Sarmento again turned the conversation to the rumors of another Jacobite uprising here in England. The topic of the followers of the deposed King was of interest to my uncle, and he had much to say. I listened intently, but I blush to own I did not follow politics very closely, and many points were lost upon me.

Adelman, whose interests were so clearly tied to the success of the current dynasty, dismissed the Jacobites as a mindless rabble, and condemned the Pretender as a Popish tyrant. My uncle nodded in mute agreement, for Adelman had merely encapsulated Whiggish sentiment. But Sarmento hung on Adelman's every word, praising his ideas as those of a philosopher and his words as those of a poet.

"And what of you, sir?" Sarmento turned to me. "Have you no thoughts on these Jacobites?"

"I concern myself so little with matters of politics," I said, meeting his gaze. I believed his question was not about my political views, but how I should respond to his boldness.

"Surely you are not a detractor of the King?" Sarmento pushed on.

I could not guess his game, but in this era in which rebellion always threatened the Crown, this was more than mere idle chatter. A public accusation of Jacobitical sympathies could ruin a man's reputation—perhaps even result in an arrest by the King's Messengers. "Must one who is not an active supporter be a detractor?" I inquired carefully.

"I am sure," my uncle volunteered hurriedly, "that my nephew has raised a bumper many times to the King."

"Yes," I agreed, "though I confess that when I drink to the King's health it is more often for the sake of the drinking than the King."

My uncle and Adelman both laughed politely, and I thought my quip should tire Sarmento. I was mistaken. He merely took a new topic. "Tell me, sir," he began when the laughter died down. "Who do you like—the Bank or the Company?"

The question confused me, and I suspected it had been meant to. The matter of this financial rivalry was of some interest to me, for I knew Old Balfour to have made investments based upon his notions of this competition, but I so little understood the terms of these companies' antagonisms that I could hardly think of how to answer. Any pretense on my part that I understood the topic should only expose me as a fool, so I spoke plainly. "Who do I like for what?"

"Do you believe the Treasury is best served by the Bank of England or the South Sea Company?" He spoke slowly and deliberately, as if giving commands to a half-witted servant.

I offered him my most polite smile. "I was not aware that a man should find himself required to takes sides."

"Oh, not everyone, I suppose. Only men of means and business must."

"Must they?" my uncle inquired. "Cannot a man of business simply observe the rivalry without taking sides?"

"But you take sides, do you not, sir?" His question, as a clerk addressing his employer, struck me as impertinent, but if my uncle took offense he showed no sign of it. He merely listened to Sarmento palaver on. "Has not your family always believed that the Bank of England should maintain its monopoly on funding government loans? Have I not heard you argue that the South Sea Company should not be permitted to compete with the Bank for this business?"

"You know, Mr. Sarmento, that I do not wish to discuss such issues on the Sabbath."

He bowed slightly. "You are quite right, sir." He turned to me again. "You, sir, feel no such restriction, I suppose. And as all men of business and means must have an opinion, may I assume that you have one that you are only hesitant to share?"

"Tell me who you like, sir, and perhaps I shall have a model that I might emulate."

Sarmento smiled, but not at me. He turned to Mr. Adelman. "Why, I like the South Sea Company, sir. Particularly when it is in such capable hands."

Adelman bowed slightly. "You know full well that we Jews may not invest in the Companies. Your assertions, while flattering, may perhaps do my reputation some harm."

"I only repeat what is spoken of in every coffeehouse. And no one thinks less of you for your interest in these matters. You are a patriot, sir, of the highest order," Sarmento continued in his dull voice, which poorly matched the passion of his words. "For while the nation's finances are protected by men such as the South Sea directors, we need little fear uprisings and riots."

Adelman appeared unable to think of a response, and merely bowed again, so my uncle stepped in, no doubt hoping to move our conversation away from matters of business, and he announced that for the second time in almost as many years the churchwardens of the parish had elected him to the office of Overseer of the Poor. This revelation produced a hearty laugh from Adelman and Sarmento that I did not understand.

"Why should they elect you to this office, Uncle? Does it not involve attending church services each Sunday?"

All three men laughed, but only Sarmento laughed with hearty pleasure at my ignorance. "Aye," my uncle agreed. "It means attending the Church on the Christian Sabbath, and it means swearing a Christian oath upon a Christian Bible. They do not appoint me because they wish me to perform the duties of the office. They elect me because they know I shall refuse to do so."

"I confess I do not understand."

"It is but a way to generate revenue," Adelman explained. "Your uncle, he cannot perform the duties they have honored him with, so he must pay a fine of five pounds for refusing. It is common for the churchwardens to appoint many Jews in the course of a year—even poor Jews. They know that others will find the money to pay the fine. In this way they raise much money."

"Can you not complain?"

"We pay many taxes," my uncle explained. "You were born here, so you are free of the alien taxes, but Mr. Adelman and I are not. And though we have both received denizenship of Parliament, our taxes are still much higher than those of freeborn Britons. This appointment is but another tax, and I pay it quietly. I save my complaints for issues of importance."

We conversed for another hour on a variety of topics until Adelman stood abruptly and announced that he must return home; I used his departure as the excuse for my own. Prior to my leaving, however, my uncle took me aside. "You are angry." His eyes glowed with a strange warmth, as though he had forgotten the anger he had felt toward me at my father's funeral, as though there had been no rift between me and my family.

"You broke your promise," I said.

"I have only delayed it. I said I would talk to you after dinner. I did not say how long after. Come to the synagogue for prayers tomorrow morning. Spend the rest of the Sabbath with your family. When the sun goes down, I shall tell you what you want to know."

I hardly knew how to respond or even how his offer affected me. "Uncle Miguel, time is not a luxury I possess. I cannot simply spend my day praying and making idle chatter."

He shrugged. "That's my price, Benjamin. But"—he smiled—"it is a one-time cost. I shall make no further demands on you, even if you need information weeks from now, or months."

I knew I could not persuade him; he would let his own brother's murderer run free rather than back down once he'd made up his mind. And I must say I liked the idea of spending the afternoon with Miriam, so I agreed to meet him the next morning.

Adelman and I stepped out the door together, and I was struck by the opulence of his gilt carriage, which was parked outside my uncle's home. Upon seeing his master, a boy of perhaps fourteen years and a brownish complexion—East Indian, I guessed—dressed in a gaudy red-and-gold livery, opened the door and stood like a statue.

"Lienzo"—Adelman grabbed my arm with a practiced congeniality—"may I drop you off somewhere? You live in Covent Garden, do you not?"

I bowed to show my acceptance and thanks.

I admit that this confinement in so small a space with a man of Adelman's prominence made me uneasy, for if my trade often placed me in the company of great men, it rarely did so under such circumstances. Here we were engaged, not in business, but in an amicable ride across town.

As the carriage lurched forward, Adelman drew the curtains along the windows, enveloping us in near-complete darkness. He kept silent for some time, and I could think of no way to begin a conversation, so I remained still, feeling the wheels of the carriage roll over the unforgiving London roads. Each time I shifted in my seat, the noise I made seemed distractingly loud. I could hear nothing from across the carriage where Adelman sat.

Finally he cleared his throat, and I believe he took a pinch of snuff. "I understand," he began, "you have had a visit from a Mr. Balfour."

"You astonish me, sir." I nearly shouted in my surprise. I own that I felt a shiver run down my spine. There was nothing in Adelman's voice, you understand, to make me fearful. He maintained his polished and measured Germanic tone. There was, however, something in the question itself—in the knowledge that produced the question. What could a man of Adelman's stature know or care of these matters? I regretted that in the darkness I could learn nothing of his face, though I suspect he was too well practiced in his expressions to have offered me any information on that front. I too could mask my feeling, however. "I cannot express my shock at learning that my dealings should attract your notice," I told him with utter calm.

"You are part of an important family, Mr. Lienzo."

"I go by the name of Weaver," I told him.

"I meant no disrespect," he explained quickly. "I thought perhaps it was a name you used only when you fought." He paused for a moment. "I shall be blunt with you. I admire you, sir. I admire that you have decided to abandon the ancient suppositions of our race and make your way on your own. Pray, don't misunderstand me. I respect your uncle to a prodigious degree, but I find his clinging to rites and rituals a dangerous hindrance to our people. You, on the other hand, have shown Englishmen everywhere that Jews are not to be mocked or laughed at. Your exploits in the ring are legendary. Even the King, sir, knows your name."

I bowed in the darkness. He spoke the truth when he said I had turned my back on the rites and rituals of my people, yet I found his celebration of this neglect made me uneasy. Perhaps because I had always viewed my neglect of matters religious something born of idleness, where he saw it as liberated philosophy. "You honor me with your words," I said after an uncomfortable moment of silence. "But I am unsure what all this has to do with Mr. Balfour, nor why my business with him should interest you, sir."

"Yes, you are a man of business. I delight in a man of business. Let me say, Mr. Weaver, that I was saddened to hear of the death of your father, but the admiration I felt for him does not make me see what is not there. His death was a tragic accident; nothing more. I knew Michael Balfour as well. He was a good man, I should guess. Good enough, at any rate. But like his son, Balfour was weak. He made mistakes in his dealings, and he could not salvage himself nor face the consequences of his ruin. To the untrained eye, the fact that two men of business who were friends died so short a time apart may appear to be strange, but there is nothing to connect them. Tell me," he said with a theatrical change of voice, "what has Balfour offered you to pursue this matter?"

I told him the nature of our agreement.

He let out a brief laugh, rather like a bark. "You will receive no money—I doubt that he can produce twenty farthings, let alone pounds. His estate, you know, cannot be recovered. Balfour lost all, and it is no secret that his mother has naught but contempt for her son. You will earn nothing for your time, sir, but the enmity of powerful men who do not like to see someone meddling in their affairs. As it happens, I may be in a position to offer you an alternative. Your skills have not gone unnoticed, and your discretion is as commented upon as your cunning. These are rare qualities, and there are many men—in the South Sea Company, in Parliament, in the Court itself—who would be glad to have at their disposal a man of your talents. What say you, Mr. Weaver, do you wish to place this unpleasantness behind you? These men I know can make your fortune."

I pretended not to find his offer intriguing. "What you propose is undeniably generous," I said, "but I am still uncertain why you are interested in my business with Balfour or why you should like me to cease perusing the matter."

"The matter is a delicate one. To begin with, I would not want to see any stench stirred up in regard to our people. Should the newspapers get wind of your search, I fear it should reflect badly upon the Jews of England, and that is bad for all of us—rabbis, brokers, and pugilists alike, yes? The second reason is that the South Sea Company involves itself in some exceedingly complex renegotiations of the dispersal of public funds. I cannot go into detail, but suffice it to say that we are concerned about the high rate of interest on the funded national debt, and we are in the process of convincing Parliament to proceed with measures to aid in lowering the interest, thus freeing the nation of a terrible financial burden. Our plan cannot work if people lose confidence in a web of credit that most find befuddling. Any public suspicion that there is some connection between Balfour's death and the funds would harm us irrevocably. If the people believe that the funds are rife with murder and intrigue, then I am afraid we shall fail in our plans to ease the national burden of debt, and you, sir, will have cost your King and your Kingdom, quite literally, millions of pounds."

"I should not like to do such harm," I said cautiously, "but there is still the matter of Balfour's concerns. He believes that these deaths are not what they appear, and I believe that I must look further into that matter."

"You will only be squandering your time and harming your Kingdom."

"But surely you can accept the possibility that these deaths are more than coincidence."

"I cannot," he told me with utter confidence.

"Then how do you explain the fact that Balfour's own clerk cannot account for the ruin of the estate?"

"Matters of credit and finance are, even to those who make their livings in dealing with them, fantastical, unfathomable things," he explained in a sharp tone, no longer so polished and friendly. "They are, to most men, on the order of the supernatural rather than the physical. I daresay there is hardly a broker in England, if his death was unexpected, whose papers would not reveal themselves to be inextricably tangled and appear to be lacking."

"Mr. Balfour's death was not unexpected," I observed. "Not to himself, if his death was indeed self-murder."

"Balfour is hardly a valid example. He took his own life, which proves his inability to order his own affairs. Come, Mr. Weaver, let us not prove our Christian neighbors correct about us by being overly rabbinical in our examination of these things." He handed me his card. "Forget this Balfour nonsense, and come visit me at Jonathan's. I shall provide you with introductions to men who will make you rich. Besides," he said, with a smile I could sense even in the darkness of the coach, "it will save you the trouble of spending the morning in the synagogue with your uncle."

I politely thanked Adelman as the coach came to a halt outside Mrs. Garrison's house. "I shall, sir, give this very serious consideration."

"It should require but little," he said. "I am glad to make your acquaintance, Mr. Weaver."

I stood and watched the coach drive away, considering his offer in my mind. Perhaps it would be a wonderful thing if I were the sort of man who could dismiss with ease what Adelman had proposed, but the thought of serving such men as he knew had a powerful allure. All he asked in return for his favors was that I not trouble his business, and what objection could I offer to abandoning an inquiry into the death of a father for whom I could recall no fondness?

I turned toward Mrs. Garrison's house and entered into the warmth of her front hall, but somehow, before I reached the top of the staircase, I had dismissed Mr. Adelman's offer forever. I could not say if it was because I did not relish the idea of dealing perpetually with men like Adelman, men who believed their wealth gave them not only influence and power, but also a kind of innate superiority to men such as myself. I could not say if it was because there was something compelling in the unexpected ease I had known in the presence of my uncle and aunt, or the displeasure I felt at the notion of severing a connection with a household wherein lived my cousin's lovely widow. Perhaps it was a combination of these, but I understood before I had even struck a single candle that my duty was clear.

It might be an awkward thing having to tell Mr. Adelman of my decision, but it then occurred to me that I should be surprised if my inquiry brought me again into contact with so busy a man. At that time I could not have even guessed how intricately his affairs would intertwine with my own.

NINE

I T WAS WITH ambivalent feelings that I met my uncle the next morning and proceeded to the Bevis Marks synagogue. Perhaps I should mention that not all Jews are so nice in their observation of the Sabbath as my uncle. Some are far more observant, of course, but an even greater number care little for this day of the week or that. Even my uncle's short beard was thought by many Jews to be of ill fashion, for it was something of a truism that any Jew with a beard upon his face was either a rabbi or a recent immigrant.

Many of the Jews of Iberian origin had long ago been robbed of the knowledge of their rituals, forced, during the time of the Inquisition, to convert to the Catholic faith. These so-called New Christians were sometimes sincere in their conversions, while others had continued to practice their religion in secret, but after a generation or two they often forgot why they secretly observed these now-obscure rituals. When these secret Jews fled Iberia for the Dutch states, as they began to do in the sixteenth century, many sought to regain Jewish knowledge. My father's grandfather had been such a man, and he schooled himself in the Jewish traditions— even studying with the great Rabbi Manasseh ben Israel—and he raised his children to honor the Jewish traditions.

I, too, had been raised with those traditions, but I had long since found them easier to ignore than to honor. For that reason I was not sure what I expected upon my return to the synagogue. Perhaps I had been making a point of expecting nothing, but I found myself somewhat comforted by the morning service. As when I was a boy, the presiding rabbi was David

Nieto, grown much older than I remembered and looking fragile and thin, but still a venerable man who cut a striking presence with his enormous black wig and his wisp of a beard that covered but the tip of his chin.

In Jewish worship, men and women seat themselves in different areas to shield the men from the distracting allure of female flesh. I always believed this custom a wise one, for I have never known Elias to attend church and not return with tales of fashionable ladies and their finery. In the Bevis Marks synagogue, the men sit downstairs in a series of pews that rest perpendicular to the rabbi's pulpit. The women sit upstairs, where they are meant to be shielded from men's sight by a latticed wooden partition. The latticing is such, however, that one can see, if not perfectly, glimpses of fair femininity through the gaps.

The synagogue was crowded that morning—more crowded than I had remembered ever seeing it as a boy. There were perhaps three hundred men downstairs and close to a hundred women in the upper section. In addition to the worshipers, there was a pair of young English bucks who came in to observe the Jews at worship. These visits were not uncommon; I recalled having seen curiosity-seekers many times as a boy, and they generally behaved themselves reasonably well, though it was not uncommon for these men to find themselves restless when confronted with hours of Hebrew liturgy. Indeed, visitors rarely hid their perplexity with a service conducted almost entirely in a foreign language and in which men appear to engage in private contemplation as much as group worship. For my own part, I found myself struggling very little with the Hebrew of the prayer book, for I had read these prayers so often when I was a boy that they remained still firmly etched within my memory, and speaking them again made me happy in a way I would not have anticipated. I felt a kind of comfortable pleasure at having a prayer shawl, borrowed from my uncle, cast about me, and I saw him offer numerous approving glances in my direction throughout the long service. I could only hope that he was less observant of the frequent glances I cast upward toward the ladies' section, where I could discern the beautiful if obstructed face of Miriam through the latticing. Indeed, there was something compelling about catching this anatomized view of her—now her eye, now her mouth, now her hand. The eye was in particular gratifying, for I could not but be pleased that it was cast in my direction as often as it was cast upon her prayer book.

After the conclusion of the service, Miriam and my aunt returned directly to the house, while I remained in the synagogue's courtyard with my uncle. He engaged in chatter with men throughout the community, while I looked on, pretending to take an interest in discussions about who had moved into and out of the neighborhood. As I stood there, I heard my name called out, and I spun around to face a handsomely dressed man whose face, disfigured from far too many beatings and blade wounds, I instantly recognized. It was Abraham Mendes, Jonathan Wild's man.

I have rarely been more astonished to see anyone in my life, and I only stared.

Mendes took some small delight in my confusion. He grinned at me like an impish child. "It is a pleasure to see you once more, Mr. Weaver," he said, with an exaggerated bow.

"What are you doing here, Mendes?" I sputtered. "How dare you follow me here."

He laughed. Not contemptuously, but out of genuine amusement. Indeed, there was something unaccountably charming about his ugly face. "I follow you, sir? You must think your business most interesting to suspect such a thing. I am here only to attend services for the Sabbath, and upon seeing an old acquaintance, I thought it incumbent upon me to greet you."

"Am I to believe you are here only to attend the service?" I asked. "I find that incredible."

"I might say the same of you." He grinned. "But you may ask around if you misbelieve me. I once again reside in Dukes Place, and have done so for several years now. And though I may not come here every Sabbath, I come often enough. It is your presence that is something of an anomaly." He leaned forward. "Do you follow me?" he asked in a stage whisper.

I could not help but laugh. "I am astonished, Mendes. You have utterly surprised me."

He bowed, just as my uncle turned to me. "Shall we return home, Benjamin." He bowed briefly to my companion. "*Shabbat shalom*, Mr. Mendes," he said, offering the traditional Sabbath greeting to this villain.

"And to you, Mr. Lienzo." Mendes grinned at me again. "*Shabbat shalom*, Mr. Weaver," he said before making his way out of the crowd.

My uncle and I took a few steps before I spoke. "How is it you know Mendes?" I asked.

"There are not so many Jews in Dukes Place that one cannot know them all. I often see him about the synagogue. Not a devout man, I suppose, but fairly regular in his attendance—and in London that is something in itself."

"But do you know what he is?" I pressed on.

My uncle had to speak more loudly than he liked, for a man selling pork pies had wandered toward the crowd exiting the synagogue to amuse himself by crying out his wares to the Jews. "Of course. Not everyone does. Ask most men, and they will tell you he works as a butler for some great man or other. But in my trade, you know, sometimes I may get a shipment of something or other that is not precisely legal to own, and if I have no buyer, Mr. Mendes can frequently offer me a fair price on behalf of his employer."

I could not believe what I heard. "Do you mean to say, Uncle, that you do business with *Jonathan Wild?*" I all but hissed the name and spoke it so quietly that it took my uncle a moment to understood what I said.

He lifted his shoulders in a gesture of defeat. "This is London, Benjamin. If I wish to sell a certain kind of goods, I do not always have a choice of buyers, and Mr. Mendes has offered me assistance more than once. I have had no dealings personally with this Wild, and I am anxious to keep my distance from him, but Mendes has shown himself a capable factor."

"Surely you are not unaware of the risks of having even indirect dealings with Wild," I nearly whispered.

"Mr. Mendes likes to say that in certain kinds of trade, one cannot but deal with Wild. I have found that to be true enough. Certainly I have heard that Wild is a dangerous man," he said, "but I trust Wild knows that I too, in my own way, can be dangerous."

My uncle smiled not at all when he said these words.

WE RETURNED TO THE house for a luncheon of bread, cold meat, and ginger cakes, all of which had been prepared the day before. Miriam and my aunt served the food themselves, and when we were finished they placed the dishes in the kitchen for the servants to tend to after sunset.

I retired to the sitting room with Miriam, and I was somewhat surprised not to find myself followed by either uncle or aunt. Miriam looked radiant that day, wearing a striking indigo gown, offset with an ivory petticoat.

I asked Miriam if she would join me in a glass of wine. She politely declined and instead sat in an armchair, turning to a volume of Mr. Pope's *Iliad*, of which I had often heard but had never inquired into. I poured myself a glass of Madeira from a handsome crystal decanter and, feigning a meditative mood, I sat across from her to watch the expression on her face as she made her way through the work. It was not my intention to stare, for I am a man not entirely unschooled in the social graces, but I found myself entranced as I watched her dark eyes follow the words across the page, her red lips pursed in appreciation.

Perhaps seeing that I regarded nothing but her at the moment, Miriam set her book aside, carefully marking her place with a small strip of cloth. She picked up a newspaper lying about and began leafing through it with an affectedly breezy air. "You have made your uncle very happy by coming here today," she said, without looking at me. "It was all he could speak of at breakfast."

"I am astonished," I said. "Frankly, I suspected he cared for me not at all."

"Oh, he values family loyalty tremendously, you know. I rather think he has taken a fancy to the idea of reforming you. By that he means, I suppose, having you move to Dukes Place, attend the synagogue with some regularity, and setting you up with responsibilities in his trade." She was silent for a moment. She turned the page. At last she looked up at me, her face an inscrutably stoic mask. "He told me that you remind him of Aaron."

I dared show neither contempt nor disagreement to Aaron's widow. "He told me the same thing."

"I can see perhaps some family resemblance in the physiognomy, but you strike me as men of different character."

"I believe I would agree with you."

There was another pause, one of the many moments of awkward silence that punctuated our conversation. Neither of us knew what to say. At last she had a new topic. "Do you ever attend dances and balls and such?" It was a casual question, or, perhaps, a question aiming to be casual. She spoke slowly and without looking up.

"I am afraid I tend to feel uncomfortable at such gatherings," I told her.

Her smile suggested that we shared a secret. "Your uncle believes London society is not for refined Jewish ladies."

I could not understand what she wished to tell me. "My uncle's opinion may be a very just one," I said, "but if you do not wish to adhere to it, I do not see what hold he has on you. You are of age and I presume of independent means."

"But I have chosen to remain under the protection of his household," she said quietly.

I wished to understand her meaning. For a widow of her standing, accustomed as she was to fine clothes and food and furnishings, to set herself up in her own household would prove an expensive endeavor. I knew not what money Aaron had settled upon Miriam; her fortune had become his at the time of their marriage, and I could not guess how much he might have left to my uncle or gambled away or wasted on a failed business dealing, or lost in any of the other countless ways that men of London see their fortunes shrivel. Perhaps independence was not an option. If that was Miriam's case, then she merely waited for the right suitor so she might pass out of the hands of her father-in-law and into those of a new husband.

The idea of Miriam's bind, the suggestion that she felt herself a prisoner in my uncle's house, made me uneasy. "I am certain my uncle only has your best wishes in his heart," I attempted. "Did you enjoy the amusements of town with your late husband?"

"His trade with the East made it necessary that he be abroad for long periods of time," she responded without emotion. "We spent only a few months in mutual company before he embarked for that voyage on which he was lost. But in that time, he showed himself, upon the issue of diversions, to be much of his father's spirit."

In my discomfort I found myself digging my thumbnail into my index finger. Miriam had placed me in a difficult position, and I wagered that she was too clever not to know it. I sympathized with her for her confinement, and yet I could hardly disagree with the rules set forth by my uncle.

"I can say from my own experience that London society is not always the most welcoming to members of our race. Can you imagine how you might feel were you to attend a tea garden, strike up a conversation with an amiable young lady, one you might wish for a friend, and then discover that she had nothing but the most contemptuous things to say on the topic of Jews?"

"I should seek out a less illiberal friend," she said with a dismissive wave of the hand, but I saw by the diminished sprightliness of her eyes that my question had not left her unaffected. "Do you know, Cousin, that I have changed my mind, and desire a glass of that wine."

"If I pour it for you," I asked, "would that not be labor, thus breaking the Sabbath law?"

"Do you then think of pouring wine for me as labor?" she inquired.

"Madam, you have convinced me." I stood and filled a glass, which I handed to her slowly, that I might watch her delicate fingers carefully avoiding all contact with my hand.

"Tell me," she said after taking a measured sip, "how does it feel to return to your family?"

"Oh," I said with an evasive laugh, "I do not feel myself to be returning so much as visiting."

"Your uncle said that you prayed with enthusiasm this morning."

I thought on how I had seen her watching me through the latticed gate. "Did you find my praying enthusiastic?" I inquired.

Miriam did not understand me or pretended not to. "It should have been very enthusiastic indeed if I could have heard you in the ladies' gallery."

"As I was feeling enthusiastic, I saw no reason the synagogue should not benefit from my mood."

"I find you flippant, Cousin," she said with amusement rather than annoyance.

"I hope you take it not amiss."

"May I ask you a question of a rather private nature?" she asked.

"You may ask me what you like," I told her, "so long as I may do the same."

My comment was perhaps a bit ungentlemanly, for she paused for a moment and appeared uncertain of how to continue. Finally she offered an expression that was not so much a smile as a thoughtful pressing together of her lips. "I shall call that a fair bargain. Your uncle, as you know, is a very traditional man. He seeks to shelter me from the world. I do not enjoy being cloistered, however, and so I try to learn as best I can." She was silent for a moment, contemplating either my words or the wine. "I was never told of the reason for your break with your father."

I had rarely spoken of the details of my rupture with my family to anyone. Part of my desire to speak of it with Miriam had to do with a wish to form a bond of trust with her, but part of it was simply the need to speak about these matters. "My father had hopes that I would follow him into business, become a licensed broker like himself. Unlike my older brother, I was born here in England, which meant that I was a citizen and would be exempt from the alien taxes, and I would be able to own land. It made sense to my father that José should return to Amsterdam to manage family affairs there, and I should remain here. But I was not very skillful at doing what was expected of me as a child. I often found myself embroiled in street fights, as often as not with Gentile boys who had tormented us only because they misliked Jews. I cannot say why I was so inclined. Perhaps because I grew up without a mother's affection. My father hated that I fought, for he feared notice. I always told him that I felt honor-bound to defend our race, but I felt an even greater thrill from striking the other boys."

I saw that I had Miriam's full attention, and I basked in her gaze. Even now it is so very difficult for me to express why this woman captivated me instantly. She was beautiful, yes, but so are many women. She had a quick wit, but women of intelligence are not so rare as some unkind authors tell us. I sometimes believe that I thought she and I had so much in common, moving as we did, each in our own way, along the borders of what it meant to be both a Hebrew and a Briton. Perhaps that was why my story had arrested her attention so fully.

"I always somehow felt that it was his fault I had no mother—you know how a child's thoughts are so nonsensical," I continued. "She died, as I am certain you know, of a wasting disease when I was still but an infant. From an early age, I sensed that my father made but a scurvy kind of parent, and I found myself almost seeking to incur his displeasure. He was a stern disciplinarian and anything other than perfection made him angry."

I paused briefly to sip from my glass, flattering myself that Miriam did not see the confusion telling my tale engendered in me.

"One day, when I was fourteen, he had entrusted me to bring payment to a merchant to whom he owed a debt. I was at the age when he was just beginning to teach me the rudiments of the family concerns. He wished to see me a trader upon the Exchange, as he was, but I fear I had little aptitude for mathematics, and I had even less interest in business. Perhaps my father ought to have begun teaching me of these things earlier, but I think he had been hoping I would mature and grow interested of my own will. But I was only interested in running about on the streets making trouble and haunting the gaming houses."

"Yet he thought you mature enough then," Miriam observed cautiously.

"So it would seem," I told her, though I had often wondered if he had only wanted to give me the opportunity to fail. "My father was determined to make me useful, and he often had me run errands. Such an errand was this payment he wished me to deliver. It was a five-hundred-pound negotiable note. I had never had so large a sum in my own hands before, and I thought it a golden opportunity. I believed that with so much money to stake, I might go to a gaming house and be sure to win—as though my luck would increase proportionate to the amount I wagered. My plan was that I should win an enormous amount of money, bring the merchant the principal and I would keep the interest. I had visited gaming houses before, and had generally come away fleeced, so I had no excuse for my optimism. I was merely young and enamored of the power of the money I had upon me. So I went to the house and cashed the note with the intention of exchanging the coin back for it on my way out. This story is predictable, I suppose; I piled loss upon loss until I had less than one hundred pounds left, and I could no longer trick myself into believing I might recover the original sum. I dared not think of returning to my father and telling him what had happened. He had many times disciplined me severely for returning late from errands—I could not even speculate how he would respond to this crime."

"You must have been terrified," she said quietly.

"Terrified, yes. But strangely liberated. I felt as though I had been waiting for that moment all my life—the moment when I would not return to that house. And suddenly it was upon me. I resolved to take the remaining money and set out on my own. To conceal my whereabouts from him, I took upon me the name of Weaver. It was not many months later that I discovered I could earn my bread—sometimes barely that and sometimes far more than that—by doing what I loved most: fighting. I sometimes fancied I might save my money and return to him with the amount I had taken, but I always postponed this project. I had become attached to my newfound freedom, and I feared that this freedom had tainted me forever. In my mind I had already returned and been cast off, so I felt in my breast as though I had been wronged and was morally obliged to stay away. I imagine that some part of me always knew this idea to be a false one—a mere excuse, for I had never liked being beholden to the laws of our people."

She said nothing, but her eyes suddenly locked on mine. I had uttered the words she had never dared to say aloud.

"On my own, I could eat what I liked, work when I liked, wear what I liked, spend my time with whom I liked. I let a youthful error grow, and my mistake became in my mind the appropriate response to the harsh and unforgiving treatment of an unjust father. And so I convinced myself until I received the news of his death."

Miriam stared into her glass of wine, perhaps afraid to look at me. "Yet you stayed away even then."

I had tried to remain detached as I told the tale; it was one I had told myself so many times that I should have been able to recount it without giving it a single thought. And yet I found myself profoundly saddened—a condition I attempted to rectify by finishing the wine in my glass. "Yes. Even then I stayed away. It is hard to change more than a decade of habit. I always believed, Miriam, that my father was an unnaturally unkind man. But it is strange. Now that I have not seen him in ten years, now that I shall never see him, I begin to wonder if it was I who was not a good son."

"I envy you that freedom," she said, eager to change the subject to one that would make me less pensive. "To come and go as you please. You can eat anything—speak with anyone—go anywhere. Did you eat pork? And shellfish?" She sounded at once like an excited child.

"They are but foods," I said, curious at my desire to diminish the thrill I had felt from the freedom to eat those victuals forbidden by our law. "What signifies one kind of meat or fish over another? What signifies its method of preparation? These things only appeal because they are forbidden, only delight because of the enticement of sin."

"Englishmen therefore do not enjoy oysters because of their flavor?" she asked skeptically.

I laughed, for I was fond of oysters. "I am not sure I mean that," I said. "But now it is your turn to answer my questions. Let us begin with your suitor, Mr. Adelman. What think you of him?"

"He is not so much my suitor as a suitor of your uncle's money," she said, "And rather old besides. What is your interest in my opinion of Mr. Adelman?"

My pride would not allow me to express the depth of my interest, though I was certainly delighted to learn that Adelman was no rival. "I shared his coach with him last night, and let us say I found his conversation a bit unsettling. He struck me as a devious man."

Miriam nodded. "He is deeply involved with politics, and many of the papers think very ill of him," she explained to me, her cheeks ruddy with pride that she knew of these things—usually the province of men. I wondered how my uncle, who cared so little for her knowing of social amusements, felt about her reading the political papers. "Much of the hatred directed against our people," she continued, "that you find to be so present in fashionable circles, stems in no small amount from a distrust of his influence over the Prince and the ministry. That is reason enough, to my mind, to have nothing to do with him. I should hardly relish being tied for life to a public villain, guilty or no."

The boldness of her way of expression utterly charmed me. She understood what it would mean to marry a man like Adelman, and I could not but applaud her wish to have no part of it. "And yet my uncle appears to permit this courtship. Does he wish to see you married to Adelman?"

"That is a topic upon which he has remained unclear. I can only imagine that the idea of his son's widow marrying another man—any man at all, I should think—must sit ill with him. Nevertheless, so near a connection to a man of Mr. Adelman's status must prove itself a powerful motivation, but Mr. Lienzo has yet to make a case to me on Adelman's behalf."

" 'Has yet to.' " I repeated her words. "You think he may yet?"

"I believe that your uncle's sentiments about his son must eventually yield to his desire to form a closer bond with Mr. Adelman."

"And what shall you do," I asked slowly, "should he attempt to force your hand?"

"I shall seek protection elsewhere," she said, affecting a lightness I sensed she did not feel.

I thought it odd that Miriam said nothing of setting up her own household; that she believed her only options were the protection of some man or another. But I could find no way to press this point without offending her, so I moved on in another direction. "You say he wishes my uncle's money, yet he is surely an enormously wealthy man."

"True, but that is not to say he does not covet more wealth. The belief that one cannot have too much money is, I am told, one of the prerequisites of a successful man of business. And he grows older and wishes for a wife. A wife to him must bring him money, but, I suspect, she must also be a Jewess."

"Why? Surely a man of his power could marry any of a number of Christian women if he so chose. Such things are not unheard of, and what little conversation I've had with Adelman suggests to me that he has no love of his own race."

"I believe you are right." Miriam pursed her lips and shrugged. "I suppose he could marry a Christian lady, but it would be unwise for a man in his position."

I nodded. "Of course. His enemies fear him as a force of consuming Jewish power. Were he to marry a Christian, his inability to . . . contain himself, perhaps, would be perceived as threatening."

"I also believe he would like to convert and become a member of the Church of England. Not that he has any religious inclinations toward that faith, but because it would be easier for him to do his business. But Adelman also recognizes, I suppose, the enmity this move would produce in both communities. And so he casts his eye upon me, a Jewess who comes with a marriage settlement and who is not tied to the ancient traditions."

I thought about Miriam's analysis for a moment. "If I may ask an indelicate question, may I inquire more about Adelman's desire to acquire my uncle's wealth? Would it not be *your* wealth that he would acquire upon marriage?"

She set down her glass of wine, nearly toppling it as she did so. I was sorry to have asked so awkward a question, but she had raised the point after all, and it was important to understand Adelman's motivations.

"I have brought this question upon myself, so I should answer it with good cheer, I suppose."

I held up my hand. "If you wish to defer, I shall in no way press you."

"You are too good, but I shall answer. Aaron, as you know, was a factor for, not *with*, your uncle. When he died, he owned very little himself, really only what had been settled upon him by my parents' estate at the time of our marriage. And much of that money had been invested in the venture that Aaron had been upon, a venture that ended disastrously, as you know. I am, myself, mistress of a very small fortune, and I owe much to your uncle's generosity."

I sensed something caustic in her last comment, but I did not believe this to be a topic that I might delve into any deeper than I had already. "So, my uncle has offered a settlement on your behalf to Adelman if he should marry you?" I inquired.

"He has not said so," Miriam explained, "but I can only speculate that is the case. Your uncle should see it as an investment to purchase such influence of Adelman. Is it true," she asked quite suddenly, now in a less dire tone of voice, as though she had changed the topic to music or stage plays, "that your father failed to consider you in his will?"

My first instinct was to wave my hand and show my lack of concern, but I knew such a gesture to be a mere façade, and one that I did not wish to erect before this woman. Instead I nodded. "I feel no resentment. Indeed, I consider it a kindness, for had he left me any sizable estate, the guilt at my neglect would surely have been more than I could endure." Miriam remained silent—not because she judged me harshly, but because, I believe, she did not know what to say. I attempted to turn the conversation to a topic less awkward. "And what of Mr. Sarmento?"

Her face betrayed what I took to be astonishment. "You are a very clever man, Cousin, to have noticed Mr. Sarmento's attentions. Yes, he too is my suitor."

"It is sometimes hard to tell if he is not, perhaps, Mr. Adelman's suitor."

She nodded grimly. "Yes, that is why I was surprised you noticed him in that capacity. Mr. Sarmento has expressed some interest to my uncle, but he is far more concerned with pursuing matters of business than matters of a domestic nature. Frankly, Mr. Sarmento is more puzzling and repulsive than Mr. Adelman. He is a self-interested and I think deceitful creature. So is Adelman, but at least he is involved in Court politics, and deceitfulness is, I should think, required. What excuse can Mr. Sarmento offer for scurrying about like a rodent? Frankly, I imagine he wishes to replace Aaron in Mr. Lienzo's heart, so in that sense he is your rival as much as Mr. Adelman's."

I chose to ignore that jibe. "He has property enough to make his match?"

"His family is not unsuccessful. They would offer to settle him, I believe, once marriage negotiations are under way. But his family would benefit far more than yours."

"And what does my uncle think of this rodent?"

"That he is an able man about the warehouse, that he keeps my father's business ordered, and that, should Sarmento decide to strike off on his own, he should be difficult to replace. I do not believe this sentiment is the same as wishing to stare across a table at him at breakfast each morning for the rest of his life."

"It is a tricky business, placing a son's widow upon the marriage market, I suppose."

"Indeed," Miriam said dryly.

"And to whom do you cast your eye, may I ask?"

"To you, of course, Cousin," she said, the words flying instantly off her tongue. I suspect she regretted her flippancy the minute she spoke, and there was a period of profoundly confusing silence in which I neither spoke nor breathed. Miriam let out a nervous laugh, perhaps suspecting she had taken too great a liberty. "Do I presume too much? We should perhaps spend two or three such afternoons thus before I may be flippant with you with impunity. I shall be serious, then. I cast my eye on no one. I am sure I am not ready to become another man's property. I have few freedoms right now, and I do not know that I want to surrender those I have. Perhaps I desire more freedoms, and I think they should be more readily attained here than in some other man's house."

I said nothing for a moment, for I felt myself still hot in the face over the unexpected exposure of the pleasure I took in her company. It took some time before I finally opened my mouth to speak, but I was cut short by the arrival of my aunt and uncle, who cheerily breezed into the room, poured themselves some wine, and told us stories of their youth in Amsterdam.

TEN

THE SUN WENT DOWN, and the Sabbath was over. After dinner I retired with my uncle to his study, where we finally came to the business
of discussing my father's finances at the time of his death. Like my
uncle's private closet in his warehouse, this room was lined with ledgers
and maps, but here he also kept histories, travel books, and even some
memoirs—all, I suspected, important to an understanding of the places
with which he traded. The walls of the room not covered with bookshelves were a distracting clutter of maps and prints he had taken from
broadsheets or pulled out of inexpensive pamphlets. Almost all available
wall space was covered; parts of prints and woodcuts overlapped one another. Some were pictures of important men, such as the King, or of
scenes of domestic life or of trade or of a ship upon the ocean. It was a
dizzying array, but Uncle Miguel took pleasure from the endless variety of
images.

He sat behind a desk, and I pulled a chair up close that I might hang
upon his words. I suppose because contacting my uncle had been such a
difficult matter for me, and because he had delayed this meeting for a full
twenty-four hours, I believed that he would have things to say that would
prove tremendously illuminating.

"The problem is not that your father kept inadequate records," my
uncle began. "He kept copious records. He simply organized his information inadequately. He knew where everything was, but no one else did. It
would be a project of months, maybe years, to organize his papers and

then cross-examine everything against the issues in his possession at the time of his death."

"So there is no way of learning whether or not his holdings were disordered, as Balfour claims his father's were."

"I fear not. At least not directly. But he was involved in something curious shortly before his death, and it is for this reason that I first became suspicious about this accident. Your father had a true gift for the funds, you know—almost a prescient ability to predict their rise and fall. He liked to discuss the funds with me—about how much this one or that was worth on the current market. I think perhaps I was the only man he could talk to and not fear I would act prematurely on his advice, and thus cause an unpredicted flux in the market. Then, shortly before he died he grew quiet and changed the subject when I asked him what he worked upon. I know that he met several times with Mr. Balfour, but Samuel never told me of their business. That the two of them should die only a day apart—I think you can see why I am suspicious."

"If I am to make any progress in this inquiry, I must have a better sense of these issues in which he involved himself. I must confess that my father never told me much about his business, and I never cared to learn much of the doings of Exchange Alley in general. What are these funds you speak of? How do they work?"

My uncle settled into his chair, and smiled like a pedant. "The process is quite simple. If you were to find yourself in need of more ready money than you had in your possession, there would be several options open to you, such as borrowing money of a goldsmith or a scrivener. Governments, particularly when they fight wars, often find themselves short of the money they require to pay their troops, manufacture their weaponry, and so forth. In the past in this country, and even today in nations oppressed by absolute monarchs, a king could demand that his wealthy nobles 'lend' him money. If the king never paid the money back, there was not much these nobles could do. And once the monarch died, heirs would usually refuse to honor any predecessor's debts."

"So this money was not lent but extorted."

"Precisely. And when the powerful landowners are oppressed by their monarch, it is ever a dangerous circumstance. When King William took the throne away from the villainous Papist, James II, thirty years ago, he immediately made war against the French in order to prevent that nation from gaining mastery of Europe. To pay for these wars, he used the Dutch method of raising revenues. Instead of demanding that men pay the Crown cash, he offered the opportunity to turn cash into investment. When the Kingdom wishes to pay for a war, money can be acquired by selling issues—promises to pay back a certain amount with a particular interest. If you invest one thousand pounds into an issue that promises to pay 10 percent interest, you receive one hundred pounds per year. After ten years, the government has repaid your loan, but you continue to receive an income. Now, this might be a bad investment for someone who has only a thousand pounds in the world, but if a man can spare the money, then the funds provide a regular and dependable source of revenue. More dependable than land, for a landowner's rents may fluctuate depending upon the economy of the countryside and the bounty of the harvest. Investments in the funds are guaranteed."

"But for how long?" I inquired. "For how long does the state continue to pay out that hundred pounds a year?"

My uncle shrugged. "It depends on the issue, of course. Some are for sixteen years, some a little more, some a little less. Some issues are life annuities, so as long as the holder is alive, the interest arrives yearly."

"But if the annuitant dies before the loan has been paid back . . ." I began.

"Then it is a good deal for the Treasury, yes."

"Is it possible that my father was killed in order to prevent some sort of loan repayment?" I asked, though I considered such a thing unlikely. It was a poor government that murdered its lenders.

My uncle laughed softly. "It is true that King Edward the First expelled the Jews from this island because he did not wish to repay his loans, but I think that things have changed somewhat in the past five hundred years. I think it unlikely that the Treasury or its agents would be so violent in its efforts to reduce the national debt."

"Adelman spoke to me the other night of reducing the national debt," I noted, not intending to speak aloud.

"It is a concern upon many men's lips."

"Yes, but I grow curious when it is upon the lips of a man who wishes to silence me. Your friend Mr. Adelman requested that I discontinue my inquiry, and that makes me wonder what he has to hide."

My uncle hardly appeared to hear me. "Adelman is a complex creature. I do not think murder is among his practices, however. He can get what he wants otherwise."

"And how shall he get Miriam, Uncle?"

He smiled impishly—the kind of smile that made me sad to have been away from him so long. "By her consent, I should suspect, Benjamin, which does not appear to be forthcoming. No, Adelman has reasons of his own, I'm sure, to ask you not to look into these matters, and I'm certain they relate to his fear that the businessmen of the coffeehouses might panic if they should hear disagreeable rumors. You see, Adelman holds an unusual place in the South Sea Company. He is not one of its directors, at least not officially, but he has secretly invested in the Company, on the order of tens of thousands of pounds—perhaps even more."

"I still do not understand why my inquiry should concern him."

"I have left much out, I see. The state does not itself broker these loans. Rather it has been the responsibility of the Bank of England to collect the money and manage the disbursal of interest. In exchange it receives certain monetary considerations from the Treasury as well as the possession of large sums of money, which, if only temporarily, may be put to use by the Bank. Now the South Sea Company has been trying to take some of this business away from the Bank."

"So, the Company and the Bank are both competing for the same trade—that of brokering government loans?"

"Correct," my uncle said. "And as I told you, when King William's wars were fought against the French, a great deal of money had to be raised, and raised quickly, and the government offered very attractive loans, such as those that I mentioned—yielding 10 percent for life. Now there is a great agitation in Parliament, which sees the debt of our fathers as the inheritance of our children. So the South Sea Company has proposed a reduction in the national debt by setting up stock conversions. One such conversion, though a very small one, took place earlier this year. Holders of government issues were offered the opportunity to exchange their annuities for South Sea stock. The Treasury gives the Company money for the stock, which eliminates a long-term debt."

"This South Sea Company must be very profitable if men would exchange something guaranteed to earn a high interest."

"Oddly, it is not profitable in the least. Its success is something of a fable of the new finance." He leaned forward and glanced at me, pleased, as always, to play the role of instructor. "Like the other trading companies, the South Sea Company was formed to hold exclusive trading rights to a particular region—in this case, the seas off of South America. Unfortunately, interference from Spain has left these rights void of much value. The Company attempted to make a profit a few years ago in the unpleasant trade of Africans for labor in South America, but from what I have heard, their inexperience in these matters made the business both unprofitable and even more cruel for the cargo than is usual."

"If it does not trade, then what does it do?"

"It has been making itself into a bank to rival the Bank of England—that is to say, attempting to participate in the funding of the national debt. And the Company has been growing in power. The stock has done very well of late, and yielded far more than these 10 percent annuities, and so it seems like a good exchange. But there are many who do not believe the conversions are sound, for in order for the stock to be profitable, the Company must make money and pay the stockholders dividends. If the company fails to be profitable, then the stock is worth nothing, and men who held government issues—real wealth—suddenly discover that they own nothing. It would be as though you woke up to discover your land had turned to air."

"That is why Adelman wishes to scare me off this inquiry? Because of a stock conversion?"

"I expect that Mr. Adelman fears your inquiry will cause a public outcry of murder and intrigue within the funds."

"You disagree?" I asked.

"Mr. Adelman has long been a friend of this family, but that does not mean that his interests and mine must always be the same. He wishes the South Sea Company to do well. My motive is justice. If these interests cannot co-exist, I am unwilling to step aside."

"I admire your spirit, Uncle," I said, for I saw a fierce determination in his face that earnestly made me wish to serve him.

"As I admire yours, Benjamin. Were Aaron alive, I know he would not hesitate to take upon himself this inquiry. Now you must stand in his shoes."

I could but nod. I believed that if Aaron were alive, he should wedge himself in the wardrobe rather than step onto the streets in search of a murderer, but if my uncle wished to remember his son as a valiant man, I would not take that image from him.

"I think perhaps we should retrace our steps," my uncle continued. "The magistrate who looked into your father's death gave naught but a harsh reprimand to the coachman who ran down Samuel. I do not believe this driver, this Herbert Fenn"—and here my uncle paused to mutter a curse in Hebrew—"would have committed this act of his own accord. If this was murder, then the coachman was in someone's employ. I shouldn't think a man of your wile would have so much difficulty making this coachman say more than what is in his best interest."

"Yes, I had thought of that," I said, "and I aim to seek him out."

My uncle offered me another smile, one not so sweet. "The conversation should not be too pleasant for him. You understand?"

"It may disincline him ever to speak again."

He leaned back in his chair. "You're a good man, Benjamin. You will find your way yet."

"Let us suppose," I continued, "that I get nowhere with this coachman. Can you think, Uncle, of any enemies my father might have had? Anyone who either stood to benefit by his death—or perhaps someone who bore a grudge sufficient to motivate revenge?"

My uncle smiled at my ignorance. "Benjamin, your father was a prominent stock-jobber. The entire nation hated him, and there are thousands who drank a bumper to his death."

I shook my head. "I do not concern myself with matters of finance, but I fail to see why my father should be so despised."

"For many Englishmen, these are very confusing times. Our family has been engaged in finance among the Dutch for a number of years now, but it is new to the English, and many see it as very dangerous, a replacement of the glory of the past with a new and honorless greed. Much of it is fantasy, naturally. It is always so when men remember the past and use it to condemn the present. But there are those who recall fondly a time when an English King was an English King, and he was chosen by God rather than by Parliament. Similarly," he said, taking a guinea from his purse, "they remember when gold was gold. Its value was contingent on nothing, and all things had value that could be measured in precious metals. Gold and silver, if you will, were the stable center of value, around which all things orbited—much as the natural philosophers have described the workings of the sun and the planets for us." He waved me over. "Now," he said, "take a look at this."

I walked to his desk and he showed me a banknote written for the value of one hundred and fifty pounds. It originated with the Bank of England and had been made out to someone I had no idea of, but this man had signed it over to another gentleman, who had signed it to a third, who had signed it to my uncle. "Which would you rather have?" he asked me. "That guinea or this note?"

"As the note is worth more than a hundred times the guinea," I said, "I should rather the note, provided you sign it over to me."

"Why should you require I sign it to you? If it is worth one hundred and fifty pounds, then that is its value. How can my signature vest it with value?"

"But it is not one hundred and fifty pounds in the way that this coin *is* one guinea. That note is merely the promise to pay one hundred and fifty pounds. It is nonnegotiable, and as it is signed to you, it is a promise to pay it to *you*. If you sign it to me, then the promise is to me. Unsigned, it should be difficult to get the promisers to agree to pay it."

"There you have the problem," my uncle said. "For money in England is being replaced with the promise of money. We in business have long valued banknotes and paper money, because they allow for large sums to be conveyed with ease and relative safety. They have allowed for the flourishing of international commerce we see today. Yet for many men, there is something most unsettling about the replacement of value with the promise of value."

"I do not see why this causes unease. If I am the merchant and can buy what I will with this banknote, or if I can easily convert it to gold, where is the harm?"

"The harm," my uncle said, "is in whom this system makes powerful. If value is no longer vested in gold, but in the promise of gold, then the men who make the promises hold ultimate power, no? If money and gold are one and the same, then gold defines value, but if money and paper are the same, then value is based upon nothing at all."

"Yet if we value paper and it buys us what we need, it becomes as good as silver."

"But can you not imagine, Benjamin, how these changes frighten men? They no longer know where value lies or how to conceive of their own worth when it changes from hour to hour. To hide your gold plate under your floorboards is lunacy in this age, for to let metal molder when it could be breeding more metal is to lose money. Yet to play the funds is to risk it as well, and many fortunes have been made and lost in speculating upon the funds. Speculation could not take place, you understand, without stock-jobbers such as your father was, but even those who have grown vastly rich upon the market turn and look at men like your father

with hatred and disdain—for jobbers like Samuel have become emblems
of these changes that make men so uneasy. Those who have lost money,
you might imagine, hate jobbers even more. There is a sense, you see, that
finance is but a game, the rules and the outcome of which have been pre-
set by men operating in secret. These men profit from the fortunes and
misfortunes of others—and they cannot lose because they themselves
dictate the values of the market. That, at any rate, is what is believed."

"Absurd," I said. "How can those who buy and sell stocks dictate their
values?"

"First you must understand that in order for stock-jobbers to make
money, the prices of the funds must fluctuate. Otherwise there can be no
buying and selling at a profit."

"If the prices of government issues are fixed," I inquired, "why do the
prices fluctuate?"

My uncle smiled. "Because the price is fixed with money, and money is
worth more at some times than at others. If there is a bad harvest and
food is scarce, then one shilling buys less than if food is plentiful. Similarly,
if there is war, and trade is inhibited, then many goods are scarce and
more expensive, so money is worth less. The threat of war or famine, or
the promise of bounty or peace, all affect the prices of the funds."

I nodded, pleased with myself for understanding this concept.

"Now, let us say that I am a corrupt stock-jobber," my uncle mused, delighted with this game, "and I have a government fund that I want to sell
that is valued at one twenty-five—that is, 125 percent of its original
value. Let us further say that there are rumors of a conflict between Prussia and France. The outcome of such a conflict will almost certainly affect
prices here, for a victory on the part of Prussia defeats a mutual enemy,
while a victory on the part of France strengthens our enemy and makes
war more likely—and if there is war, then money buys less."

"I understand," I said.

"Our corrupt jobber believes that France will win and that the prices of
government issues will fall, so he wishes to sell. What does he do? He
plants false rumors that the Prussians cannot but win—that is, he con-
vinces others of the opposite of what he believes to be true. He has writings to this effect appear in the newspapers. Suddenly 'Change Alley is full
of bulls who wish to buy all they can. Our friend sells at one thirty-five,
and when the Prussians actually lose the battle, the price of the issue

drops, the jobber has sold at an unreasonable rate, those who purchased when the price was elevated now suffer a great loss."

"Surely you do not suggest that men truly practice such schemes, or that my father did?"

"Bah." He waved his hand. "Do jobbers manipulate rumors to alter stock prices in their favor? Some do and some don't. If so, it is the province of well-placed men who have the ear of governments. Directors at the Bank of England and so forth. These men do have control over what is valuable and what is not, and that is indeed a great deal of power."

"But did my father resort to such deceptions?" I asked pointedly.

He showed his palms to the ceiling. "I never meddled with his business. He managed his affairs as he thought best."

I ignored the fact that my uncle had maneuvered out of answering a question. It was no matter; I knew the answer but too well—that is, I knew of at least one incident, from when I was a boy, when my father had cheated another man. When I had learned of that cheat, though I was but a child, I could not understand how he might have deceived other men—he had no ability to charm or cajole as my uncle did. Perhaps his bland impatience had been misunderstood as earnestness.

"Even if he did not engage in any manipulations," I continued, "he would sell when he suspected prices would soon fall. Is that not deceitful?"

"He never *knew* that prices would fall, and assuredly he was wrong many times, though never so often as he was right. If I buy something of you, there is much uncertainty on my end, but one thing I may be sure of is that you are willing to part with what you sell. When your father sold he took a chance, much like the men to whom he sold."

"Yet when he was right, and prices fell, men cried dishonesty."

"Inevitably. It is the way of things when one loses, is it not?"

"Then," I said with some agitation, "you think every man my father ever did business with should be suspected? That seems like a great number of men. Is there perhaps a record of some of the men with whom he dealt most recently?"

My uncle shook his head. "Not that I have been able to discover."

"And can you think of no one in particular—a great enemy who might have delighted in the destruction of my father?"

My uncle shook his head vigorously, as though trying to dispel an unpleasant thought. "I cannot. As I say, your father was hated by many men, men who feared the new financial mechanisms. But a great enemy? I think not. It is Herbert Fenn, this coachman, who ran him down. That is where your inquiry must begin." He slammed his fist into his palm.

Sensing that my uncle had no more to tell me, I rose and thanked him for his assistance. "I shall, naturally, keep you informed of my progress."

"And I shall continue to look for anything that may be of use."

My uncle and I shook hands warmly, perhaps a bit too warmly for my comfort, for he looked at me with something like paternal affection, and I could only choke back the urge to tell him that I was not his son, and his son was most certainly not to be found within me.

After a formal farewell to my aunt and to Miriam, I left the house and made my way to the High Street, where I procured a hackney to take me to my home.

I was pleased that I had acquired so much information, even if I was not sure how I would now proceed. One thing was certain, however. In the time since I had first spoken to Mr. Balfour, I had come around to his way of thinking. Perhaps it was the conversation I had had in Adelman's coach, or perhaps it was my understanding of the depth of confusion produced by the financial markets that my father had understood so well. I could not say why precisely it had happened, but I realized that I now acted with the belief that my father's death had been a murder.

There remained in my mind, however, one question that I could not set aside. It was on the matter of my father's enemies. I could not understand why my uncle had lied to me so boldly.

ELEVEN

I RETURNED TO my rooms in Mrs. Garrison's house, and after pouring myself a glass of port, I sat in the dim light of a cheap tallow candle and wondered if my uncle and I had simply misunderstood each other. I had asked him if my father had any great enemies, and my uncle had said no. Could it be that he had no wish to bring up an unpleasantness from the past? That he believed an enemy whose hatred had been born so many years ago could be no true foe today? Or was it that in the ten years since I had left Dukes Place my father had achieved some kind of peace with a man who had sworn to undo him?

I had thought to clarify the question—to ask my uncle if there had *never* been any such enemy, but I feared that if I forced the issue, he would answer with the name I had in mind, and I was far too curious of his silence to force him to speak. Had he withheld that information because he believed that I never knew of this enemy? That my father had never bothered to speak of him to me, the disobedient son? Or had my uncle hoped that my recollection of this enemy had slipped through the fissures of a memory made unreliable by intemperate living and misadventure?

Whatever the reason my uncle might have had to withhold this name, I could never hope to forget Perceval Bloathwait.

I never entirely knew the nature of my father's conflict with Bloathwait, for it had happened when I was perhaps eight years old, but I knew enough to understand that either my father had cheated Bloathwait out of a sum of money, or Bloathwait believed he had. All I knew as a child, and all I knew that night, as I sat in my room, was that Bloathwait had come to my father on a matter of business—either to buy or to sell, I know not which. I understood this much when, one cold evening in midwinter, snow pushing up toward the windows on the ground floor of our house, Mr. Bloathwait had arrived in the middle of our dinner and demanded to speak with my father. We sat about the table, my brother José and myself, while my father, looking stern in his white wig and drab, slightly soiled clothes, told his servant to refuse the man. The servant disappeared with a bow, but only seconds later, it seemed to me, a fat, sturdy man in a black, flowing full-bottom wig and a scarlet coat, burst into the room, snow still dripping from his outer garments. He seemed a giant of a man, made huge by indignation—a massive bulk of animated contempt for my father.

"Lienzo," he hissed like a cat. "You have ruined me!"

We were all silent. I waited for my father to rise up with outrage at this rudeness, but he only sat motionless, staring at his plate, avoiding eye contact with the man as though to look at him would be to invite some kind of violence. "You may speak to me in my place of business on the morrow, Mr. Bloathwait," he said at last. His voice was subdued and tremulous. Perspiration, reflected in the orange light of the fireplace, glistened upon his face.

Bloathwait spread his legs a bit as though to steady himself against an assault. "I fail to understand why I should not destroy your domestic quiet when you have utterly ruined mine. You are a scoundrel and a thief, Lienzo. I demand restitution."

"If you believe you have been wronged, you may take your concerns to court," my father replied with uncharacteristic fortitude. A crack in his voice betrayed his fear, but he responded to the desperation of the moment with a kind of noble resignation. "Otherwise, you must consider yourself a victim of the changeable nature of the funds. We all suffer from time to time, at the whim of Lady Fortune: there is no avoiding it. I believe a man should always invest no more than he can afford to lose."

"My enemy was not Fortune. It was *you*, sir." He pointed at my father with a great walking stick. "It was you who encouraged me to invest my fortune in those funds."

"Mr. Bloathwait, if you wish to discuss this matter, you may come see me upon the 'Change, but I wish to spare you the indignity of being escorted out by my servants."

Bloathwait twisted his mouth as if to speak, but it suddenly grew slack—like a wine bladder gone empty. He lowered his walking stick and tapped it once upon our floor. He then stretched out his shockingly small mouth to show us a grin. I say *us*, for he flashed it at me and José as much as at my father. "I think, Mr. Lienzo, that I shall wait for you to seek me out." He offered a short and formal bow, and then departed.

Had that been the end of the affair, I suppose I might have forgotten it. But it did not end there. Only a few days later, as I returned home from my school, I spotted Mr. Bloathwait upon the street. At first I did not recognize him, and walked on, noticing an enormous figure directly before me who stood shin-deep in snow, trailed by the flapping of a great black overcoat. He stared hard upon me, and his black eyes sunk into a face that appeared to me an enormous expanse of skin peppered with tiny eyes, a bud of a nose, and a mere slash of a mouth. The harsh gusts of wind had turned his skin red and sent his dark wig upon the air like a military banner. He wore somber clothes—for Bloathwait was a Dissenter—and those of his sect had learned from their ancestors, the Puritans, to use their attire to signify a disregard of vanity. On Bloathwait, however, these dark colors held more of menace than of abnegation.

I moved to step out to the street, to cross and thereby avoid him, but a hackney barreled down, and I had no opportunity. So I walked on, even then foolishly thinking bravado should serve me where luck might not. Perhaps if I only walked by him, ignored him, the incident would pass.

It was not to be so. Bloathwait reached out and grabbed my wrist. It was a firm grab, but not a strategic one. I understood that, as an adult, he was not in the custom of grabbing people by the wrist, and as a boy with an older brother, I knew well how to break such a sloppy hold. For the moment I held my ground, unsure if I should break free and run or listen to what this man, who was, after all, an adult, had to say. He frightened me, yes, but I recognized in his anger with my father some commonality with him—as though he had found a way to give voice to my own ideas and experiences. For this reason, I wished to know more of him, but because he made me recognize my father in a way I never had before, I wished to flee.

"Let go of me," I said, trying to sound nothing so much as irritated.

"I'll let go of you, sure," he said. "But I want you to tell your father something for me."

I said nothing, and he took that as acquiescence. "Tell your father I want my money returned, or sure as I stand here I shall let you and your brother know my outrage."

I would not show him that I was frightened, though there was much in his look to frighten a boy my age. "I understand you," I said, raising my chin. "Let go of me now."

The wind blew fresh snow in his face, and I believed there to be something villainous about even the uncaring gesture that wiped it aside. "You've more courage than your father, boy," he said with a grin that spread out his tiny mouth.

He released my wrist and stared at me. I, refusing to run, turned my back to him and walked slowly home, where I waited in silence until my father returned from 'Change Alley. It was not until late, well after dark, that I saw him, and I sent one of the servants to request an audience with him. He refused until I sent the servant back, telling him that it was of the greatest importance. I think my father must have recognized that I rarely requested time with him, and never before had asked again when first refused.

Once he admitted me to his closet, I told him with a steady voice of my encounter with Bloathwait. He listened, attempting to show no emotion upon his face, but what I saw there frightened me more than the vague threats of a fat and pompous man like Bloathwait. My father was frightened, but he was frightened because he knew not what to do, not because he feared for my safety.

I wanted to keep this encounter a secret, even from José, but at last, later that night, I told him, and to my horror he revealed that he had had a nearly identical encounter. From that moment on, Bloathwait became to us more horrific than any goblin or witch used to frighten a child. We saw him regularly, as we came out of school, upon the street, in the marketplace. Grinning at us, sometimes hungrily, as though we were no more than morsels he might devour, and sometimes with a kind of inclusive amusement, as though we were all victims of the same ironic twist of fate—that we were somehow comrades and partners in this ordeal.

I once believed that these encounters went on for months, maybe years, though when I was older, José insisted it had only been for a week or two. I suppose he must be right, for a grown man cannot spend too large a part of his life following children around in order to frighten their father, and I had no memories of Bloathwait in which he was not surrounded by snow or red-faced from the cold. Even now, when I have seen far more of Bloathwait to frighten me as an adult than I had as a child, when I think of him I see him in his great coat, a mass of black in the white of winter.

But Bloathwait's terror did at last end. When I had not seen him for some time, I asked my father about it, but he only slammed his fist upon the table and shouted that I was never to speak that name aloud again.

I cannot say the name was never spoken of in the house, though. Sometimes, among my father's business associates, I would hear the word *Bloathwait* mentioned in hushed whispers, and always my father looked over his shoulder to see if there was a witness, a witness who might strip away his mask of indifference and take note of the secret shame beneath.

Until the day I quit that house, I never dared utter his name to my father, but this great, sinister enemy—this man who had been my antagonist, and in a strange way an ally, exposing to me in the most irrefutable terms the failures of my father—remained firmly set in my fancy. I had no difficulty in recognizing him when I saw him next, now grown older, fatter, a lampoon of his former self. I had last looked upon his face, not as a child, but at my father's funeral, when I had turned away from the service, and walked though the damp London afternoon, and seen him standing at a distance of perhaps fifty feet, looking at us, his little eyes fixed upon the huddle of Jewish men muttering their prayers. Strangely, I knew neither fear nor horror, though in retrospect I believe he looked a horrific figure, wrapped as I remembered him in a black outer coat, his wig, wet with rain, pressed against his face. A servant stood, ineffectually holding an umbrella above his head, and two more stood at the ready, awaiting his commands. When I noticed him, my initial thought was of recognition, as though he were a great friend and one I should be glad to see. Driven by instinct, I almost raised my hand in a wave, but in an instant I recollected his face, and froze, staring at him. He met my gaze and did not flinch. Rather, he offered me a slight smile, amused and menacing, and then turned to enter his carriage.

I devoted little attention to matters of politics and commerce, but London is a city in which great men are known to all, and I could not but be aware that this man who had once been so monstrous an enemy of my father was now a figure of some prominence—a member of the Court of Directors for the Bank of England. The Bank of England was the enemy of the South Sea Company, and the Company wished my inquiry to cease. I could not tell what it was, or how these matters fit together, but my uncle's refusal to name Bloathwait, to allow his name to cross his lips, made plain to me that I had no choice but to talk to this enemy once more to learn if a villain from the past had returned to take my father's life.

I DO NOT WISH to produce in my reader the impression that I had no pursuits but those described in these pages, nor any acquaintances than those herein detailed. I knew my nature to be a single-minded one, however, and I thought it best to clear myself of all outstanding obligations before I plunged myself further into this inquiry. In the days that followed my visit to my uncle's house, I completed some business I had with a regular patron of mine—a tailor who catered to the city's quality and who often found his bills neglected by gentlemen whose fortunes had turned. Many such gentlemen take advantage of this country's liberal statutes and appear in public on Sundays when they know the bailiffs cannot arrest them for their debts. Thus, their creditors suffer while debtors parade about under the denomination of *Sunday Gentlemen.* I, however, in the service of my patrons, chose to maintain a much more flexible view of the law than did the bailiffs. I had a long-standing agreement with Bawdy Moll, who allowed me to pluck debtors off the streets on Sundays and deposit them in her gin house until Monday reared its more agreeable head. Rare was the man who would not accept of Moll's liquor once locked in her dungeon, and with our debtor disoriented and unable to produce a coherent story of his illegal arrest, I would contact a proper bailiff—unaware of the larger scheme—who would make the arrest. It was a simple operation, for which I received an amount equal to 5 percent of the outstanding debt and Moll received a one-pound gratuity.

Having secured a slippery fellow who owed my tailor friend in excess of four hundred pounds, I canvassed a few of my acquaintances to see if they knew something of the elder Balfour or his death, but that proved a fruitless venture. More successful was a visit to a young actress—whose name it would be indelicate to mention—with whom I kept some small acquaintance. She was a beautiful girl with bright blond hair and azure eyes and a sly smile that always made me believe she should play a trick upon me at any moment. I often took comfort in her idle chatter, for the world of the stage was so far from the world of my ordinary exploits, but on this occasion I could take no such refuge, for I listened to her tell me that she had learned she would play Aspasia in *The Maid's Tragedy* only because the role had been abandoned by a woman who had fled the theatre to become Jonathan Wild's whore. But I soon forgot the name of this enemy as I enjoyed several delicious hours in this woman's company. It was something of a shame that she always found herself cast in tragic roles upon the stage, for she had a kind of wit about her that I found irresistible. An evening with this charmer was spent as much in laughter as it was in amorous intrigues. But I digress, for these adventures are of little relevance to this history.

What I believe is relevant, however, is that on my late-night retreat from her lodgings I met with a misadventure I could only assume to be tied to my inquiry. My actress lived not far from my own lodgings, across the Strand, in a small outlet off Cecil Street, an area I thought too isolated and too near the river for an attractive lady's comfort. It was her habit to send me home late at night, after her landlady had gone to sleep and before she rose again, and I had no great objection to the arrangement, preferring the comfort of my own rooms. That night, having paid my tribute at the temple of Venus, I set out to make my way back to Mrs. Garrison's. It was dark as I walked up toward Cecil Street, and not a soul stirred that I could see. I could hear the waters of the river, and I could smell its dank, fishy odor. It had begun to rain slightly, and a cool mist filled the air. I pulled my coat about me and headed into the darkness of my ill-lit way home. When I was a boy, the streets of London had been reasonably lighted with lamps, but in the few years before this tale those lamps had fallen into disuse. These dark streets had become lost to honest folk, taken over by the wretched denizens of the alleyways, gutters, and gin houses.

If my reader lives in London, he will understand that no man, no matter how formidable and no matter how well armed, can walk the dark streets of this city without trepidation. Such had always been the case, I suppose, but matters had grown far worse as Jonathan Wild's rascals began to take for themselves the freedoms of the city. Had I lived farther from my paramour than I did, I should have sought to procure a hackney, but I would not be able to do so until upon the Strand, and from there I felt I could safely make my own way. Thus I walked cautiously, attempting to keep my wits about me, though my mind was distracted by the memories of a pleasant evening as well as a bit muddled from two or three bottles of a pleasing vintage.

I had walked only a few minutes when I heard footsteps behind me. Whoever followed was skillful, for he matched his gait precisely with my own, making his footfalls all but impossible to discern. I could only presume it was a footpad who had made his way up from the river and had been delighted to find fair game upon these streets. I kept my pace steady, not wishing to let him know that I heard him, but I grabbed the handle of my hangar with a resolve to be ready for him with my blade. I thought about bringing forth my pistol, but I had no desire to fill yet another prig with lead, and it was my hope that I could defend myself without killing my assailant. It was certainly not overly optimistic to believe that the sight of a brave man with a drawn weapon would be enough to end the matter. The city, this prig might realize, was surely full of easier prey.

I continued to walk, and he continued to keep apace. The mist began to turn into a steady rain, and a strong wind picked up from the river. I found myself shivering slightly as I walked, hearing my heart pound as if behind my ears, just as I heard the rhythmic tapping of the stalker's footfalls. I could not tell when he would strike, but I found it strange that he waited so long. We were alone, and no footpad could hope for more favorable conditions. Indeed, he had nothing to gain by waiting, but he continued only to keep pace. I thought to turn around and challenge him to force the issue and to end the conflict, but I flattered myself that I might reach the Strand—and safety—without risking a struggle. I should have loved to have faced any ruffian of this order in a fair match, but I had no knowledge of his weaponry. He might have a brace of pistols pointed at me, and by frightening him I would only secure my demise. Perhaps, I thought, he was new at his trade and did not understand how ideal the conditions were. If so, I might keep walking until I should find company and the matter would end without confrontation or violence.

At last I saw a hackney coach up ahead, barreling in my direction. I could not imagine where it headed at such a speed, for the street went nowhere one might need to get to quickly. Despite its frenzied pace, I felt certain that if I signaled to him, the coachman would stop and permit me to ride at least to the nearest well-lit spot, where I might procure my own transportation. I feared he might not see me in the dark, so I stepped forward into the road, and drew my hangar, hoping that such light as there was would reflect off the thin blade and signal my distress.

I waved my arms as the coach drew nearer, but it did not slow down. Indeed, I realized as it approached that the horses were not going to run by me, but rather into me, and so I took myself a few steps backward, continuing to wave as I did so. As I changed my course, so too did the horses, and I could not but conclude that this madman meant to trample upon me. I hope my reader will think me no coward, but in an instant I was filled with terror, for I believed in my heart that this was the coach, and this the very coachman, who had run down my father. This terror sprang not only from the fear I now felt for my own life, although that was certainly no small part of it, but from the recognition of the enormity of what I faced. I sought to know what had happened to my father, and now his fate might well be my own. There were forces at work that I could not comprehend, and because I could not comprehend, I felt I could not defend myself.

I took another few steps backward, away from the road, where the murderous coachman would never dare to drive his horses but at his own peril. I discovered, however, a difficulty I had not bothered to consider—that the coach and the thief were but of the same party, for the thief had managed to sneak his way behind me, and, taking advantage of his surprise, he gripped me hard upon the shoulders, twisting my body roughly before throwing me to the ground. As I landed, the coach sped by at a frightening pace, the horses screaming with what sounded like sinister pleasure. My assailant lost no time raising up and holding forth his own blade over my dazed and prostrate form.

"I thought to say 'stand and deliver,' " he told me with a grin dully reflected in even the minimal light, "but in your case, delivering will be enough."

I could not discern his features clearly in the darkness, but he was a stout, gritty-looking creature who, by the width of him, might have acquitted himself reasonably well in an honest fight. Now that he had the advantage, I thought hard for ways I might remove myself of his mercy.

"I have little money about me," I told him truthfully, hoping to prolong the conflict that I might find a way to reverse his obvious advantage. "If you will let me return to my lodgings, I shall pay you for your consideration."

Even in the darkness, I could see him grin. "That's all right," he said in a thick country accent. "My business is somewhat seriouser'n robbery. I was just hoping to get myself a little something extra."

He thrust forward with his weapon, which surely would have pierced my heart had I not raised a leg and, with my heavy boot, stomped hard into his manly parts. It is a painful thing to be struck thus; I know so from experience, but a man who fights in the ring must learn to ignore a pain that, while distracting, is rarely harmful. This prig had never learned that lesson. He let out a howl, staggered backward, and dropped his own weapon that he might helplessly support his injured flesh.

I quickly retrieved both my blade and his own, but I was in no haste to run him through. I walked rapidly toward him as he crouched, clutching at his cod. I could discern that he was dressed not so poorly as the average prig, but I could not see the specific details of his attire, or those of his face.

"Tell me who sent you," I gasped, my breathing having been much disordered by the adventure. I took another step forward.

I heard the clattering of hooves and the grinding of wheels, and I knew the hackney coach was returning. I had little time.

He groaned. He clutched. He said nothing. I thought I should get his attention, and do so quickly, so I kicked him again, this time in the face. He went flying backward into the street, and landed hard upon his posterior. I heard a groan and then a scraping in his throat as he struggled for air.

"Who sent you," I again demanded. I hoped my voice conveyed the urgency of the question.

I thought that if my blow to his tenderest part had so disabled the thief, my second should have all but mastered him, but such proved not to be the case. "Kiss my arse, Jew," he said, and then, audibly sucking in his breath as he mustered his strength, he ran after the coach. He ran slowly and awkwardly, but he ran all the same, and he kept himself just out of my reach as he jumped, or I should say threw himself, onto the back of the coach as it barreled toward the Strand. I took a step farther backward, that the coach could not threaten me, though I did not believe it would try to do so again. It sped off, leaving me standing unhurt if confused and weary.

In such moments, one wishes for some sort of dramatic resolution, as though life were but a stage play. I cannot say which I found more disorienting: the attack upon my person or the fact that, once the attack had ended, I simply continued my walk toward the Strand. And in the silence of the night I could almost believe the assault had been but a fantasy of my mind.

But it had not been. Nor had it been a simple attempt upon a man foolish enough to be caught by himself at night. The hackney coach told me that these were not poor and desperate men, for where would thieving knaves have acquired so expensive a piece of equipment? What frightened me more was that these men knew me—knew me to be a Jew. They had been set upon me, and that I had let them escape filled me with a twisting anger that I vowed to unleash upon my assailants, whom I firmly believed to be my father's killers.

TWELVE

WITH THE CLARITY that comes with the light of morning, I realized precisely the gravity of my situation. If my assailants had desired to murder me, they had certainly failed miserably, and if their desire had been to frighten me away, I resolved that they should fail just as thoroughly on that score. I took this assault as incontrovertible proof that my father had been murdered, and that men of violence and power wished to keep the truth of his death a secret. As a man well used to danger, I determined only to exercise more caution and to continue upon my course.

My thoughts were interrupted by the arrival of a messenger, who brought me a letter addressed in a feminine hand I did not recognize. I tore it open and found myself astonished by the following communication:

Mr. Weaver,

I trust you can easily imagine the extraordinary discomfort at imposing upon you, particularly as we have met but recently. I call upon you, however, because though you and I are but newly acquainted, I can see that you are a man of both honor and feeling, and that you are as generous as you are discreet. We discussed briefly the limitations with which I find myself in your uncle's house, but I hoped to spare you the discomfort and myself the mortification of mentioning that these limitations are both urgent and

real. I find myself short of ready money and threatened by villainous creditors. I dare not risk Mr. Lienzo's disapproval by begging his
assistance, and with nowhere else to turn I am forced to reveal myself to you in the hopes that you will have both the means and the
willingness to advance a small amount that I shall repay in silver
upon the earliest possibility, and repay in gratitude immediately
and eternally. The sum of £25 will perhaps not be missed by a man
of your station, but it will save me from a shame and discomfort I
hardly dare imagine. I hope you will give this note all due consideration, and take pity on a most desperate

Miriam Lienzo

My response to this note was a mixture of surprise, perplexity, and delight. Having been reimbursed by Sir Owen for what I had advanced in the
service of Kate Cole, I could scarcely have endured myself if had I let
Miriam suffer under the threats of her creditors. I had no doubt that my
uncle would never allow her to visit the inside of a debtor's prison over so
niggling a sum, but I believed that she had reasons for wishing to keep
him ignorant of her troubles.

I immediately collected the sum she required from my hidden store of
silver and dispatched Mrs. Garrison's boy with the coins and the following
note.

Madam,

I shall long remember this day as a great one, for on it you have
given me the opportunity to perform for you some small service. I
ask that you consider this insignificant sum as a present and think
no more of it whatsoever. The only consideration I require is that
should you again find yourself in need of assistance of any kind,
you will think first to call upon

Ben. Weaver

I spent much of the next hour wondering about what sorts of debts
Miriam could have accrued and how she might show me her gratitude.
Unfortunately, I soon had to turn to other matters. This was the day I had

appointed to meet with Sir Owen at his club, so after concluding some routine business about the metropolis, I returned to my home in Mrs. Garrison's house to wash my face and change into my best suit of clothes. I even briefly considered wearing a wig, that I might endeavor to appear as one of these men, but I quickly laughed at my own foolishness. I was not a fashionable gentleman, and my pretending to be one should only earn their contempt. And it was with a certain amount of pride that I reminded myself that I did not require a wig as most English gentlemen do, for I, being mindful of cleanliness, washed my hair several times each month and thus avoided the plague of lice. I did not neglect to wear a hangar, however, even though most men consider a fashionable sword to be a sign of gentility. Indeed, it was not many generations ago when the laws of the Kingdom would have forbidden a man such as myself from wearing a weapon, but despite the harsh looks my hangar at times brought me, I never thought to leave it behind. Its protection proved far too valuable, and no stranger ever dared to express his disapproval with words uttered above a whisper.

It was nearly nine o'clock, the time I was engaged to meet with Sir Owen at his club, and after my adventures the previous night, I could feel the dull torpor of exhaustion in the core of my muscles. I considered Sir Owen's invitation a fine opportunity, and I certainly had no wish to insult him by not acknowledging it as such, but as I approached his club, located in a beautiful white town house of Queen Anne's time, I wondered why precisely he had invited me to join him there. I could not but think that in a club to which Sir Owen belonged I might expect to find no shortage of men to raise their eyebrows at a Jew guest. Did Sir Owen want to do me a good turn, or did he have another motive? I wondered perhaps if he might have enemies within his club, people whom he hoped to intimidate by flaunting his connection with me. Was it possible that he thought there would be some sort of prestige in showing he had a man of my stripe in his orbit? Or was it no more than that an exuberant gentleman like Sir Owen felt that I had done him a good turn and wanted to do me one as well—even if such a good turn were in bad taste? Based on what I knew of him, this explanation was hardly unlikely, so I chose to believe in his goodwill, and I knocked heartily upon the door.

After but a moment I was greeted by a very young footman—perhaps no more than sixteen—who had already learned to affect the snobbish manner of his employers. He peered at me, no doubt noting my darkish skin tone and natural hair, and screwed up his face into a foppish disgust. "Can it be that you have some sort of business here?"

"It can," I said with a tight sneer. Five years earlier, perhaps, I would have been considering whether or not to provide the spark with a painful lesson in manners, but age had tempered my passions. "My name is Weaver," I told him wearily. "I am a guest of Sir Owen Nettleton."

"Oh, yes," he droned, his face not yet ready to abandon its conviction of superiority. "Sir Owen's *guest.* We've been told about you."

The "we" I thought an adventurous touch on his part. I was sure if I mentioned it to Sir Owen the boy would have received a good beating for presuming to number himself with his betters, but reporting the spark's insolence was a task I would leave for another man. Instead I followed this servant into an exquisite hall paneled with a dark wood the likes of which I had never seen before. On the floor was a rug of Indian origin, and no inexpensive one I guessed from the intricacy of the work. Not knowing much of the arts, I could not offer an opinion of the paintings on the wall, but they were pastoral scenes of fine workmanship—Italian, I guessed, based on the costumes of the figures. It was clear that Sir Owen kept sophisticated company.

I followed the boy through an equally exquisite drawing room, where three men sat drinking wine. Their close conversation broke as I passed, for they took the opportunity to stare hard at me. I smiled and offered them brief bows as I moved to the main room. This was a large area with perhaps four or five tables, several sofas, and countless chairs. Here a good twenty or so men were engaged in a variety of activities—playing card games, conversing gregariously, and reading the papers aloud. One man stood in the corner, making water into a china pot. The furniture was all of the highest quality, and the wood-paneled walls were decorated with the same style of Italian paintings as I had seen outside. Toward one wall stood an enormous fireplace, but only a small fire burned within.

Sir Owen spotted us before we saw him. The baronet had been sitting at one of the card tables, his face invisible as he contemplated a hand. As he saw us he made some brief apologies to the men with whom he had been playing and stood to greet me.

"Weaver, so good of you to show." Sir Owen's affable face was bright with portly good cheer. "So very good. A glass of port for Mr. Weaver," Sir

Owen shouted at a liveried servant across the room. The footman who had led me in had already melted away.

I felt the hum of conversation die down to a quiet whisper; all eyes were upon me, but Sir Owen either did not note the suspicion with which I was regarded or he did not care. Instead he clapped his arm about my shoulder and led me over to a group of men seated in a few chairs arranged to face one another. "Look here," Sir Owen nearly bellowed at these men, "I want you to meet Benjamin Weaver, the Lion of Judah. He's helped me out of a tight spot, you know."

The three men rose. "I should think," one of them said dryly, "you refer to just this moment, for Mr. Weaver's arrival saved you from your ill luck at play."

"Quite so, quite so," Sir Owen agreed jovially. "Weaver, these men are Lord Thornbridge, Sir Robert Leicester, and Mr. Charles Home." All three men greeted me with rigid politeness as Sir Owen continued to talk. "Weaver here is as brave and stout a man as you're likely to meet. Here's a fellow who's a credit to his people, helping folks rather than tricking them with stock and annuities."

Sir Owen's was a sentiment I had certainly heard before. Men who did not know that I was the son of a stock-jobber frequently felt free to compliment me for having nothing to do with finance or Jewish customs, which were often imagined to be one and the same. I wondered if Lord Thornbridge knew of my family connections, for he took what I believed an ironic amusement at Sir Owen's raillery. He was of about five-and-twenty years, I guessed—a striking-looking man, astonishingly handsome and ugly simultaneously. He had strong cheekbones, a manly chin, and striking blue eyes, but his teeth were rotted black within his mouth, and he had a distracting red and bulbous growth upon his nose.

"Do you feel yourself to be a credit to your people?" asked Lord Thornbridge, as he sat down. The rest of us followed suit.

"I think, my lord," I said, choosing my words with the utmost care, "that any man of a foreign nation must serve as an ambassador among his hosts."

"Bravo," he said, with a slight laugh that appeared to me as much out of boredom as appreciation. Then he turned to his friend. "I should like if your brother Scots felt thus, Home."

Home smiled with pleasure at the opportunity of contributing. He was approximately Lord Thornbridge's age, and I sensed the two were com-

panions, if not friends. He was more fashionably dressed than the noble-
man, and his handsome appearance was unmitigated by any defect
whatsoever. The confidence that Thornbridge derived from his nobility,
Home derived from his appearance. Both, I quickly surmised, derived confidence from money. "I think you do not understand the Scots, my lord,"
Home droned. "Mr. Weaver perhaps feels that his fellow-Jews must be
careful not to disoblige their hosts, for they know their hosts may all too
readily feel disobliged. We Scots, however, feel a more fraternal obligation
to teach the English in the areas of philosophy, religion, medicine, and
manners in general."

Lord Thornbridge affected amusement at Home's repartee. "Just as we
English teach the Scots how to—"

Home cut him off. "How to learn from French dancing masters, my
lord? Really, you must know that any culture England boasts of comes
from the north or from across the Channel."

Lips pursed petulantly, Lord Thornbridge muttered something about
Scottish barbarians and rebels, but it was clear who was the wittier man.
Thornbridge opened his mouth to begin speaking again, no doubt with
the intent of recovering some of his honor, but he was cut off by Sir
Robert, a much older man of fifty or more who sat with the stony superiority of someone who had never been in want of anything. "What think
you then, Weaver, of the Shylocks of your race?"

"I say, Bobby," Sir Owen cut in, "let us not roast our friend upon the
fire. He is my guest, after all." His tone bespoke more amusement than
censure, and I could not think his words were calculated to have any effect upon his friends.

"I see it not as roasting," Sir Robert replied. He turned to me. "Surely
you must acknowledge that many of your people are schemers who seek
to trick Christians of their property."

"And their daughters?" I asked. I hoped to defuse this topic with a bit of
humor.

"Well," Lord Thornbridge chimed in, "it is no secret that the circumcised among us have a voracious appetite." He laughed heartily.

Certainly I felt uncomfortable, but I had long understood what such
men thought of my race. "I cannot speak for all Jews, as none of you could
speak for all Christians. But we have the honest and dishonest among us
as you do."

"Diplomatic but false," Sir Robert said. "Any man who has lost money in the funds knows he can follow the trail of his loss to the hand of a Jew—or a man in a Jew's service, to be sure."

The sophistry of this argument fairly filled me with rage. I knew not how to counter such nonsense. I was therefore shocked to hear Home respond for me. "What rubbish is that, Sir Robert? To say that any transaction might be traced to a Jew is the same as saying that, as you have made it a habit to attend the opera, I can trace you to a buggering Italian, and thus you must be a sodomite."

"Clever wordplay from a Scot," Sir Robert said, visibly angered by Home's analysis. "But I've often wondered about you Scots—refusing to eat pork as you do and clinging so tightly to your funds. I have heard it said that you yourselves are one of the Lost Tribes of Israel."

"Let us not give Mr. Weaver the wrong idea of friendly commerce among Christian gentlemen," Lord Thornbridge proposed cautiously, in an effort to keep tempers in check.

Sir Robert coughed into his hand and then turned to me. "I do not mean to insult your people. I suppose there are reasons—historical reasons—that explain why you are the way you are. The Popes never permitted members of the Romish faith to engage in usury," he explained to the others, perhaps believing that I was familiar with all aspects of Christian history that related to Jews. "And thus Jews gladly took the trade for themselves. Now, Weaver, your race seems tainted by that trade. And here your people are, working your stock-jobbery in this country. One wonders if you are not trying to take the very nation itself away from us. Must we say farewell to Britain and greet instead Judea Nova? Shall St. Paul's be turned to a synagogue? Are we to see public circumcisions in the streets?"

"Gad, Bobby!" Sir Owen exclaimed. "You make me blush with your illiberal words."

"I heartily hope Mr. Weaver is not insulted," Sir Robert said, "but we so rarely have an opportunity to address Jews upon these gentlemanly terms. I feel that we have much to learn from one another under these circumstances. If Mr. Weaver can disabuse me of false notions, I shall not only be willing to listen, but grateful to have the scales lifted from my eyes."

I attempted to smile politely, for there was nothing to be gained from showing this man my anger, and I took a certain comfort in the contempt his opinions earned him from his fellows. "I feel there is little I can say," I began, "for I cannot claim to be an expert on either Jews or money. But I can assure you the two terms are not synonymous."

"No one should claim they are," Sir Robert rejoined. "I think that we only wish to have some points clarified about what Jews want in our country. This is, after all, a Protestant country. If that were not important to us, we would not have imported a German King—we would have been contented with a Popish tyrant. And our Romish citizens understand their precarious situation, but I often feel that you Jews do not—always wanting special dispensations from taking oaths for office and so forth. It's as though you want to become *English* yourselves. And despite what our friends in North Britain may think, being English is no simple matter of how one dresses or speaks."

"I fear I must agree with Sir Robert here," Lord Thornbridge told me, "for while I do not begrudge any foreigner his manners or ways, I do wonder about your brother Jews, who come to settle here in this nation, who wish to remain separate from us, yet clamor for special treatment. There are any number of men I know whose forebears were French or Dutch or Italian, but, from having lived here for a generation or two, they have become engrafted onto our English stock. I am not sure that is the case with your people, Weaver."

"Indeed," Sir Robert chimed in, "suppose stock-jobber Isaac, after earning a plumb in 'Change Alley off the misfortunes of honest Christian gentlemen, decides he wants to take his hundred thousand pounds to the country and become Squire Isaac. He buys an estate and builds up his rent rolls, and lo! he finds himself in charge of appointing a living for a clergyman. Is a Jew to appoint a priest of the Church of England, or are we to expect the good citizens of Somersetshire to follow the teachings of the rabbis? When Squire Isaac, who must serve as the law upon his property, is approached by tenants with a dispute, does he turn to the law of England or the law of Moses?"

"These are questions I cannot answer," I told him, holding my voice steady. "I cannot speak for your Squire Isaac, for no such creature exists. And it has been my experience that rather than seek to take our host nation for as much as we can, we seek to live in peace and gratitude."

"There," Sir Owen said cheerfully, "you have the honorable sentiments of an honorable man. And I can vouch for Mr. Weaver's honor."

"Indeed," Sir Robert said, "Mr. Weaver may not be the perfect speci-men of his people. You recall, I believe, the story of Edmund West?" The other men nodded, so Sir Robert turned to me and explained. "West was a successful merchant who took to playing the funds. He became rather set on the idea of retiring worth a plumb, you know, like so many other men. His fortune rose such that he could have easily retired from the busi-ness of the Exchange, but he would not quit until he had that hundred thousand pounds in pocket. So, worth perhaps eighty thousand pounds, he made some investments of Jews and watched in horror as his fortune was diminished by a full third. These Jews scented out his panic and took advantage of it. Soon this amount was halved and then halved again until he was worth nothing and less. And if you doubt this story"—Sir Robert looked at me squarely—"you may visit Mr. West among the lunatics at Bedlam itself, his losses having quite undone his mind."

Though much of my work required that I bear the abuses of gentle-men, I found my patience all but at an end with this lot. I also grew angry at Sir Owen for allowing this calumny to be launched at me with naught but an ineffectual guffaw. For a moment I thought on taking my leave and showing this buffoon that a Jew is as capable as any man of feeling indig-nation and responding to it as it deserves. And yet something held me back, for I had rarely had a man of Sir Robert's stature lay open his thoughts to me at length, and I wondered what there was to be learned in this conversation. I therefore chose to choke upon my pride for the mo-ment and to consider how to turn this unpleasant conversation to my best advantage.

"All men risk losing their fortunes in the funds," I replied at last. "I can-not think that the dishonesty of Jews can be blamed. Because one man sells to another in hopes of gaining advantage does not make the seller a villain," I said, confidently repeating the words of my uncle.

"I rather agree," Home said. "To blame Jews for the corruption of 'Change Alley is much the same as blaming a soldier for the violence of a battle. Men buy and sell upon the Exchange. Some men make money and some lose—and some of these men are Jews, but I think you know too well, Sir Robert, that most are not."

"Many, however," Lord Thornbridge added, "are foreigners, and there Sir Robert is not wrong to be concerned. I think," he said, turning to his friend, "you are too much the victim of popular prejudice to blame the sons of Abraham exclusively, but they are certainly there, along with many other men of many other nations, and a host of Englishmen with a loyalty to no nation, who would stock-job away the entire country if they could."

Sir Robert nodded in solemn agreement. "Now you talk like a man of sense," he said, waving his hands about excitedly, "but the true villainy of all of this is what it does to our nation. When men begin to trade things of real value for all of this paper, it turns them into frenzied, fanciful women. The rugged and manful values of the ancients are set aside in favor of frivolousness. These loans and lotteries and annuities run our nation into a debt that can never be paid, because we care not to give a fig for the future. I tell you, all this Jewish stock-jobbery shall destroy the Kingdom."

"In my mind," Lord Thornbridge noted, "far more pernicious is the effect of paper money upon the lower elements. Why should a man labor hard for his daily bread if he owns a lottery ticket that may transport him to sudden wealth? In the end I fear that stock-jobbers"—he turned to Sir Robert—"and I mean stock-jobbers named John and Richard as much as those named Abraham and Isaac—threaten to replace birth and gentility with money as the measure of quality."

Here I saw my opportunity. "I wonder, my lord, if Jews or anyone else need to plot the demise of those who are so effective at undoing themselves. I do not wish to speak ill of the dead, but I need only point out Mr. Michael Balfour, who was ruined not by schemers but by his own greed."

Sir Robert stared hard at me. Sir Owen, Home, and Lord Thornbridge exchanged glances. Had I gone too far? Had Balfour perhaps been a member of this club? I felt a flicker of remorse, as though I had been guilty of some *faux pas*, but I soon recollected the indignities these men had laid upon me, asking me to smile like an ape as I received their insults.

Finally, as I might have anticipated, it was Sir Robert who spoke. "It is certain that Balfour was killed by Jews, Weaver. I say, you astonish me by mentioning his name at all."

I opened my mouth to speak, but Sir Owen, not suffering from the shock and excitement I felt, spoke first. "In what capacity, sir? All of London knows that Balfour died of his own hand."

"True," Sir Robert agreed, "but can we doubt that there was a rabbinical influence behind it all? Balfour had a connection with a Jew—that stock-jobber who was killed the next day."

"I believe you misrepresent matters," Home said. "I heard that Balfour's son had the Jew run down to avenge his father's death."

"Nonsense." Sir Robert shook his head. "Balfour's son would have helped the Jews to kick the stool from under his dangling father, but there can be no question that this Jew was involved."

I looked about me carefully to see if anyone stared at me. I felt reasonably sure that no one knew the identity of my father, but I also felt that I was perhaps being tested in some way. I speculated that it would be best if I said nothing, but it then occurred to me that I had nothing to fear of failing the test. "Why," I asked, "is there no question that there were Jews involved?"

Other than Sir Robert, who stared at me with mute amazement, the others simply looked embarrassed and inspected their shoes. I felt embarrassed and awkward, and their embarrassment did nothing to put me at my ease, but I had no choice but to press the inquiry. Sir Robert did not shrink from my gaze. "Really, Weaver, if you wish not to be insulted, then you should not ask such questions. The matter does not concern you."

"But I am curious," I said. "How is Mr. Balfour's death related to Jews?"

"Well," Sir Robert said slowly, "he was friends with that Jew broker, as I told you. And it is said that they were plotting something."

"I have heard this as well," Home chimed in. "Secret meetings and such. This Jew and Balfour surely involved themselves in something to which they proved unequal."

"Are you saying," I said, almost whispering, "that you believe these men were murdered because of some financial scheme?"

"Balfour involved himself with these"—Sir Robert waved his hand in the air—"these fiends, sir, these stock-jobbers, and he paid the price. I can only hope others will learn from him. Now, if you will excuse me."

Sir Robert rose abruptly and Thornbridge, Home, Sir Owen, and I instinctively followed. He walked halfway across the room with his friends, leaving me to stand, by myself, with all eyes upon me, for an excruciating minute or two. Then, with a broad smile upon his face, Sir Owen strolled over to me. "I must apologize for Bobby. I thought he would be more welcoming. He really meant nothing, you know. Perhaps he was a bit warm from too much drink."

I admit I was not as profuse in my expressions of unconcern as I might have been had I been truer to the dictates of fashion rather than those of feeling. I only thanked Sir Owen for inviting me, and took my leave.

I found myself overcome with relief when I finally stepped out of the building. Wishing to avoid even the potential unpleasantness of attacks upon my person, I asked the footman to procure me a hackney, and I rode home in a foul disposition.

THIRTEEN

T HE NEXT DAY, after a hasty breakfast of coarse bread and Cheshire
cheese, washed down with a mug of small beer, I rushed over to Elias's
lodgings. Though it was rather late in the morning, I found my friend still
asleep. Such was often his way. Like many men who thought themselves
more blessed by the gods of wit than those of money, Elias would often
sleep away whole days at a time that he might avoid the consciousness of
his own hunger and poverty.

I waited as his landlady, Mrs. Henry, roused him, and I considered myself honored that he rushed to dress himself in all due haste.

"Weaver," he said, hurrying downstairs, still thrusting one arm
through his deep-blue laced coat that matched perfectly a blue-and-
yellow waistcoat beneath. Short of money though he was, Elias owned
some handsome suits. He struggled to finish dressing himself, as he shifted
from hand to hand a thick pile of papers tied together with a green ribbon.
"Monstrous good to see you. You've been busy, yes?"

"This business with Balfour consumes my full attention. Have you
time to discuss it?"

He studied me with concern. "You look tired," he said. "You have not
been getting enough sleep, I fear. Shall I take some blood to refresh you a
bit, sir?"

"Someday I shall let you bleed me just for the pleasure of astonishing
you." I laughed. "That is, I shall let you bleed me should I believe you will
not kill me in the process."

Elias rolled his eyes at me. "It is a wonder you Jews ever survived at all.

You are like savage Indians in your medical beliefs. When one of your tribe grows ill, do you send for the physician, or for the shaman dressed in a bearskin?"

I laughed at Elias's retort. "I should love to hear how you Scots, who run around the Highlands naked and painted blue, are more civilized than the authors of the Scriptures, but I had hoped you would have time to discuss the Balfour matter. And I should very much like to talk with you about all this stock-jobbery and such, of which I believe you know something."

"By all means. And I have much to tell you. But if it's stock-jobbery you wish to discuss, I can think of no place better than Jonathan's Coffee-house, the very heart and soul of 'Change Alley. If you should only agree to pay for a hackney to drive us there, then I shall allow you to buy me something to eat. Or better yet, why not bill our expedition to Mr. Balfour?"

There would be no expenses billed to Mr. Balfour. From what Adelman had told me, I should be lucky to receive anything of him, but I had no desire to dampen Elias's enthusiasm. I felt the jingle of silver in my purse, owing to Sir Owen's kindness, and I was happy to pay for my friend's morning meal as well as his good advice.

In the hackney on the way to 'Change Alley, Elias chatted constantly but said relatively little of import. He told me of old friends he had seen, of a riot in which he had nearly been caught, and of a ribald adventure he'd had involving two whores in the back room of an apothecary's shop. But my mind wandered as Elias prattled happily away. The day was cool and overcast, but the air was clear, and I watched out the window as we headed east on Cheapside until it turned into Poultry. I saw in the distance Grocers Hall, home of the Bank of England, and before us the enormity that was the Royal Exchange. I must say this mammoth structure always filled me with awe, for though my father had not done business within since I had been a very small child, I still associated it with sullen and mysterious paternal power. The Exchange, as it was rebuilt after the Great Fire destroyed the old building, is essentially a large rectangle, the exterior surrounding a great open-air courtyard. Though only two stories, the walls reach upward three or four times as high as any other two-story structure one might think of, and the entrance is hovered over by an enormous tower that spires into the heavens.

Many years ago, stock-jobbers like my father did their business in the

Royal Exchange, and Jews even had their own "walk" or place of business in the courtyard, along with clothiers and grocers and all manner of men engaged in foreign trade. But then Parliament passed a law forbidding stock-jobbing within the Royal Exchange, so jobbers had moved to nearby Exchange Alley, taking up residence in coffehouses such as Jonathan's and Garraway's. Much to the anger of those who had fought against stock-jobbing, the greater share of London's commerce moved along with them, and while the Royal Exchange stood as a monument to Britain's financial soundness, it was but a hollow monument.

In comparison, the real business of 'Change Alley took place in a few tiny and seemingly insignificant streets that one might circumnavigate in but a few minutes. On the south side of Cornhill, just across the street from the Royal Exchange, one entered Exchange Alley, and proceeded south past Jonathan's and then Garraway's, while the alley wound east to Birchin Lane, and a traveler passed the old Sword Blade Bank and a few other coffeehouses in which one might do business with lotteries or insurance or projects or trade abroad. Birchin Lane took one north, back to Cornhill, thus completing the simple tour of the most confusing, powerful, and mysterious streets in the world.

Our hackney encountered traffic near the Royal Exchange, so I bade the coachman stop by Pope's Head Alley, and from there we walked the short distance, pushing our way through the crowds of men who swarmed about us. If Jonathan's Coffeehouse was the center of commerce, it was also the purest standard of commerce, and the farther one pushed outward, the more one found strange hybrid shops, rooted in both the monetary frenzy of 'Change Alley and the more mundane business of everyday life. One could see lottery butchers, where the purchase of any chicken or coney registered a customer for a prize. A tea merchant promised that a treasure of East India Company stock was hidden in one out of every hundred boxes of his goods. An apothecary stood outside his doorway, shouting to all who passed by that he offered inexpensive advice on the funds.

It would be unfair of me to suggest that the area surrounding the Exchange was the only place in the metropolis into which the new finance had sunk its teeth. Windfall mania had swept the city with the legal reintroduction of the lottery in 1719, the year of this tale, and illegal lotteries had long been popular everywhere. I confess that I myself did business with a lottery barber who registered me for a prize each time I took a shave, though my almost daily visits, for upward of two years, had yet to yield me any bounty.

I had seen the sights of the Exchange before, but now they held a new wonder for me. I kept my eye alert, as though each man I passed might hold the key to my father's murderer; in truth it was far more likely that any man I passed cared not a fig for my father's death unless I could show how it might make or cost him money.

Elias and I forced our way to the Alley, and quickly reached Jonathan's, which was quite full and bustling with the business of the day.

Jonathan's, the stock-jobbers' coffeehouse and the very soul of Exchange Alley, seemed to me more animated than any coffeehouse I knew. Men clustered around one another, arguing vehemently, laughing, or looking grave. Others sat at tables, hurriedly thumbing through piles of papers, gulping their coffee. And the din was not merely that of conversation. While some slapped friends upon the back with warm benevolence, others shouted out their wares: "Selling for the upcoming lottery, eight shillings a quarter ticket!" "Anyone to sell 1704 issues?" "I have an astonishing money-maker here for the man who will but lend me five minutes of his time!" "A project to drain the marshlands! Guaranteed!"

Looking about me, I could see why my Christian neighbors were so quick to associate Jews with 'Change Alley, for there was a superfluity of Israelites in the room—perhaps as many as I had ever seen together outside of Dukes Place. But Jews were hardly dominant in Jonathan's and by no means the only aliens. Here were Germans, Frenchmen, Dutchmen— and Dutchmen aplenty, I assure you—Italians and Spaniards, Portuguese, and of course, no shortage of North Britons. There were even some Africans milling about, but I believed they were servants, and not upon the 'Change for business. The room was a cacophony of different languages, all being shouted at once. It was a dizzying array of papers changing hands, of pens signing, of envelope-stuffing, of coffee-pouring, and of coffee-drinking. I thought it the very center of the universe itself, and I admired in no small degree any man who could conduct business in a place of such distraction.

Fortune favored us, for no sooner did we step inside than a trio of men vacated a table just before us, and we moved quickly to beat out a large crowd that had been waiting longer, all the while conducting their business afoot. Shouting above the din, I asked one of the boys who passed by us with a tray full of dirtied dishes to bring us coffee and some pastries.

I looked about in amazement. I had not been inside Jonathan's since I was a child and my father had dragged me and my brother along to watch him conduct his affairs. We had sat in mute discomfort, half stemming from the dull terror a child feels in the presence of inexplicable adult mania, the other half from pure boredom. Now, in Jonathan's as a grown man, and in my own way here upon business, I still felt small, towered over, and a bit awed. At least I was not yet bored.

The boy brought us our coffee and food, and Elias wasted no time stuffing one of the pastries into his mouth. "Do you know Mr. Theodore James, the bookseller upon the Strand?" he asked me, his words muffled by dough and jam.

"I have passed by his shop," I said.

Elias bubbled with excitement as he spoke. "You might try stepping inside sometime. He's a grand man. He printed my volume of verse, you know. Mr. James possesses no small amount of influence, which he has used to obtain for me an audience with Mr. Cibber at the Theatre Royal, Drury Lane, who is to consider staging my play. It is an astonishingly exciting thing really. I grow giddy at the idea of having my play acted upon the stage. It is truly marvelous, don't you think?"

I could not help but smile. Elias was, after all, a man of many talents. "I had no idea you had a play to stage." I shook his hand with pleasure.

He giggled foolishly. "I hadn't. I shall tell him I have labored hard. Not too hard, for I don't want him to believe me one of those silly playwrights who think themselves a Jonson or Fletcher. I wrote it yesterday," he added in a whisper.

"An entire play in a day?"

"Well, I've seen enough comedies to know how to order these things. And yet, despite its haste, it is not without some very original turns. I call it *The Unsuspecting Lover.* Who could resist a play with so merry a title? Come, Weaver, I consider you a man of taste. Let me read it to you."

"I should love to hear your work, Elias, but I admit I am a bit preoccupied. I promise to attend to it on another occasion, but now I must seek your guidance regarding this Balfour business."

"Of course," he said, sliding out of sight the bundle of papers he'd pulled from his pocket. "The play can certainly wait. It has but so recently hatched into the world that perhaps a rest shall do it some good."

I could not help but find Elias a marvelously agreeable friend. "Thank you," I said, hoping that I had not hurt his feelings by shunting aside his literary efforts, "for I very much require your assistance in this matter. I am somewhat at a loss. Here, after all, we have two men who had some sort of acquaintance, if not a friendship, who died within twenty-four hours of each other. One under mysterious circumstances, the other under scandalous circumstances. I can assure you that the talk about the town is that there is something amiss in this matter, but I have no idea how to begin to settle upon what precisely that is. I shall attempt to locate the man who ran down my father, but I cannot imagine he will allow me to find him too easily."

Our conversation was momentarily interrupted by one of the boys, who walked past us ringing a bell. "Mr. Vredeman. Message for Mr. Vredeman." These interruptions were but part of doing business at Jonathan's.

Elias had no difficulty ignoring the distraction. "Yours is a complicated matter," Elias agreed as he sipped at his coffee. I could tell he wished to talk more of his play, although there was something in this affair he found irresistible.

"It seems," I explained, "that there are those who do not wish me to seek out the truth behind these deaths. My life was attempted two nights ago."

I now had Elias's full attention, to be sure. I related to him the story of my encounter with the hackney coach, giving particular emphasis to the coachman's parting words to me.

"It can have been no random assault," he noted, "for you say the culprit knew you to be a Jew. Those who murdered Balfour and your father clearly do not wish you to expose their doings." I had seen such a sparkle in his eye before when he had helped me out. In truth, I was used to seeing that sparkle when he helped me in matters that concerned amiable young women. Nevertheless, this inquiry obviously awakened Elias's voracious curiosity.

"These villains have gone to great lengths to disguise their work, and now it seems they will go to greater lengths to keep their secrets hidden. It will be difficult for you to find them out."

"Not difficult." I nearly sighed. "I fear impossible. I am used to following trails that men foolishly leave behind. Now I am upon men who have been careful to leave no trace of their presence—indeed, who have gone to some lengths to obfuscate their business. I do not know that there is a way for me to proceed."

"I wonder." Elias lifted up his head thoughtfully. "There has to be a trail, just not the type you are used to looking for. A trail of ideas and motives, if not one of witnesses. You will have to do some guessing, you understand, but that is no matter."

"Guessing will get me nowhere." I now wondered if Elias was not off on some flight of fancy when I needed his clarity. "When a man comes to me for help in finding a debtor, do I guess where I shall find him? Certainly not. I learn what I can of his life and his habits and then look for him where I know I shall find him."

"You look for him where you *guess* you will find him, for you do not know that he will be where your reasoning directs you. You guess every day, Weaver. I only suggest that you make some bigger guesses. Locke, you know, wrote that any man who admits to nothing but that which can be plainly demonstrated may be sure of nothing but perishing quickly. In your case there may be more truth to that than Locke intended."

"This is but wordplay, Elias. These games do not help me."

"Not so. I believe you are more used to acting upon speculation than you realize. In this case you are going to have to make some reasonable assumptions and then proceed as though they might be true. Your task is to look at the general and conclude the particular—for generals and particulars are always related. Consider what Mr. Pascal says of Christianity—he writes that since Christianity offers rewards for adherence to its tenets and punishments for the failure to adhere to its tenets, and the absence of Christianity offers neither, a reasonable man would opt to become a Christian because by doing so he receives the maximum chance of reward and the minimum chance of punishment. Now, the Christianity business does not apply to you, and I should think Pascal was more or less pretending that Christianity was the only religion available to a reasonable man. His thinking is precisely what will allow you to resolve this matter, for you must work with probability rather than facts. If you can only go by what is probable, you will sooner or later learn the truth."

"Are you suggesting I conduct this matter by randomly choosing paths of inquiry?"

"Not randomly," he corrected. "If you know nothing with certainty, but you *guess* reasonably, acting upon those guesses offers the maximum chance of learning who did this with the minimal amount of failure. Not acting offers no chance of discovery. The great mathematical minds of the last century—Boyle, Wilkins, Glanvill, Gassendi—have set forth the rules by which you are to think if you are to find your murderer. You will act not on what your eyes and ears show you, but on what your mind thinks probable." Elias set down his coffee and fidgeted with his hands. When he believed himself to be brilliant, he instantly turned into a great fidget. I wondered how he dared ever bleed a patient, since he believed so strongly in the curative powers of phlebotomy that I fancied his hands would grow unmanageable at the very idea of the powers of blood-letting.

I confess I did not even vaguely suspect the importance of what it was that Elias told me. I did not see that he was helping me to change the very nature of my reasoning. "And how might I know where to begin my guessing and my acting upon probability?"

"You don't credit your own intellect sufficiently. I think you reason in this way all the time, but because you have not read in philosophy you don't recognize the types of thinking you engage in. I shall be happy to lend you some of my books."

"You know I have no head for your hard books, Elias. Fortunately I can depend on you to look into them for me. What does Mr. Pascal's philosophy tell us we should guess about the matter at hand?"

"Let me consider," he said slowly, and looked up to study the ceiling. I must say that I never grew tired of my friendship with Elias, for he was a man of so many different aspects. Were a comely whore to walk by at that moment, he would have forgotten that men such as Pascal had ever trod the earth, but for that moment I had the full powers of his intellect at my disposal, and I believe that he took the greatest pleasure in applying them to my cause.

"We have a man," he intoned slowly, "whose death has revealed the ruin of his estate. His son thinks this self-murder a ruse and that the ruin of the estate is connected with the death—indeed, the death was brought about to accomplish the ruin of the estate. Certainly," Elias mused, "the killer could be no ordinary thief. One cannot simply take another man's stocks—they must be brought to the issuing institution and transferred."

"Which institutions issue stocks?" I asked.

"The Bank of England has a monopoly on issuing government funds, but there are of course the companies—the South Sea Company, the East India Company, and so forth."

"Yes, I have recently come to hear much of these companies. Particularly of the Bank and the South Sea. But how came you to know so much of these matters?"

"You know I am a bit of a dabbler in the funds." He puffed himself up, looking about Jonathan's as though he owned the place. "And as I am something of a coffeehouse denizen, I cannot but learn a thing or two of the business. I have held some issues that have yielded a pleasing return, although my interests lie predominantly in projects."

I believe that when Elias was born the projectors and schemers of the world drank a bumper to his health and another to honor his parents. Since I began my friendship with Elias, he had invested in, and lost money on, projects to fish for herring, to grow tobacco in India, to build a ship that sailed underwater, to make salt water fresh, to produce an armor for soldiers that would resist musket fire, to create an engine that runs on steam, to make a kind of pliable wood, and to raise a species of edible dogs. Once I had mocked him mercilessly for investing fifty pounds (which he borrowed of a group of unsuspecting gulls, myself included) in a project "to produce enormous sums of money through means that, once revealed, will utterly astonish."

So, while I did not believe Elias to be the most cautious investor in the world, I believed he understood something of the financial marketplace. "If a mere thief could not rob a man of his funds," I continued with my querying, "who could, and for what purpose would he do so?"

"Well"—Elias bit his lip—"we might consider the lending institution itself."

I guffawed as though I found the idea preposterous. But I could not forget my father's old enemy, Perceval Bloathwait, the Bank of England director. "You mean you think the Bank of England, for example, could kill two men for some purpose—that the Bank of England was responsible for the attempt upon my life as well?"

"Mr. Adelman!" the coffee boy shouted as he walked past our table. "A hackney awaits Mr. Adelman!"

I watched from afar as my uncle's friend made his way across the coffeehouse, trailed by a cluster of sycophants who hounded him even as he tried to pass through the doorway. For a moment I felt startled, as though it were a strange coincidence that he should be in the very place I chose to drink a dish of coffee. I then recalled that I chose to drink a dish of coffee in his place of business. It was not he who haunted me, but much the other way around.

I turned back to Elias, who had, while I had been lost in my thoughts, speculated on the murderous intent of the nation's most powerful financial institution.

"Perhaps the Bank realized it could not afford to pay the interest and had to dispense with all the investors," he proposed. "What better way to order the books than to make some of the issues disappear? Perhaps your father and Balfour had large holdings from a particular institution."

I felt something of a chill. Elias raised a specter that my uncle had dismissed as preposterous. "I am told such a thing is unlikely. I do not believe the Bank of England goes about murdering its investors. If it needed to renege on a loan, I am sure there are more effective ways of handling it."

Elias gesticulated. "Good Lord, Weaver. What do you think the Bank is about?"

"Not murder, surely."

"Such is not its function, but there is no reason to believe that murder is not among its tools."

"Why so?" I asked. "Is it not more *probable* that these murders are the work of a man or perhaps a group of men rather than the program of a company?"

"But if this man or men is acting to serve a company, then I am not certain I see the distinction. The company remains the villain. And what is the life of a man or two in the eyes of an enormous institution such as the Bank of England? If the death of a man suggests a strong probability of a good financial return, what is to stop the Bank or one of the other companies from making such a bloody investment? You see, the very devil of it is that this kind of probability theory, which will help you learn the truth behind these atrocities, has allowed for the rise of the institutions most likely involved in your father's murder. The Bank and the companies but engage in large-scale and organized stock-jobbery, and what is stock-jobbery but an exercise in probability?"

"Between you and my uncle, Elias, I feel as though I have enrolled in one of the universities. I know not that I can fathom all of this probability and government issue and heaven knows what else." I paused for a moment and considered that I perhaps rejected what Elias said too quickly. "How does your probability relate to these companies?"

The smile upon my friend's face told me that he had been hoping I would ask this question. "It is the theory of probability that has allowed for the rise of the funds. To invest, you must think of what is probable, not what is known, and act accordingly. Consider the business of insurance. A man pays out insurance because he knows something might happen to his goods. The insurance company, in turn, accepts the money, knowing that in each individual case, it is *probable* that nothing will happen, so when it is forced to pay out, the bulk of its money is secure. Now it is possible that every ship a company insures might sink to the bottom of the ocean, and the insurance company would then go bankrupt, but so monstrous an event is not probable, and so our wealthy friends at the insurance companies sleep well at night, indeed."

I felt as though Elias was on the cusp of something that I still could not understand. "None of this explains why the Bank of England should involve itself in murder."

Elias's eyes lit up like twin candles as he returned to the topic of the Bank's villainy. "Again, you must think in terms of probability. What could, in all probability, explain these two murders? Old Balfour died under mysterious circumstances, and his estate proved to be missing a great deal of money. We do not know how much, but if it is an amount that could be the difference between his very large estate being ruined or no, we must assume at least ten thousand pounds. Perhaps more. Do you agree?"

I told him that I did.

"Now, funds of this value would either be stock of one of the trading companies, or government shares issued by the Bank of England. In either case, those shares would be nontransferable, meaning that in order for someone other than the holder to own those stocks, he would have to officially transfer ownership in the company or the Bank during designated transfer hours. I cannot simply pick up old Balfour's holdings and claim them as my own. He or his heirs must sign them over to me."

"I believe I begin to understand you. No common thief would gain anything from these stocks, so the murderer must be someone involved with the company—for only such a person could turn the stocks to gain."

"Exactly," Elias said.

"But that does not tell me why an institution itself must be involved. Could not the murderer be a company clerk—someone who could transfer the stolen issues to himself or a partner?"

"A solid conclusion." Elias smiled somewhat patronizingly. "But you told me that old Balfour and your father had some mysterious business together before their deaths. Your father's estate does not seem to be missing any issues. To my mind, it is therefore probable that these murders are about more than a theft. Old Balfour and your father knew something or they were planning a venture or involved themselves in a scheme that made them dangerous to some very powerful men. You see, you keep considering old Balfour's death and then your father's death—not both of them together. And if these deaths are related, then the motive is more than money—and that to me suggests a plot, and plots suggest power."

I remained silent for a moment as I considered Elias's dexterous hops from conclusion to conclusion. I did not fully believe what he said, but I could not deny the power of his ability to draw possible answers from what I had seen as a jumble of facts. "What sort of plot do you envision?"

Elias sucked on his lower lip. "Give me a shilling," he said at last. He waved his hand impatiently at my quizzical look. "Come now, play along, Weaver. Put a shilling on the table."

I reached into my purse and felt around for a shilling, which I slapped down.

Elias picked it up before returning it to the table. "That's a sorry shilling," he observed. "What's happened to it?"

It was indeed a sorry shilling. Most of the edges had been filed away until it was a shapeless hunk of metal and only a fraction of its original weight.

"It's been clipped," I told him. "The same as every other shilling in the Kingdom. Are you suggesting that the companies are involved in coin-clipping?"

"No, not as such. I merely wish to demonstrate the idea of what these companies are doing. Our shillings are clipped and filed, and the excess silver melted down and sold abroad. Now you have a shilling that contains perhaps three-fourths of its original metal. Is it still worth a shilling? Well, it is, more or less, because we need a medium of exchange for the nation to function smoothly." He held up the coin between his thumb and index finger. "This clipped shilling is but a metaphor, if you will, of the fiction that the idea of value has become in this Kingdom."

I pretended not to see him slip the coin into his pocket. "Thus the rise of the banknote," I observed. "At least in part, from what little I understand. If the silver does not circulate, but stays safely where it cannot be harmed, the representation of the silver provides a secure measure of value. The fiction is thus replaced by reality, and your anxiety over these new financial mechanisms undoes itself."

"But what would happen, Weaver, if there was no silver? If silver was replaced by banknotes—by promises? Today you are used to substituting a banknote for a large sum of money. Perhaps tomorrow you may forget that you ever dealt in money proper. We shall exchange promises for promises, and none of these promises shall ever be fulfilled."

"Even if such a preposterous thing were to happen, what would be the harm? After all, silver only has value because everyone agrees it has value. It is not like food, which has a use unto itself. If we all agree that banknotes have value, how are they less valuable than silver?"

"But silver is silver. Coins are clipped because you can take your silver to Spain or India or China and exchange it for something that you desire. You cannot do that with a banknote, because there is nothing to support the promise outside of its point of origin. Don't you see, Weaver, these financial institutions are committed to divesting our money of value and replacing it with promises of value. For when they control the promise of value, they control all wealth itself."

"Is this the plot you are talking of? Do you mean to say that you believe that one of the companies is scheming to control all of the wealth in the Kingdom?"

Elias leaned forward. "Not one of the companies," he said in a low voice. "All of them. Separately, together—it makes no difference. They have seen the power of paper, and they wish to exploit it."

"And you believe that my father and old Balfour somehow thwarted such a scheme?"

"More likely some small part of a greater scheme. A system of credit is like a great spiderweb—you cannot see it until you are trapped within it, and you cannot see the spider until she dangles above you, poised to devour. I do not know who the spider is, Weaver. But I assure you, it is the spider that killed your father. It is money that killed your father. Money inspires action, and money creates power. Somewhere in this Kingdom are the men who create money, and they, for reasons we do not yet understand—perhaps even for reasons *they* do not understand—have killed your father."

"I say, Elias, I cannot think why, if you view the funds as so very wicked to the core, you invest in them yourself."

"That's the very devil of it," he breathed. "One *must* invest in the funds these days. Look about you in this coffeehouse. Do you think these men are here out of a love of stock-jobbery? There is no other thing to do with one's money. Money breeds money, and we are all caught within the spiderweb, even those of us who see it for what it is. We cannot help it."

"None of which tells us in what plot my father and old Balfour found themselves entangled."

"We can't weave facts out of the air, Weaver. I only wish you to see that these companies have much to gain, and they may have good reason to harm someone who stands in their way."

"As you are so well versed in these matters," I said, mustering the courage to bring up a topic I wished heartily to avoid, "can you perhaps tell me what you know of a gentleman called Perceval Bloathwait? He is a man deep within the funds, and therefore, no doubt, one of the nation's great enemies."

To my astonishment, Elias suddenly lit up. "Bloathwait, the Bank of England director? A devilish good man for one of your English Dissenters. Knows how to show his gratitude at any rate. I had the good fortune to be close at hand during a production of Addison's *Cato* when Bloathwait was overcome with an attack of stomach gout. He nearly fell into the pit. Fortunately, I was there to bleed him on the spot—neatly turning a near-fatal accident into a lucky bit of business indeed. He rewarded me with no less than twenty guineas."

"Your suspicions of moneyed men," I observed, "are considerably tempered when they do you a good turn."

"I should say so!" Elias responded with exuberance. "Many's the man of greater birth who would think himself above paying the surgeon whom providence has placed in his way. Bloathwait is a good man, I say. If," he added after a brief pause, "vested with too much power and probably corrupt and villainous."

"It is clear that I shall have to pay a visit to this devilish good, corrupt, and villainous fainter," I muttered, "for he has long been an enemy of my father."

"You will forgive me if I don't accompany you. I do not wish to have so powerful a man speak ill of me in the best circles."

"I understand," I said. "Perhaps you can use the time to polish *The Unsuspecting Lover.*"

"A splendid idea. Would you care to hear a few particularly effective scenes?"

I finished my coffee and rose. "I would like nothing better, but I must make this business my first priority." I paid our reckoning, and left Elias at the table, scribbling busily upon his play.

FOURTEEN

I FOUND ELIAS'S ARGUMENTS based upon probability both fascinating and seductive, and I longed to find some way to put them to use. Until I could do so, however, I thought it time I applied some of the more basic powers upon which I had long depended.

I knew that Herbert Fenn, the scoundrel who had run down my father—and who, in my mind, had attempted to run me down as well—drove a cart for the Anchor Brewery, so it was to the brewery I went in search of this villain. As the hackney coach approached, I felt that I passed not only through neighborhoods, but through the dozens of different worlds that combined to make the great metropolis: the worlds of the rich and the privileged and the poor and the criminal, artisan and beggar, beau and belle, foreigner and Briton, and, oh yes, the world of the speculator, too.

I had, for the past two days, inhabited the world of speculation—I had tried to imagine who had killed my father and old Balfour, and I had tried to imagine what the motivation for these murders might be. According to Elias, it was conspiracy and plot and intrigue. His ideas were fantastical to me, and yet now I was on my way to confront the man who had trampled my father in the street. I cannot say that I looked forward to this confrontation, and my experience at Jonathan's made me feel twitchy and violent, as though I could not depend upon myself to keep a mastery of my passions.

I cannot quite say what I felt when the foreman in charge of the delivery wagons assured me that Berty Fenn had not worked at their brewery for many weeks. " 'E run over an old Jew," the foreman said. "Not on purpose, 'e told me, and no reason to think otherwise, but you can't keep a man around who'd run over folks, accident or no. Jew or no," he added as an afterthought. "Trampling folks to death is no good, and I send such men away, I do, without the by-your-leave they might think themselves entitled to."

"Do you know where Fenn went?"

He shook his head. "Couldn't say. Someplace where running over old Jews isn't so frowned upon, I reckon. You a bailiff? I don't think so—you don't smell bad enough. Besides, no one would let 'im get so far into debt as to need a bailiff to find 'im out. What's Fenn to you, anyhow?"

"The old Jew he ran over was my father."

"That would make you—"

"A young Jew, yes. At least a younger one." I handed him my card. "Should you hear of his whereabouts, please let me know. I assure you I shall pay fairly for any information."

I started to turn away when the foreman called after me. "Wait a moment, Sir 'Ebrew. You didn't say nothin' before about payin'. You understand that we have to look after our own, but if you've some silver upon you, I might be persuaded to look after meself."

I handed him a sixpence. "That's to loosen you up. Tell me something useful and I'll make it worth your while."

"A sixpence? You're as tight-fisted as they say. I reckon I should be more civil, eh, Sir 'Ebrew. Otherwise you might put the knife to me an' circ'cize a beggar."

"Might you please simply tell me what you know?"

"Right. Well, Fenn, 'e didn't take so kindly to being given the boot, and 'e bragged on 'ow it didn't matter to 'im none, now as 'e got 'imself a position, 'e did. With a Mr. Martin Rochester, 'e said. 'I'll do a turn with Mr. Martin Rochester,' 'e said. 'Mr. Martin Rochester don't treat a man so,' 'e said. Like Mr. Martin Rochester was first arse-wiper to 'is 'Anoverian Majesty 'imself."

"Who is Martin Rochester?" I asked.

"That's the point, don'cha see? No one ever 'eard of the bugger, but Fenn thinks 'e's the Second Coming." He flashed me a grin. "Or the First, depending upon your perspective, I reckon."

"Did he say anything else? Give you any other information about this Rochester?"

"Aye, 'e said 'e was a bigger cove than Jonathan Wild. This buck no one's ever 'eard of a bigger man than the big prig-nabber 'imself. Course, I figured 'e was talkin' to 'ear 'imself since I'd givin 'im the shove and all. But I reckon this Rochester spark is some new man or t'other who took Fenn in for a driver or some such."

"How long after the accident did all this happen?"

"A few days. Soon as the matter cleared the magistrate, I sent him on 'is way, I did."

"So it seems reasonable to suppose that Fenn knew this Rochester prior to the accident."

"I suppose it does, not that I ever gave it much thought."

"Did Fenn have any family, friends, anyone who might know where to find him?"

He shrugged. "I just worked 'im, I didn't like 'im. Can't say none of us much did, and I can't say as I felt too bad 'bout 'aving a reason to send 'im on his way. 'E was foul-tempered, 'e was. Didn't take to followin' orders much, had a pair o' gums on 'im that 'e'd flap at you for no cause but the pleasure of flappin'. None of the boys 'ere took their pints with 'im. When 'e was done with what 'e 'ad to do, 'e made 'is way to wherever it was 'e went to."

I gave the man a half crown with a reminder to contact me if he had any more information. Based on the look upon his face, he had now changed his mind somewhat about the generosity of the Hebrew.

I stopped into a public house and called for a lunch of cold meat and ale—a meal that was interrupted when an urgent-looking fellow rushed in demanding to know if there were a man inside called Arnold Jayens. He further announced that he had been sent because Jayens's boy had been injured at his school, that he had broken his arm and that the surgeon feared for his life. A man in the back jumped up and ran for the door most furiously, but before he had even taken a second step outside, two bailiffs grabbed him and explained that they were sorry for the deceit, but that his son was well, and they merely wished to escort Mr. Jayens to debtor's prison. It was a sad trick—one I had used myself in the past, though always with great regret. As I looked through the window and saw this unfortunate taken away, I could not but think of the money Miriam had borrowed of me, and I fairly puffed myself up with pride to think I had saved her from such a fate.

I shook myself from thoughts of my cousin-in-law in order to reflect upon the information I had acquired. Fenn had moved rapidly from his employment at the brewery to work for the great Martin Rochester, a bigger man than Jonathan Wild. I could only hope it was all a lie, for I needed no more great enemies.

I SPENT MUCH OF the rest of the day and night pondering my next move, and the following morning I determined to seek out old Balfour's clerk, this d'Arblay of whom Balfour had spoken. I recalled that Balfour had told me that d'Arblay made his home at Jonathan's, so learning from my experiences the previous day, I sent Mrs. Garrison's boy to the coffeehouse with a note addressed to d'Arblay, identifying myself only as a man who wished to see him upon business. The boy returned within an hour with a message from d'Arblay, indicating that I should find him at Jonathan's until late this afternoon and that he awaited my commands.

I therefore procured a hackney and once again made my way toward 'Change Alley and the buzzing hive of Jonathan's. Such places generate their own pleasures, I think, for the moment I stepped through the door, and took in the sounds and sights and pungent smells of that house of commerce, I wanted nothing so much as to drink a strong dish of coffee and to feel the taut excitement of doing business with a hundred men who have all taken too much of the same drink.

I asked a boy to point out to me Mr. d'Arblay, and he gestured toward a table at which two men sat, hunched over a single document. "He's the bullish one," the boy mumbled, using the language of the Exchange. Bullishness signified that a man had an interest in selling, while bearishness meant that he pursued buying. And looking at these men, it was not difficult to determine which animal was which. With back angled toward me, but such that I could see half of his face, sat a man who had lived perhaps fifty years, each of which had left its mark upon a gaunt visage tightly wrapped with blotchy pale skin. A bit of snuff was encrusted about a nose that had been well eaten by the ravages of the French pox. His attire, fashionable in its cut, informed me of a desire to appear the gentleman, but the flimsy fabric of his red-and-black suit of clothes, also sprinkled liberally with snuff, and even the weave of his wig, were of poor quality.

The bear he spoke to was perhaps twenty years his junior. He possessed one of those wide-open, happy faces, and hung upon each of d'Arblay's words with the intense, almost drooling attention of a man born to idiocy.

I moved in as closely as I might and attempted to make myself discreet as I listened to the conversation.

"I think you will agree," d'Arblay was saying in a voice I found unusually high and shrill for a fully grown man, "that this is the soundest method of protecting your investment."

"But I do not see that the investment needs protecting," his interlocutor responded, sounding more confused than resistant. "Is not chance the very purpose of the lottery? I must risk losing if I am to have a chance of winning."

D'Arblay flattened out his lips into a condescending smile. "You are not tempting fate by protecting your investment. Your tickets cost you three pounds each, and if you draw blanks, the amount will be repaid over a period of thirty-two years. This is a very small investment indeed. I simply offer you the chance to insure your lottery tickets for an additional 2 percent for ten years."

"But it is a chance?" the man inquired. "It is not guaranteed?"

D'arblay nodded. "Like you, we wish to keep intact the spirit of the lottery. You may insure your lottery tickets with a kind of lottery insurance—each losing ticket places you in the drawing for the additional revenue, and at only one shilling per ticket I think you will agree that it dramatically increases your chances of winning without to any great extent increasing your risk."

His associate bobbed his head. "Well, you make a compelling case, sir, and I think of myself as a sporting man." He slid some coins across the table. "I should like five tickets insured."

The men made an appointment to meet again for the purpose of recording the ticket numbers, and, shaking d'Arblay's hand, the other man made his way out of Jonathan's.

I had, during this exchange, been standing behind d'Arblay, who now, alone at his table, looked straight ahead and said, "As you have been attending my conversation so nearly, may I presume that you have business of me?"

I stepped forward to where he could see me. "You may." I gave him my name and reminded him that I had inquired of him earlier in the day.

D'Arblay rose just enough to offer me a bow. "In what capacity may I serve you, sir? Do you wish to buy or sell?"

"If I wished to buy," I said slowly, wishing to know more of the man before I pressed him, "what would you have to offer me?" I sat at the table and faced him, attempting to imitate the ingenuous appearance of the man who had just left.

"Why, anything that one may sell, of course. Name what issue you seek, and I shall provide it for you within two days."

"So you will sell me what you do not have?"

"Of course, Mr. Weaver. Have you never done business upon the 'Change? Why, you are very fortunate to have found me as you have, for I can promise you that not every man you come across will serve you as honestly as I. Nor can you easily expect to find a man as well situated as I. You need but name your interest, sir, and I can promise you that I shall procure it within an acceptable time, or I shall return your money with my good wishes. No man has yet had cause to call me a lame duck," he boasted, using the language of the Exchange to signify a man who sold what he could not provide. "I think you will further find that, once we complete our business, my fees are competitive. May I ask how you learned my name?"

"I learned your name of William Balfour," I explained, "and what I seek is information, not government issues."

D'Arblay sucked upon his already hollow cheeks, took a bit of snuff, and folded his hands neatly upon the table. "I fear you must misunderstand me. I do not trade in information of any kind—there is so little to be gained and so much to be lost."

"I seek only justice, Mr. d'Arblay, for your late employer. Young Mr. Balfour has come to me with the belief that his father's death was not what it appears, and he suspects there may be some machinations in the Alley to explain the deceit."

"I dismiss the very notion," d'Arblay said. "Now, if you will excuse me, I believe I have business to attend to."

He began to rise, but I stopped him with a single look. "I do not think you understand me, sir. Mr. Balfour has explained to me that his father's estate was missing a prodigious quantity of money for which he cannot account. As the late Mr. Balfour's clerk, you would have been the first man to notice such an absence. And yet, apparently, you did not. I wonder how you can account for that."

"If you accuse, I would prefer you did so in plain language," d'Arblay said haughtily. "I can assure you that I cannot account for missing money from Balfour's estate—unless one accounts for gambling, excessive drinking, living beyond one's means—and, I might add, three expensive mistresses, not one of them worth her upkeep, to my mind. I am surprised Mr. Balfour would send you upon so foolish a quest. He of all people despised his father for being a wastrel. Mr. Balfour—the elder, that is—was once industrious and successful, but as he grew older he felt that he had earned the right to waste all that he had accomplished, and as his son watched his estate disappear, he began to hate his father."

I nodded, thinking about the discrepancy in Balfour's version of the tale. "Yet you told young Mr. Balfour that you believed some issues to be missing from his father's estate."

"I did no such thing. Who told you this preposterous lie?" D'Arblay did not wait for me to answer. "Missing issues, indeed. My late employer was certainly capable of losing valuable pieces of paper, but fortunately I ordered those affairs, not he. It is only owing to my skills that I was able to keep his estate afloat as long as I did. In the end, however, he was quite ruined, and as you know he could not endure his shame. There really is very little to this history that should surprise you, although it is a cautionary tale from which many could learn." D'Arblay folded his arms, pleased with the wisdom of this observation.

"Can you think of anything to suggest that Mr. Balfour's death was not what it appears?"

"Nothing," d'Arblay replied adamantly.

"And for whom do you work now, Mr. d'Arblay?"

"I have offered my services in putting Mrs. Balfour's affairs in order. She is a foolish woman who has long held her money in gold plate and precious jewels. I have convinced her that the funds shall serve her more justly."

"And can you tell me what Mrs. Balfour stood to inherit from her husband—assuming he died solvent, that is?"

D'Arblay screwed his face into a skeletal attitude of disgust. "Not a thing," he said. "Mrs. Balfour had a separate settlement upon her. She would have inherited nothing. Balfour's mismanagement was an embarrassment to her, but nothing more."

That was precisely what Balfour had told me, but as their stories had several discrepancies, I wanted to see how d'Arblay characterized the financial arrangement between the spouses. "I see. Where might I reach you if I have any more questions regarding this matter?"

"Allow me to be blunt with you, sir. I have no desire to have you ever visit me in my places of business or residence. I have endured this conversation only out of courtesy to the late Mr. Balfour, who was a kind gentleman, if a foolish one. I can offer you no further information, so there is little reason for you to seek me out."

"I shall then thank you for your help." I rose and bowed at him before heading farther into the thick confusion of Jonathan's. As I wandered, pushing my way through the crowds, I attempted to understand the conversation. If old Balfour's estate had been robbed, then there could have been no one in a better position to perpetrate the robbery than d'Arblay. Elias's suspicions of plot and scheme might go no further than this one clerk, who, for all I knew, might have had the power to rob his employer freely. On the other hand, I had only young Balfour's belief that the estate had been robbed. Surely one of them lied, but if d'Arblay was the liar, he might still not be the thief. Such a man could obscure a crime that he might protect his own reputation.

I would not understand this crime, or this purported crime, unless I better understood the Alley itself. So I thought it a fine idea to take advantage of the library available in the coffeehouse, and made my way over to the shelves, where I began to search through the mountains of material, organized in no way I could discern. The proprietors showed little worry about insulting their patrons, for many of the pamphlets decried stock-jobbers as villainous Jews and foreigners who made Englishmen effeminate with their financial legerdemains. I dismissed titles that I thought too narrow in their focus, such as *A Delineation of the Complaints of the New East India Company Lodged Against the Old.* I similarly rejected the works too complex in their intent, like *A Letter from a Gentleman in the Country to a Friend in the City on the Recent Legislation*—I can remember no more of that title, for the very word *legislation* makes my brain feel as though it is covered with grease.

Even as a boy I had been shockingly inept at matters of hard books. My teachers had refused to understand why I could not master what came far more easily to other boys. More often than not, words would simply blur upon the page as I looked at them, and I found myself thinking of engaging in anything other than my studies. It was not as though I took no pleasure from reading, for I often enjoyed the illicit pleasures of romances or adventure stories—I merely wished never to read what others wished to make me learn.

Perhaps that was why I now finally settled on a slim volume of some thirty or so pages that I believed to be as approachable as it was inflammatory: '*Change Alley Laid Open; Or, the Crimes of that Sinister Race of Beings, Called Stock-Jobbers, and the Truth of Their Villainous Operations.* It had been put out but recently by a publisher called Nahum Bryce, whose name I knew from some novels and romances in which I have indulged. Here, I thought, was precisely what I wished for: a history of the 'Change written as an adventure.

Clutching the little booklet, I slid myself into a chair at an open table and began to make my way through. I was disappointed to discover that the book was more full of invective than information—or adventure for that matter; it railed against the mortgaging of the future with the national debt, the corruption of the Parliament through bribes, and the unmanning of the nation from the mania of stock-jobbing. I found it shocking to discover a fleeting reference to my own father in these pages, hidden with the pretense of disguise as "S——l L——n——o, that notorious jobber of the Hebrew race, who can be seen everyday upon the 'Change, draining the purses of honest Englishmen with his promises of untold wealth."

To discover one's own father maligned is no easy thing. I had seen my own name in print before—many times, in fact, and there has always been something disorienting to be sure, for a man's business is a private thing, and print is a very public affair. But here these names were not printed in transient and ultimately insignificant newspapers. This was a pamphlet, a permanent thing that a man might keep in his library. These accusations the pamphleteer made—I understood they were mere hyperbole, the rhetoric of the anti-jobbers, but the fact that my father should be so important a figure in their thinking took me by surprise. I could not say that I recognized no other names, for here were references to the schemes of N——n A——l——n, who could only be Nathan Adelman; and the pamphlet had much to say on the villainy of P——l B——th——t, whom I could not but conclude to be my father's old enemy, Perceval Bloathwait. This scoundrel, according to the pamphlet, delighted in trickery, manipulating the markets to his own profit, caring not what ruin he brought upon others and the nation. It was odd to me that men who lived far from the metropolis, men who knew 'Change Alley only from such pamphlets as these, would think of men such as my father and Adelman and Bloathwait much as they would of fictional characters in a novel or romance.

My musings on this subject were shattered when I noticed the short, round form of Nathan Adelman standing near me with a kind of wry smile. "Have you come to follow in your father's footsteps?" he asked me, hovering over my table. He struck me as entirely different from the person he had been at my uncle's or in his coach. Here he was in his element, and he fairly drew strength from the chaos around us. Despite his obvious smallness, Adelman appeared to me grander, more powerful, more confident; and why should he not have appeared so when all those around him behaved as though he was a monarch in his own little kingdom? Perhaps ten feet behind him, a crowd of jobbers had gathered. All desired a few minutes of his attention, and I must say I enjoyed being important enough to divert the great financier from his pressing concerns. I took no personal pride, mind you, but Adelman's interest in me only confirmed that I was not wasting my time or chasing shadows.

I greeted him, and he casually asked me with what pamphlet I passed the time. "Ah," he said, looking it over. "I fear the author thought little of me. Or of your father, for that matter."

"And do you believe what the author writes? Do you believe in the corrupting power of greedy jobbers?"

"I believe the issue here is not the greed of jobbers but the greed of the booksellers," Adelman said. He casually placed his hands behind his back and balanced on the balls of his feet.

"These are lies you say that the author has written of you and my father. What do you know of Perceval Bloathwait?"

"Bloathwait." Adelman's good cheer dripped away like the fat from a roasting hare. "Yes, he rather deserves the abuse he receives. He's a tricky rascal, and he gives the rest of us a bad name."

"I do not suppose you say that because he is a member of the Court of Directors of the Bank of England, and thus the enemy of your South Sea Company."

"The Company is hardly mine, but I do, as you say, take an interest in it. I look to the Company because its practices are laudable; I do not defend the practices because of my association."

"Your loyalty is commendable, but I wonder how far it extends. This pamphlet I've been reading makes some convincing points. I do not believe its assertion that jobbery is itself evil, but I cannot but be swayed by the argument that greed—in any form, I suppose, but in this case stock-jobbing—can shift villainy from one venue to another. It is, perhaps, only a short step from trickery in what one buys or sells to, perhaps, murder."

Adelman stiffened considerably. "I see you have not taken my advice to heart, Mr. Weaver. Do you have any idea how much one Jew crying *murder* will injure us all?"

Our conversation was then interrupted by a ruddy-faced gentleman who looked to be about five-and-twenty, who rushed into the center of the coffeehouse. His wig was askew, and his chest heaved as he struggled for air. Yet he managed a deafening bellow. "I have just come from the Guildhall," he cried to all who would listen. "No one does business within the lottery ticket office. The drawing is grossly undersubscribed. It shall all be a disaster!"

A swarm of men jumped from their seats and all shouted at once. Yet I could hear one name repeated again and again. *D'Arblay.*

I looked over to where he sat and observed that his table was now surrounded by a host of men who would sell their holdings: "Do you still wish to buy tickets, sir? Take these. I shall give you a very fair rate." D'Arblay dealt with each man calmly, looking at what he had to sell and negotiating a price.

Adelman laughed softly. "I cannot believe that ruse still works. Note that the men buying from Mr. d'Arblay are all younger. They have not been long upon the 'Change."

"Do you mean to say that the man who made the announcement is in league with d'Arblay?"

Adelman nodded. "Of course. He creates a panic, makes the gullible believe the lottery is undersubscribed. These men sell at a loss, and d'Arblay makes a handsome profit. It is but a primitive stock-jobber's trick, yet it clearly continues to earn a profit for those who dare to do the unthinkably silly."

I looked at the frantic scene with a kind of distant amusement.

"Are you prepared to involve yourself in such matters?" Adelman asked, distracting me from the mayhem of frantic selling. "All this stock-jobbing that you see—you do not understand it, and there is no reason you should trouble yourself with it. Why not think on my offer to do business with gentlemen I know?"

"I am thinking about it, Mr. Adelman, and I appreciate your attention, please make no mistake. In the meantime, I think you will understand that I am interested to uncover the truth about what happened to my father. Could a son do less? Especially," I added by way of cutting off any stinging retorts, "a son who has much to make up for. And now that we have sorted out why we do the things we do, can you tell me, sir, what you know of a man called Martin Rochester?" I could not think why I asked if he knew the man who had taken into employ my father's killer, but the idea to do so entered my head and found expression in my mouth before I had time to consider of it.

I should like to say the expression of Adelman's face betrayed something, but it did not change at all. So frozen was his face in the blank amusement of our conversation, so much did he not twitch or narrow his eyes, that I could not but suspect that this lack of movement was a practiced impenetrability. Adelman made every effort to hide what he was thinking.

"I've never heard the name," he said. "Who is he, and what is it to me?"

"You've never heard the name?" I asked incredulously. I had considered what Elias had explained of probability, and it occurred to me that if I was to believe that my father had been murdered, then I must act as though the events surrounding his murder were connected. Rochester had hired away the man who had run my father down, and here was Adelman, who wished me to discontinue my inquiry of that event. Was it not probable, I wondered, that Adelman should at least know of Rochester? "You, sir, perhaps the best-known and best-informed man upon the Exchange," I pressed on, "can it be that you have never *heard* of him?"

"Well, I have *heard* of him," Adelman said, a slight smile upon his lips. "I simply meant that he was not worth hearing of," he continued. "My use of Court language has confused you—I quite apologize. I should have realized you are not used to this bombastic method of talking. But as for this Rochester, one hears so little of small men that the names are not long retained in one's mind."

"And what little have you heard of him? Who is he?"

He shrugged. "A small man upon the Exchange. No more. A jobber."

A jobber. This Martin Rochester was a jobber, and the man who killed my father was in his employ. The man at the Anchor Brewery had likened Rochester to Jonathan Wild—not a jobber, but a master thief. Perhaps Elias was right about the corruption of 'Change Alley, for now it seemed that in the person of Martin Rochester, finance and theft found a single voice.

"I have heard," I said, pushing as far as I might, "that he is a great man."

"From whom have you heard this arrant nonsense?"

I spoke without pause. "From the man who killed my father."

Adelman pursed his lips into an ugly and twisted shape. I could only presume he wished to display this disgust, for he was quite clearly a man who knew how to disguise his feelings. "I shall not linger long," he said, "for if you keep the company of such men, I do not wish to be numbered among them. Let me only say this, Mr. Weaver: you sail your ship upon treacherous waters."

"Perhaps I require insurance." I grinned at him.

Adelman responded to my gibe with characteristic seriousness. "No company will insure you. You are in danger of foundering."

I thought to make another quip, but changed my mind and considered his words. The man I spoke to was no street filth whose threats could be laughed off. He was one of the wealthiest men in the Kingdom and one of the most powerful, too. Yet he took the time to speak with me, to attempt to frighten me off my course. I could not take this matter lightly, nor could I dismiss it with clever phrases. I had not the slightest idea of what Adelman's interest was in my inquiry nor what his involvement might be in the deaths of my father and Balfour, but I could not ignore the fact that a man of his position hovered above me in a public place, speaking of my doom.

I stood up very slowly, until I dwarfed him at my full height. We stared at one another, each like a fighter sizing up his opponent in the ring. "Do you threaten me, sir?" I asked after a moment.

He impressed me greatly, for he showed no sign of intimidation. He did not merely pretend to disregard my greater size and the anger upon my face. He truly cared nothing for it. "Mr. Weaver, the difference between us in family, fortune, and education is so great that your question, asked in so bellicose a manner, truly does you little credit. You must recognize that I condescend to speak to you as an equal, and you have now taken advantage of my generosity. No, I do not threaten you. I merely wish to advise you, for you neither see nor care to see the path upon which you embark. Exchange Alley, sir, is no game of fists within a ring, in which might prevails. It is not even a chess game, in which all pieces are laid upon the board and each player sees all and the most accomplished man sees best. It is a labyrinth, sir, in which you will see only a few feet before you; you can never know what it is that lies ahead, and you can never be sure from which direction you came. There are men who stand above the labyrinth, and while you try to learn what is beyond the next turn, there are those who see you and the path you seek with perfect clarity, and it is but a small thing to block you. Please make no more of what I say. I do not suggest that your life or your safety are in danger. Nothing so dramatic. But to learn the things you wish to know—even if none of your suspicions are true—you may have to cross men who share no direct guilt in your father's death, yet believe that your inquiries will expose them in ways they have no wish to be exposed. These men can and will block your passage. You will never see their hands or suspect how they move the pieces. You cannot succeed."

I did not lower my gaze. "Are you one of these men?"

"Should I tell you if I were?" He smiled. "Perhaps so. I would have nothing to lose."

"Such men," I said, my quiet voice hardly audible above the din of the room, "attempted my life two nights ago. If you know who they are, inform them that I shall not be deterred."

"I know not men who would execute so foul a plot," he said hastily. "And I am sorry to hear of the attempt. I can promise you that no man of business engages in such tricks. You must have been the victim of an enemy from one of your other ventures."

I said nothing at this speculation that was, after all, not improbable.

Adelman now attempted to soften slightly. "I do admire you, sir; I have not lied about that. Despite your enthusiastic rudeness, I wish you well. You show the world that not all Jews are loathsome beggars or dangerous schemers. I believe that your father would want you to use your talents to enrich yourself and to strengthen your family, not to waste your time upon a fool's errand that will make you enemies you will never know and harm you in ways you will never see."

I bitterly thanked Mr. Adelman for his good wishes and watched him effortlessly insinuate himself into the conversation of a group of grim-looking gentlemen. I sat staring blankly for some time, thinking on what Adelman had said, and then returned to the pamphlet, though my concentration was now shattered. So I thought on the things I had now learned.

My mind wandered fitfully, and I took to scanning the room, wondering who among these men knew who I was and what I was after. Who among them could perhaps easily tell me something of use, but would not do so because a fund might fall by ten points should the truth out? What would my father have done? I wondered. Would he have spoken the truth, uncovered a terrible crime, if it had meant losing a great deal of money? What about my uncle? Indeed, what about me?

I had nothing to gain from remaining at Jonathan's, though I thought it might be worth my while to make an appearance with some regularity until I resolved the current inquiry. Tired and somewhat frustrated, I made my way home, where I hoped to take some sleep.

When I walked through the door, however, I was astonished to hear what I took to be my uncle's voice coming from the parlor. I approached slowly, unsure what to make of his presence in my home, but the tone of his voice was light, even cheerful. And I thought I even heard Mrs. Garrison laugh.

"I do not believe now is the time to look to East India funds," my uncle was saying as I entered the room. My landlady and my uncle, playing cards clutched in their hands, were seated at the small table, whose velvet top was strewn with piles of small coins. "And I cannot support the South Sea Company. Government issues, madam, funded by the Bank of England, are your wisest investment." He sipped at a dish of chocolate that had been laid out for him.

"Oh, Mr. Lienzo, you are so very learned in these matters," she said with a puerile titter, the likes of which I had never heard burst from her mouth, "but I fear that right now you have rather lost your investment." She set her cards upon the table. "You owe me four pence, sir," she announced, in a tone that made it clear that her designs on my uncle were of the amorous variety.

My senses had been too heavily assaulted in the past few days, and I could in no way consider allowing this silliness to continue. "Uncle," I announced as I walked into the room, "I am astonished to see you here."

"Mr. Weaver, sir," Mrs. Garrison cooed, "you never told me you had such a charming uncle."

"That is because I knew you would attempt to beat him at cards. Now the secret is out."

My uncle cleared his throat and stood up. He stroked his beard as he ran through a gamut of facial expressions, searching, perhaps, for the one that best fit the moment. "Benjamin, we must speak at once." He bowed to Mrs. Garrison. "I thank you for your entertainment, madam. You have been most kind. And if you wish to look into the funds, please let me know, and I shall find an honest man who shall meet your needs admirably."

Mrs. Garrison curtsied. "You are too kind, sir."

"Shall we talk in my rooms, Uncle?" I suggested.

"By all means." He collected a bundle of papers pressed into a sheepskin folder and then followed me up Mrs. Garrison's narrow and steep stairway. When we reached the top, I saw my uncle was agitated and breathing hard. I opened the door, invited him to sit, and opened a bottle of claret that I hoped he would find refreshing.

He clutched his wine in both hands and stared straight ahead, his eyes suddenly having lost their focus. "I am no longer a young man to muster this kind of energy. But still I am clever enough to impress myself," he said with a smile. He studied the look upon my face and saw that I did not smile in return. "You have no curiosity about what I have to tell you?"

"I am curious at any business that leads you to turn my landlady into a coquette, Uncle."

He smiled. "She is a bit of a talker, is she not? But there is no harm in kindness to the ladies, I believe. It is what I always told Aaron, and I hope it is a lesson you may learn as well. But I have come to talk rather about the matter of Samuel's death and to review our progress."

"There has been little progress, I'm afraid. I grow discouraged," I said as I took a seat across from him. "I have learned many things, developed many suspicions, but I cannot know if they have anything to do with the matter at hand, and I'm not sure I shall ever know. I wonder if this inquiry will yield anything at all."

"You discourage too easily," he said. "And while you get discouraged, I make progress. Benjamin," he said, tapping the bundle of papers on the table beside him. "I now know why your father was killed."

FIFTEEN

I STARED AT MY uncle in astonishment.

"Yes," he repeated as he tapped the envelope with satisfaction. "I believe I now know why your father was killed. We are now closer to learning who is responsible."

I set down my wineglass and leaned forward, but I said nothing.

"Our conversation the other day," he continued, "inspired me to return to my brother's papers and look for anything that might suggest what manner of investment had made him so secretive in his last days. I thought perhaps he had inadvertently become entangled in some kind of scandalous project whose architects had killed him to conceal their treachery. But as I looked and discovered nothing, I became convinced that an investment of this kind was unlikely. Your father was far too canny to involve himself with something not founded upon a solid bottom. As I searched, I wondered if what I sought was not an investment he had made, but rather an investment he had not made, and when I began to look through other kinds of papers, I discovered this."

He opened the envelope and removed a pile of manuscript pages—perhaps forty or fifty of them—covered with the wide, looping handwriting of my father. "What have you found?"

"It is called *A Conspiracy of Paper; or, the South Sea Company Expos'd.* It appears to be a pamphlet your father sought to publish."

"My father publish?" I asked incredulously.

My uncle laughed softly. "Oh, yes. He authored perhaps four or five short works—all on financial matters, and all published anonymously, as is the custom. Two or three of his pamphlets were received with great enthusiasm. He wrote several on behalf of the Bank of England, you know, for it was an institution he saw as vital to the nation's economy."

My confusion was now complete. "The Bank of England," I repeated, hardly above a whisper. "*He* was a defender of the Bank? I cannot understand it."

"But why?" my uncle asked. "Your father was a clever man, and he studied the banks of the other great nations, especially those of Holland. He became firmly convinced that the Bank offered the greatest security for the nation's finances."

That my father could take the time to write something for the benefit of others shocked me. "Why should he bother to undertake such a project? What had he to gain?"

My uncle shook his head. "Your father loved nothing so much as convincing others that he was right."

I nodded. I had seen him do so a hundred times at dinners and gatherings. That he should try to convince the world of something made more sense than I had first credited. But if this explained why he should publish his views, it did not tell me why he should publish *these* views. "Is not his enemy, is not Perceval Bloathwait, a Bank director?" I asked cautiously.

"Bloathwait," my uncle repeated as though I had uttered something nonsensical. "What do you know of him?"

The blankness of my uncle's face chilled me. If he could so effectively act as though there had been nothing between my father and Bloathwait, what else might he be concealing? I remembered that when I was a boy my uncle and my father had sometimes argued over these matters of prevarication. Indeed, taking pride in his importation of contraband commodities, my uncle often played the wily Jacob to my father's stoical Esau. "You fear the worst," my uncle once told my father, "because you are such a poor deceiver. In matters of finance it is easy enough to confuse—all those hard terms and such—and men are often blinded by their own greed. But to deceive a customs inspector, a man whose very livelihood depends upon his ability to find you out—now *that* is an art."

It was no difficult thing for me to imagine how my uncle could deceive customs inspectors. He had an ingenuous quality that made it hard not to do aught but like him. For the first time, however, I could not but wonder if he practiced his deceptive arts upon me for some purpose. I was not so suspicious as to assume the necessity of villainy where I found concealment. Perhaps, I considered, my uncle sought to protect some secret that had no connection to the inquiry.

"How can I not know of Bloathwait?" I demanded in a voice with which I hoped to impress upon him that I would not be distracted. "He tormented my father, he tormented me when I was but a boy. Since I have begun this inquiry I have wondered if he might not be in some way involved with what happened to Father."

"I am surprised you knew of Samuel's problems with Mr. Bloathwait. He rarely discussed matters in which he appeared at a disadvantage. You say you had some contact with Bloathwait?"

"I did—enough to show me that Bloathwait is a madman, I would put nothing past him. And that is why I am shocked to learn my father defended the Bank."

"The difficulties with Mr. Bloathwait happened long ago. And your father's troubles were with the man," my uncle explained, "not the Bank. Samuel did not change how he felt about something like the Bank simply because one of its directors wished him ill."

"And is this pamphlet in support of the Bank of England?" I asked.

"Oh, it does indeed support the Bank, but, more important, it exposes the South Sea Company. You will read it for yourself, but your father makes three major points in this pamphlet. First, he argues that for several years now the South Sea Company has been growing in power, despite the fact that its patent to trade in the South Seas has yielded very little real wealth."

I thought on all of this. "But you have told me as much yourself. I can hardly believe that any organization would propose to kill all men who uttered common knowledge."

"You are quite right," my uncle said, "but there is more." He began to leaf through the papers, looking for nothing at all, I suspect, but drawing some comfort from the sight of the handwriting. "Your father believed that the security of the South Sea Company has been compromised—that someone has been circulating fictitious South Sea stock, and that these activities could be possible only with the aid of men working within the Company itself."

I own I did not fully understand the implications of such a forgery. "If this were true, would not the Company want the forgery of its stock put to an end?"

"Of course, but it would want to do so quietly. Your father wrote that this counterfeit stock represents a complete failure on the Company's part to regulate its own business and that the Company should not be trusted with millions of the nation's pounds."

I could not but think of what Elias had said, of how his ideas of probability had led him to suspect the involvement of a company. Now it appeared that my father had indeed involved himself in something dangerous, something worthy of the kind of plot Elias had envisioned. "Is it your belief that my father was killed by the South Sea Company in order to keep him from exposing the counterfeit stock?"

"I am not certain I would put it so bluntly." He spread out his hands. "But I do believe that there may be a relationship between his death and this information."

I picked up the manuscript and began to leaf through it. "I suppose," I said absently, "I shall have to pay a visit to the South Sea Company."

My uncle laughed. "Will you march in there, manuscript in hand, and demand what information they have of your father's death? This is one of the most powerful institutions in the Kingdom, and it grows more powerful all the time. You must not take it lightly."

"You sound like my friend Elias. He believes these companies capable of anything."

"Never underestimate the power and the villainy of stock-jobbers." His voice held something ominous that I misliked.

"Your brother was a stock-jobber," I pointed out hesitantly.

"I do not mean to suggest that to work in the funds is to be corrupt, but it is a course that can lead to corruption, and there is power enough to make that corruption dangerous indeed. Your friend is right to advise caution."

"What of your friend Mr. Adelman?" I asked pointedly. "Can he not help us? If he is connected to the South Sea Company, then perhaps he can offer some insight."

"Mr. Adelman and I live upon very good terms as men of business. I know him for what he is, and I respect him as such. But I cannot expect that he would think of exposing the Company for the good of our search for justice. He might be just the man to do so, but then he might not. If I must learn which of these he is, I should like to learn upon very safe terms."

"If," I said, wondering aloud, "my father was killed for authoring this pamphlet, we still don't know why Balfour was killed or what the connection was between the two men. I wonder if there is any way at all to speak to Adelman about this matter. I do not suggest you ask him if he had two men murdered, but there might be a less inflammatory way to broach the subject."

My uncle shook his head. "I think not. Adelman is no fool. He will know precisely what I am doing. There is no point agitating such a man unless we have need to do so."

I sighed, but I agreed with his sentiments. "Yes. But I wish we could make more sense of it all. To my mind, none of our suspicions quite ring true. I know what you and Elias have told me about these companies and their power, but to murder men over a business transaction—it strikes me as preposterous. I can understand how one man might murder another over business if it was a crime of passion, but this is quite another matter. We are talking about men planning and carrying out murders as *part* of a business transaction. It is a kind of commercial assassination."

My uncle nodded. "That may be precisely what it is," he said. "The scale of this transaction is unprecedented. According to *A Conspiracy of Paper*"—he gestured toward the envelope—"the South Sea Company is considering offering the Treasury a three-million-pound gift as a bonus for permission to allow holders of certain government bonds to exchange their issues for South Sea stock. They plan, in other words, to encourage the public to trade their valuable holdings, which put the state in so much debt, for the empty promise of South Sea Company profits. Do you understand the magnitude of this exchange? Three million pounds, just for agreeing to the transaction. What can the profits be if they are willing to part with this sum? This is perhaps the largest business transaction in history. Surely men who have so much to gain might kill to protect their interests."

I put a hand to my forehead as I thought. "I cannot even conceive of such amounts. Who could desire so much? What opulence would be enough for these men?"

My uncle looked grave. "I fear we face a new kind of man along with this new kind of affluence. When lands meant wealth, men could perhaps have enough. Too much land was difficult to govern. But with paper money, more is simply more. In France, you know, where they suffer from their own financial mania, they have a word—the *millionaire*—to denote men whose wealth is measured in the millions. Millions. It is inconceivable, but there are more than a few men who hold this title."

"And how do we track men of such great wealth and ambition?"

"That is yet to come," my uncle informed me confidently. "We must start with a simple conviction—the belief that these two deaths are connected. It will take time to sort out why and how. We must move in small steps, I think."

"I understand." I leaned back in my chair and tried to think how I might ask a question I knew my uncle did not wish to answer. "Tell me," I said after a pause, "what exactly happened with my father and Bloathwait."

He shook his head. "That was a long time ago, and it is of no consequence now. Your father is dead, and I can assure you that Mr. Bloathwait no longer cares to remember that unpleasantness. He is but an old bachelor now, with a passion for nothing but business."

"But I should like to know. If I am to find out what happened to my father, does it not make sense that I should know more of him?"

"It does," my uncle said. "But you should understand him as he was in the days before he died, not when you were a child."

"I should like to know the truth," I said solemnly.

My uncle nodded. "Very well, but you must consider that your father was younger in those days. It took him a long time to establish himself in the Alley, and, like many men, particularly men with families they wished to see prosper, he was anxious that his efforts yield fruit. He was perhaps not always as thoughtful of the profits of those he served as he later became."

"He deceived Bloathwait in some fashion?"

My uncle gave me a half nod. "He sold Bloathwait a large quantity of stock whose value plummeted within a few days of the sale. Your father had been somewhat zealous in insisting that Bloathwait buy, and when the value dropped, Bloathwait blamed your father."

"Did my father know the value would fall?"

My uncle shrugged. "No one knows anything for certain with these issues, Benjamin. You know that. But he had his suspicions."

"And Bloathwait hated my father for it."

"Yes. It took some years for Bloathwait to recover his losses, but he did recover, and grew richer than ever. But he never forgot your father. He made a point of appearing at Jonathan's, staring at him in a menacing way, of sending him cryptic and vaguely threatening notes. He would ask about Samuel, tell distant acquaintances to give Samuel his regards so that your father would think that Bloathwait was always watching him. And then, after spending so much time and energy following your father about, something rather unexpected happened. Bloathwait became a job-ber of sorts himself. All that time in the Alley was not lost on him. He began to buy and sell—to make a success of himself, and now he is one of the Bank of England directors. I am sure he wishes more than anyone to forget the matter with your father, for it only made him look foolish and weak."

I was not certain I believed that. In fact, I was sure I did not. Hatred did not die so easily, not a hatred that Bloathwait had found so consuming.

My uncle's eyes wandered about the room; he wished to speak on this matter no more. "Keep the pamphlet," he said, pushing it toward me. "You should read your father's words."

I nodded. "I wonder if we might not consider publishing it."

"No one knows we have this pamphlet. Keeping it a secret may protect us."

I agreed, but I thought we might look into the matter just the same. I asked whom my father had sought out as a publisher in the past, and my uncle gave me the name of Nahum Bryce of Moor Lane, whose imprint, I recalled, I had seen on the pamphlet I'd been reading at Jonathan's.

"I must go," my uncle said. He stood slowly and cast a glance at my fa-ther's pamphlet, as though afraid to leave it with me.

I stood as well. "I shall take good care of it."

"These are your father's words from beyond the grave, and I believe they will tell us, however cryptically, who did this thing."

And then, to my surprise, my uncle embraced me. He wrapped me in his arms and pulled me close, and I felt the surprising damp of his tears press against my cheek. He broke the embrace just as I moved to return it. "You are a good man, Benjamin. I am glad you have come back." With that, he opened the door and hurried with surprising agility down the precipitous stairway.

I closed the door to my rooms and poured myself another glass of claret. Feeling that I had much business yet before me, I lit a tallow upon my desk and settled down to look at my father's pamphlet, but I could not retain the words. And I could not let the emotion of my uncle's departure entirely eclipse my feeling that he wished to avoid my seeking out Perce-val Bloathwait, a man who had made himself my father's great enemy. Maybe my uncle truly believed that the enmity between these men had been long forgotten, and maybe it was only the mythic proportions that children give to conflicts that made me doubt that such a hostility could ever dissipate.

It would be pleasant if we could take comfort in these firm resolutions of ours, but that is rarely the case. I was uncertain of how to deal with this man. I had interacted with men as powerful as Bloathwait in the past, but always because they had called upon me. I had never had to knock on a gentleman's door to demand answers before. My inquiries always moved downward in status. Now I found myself below, looking upward, wondering what means I had to obtain the information I required. Perhaps a member of the Court of the Directors of the Bank of England would find my calling upon him presumptuous. But if social rank, as Elias claimed, was another value undone by the new finance, then my presumption served as a pretty piece of irony.

Sixteen

I SPENT THAT NIGHT visiting a few taverns and alehouses, hoping to learn something about Bertie Fenn, the driver who had run down my father. No one I knew could provide me with what I needed to know. Most had not heard of him, a few had, and an even smaller number knew of his association with a shadowy figure called Rochester. I could find no one who knew where he was, but I let it be known that I would pay handsomely for the information. I knew that by being so bold there was a chance that the man I pursued might learn of my search. This knowledge might entice him further into hiding, or he might come looking for me himself.

Having given up hope of learning anything more that night, I settled myself with a comforting ale at the Bedford Arms tavern upon the Little Plaza in Covent Garden. This tiny, dank stewpot attracted the regular jades and ruffians of the neighborhood, most of whom earned their keep through thieving and thus kept a cautious eye upon me as I sat at my corner table and drank my mug in silence. Sometimes, in such places, an acquaintance or two would stumble upon me and most times I would welcome the company, but I had no wish to drink with friends that night. I had too many puzzles through which to sort.

Chief among these was my father's pamphlet and its implications. Could Elias's philosophical musings have proved true? Could a chartered company like the South Sea truly turn to murder to further its business? I continued to find the idea fantastical, but I could not shake Elias's conviction in light of the claims put forth in *A Conspiracy of Paper*. This pamphlet, however, ultimately explained little and raised many questions. Even if my father had made a deadly enemy at the South Sea Company, I still needed to learn how old Balfour became involved. For that matter, I needed to understand the connection with Bertie Fenn, who had run down my father, and Fenn's new master, Martin Rochester.

The other principal concern upon my mind was the dark-eyed beauty who had just walked into the tavern with the clear intent of finding a man who would buy her a mug of wine. I do not wish for my readers to think that while I considered this lass I had lost all regard for Miriam; nothing could be more false. Indeed, I considered the pleasures of this accessible creature precisely because I believed Miriam's charms to be forbidden. The twenty-five pounds I had sent to my cousin-in-law might purchase on my behalf some small measure of gratitude, but the matter of a few shillings here could have provided me with a much more intimate gratitude in a much more immediate way.

As I moved to raise my mug to this charmer, the door of the tavern burst open and a half-dozen men, most with pistols drawn, marched into the room. I instinctively reached for my hanger, but I saw at once that their business would not concern me, for at the head of this crowd stood none other than Jonathan Wild. His lieutenant, Abraham Mendes, scanned the room and then pointed to a scurvy-looking cove sitting with a pair of doxies at the far end of the tavern. If Mendes saw me, he made no sign of it. He shoved a few chairs out of his path and marched toward his prey.

This old fellow, a skinny mass of pocked skin and wisps of gray hair, could do naught but finish his ale and await Mendes and the others. Perhaps he had withheld booty from Wild, as Kate Cole had done, or perhaps he had simply grown too old to be an effective enough thief for Wild to justify keeping him about. It made no difference—Wild would now have him carted off to be tried and inevitably convicted. The great thief-taker would earn his reward and such public nabbings as this one would only enhance his reputation as a heroic enemy of crime.

Two of the men, under the supervision of Mendes, gripped the resigned sacrifice under the arms and hoisted him to his feet. Wild held back and scanned the room, hoping perhaps to gauge the mood of the tavern, and as he looked about, his eyes met with mine. I expected him to turn away, but instead he limped forward that he might speak to me.

"Good night to you, Mr. Weaver." He bowed deeply. His smirk suggested that he knew of something funny—almost as though we shared a joke between us.

I lifted my mug in salute, but the look on my face made it clear that I meant not to honor him.

"I trust your current inquiry proceeds apace," he said with roguish cheer.

I did not consider but that he meant the business with Sir Owen, for he had involved himself, if only indirectly, by 'peaching poor Kate. Was that the source of his delight? That he had sent a woman almost certainly to hang that she might be punished for something I had done?

"Such a tricky business, murder," he continued.

"Your prosecution of Kate has shown it to be the trickiest business in the world," I countered.

He laughed softly. "You misunderstand me. I care not for that business with Kate Cole. I talk of your present inquiry. As I say, a very tricky business. There are those who believe that if the villain is not found immediately he shall never be found, but I have every faith in your skills."

I opened my mouth to respond, but nothing came forth.

It mattered not that I had no words. Seeing that his men awaited him, Wild bowed again and turned to lead them from the tavern.

The place erupted into a buzz the moment the thief-taker departed; for most of the patrons here, this arrest was more than a matter of gossip, it was a matter of business. I could hear the speculation on why Wild had chosen this man, why this old fool had it coming, and why, ultimately, each of these men who remained believed that they would never meet such a fate.

I looked up from my drink and saw that the dark and pretty lass sat now a few tables over, and she cast her eyes in my direction, hoping to catch my attention. I turned away, for my amorous mood had departed along with Wild. It was not the tyranny with which Wild ruled his soldiers that had soured my disposition, for in truth I had grown accustomed to such scenes. Rather, I could not but wonder about the words Wild had spoken to me. How had he become familiar with my inquiry into my father's death? And, perhaps more important, why did he feel compelled to make sure I knew he had become familiar? I tried to make myself believe that his only concern was based upon our business rivalry, but there had been too much mischief in Wild's expression for me to accept that explanation. I did not even dare guess why, but my inquiry surely meant something to him. If I were right, if I might trust my instincts, then before I could learn who had killed my father, I should inevitably have to contend with the most dangerous man in London.

I WASTED NO MORE time in approaching Perceval Bloathwait at his town house in Cavendish Square. Rather than writing him a sycophantic letter in which I begged him to meet with me, I took a more direct approach—one that worked more effectively than I had reason to hope. I simply arrived in the early afternoon and handed my card to a shabbily clad footman, who invited me to wait in a cramped parlor. The room suffered for a want of windows, and what little light it received was dampened by furnishings of dull brown and red tones and by the somber portraits of Puritans—no doubt Bloathwait's ancestors—that hung crookedly upon the wall. I could find no books with which to pass the time, so for want of any other occupation I began to pace with slow intensity. I thought my footsteps might kick up a cloud of dust upon the old carpet, but Bloathwait's furnishings were merely old, not dirty.

The modesty of the house surprised me, for as a member of the Court of Directors of the Bank of England, Bloathwait could only be opulently wealthy. Though he hardly lived in squalor, I had anticipated something more along the lines of splendor—large, open, sunny rooms, classical columns, splendid furnishings, and handsomely dressed servants. Perhaps, I thought, an older, unmarried man who dedicated himself to his business had no opportunity or inclination for pleasures.

I reassessed my position, however, when, after perhaps three-quarters of an hour, the entrance of a pretty servant girl interrupted my pacing. This lass was slightly plump, but pleasing in a dress whose neck was cut low to delight what I supposed to be the lascivious oglings of her master. She had pale yellow hair, delicious hazel eyes, and milky skin bespotted with freckles. At first oblivious to my presence, she stopped halfway through the room and yelped when she abruptly noticed me.

"Bless me," she said as she pressed one hand to her breast. "I beg your pardon, sir. I didn't see you there, nor knew you was there at all, or I wouldn't have come passing through, with a visitor here and such. But it's a long way to go 'round, and when there's no one in here, I don't see that there's a harm in it, though Mr. Bloathwait, he'd have my hide if he knew I'd done it."

I smiled at her and bowed. "Benjamin Weaver, at your service."

"Oh," she breathed, as though a man in a handsome coat had never before plied her with gallantries. She stared at me and then, remembering her place, perhaps, she cast her eyes downward. "I'm Bessie." She curtsied, and I took some pleasure as her pale and freckled skin reddened. "The laundry maid."

I knew it unusual for a bachelor like Bloathwait to employ female servants unless he required more of them than their scrubbing and their washing. If such was the case with Bessie, I thought, then her presence here suggested that she was just the sort of willing lass who could prove useful.

"Do you like working for Mr. Bloathwait, Bessie?" I strolled over toward her, that I might stand directly in front of this pretty little laundry maid.

"Oh, aye, I do." She nodded with a little too much enthusiasm, as though I might report her should she seem unhappy.

"What kind of a man do you think him?"

Her mouth dropped a little. She knew I was probing, but she could not tell for what. "Oh, I couldn't answer a question like that. But he's a great man, sure." She looked up as though she had recalled something. "I best be getting on, sir. If Mr. Stockton, Mr. Bloathwait's butler, finds me standing here talking with a fine gentleman, there'll be no end to his questions, for sure."

"I certainly wouldn't want that. But I would think it rather pleasing, Bessie, if I might see you again sometime in the future. Perhaps we might arrange a meeting during which we would have no fear of Mr. Stockton. Would you like that?"

That charming redness spread across her face and neck and bosom again. She dropped into a curtsy as low as it was quick. "Oh, yes, sir. I would, sir."

"How much would you like it?" I asked her, as I took a shilling from my purse and placed it in her palm. I held the back of her hand with my palm while my other hand closed her fingers around the coin. I gently stroked her fleshy digits with my thumb.

"Very much," she breathed.

"I would like it very much too." I removed my hand from hers and gently ran the backs of my fingers along her face. "You had better run along, Bessie, lest Mr. Stockton come after you."

She curtsied again and then ran off.

Now, I am hardly the sort of man who considers himself above using a shilling or two to conquer a gentleman's laundry lass, but I had more than the pleasures of the flesh on my mind. It seemed to me a useful thing to have a pliable confederate inside Bloathwait's house, and if she was a compliant beauty, so much the better.

Not more than ten minutes after Bessie's departure the unkempt foot-man returned and announced that Bloathwait would see me. I followed him out of the parlor and down the hall to a closed door. He knocked once and opened it to reveal a cramped room, furnished in the same dull tones as the parlor.

The study let in more light, however, but the brightness that came through the windows did little to dispel the feel of duskiness—just as the evident neatness of these rooms did little to dissuade me that I kicked up dust as I walked. Bookshelves covered the walls, and within them volumes were arranged according to size, of all things. Upon the floor near many of the shelves, ledgers were stacked, without any apparent attention to detail, and loose sheets of paper sat upon the shelves and were wedged be-tween volumes.

For a man whose home suggested that he gave little credit to appear-ances, Bloathwait had designed his study with a brilliant attention to detail. He was an enormous man, and his oversized desk prevented him from looking like a foolish adult sitting upon a chair furnished for a child. He sat with an air of dignity that suggested his enormity, this man who was, after all, among the principal figures of the world of London finance.

Bloathwait sat with a formal stiffness, his somber black wig and black suit hovering like a storm cloud about his bulk as he engaged in some business or other. His ink-stained hand sailed across paper after paper in a furious hurry, as though there could never be enough time for all the work he had yet to finish, and in his mania he seemed to me half a fool, half a villain—a man equally likely to order my death as to spill his ink upon his lap.

I suppose he looked little different from the man I remembered from my boyhood; that creature had been enormous, full of grotesquely under-sized features: mouth, teeth, nose, eyes—all adrift upon a wide, fleshy face. Now there was something that seemed more unpleasant than terri-ble, better able to incite distaste than fear. Still, I knew that if I had just passed him upon the street, spotted him upon the peripheries of my vi-sion, my blood should have run cold.

Casting only a momentary glance at me, Bloathwait used his forearm to wipe a space clear of papers, and then grabbed a paper to attend to. Piles upon piles covered the entire surface of his desk; some documents were entirely filled with a tiny, close hand, others with only a few words. I could not imagine that a man so important in the management of the Bank of England could thrive in this chaos.

"Mr. Weaver," he said at last. He set his pen down and looked at me. An old clock, as wide as a man and half again as tall, began to emit a rusty chime, but Bloathwait raised his voice to speak over the contraption. "Please sit. I trust you will state your business with all possible haste."

As I moved to seat myself in an unsteady-looking chair that faced the desk, I saw him stretch out his arm for a piece of foolscap that rested at the outermost limit of his reach. It was a subtle movement, cautious and casual at the same time, but it caught my eye, as did the piece of paper he covered. I cannot say what was there, written in a scrawling hand, but some word or idea or phrase upon the page drew me in the very moment Bloathwait hid it from my view. With his free hand he took a folio volume and set it atop the paper. He then turned to me.

Observing that I watched his movements, he squinted disapprovingly. "I await your commands," he said tersely. "I have allotted a quarter of an hour at the utmost for this meeting, but I reserve the right to abridge that amount of time should I determine our conversation to be unproductive."

I could never be certain with a creature like Bloathwait, but I believed that my presence unnerved him, and I felt a strange thrill, pressing upon this man who had so pressed upon me when I was a boy. We sat here as equals, or at least something not entirely unlike equals. At any rate, he felt it in his interest to listen to what I had to say. "And what is it you wish your conversation to produce?" I asked, opting to be deliberately elliptical.

Bloathwait blinked like an uncomprehending beast. "What expectations should I have? You have called upon me."

Anxious to remove myself from his cold scrutiny, I thought I should avoid the issue no further. "I am here, Mr. Bloathwait, because I am inquiring into the matter of my father's death."

His face displayed no emotion, but he scrawled a note upon a piece of paper. "How very odd you should come to me." He did not look up while he spoke. "Do you believe I know something of the operation of hackney coaches?"

I stung a bit at this rebuke. It occurred to me that, despite my efforts to puff myself up, I still felt somewhat childish in Bloathwait's presence, as though he were an older kinsman or a teacher; unnerving him, I realized, left me feeling naughty, not powerful. I would get nowhere if I cringed each time he looked at me with disapproval, so I involuntarily clenched the muscles in my chest as I determined to treat him as I would any man.

"Hardly," I said, affecting a bit of impatience. "But it is my recollection that you did know something of my father."

He raised his head once more. "Your father and I both worked upon the 'Change, Mr. Weaver—each in his own way. I attended your father's funeral as a courtesy, and no more."

"But you knew something of him," I pressed on. "Such is what I have heard."

"I will not answer for what you have or have not heard."

"Then I shall tell you," I said, thrilled now to have taken control of our conversation. "I have been told, sir, that you made it a habit all your life to inquire into my father's affairs. That you familiarized yourself with his business, with his acquaintances, with his comings and goings. I know that at least once you took some small notice of the comings and goings of his children, and that later you transferred your interest to the father himself."

He offered me the slightest of smiles, exposing a wall of improbably large and crooked teeth. "Your father and I had been enemies. I see you have some recollection of our animosity. Though that enmity ended long ago on my part, I have learned that it is wisest to assume one's neighbors less generous than oneself." He paused for a moment. "I maintained a distant familiarity with your father in the event that he wished me harm. Such never proved to be the case."

"I hoped," I continued, "that because you did maintain such a familiarity you might have some idea on who should wish him harm."

"Why do you believe anyone should wish him harm? I was led to believe that his death was an unfortunate accident."

"I have been led to believe otherwise," I explained. I proceeded to inform him of the suspicions of William Balfour.

Bloathwait listened like a student at a lecture. He took notes as I spoke, and appeared to ponder confusing aspects of my narrative. Then I finished, and he changed his attitude to one of mild amusement, shaking his head and displaying a condescending smile upon his little mouth. "If

Balfour-the-son is only half as much a fool as Balfour-the-father, then he is twice as much fool as should be heeded. I shall tell you, I have no contempt for poverty—none whatsoever. If a man begins with nothing and ends with nothing, he is like most men upon the earth. Some men who grow rich become contemptuous of men who are poor or of men who began as poor. I only have contempt for men who were once rich and became poor. I have had my reversals—of course *you* know that—but a true man of business can reverse his reversals. Balfour squandered everything upon nonsensical pleasures, and he left nothing for his family. I scorn him."

"I believe there is some merit in what his son claims. If not in the son himself," I added after an instant.

He fingered the corner of a piece of paper. "Have you any proof of these suspicions?"

I thought it best to share no information yet. I wished to know what Bloathwait knew—not how he would react to what little information I already had. "Had I proof," I said, "I should not require your help. I now only have suspicions."

He leaned forward, as though to signal that he now wished to give me his full attention. "I shall tell you that I had something of a personal dislike of your father. I do not hesitate to say so. In matters of the Exchange, however, I could not but respect him, as I respect any man who supported the Bank of England. I shall therefore do all that I can to aid you, that I might honor all men who honor the Bank. I cannot say I believe your fantastical tale of plotted murders and missing issues, but if you wish to make some sort of inquiry, I shall in no way hinder you."

I thought it best to acknowledge what he clearly believed to be his generosity. "Thank you, Mr. Bloathwait."

He stroked his chin thoughtfully. "I also do not like the idea that someone might murder one of your race with impunity," he continued. "I hardly need tell you that we Dissenters suffer from nearly as many disabilities as you Hebrews, and I should hate to think that any man might strike down another without fear of punishment so long as his victim is not a member of the Church of England."

"I respect your sense of justice," I said cautiously.

He leaned back in his chair and spread his hands upon the expanse of his chest. "I wish I knew of something that might help you. I can only tell you this: in the weeks before his accident, I heard some rumors about your father. I heard that he had somehow become an enemy of the South Sea Company."

I concentrated on looking no more than mildly curious, though I wished to ask a thousand questions—none of which I could formulate. That Bloathwait had heard talk of enmity between my father and the Company proved little, but it confirmed the importance of the pamphlet that my uncle had uncovered.

"Tell me more about what you heard."

"I fear there is no more," he said with a casual wave of his hand. "Men do not speak openly against the Company, Mr. Weaver. It is far too powerful to cross. I only heard that your father had engaged himself upon some business that might injure the South Sea. I never learned the nature of the business or the injury."

"From whom did you hear these things?"

He shook his head. "I could not say. It was long ago, and I thought nothing of it at the time. Men who do business often exchange information casually. I regret that I took no further notice."

"I regret it too."

"Should I learn anything further, I will certainly contact you. I can only advise you that if you truly believe your father to have been murdered, then you must look to what he might have done to anger the men of the South Sea Company. You must then determine what course of action such a Company might take."

"What *could* a man have done to anger the Company?"

Bloathwait exposed his palms in a gesture of ignorance. "I cannot say how the managers of the South Sea think, sir. If a man were to threaten their profits, would they lash out against him? I do not know. But I can think that your father had no greater enemy when he died."

"Do you believe, then, that the Company would have its agents kill a man who threatened profits?"

"I never said so," Bloathwait responded coolly. "I merely state that the directors of the South Sea are ambitious men. I would not guess to what lengths they might go to protect their ambitions."

I could not trust the disinterested air with which he hinted at the villainy of the Company. When I was a boy, Bloathwait had proved himself to be an ambitious plotter, and he had not become a man of such importance without learning subtlety. His caution in discussing the Company surely disguised the extent to which he wished me to believe his implications.

"These ambitions," I said, using the same easy tone as Bloathwait, "threaten the Bank of England, do they not? The South Sea Company is your most dangerous rival. I should think you would benefit greatly if I discover any wrongdoing on the Company's part."

Bloathwait's face darkened, and in an instant I saw the man of my boyhood—enormous, determined, and terrifying in his intensity. "I think you go too far." He spoke in a deep, hostile whisper. "Do you suggest that I would threaten other men's business out of petty motives? You came here looking for my assistance, and I have told you what I know. I find your insults as inexplicable as they are rude."

"I meant no rudeness." I attempted a conciliatory tone, though what came from my mouth sounded like an angry retort.

He shook his head to show his contempt for my clumsy effort at recovery. Our discourse now resembled lines in a stage play more than it did conversation—neither of us spoke anything like truth, but we dared not venture too far from our roles.

"You may show yourself out," he said quietly, hoping to convey the demands of his affairs rather than the insult of my accusation. "I have no more time for you. I wish you well of your inquiry, and if I stumble upon information that might help you, I shall send it along."

I pushed myself to my feet and bowed. I had just turned when he called my name.

"I cannot guess what your inquiry will yield, Weaver, but should you learn anything of the South Sea Company that seems to be of"—he paused to consider his words—"of an incriminating nature, I beg that you will come to me with your information before you go elsewhere. I promise you that the Bank will pay you handsomely for your consideration."

I bowed again and left the study.

I felt some relief as I made my way out, for I believed that I should always relish keeping my distance from Bloathwait. For now, however, I knew that I might not enjoy so much of a distance as I should like. He had confirmed what I already knew—that my father had made the South Sea Company his enemy. The mere existence of this enmity did not prove a murder, but it gave me somewhere to press my inquiry. More to the point, Bloathwait had shown himself willing to aid me in my efforts, so long as the South Sea Company suffered for it. I comforted myself with the thought that should I become convinced of the guilt of the Company or its agents, I should have a powerful, if dangerous, ally.

As I walked toward the door, I stopped and asked a stooped man of middle years if he knew Bessie's whereabouts, but this worthy shooed me away. "Off with ye," he snapped and bared his teeth like a goat. "Bessie's fool enough without having her head turned by the likes of ye."

I bowed meekly and made my way from the house. But I had an idea in my head that I would be back, and the next time I would not go through such formal channels.

Seventeen

T HE NEXT AFTERNOON, Elias came to pay me a visit, puffed up with joy and quite ready to hug himself. He had hardly walked through my door before his news exploded forth. "There's been a terrible misfortune with a brother playwright," he said with pleasure. "Some blockhead named Croger, who was to have had a play completed for Cibber, has gone and died without finishing his work. Absolutely dead. My play has been accepted and is to be performed next week."

I heartily congratulated my friend upon his good fortune. I turned to reach for a decanter that we might share a celebratory drink, but Elias had somehow reached it before I turned around, and he handed me a glass. We drank to his success, and he threw himself down in one of my armchairs.

"Is this not unusual, for a play to be rushed into production so quickly?" I asked.

"Shockingly uncommon," he assured me, "but Cibber is the sort of theatre manager who is always determined to have something new early in the season, and when he heard my *Unsuspecting Lover*, he was entirely taken with it. In no small part, I think, because I designed the character of Count Fopworth to be played by Cibber. As I read through the play—and I can tell you, reading through an entire play by one's self, trying to get all the inflections just so, is no easy task—he kept interrupting when I read Fopworth to exclaim, 'I think there may be something in this piece,' or 'That has a delightful turn.' The key is not to write plays that are good, but rather to write plays with roles for the manager. I am so very pleased with myself I shall burst."

I listened to him talk at some length about Mr. Cibber, about the The-atre Royal, Drury Lane, about the actresses he liked there, and so forth. Elias then explained to me that he would be exceptionally busy with the rushed rehearsals, but that he still wished to assist as best he could with the inquiry. I then told him of my encounter with Bloathwait, and I asked if he had ever heard of Martin Rochester, the man my father's slayer now worked for, but Elias shook his head.

"I cannot think how to track him down," I complained. "A man no one can find working for another no one knows. Perhaps if I haunt Jonathan's I might learn something of use."

Elias smiled. "Can you be certain that you will be spending your time wisely?"

"I cannot," I explained. "It merely appears to me to be my best option. I hope," I said with a smile, "to study the general and to learn the par-ticular."

He nodded. "Very good, Weaver. In the absence of knowledge, you seek out likelihoods. There is hope for you yet."

Elias pushed himself out of his chair and walked with an unsteady gait to my decanter, which he was displeased to find spent. "What say you, Weaver, that we go forth and celebrate my success? We shall visit the bagnio of your choice and talk probability with the whores." I saw him looking about my shelves for another bottle of wine.

"I should like nothing better," I assured him, "but I fear I must con-tinue with this inquiry."

"I suspected as much," he replied, having no small difficulty with the word *suspected*. He then treated me to several soliloquies from his comedy, and though he forgot most of his words, I applauded vigorously. He then announced that he had whoring to attend to and more game bucks than I with whom to share his amusement. He made several attempts at the door handle, and then clumsily departed.

I listened to Elias make loud work of Mrs. Garrison's stairway, and then sat myself at my desk and once again attempted to read through my fa-ther's pamphlet. I cannot pretend to be shocked to say that my father was no more accessible in prose than he was in conversation. Consider the very first words of this document:

> We cannot but be aware that in recent years there has been a
> general cry, indeed an uproar, over the growing powers in certain

factions of Exchange Alley—factions that have made their intentions clear and have striven, against the better wishes of those who would see the nation prosper, to undo that which has been so boldly done in the Kingdom's interest.

After this first sentence, I determined to begin a course of judicious skimming, which produced a flurry of accusations about the South Sea Company and praise of the Bank of England that swam mercilessly before my eyes. Some portions held my interest more than others; I could not but read closely where my father postulated a conspiracy within the great Company itself: "This forgery can only have been perpetrated with the co-operation of certain elements within South Sea House itself. The Company is as a piece of meat, rotted and crawling with maggots."

I spent perhaps another hour with the manuscript, skimming about, hoping that somewhere my father had distilled his ideas into an apprehensible conclusion. Once disabused of this hope, I then determined that to understand the issues, my time should be spent not before my father's pamphlet but in the heat of the fire. So I dressed myself in my best waistcoat and coat, carefully combed and tied my hair, and left my rooms with a very neat appearance. I then made my way to Jonathan's Coffeehouse, where I was determined to spend a few hours among the engineers of the London financial markets. If I was to understand their intrigues, I reasoned, it was necessary I gain a better feel for these stock-jobbers.

I found the coffeehouse just as vibrant as it had been the day before, and though it was a less entertaining place to spend an afternoon than in a house of pleasure with a drunken Scot, I found myself of the opinion that Exchange Alley, with its bustle of activity, had much of interest. I took a seat at a table, called for a dish of coffee, and began leafing through the papers of the day.

I listened to men shout at one another across the room, debating the merits of this issue or that. Voices cried out to buy. Voices cried out to sell. I could hear arguments conducted in every living language and at least one dead one. Yet, confusing though it may have been, I felt I learned a great deal, and I took a certain pleasure at remaining there, feeling as though I were a bit of the stock-jobbing Jew upon the 'Change. There was something truly infectious about the exuberance of this place where momentous events were always about to happen, a fortune was always about to be made or lost. I had been in many a coffeehouse before where men argued about writers or actresses or politics with unbridled vehemence. Here men argued about their fortunes, and the results of their arguments produced wealth or poverty, notoriety or infamy. The stock-jobber's coffeehouse turned argument into wealth, words into power, ideas into truth—or something that looked strikingly like truth. I had come of age in an unambiguous world of violence and passions. I felt myself to be among a different species of man now, in a strange and alien land ruled not by the strong but by the cunning and the lucky.

After perhaps three-quarters of an hour, I noticed my uncle's clerk, Mr. Sarmento, among a group of men I did not recognize, vigorously engaging in their business. A series of documents lay upon a table, and several of the men were reading over these papers. This ritual continued for some time, and then the men all departed on seemingly amicable terms.

Sarmento had in no way indicated that he had seen me, yet when he was done with his business, he folded up his papers and walked purposefully over to my table.

"Shall I join you, Mr. Weaver?" he asked in a tone as blank and inscrutable as his face. I could find nowhere any trace of the puppy who had bounded after Mr. Adelman at my uncle's house. Here I only saw the grim visage of a man who found life but a series of greater and lesser tensions.

"I should be delighted," I said with a politeness that hung in the air like a foul odor.

"I cannot imagine what business brings you to this coffeehouse," he said absently. "Are you thinking of involving yourself in the funds?"

"Yes," I said dryly. "I believe I shall pursue a life as a licensed broker upon the 'Change."

"You are mocking me, but you have still not answered my question."

I took a sip of coffee. "What do you think I am doing here, Mr. Sarmento?"

He appeared astonished at this question. "I would not think you so bold as to speak of it openly. I never presume to judge Mr. Lienzo's business, but I should hope for his sake that you would be subtle. You still recall, I hope, what your family is."

Sarmento was hard to read, but he had the look of satisfaction that comes with having pieced together a complex puzzle. "What do you know of the matter?" I asked gently. I thought perhaps I could mislead him into telling me—I do not know what. I only knew that I did not trust him nor he me, and that struck me as reason enough to push onward.

"I assure you I know enough. Perhaps more than I ought."

"I should very much like to know more than I ought," I said with great calm.

Sarmento smiled in return. It was the crooked and misshapen smile of a man to whom mirth came unnaturally. "I do not believe you would. Do you know what I think, Mr. Weaver? I think you have ambitions that are well beyond your abilities."

"I am grateful for your good opinion of me." I bowed slightly.

"What? Must we conduct ourselves with the duplicitous politenesses of our English neighbors? That is not our way—all of this 'you honor me' and 'I am your servant' rubbish. We say what is on our minds."

I rankled at the idea that I performed the Englishman, that I pretended to something I was not. That this man was a member of my race filled me with a kind of shame. It was a strange thing, for I had grown so used to thinking of myself as a Jew in a very particular way—listening to what the Britons around me had to say about Jews, wondering how I should feel about their words. But here was something else; over the last decade I had little experience of thinking of myself as a Jew in relation to other Jews. Now Sarmento made me feel something else—a kind of strange defensiveness, as though I were a member of a club, and I wished to see him cast out.

"Of what do you wish to speak, Mr. Sarmento?" I asked at last.

"Tell me about your conversation in Mr. Adelman's carriage the other night."

I pressed my hands together so as to appear a man deep in thought. In fact, I *was* deep in thought, but I wished to appear thinking thoughts of cleverness, not of confusion. "First, sir, you speak of my business with Mr. Lienzo, and now you inquire of my business with Mr. Adelman. Is there any business I have of which you do not wish to speak?"

"Business?" he asked in astonishment. "Is it business you conduct with Adelman?"

"I did not say that we had reached any agreement," I explained. "Only that we spoke of business. But I would still very much like to know why you inquire so nearly into my affairs."

"You misunderstand me," Sarmento stammered, suddenly attempting to appear obsequious. "I am merely interested. Even concerned. Adelman may not be the man you think him to be, and I do not wish for you to suffer."

"To suffer, you say? Why, did I not see you fawning all over Adelman the other night, and now you wish to warn me off him? I cannot claim to understand you."

"I am a man who knows his way about 'Change Alley, sir, and you do not. You would be wise to remember this. But men such as Adelman and your uncle are men of business, trained in the arts of deception and flattery."

I abruptly sat up straight, startling Mr. Sarmento. "What say you about my uncle?"

"Your uncle is not a man to be trifled with, sir. I hope you do not take him lightly. You perhaps see him as a kindly older gentleman, but I can assure you he is extremely ambitious, and it is an ambition I have come to admire and to emulate."

"Explain yourself more clearly," I demanded.

"Come, come. I know you are steeped now in your family *business*. Your uncle throws you a few coins, and you fetch them like a dog. But even you must surely see that it is strange that your uncle should have such a fond friendship with a man hated by your father."

My uncle throw me coins? Adelman hated by my father? I wanted to know more, but I dared not expose myself by asking.

"Do not play with me," I said at last. "And I should remind you to watch your tongue when you speak to a man who would not think twice about ripping it from your head."

"I have no time for games, *Weaver*." He mocked my name with his pronunciation. "I am also, I promise you, not a man to be trifled with. You are no longer in the ring, and you cannot beat men out of your way. If you wish to fight in 'Change Alley, sir, you will find you are outmatched by men such as myself, and here we use far more dangerous weapons than our fists."

He looked at me in the most unanimated fashion, as though he shared a table with a piece of vegetation. There was nothing threatening about the gestures of his body, nor the look in his face. "I confess I don't know how to understand you, sir," I said finally. "You seem for all the world to wish to threaten me, and yet I know of no reason why you should be my enemy."

Sarmento again offered me something not entirely unlike a smile. "If you have no wish to be my enemy, then I have no wish to threaten you."

"What is it you fear of me?" I asked him. "That I shall assume your place in my uncle's business? That I shall marry Miriam? That I shall challenge you to fight me? Let us be honest with each other."

"I scorn your mockery," he said—I cannot say angrily, for his tone changed not a whit. "You would be well advised to be cautious of me. And of your uncle—and his friends."

Before I could respond, Sarmento had risen to his feet, shoved a short trader out of his way, and forced his way into the crowd. I was unsure of what he meant to imply about my uncle, but his warning me of Adelman troubled me more than anything else he had said, for Sarmento now wished to make insinuations of a man whom, at my uncle's house, he had wished nothing more than to please.

Driven by curiosity, I arose from my table and made my way toward the exit, where I saw Sarmento just leaving. Waiting a moment, I followed suit, and watched him head north toward Cornhill. Once upon this busy street, it was easy for me to follow closely. He walked briskly, weaving in and out of the greedy mobs come to do business upon the 'Change.

He made his way west, to where Cornhill intersects with Threadneedle and Lombard streets, and here the thickness of the crowd began to thin out a little, so I hung back, took an instant to throw a penny at a beggar, and continued to follow at a safe distance.

By now Cornhill had turned into Poultry, and Sarmento made a right upon the much more sparsely populated Grocers Alley. I waited a moment and followed him into the alley leading to Grocers Hall, which I reminded myself was the home of the Bank of England. Sarmento veered off toward the massive building, which, like the Royal Exchange, stood as an architectural testament to the excesses of the last century.

Sarmento hurried toward a coach standing before the Hall. That I might move closer, I approached a group of gentlemen nearby and, keeping one eye upon this coach, I affected a country accent and explained that I had lost my way and required the quickest route to London Bridge. Londoners may not be the most gregarious lot in the world, but there is little they love so much as to give directions, and now, while these five gentlemen vied with each other to provide me the shortest walk, the coach began to move slowly, making its way past me. Sarmento, I could see, engaged himself in deep conversation with a man with a wide face full of undersized features. The smallness of his nose and mouth and eyes was made even more absurd by an enormous black wig that piled almost to the ceiling of the coach and undulated down in thick ringlets. It was a face that I had seen but recently and one that I recognized with little difficulty. I cannot say I felt anything so much as utter confusion as I watched Sarmento drive off with Perceval Bloathwait.

Eighteen

I COULD NO LONGER pretend to myself that my suspicions of Bloathwait were born of the vague ghost of a childhood terror. He had covered something on his desk, something he had not wanted me to see. That in itself might mean little—it might have been a reminder to himself about private finances or whores or a taste for young boys for all I knew. It would be very strange if a man like Bloathwait had nothing on his desk worthy of hiding from a potential enemy. But a connection with Sarmento, a man employed by my uncle, was an entirely different matter. Bloathwait maintained a secret connection to my family, and I felt I had to know what it was.

My youthful adventures as an outlaw had left me well prepared for this business of inquiring into murder, and I knew that it was time to call upon my skills as a housebreaker. I had long ago learned that there was no more useful tool for the illegal entering of a house than the interests of a silly maid, so I composed an enchanting little *lettre d'amour*, which I sent wrapped around a shilling. I had little doubt that Bessie the laundry lass would respond kindly to my missive, and when I received the answer I desired within the hour, I rubbed my hands together with excitement.

My next stop was Gilbert Street, where I was delighted to find that Elias had returned from his celebratory debauch, but he slept so soundly under the influence of a wine which still stained his teeth and tongue a bright purple that it took Mrs. Henry and me nearly half an hour to bring my friend to consciousness. He lay on his back, his bob-wig remaining affixed to his head, but pushed forward down his brow. His clothes were mainly still upon his body, but he had fallen asleep after removing one arm from his coat. His shoes and stockings were speckled with mud that he had smeared all over Mrs. Henry's sheets, and his cravat, loosened but not untied, was strewn with brown meat drippings.

When he at last came to something like consciousness, Mrs. Henry left the room with performative disgust, and in the flickering of two inadequate candles I watched my friend open and close his mouth like a Bartholomew Fair puppet. "Gad, Weaver. What time is it?"

"Nearly nine o'clock, I believe."

"If the house is not on fire, I shall have to be very angry with you," he muttered, and pushed himself to sit upright. "What do you want? Can you not see that I am celebrating?"

"We have work to do," I told him bluntly, hoping the force of my intent would help to awaken him. "I need to break into the house of Perceval Bloathwait, the Bank of England director."

Elias rolled his head from side to side. "You're mad." He pushed himself to his feet and stumbled across the room to a basin filled with water and discreetly covered with a pretty piece of linen. He stripped himself of his coat and waistcoat and then removed the cloth from the basin and began splashing his face. Even in the dark I could not but notice what appeared to be grass stains across the rump of his breeches.

He turned to me, his face now glistening with water. "You wish to break into Bloathwait's house? Good Lord, why?"

"Because I believe he's hiding something."

He shook his head. "Break into his house if you wish. I shan't stop you. But I don't know why you should wish me to go with you."

"Because I'm gaining access by the good graces of a pretty little servant girl, and I shall need someone to keep her occupied while I search Bloathwait's papers."

I now had Elias's attention. "How pretty?"

An hour later Elias had cleaned himself up, changed his clothes, fixed his wig, and demanded that I buy him a few dishes of coffee. We thus made our way to Kent's, a favorite coffeehouse of Elias's; it was filled with wits and poets and playwrights—none of whom had a farthing about them. I should think the serving girls must have had the very devil of a time getting this band of self-inflated rogues to pay their reckonings, but the coffeehouse, for all the poverty of its patrons, appeared to thrive. On this particular night, nearly every table was full, and conversations buzzed all about us. The new theatrical season was upon every man's lips, and I heard critiques of this play and that author and praises of the beauty of half-a-dozen actresses.

"Tell me again what you hope to gain from breaking into this man's house." Elias hesitantly raised his dish of coffee to his lips like a servant presenting a platter.

"He's hiding something. He has more information than he's willing to share, and I'll wager that we can find what we need in his office, and probably upon his desk."

"Even if there was something there when you went to see him, would he not have locked it away by now?"

I shook my head. "Bloathwait doesn't strike me as the sort of man who would believe anyone might dare to violate his home."

"I wish he were right," Elias sighed. "You do realize that housebreaking is a hanging offense?"

"Only if we are there as thieves. If we are there to prey upon the virtue of a young girl, there's not a man in England who would stand to see us charged, let alone convicted."

Elias grinned at my ingenuity. "True enough."

My friend began to look more alert, and though it was perhaps not the best time to seek his advice, I could not subdue the urge to ask of him what I hoped he would know. "What," I began, "can you tell me of insurance?"

He raised but one eyebrow.

I pressed on. "Would a merchant ever send a ship upon a trading mission uninsured?"

"Not unless the merchant was a dunce," he said. He left the *why* unasked.

"My cousin's widow," I explained hesitantly. "She had a fortune—not an insignificant one—when she was married, and my cousin invested in my uncle's business. His ship, which represented much of the investment, was lost, and so, she presumes, was her portion. But if the ship was insured, then surely someone has that money."

"An intrigue with a pretty widow!" Elias nearly shouted. He was now fully awake indeed. "Gad, Weaver, I should kill you for holding back this information. I must know all about her."

"She lives in my uncle's house," I said, careful of how much ammunition I wished to provide for his raillery. "I believe she wishes to set forth on her own, but she has not much money."

"A widow," he mused. "I love a widow, Weaver. None of that niggardliness with their favors. No, widows are a generous race, and I applaud them." He saw my displeasure and reined himself in. "It is a sad matter," he observed.

"I would like to help her somehow."

"If she's pretty, I'll help her soundly!" he exclaimed, but then soon recovered himself. "Yes, well, do you suspect your uncle of withholding what is rightly hers?"

"I do not think he has taken anything not his by contract," I said. "But it pains me to think that he keeps her a near-prisoner in his house by taking advantage of the laws of property."

"Do you believe your uncle to be entirely trustworthy?" he asked.

I had no answer, not even for myself. Instead I checked my watch and announced that it was time for us to go. I paid our reckoning and procured a hackney, which took us a few blocks from Bloathwait's house. From there we walked to Cavendish Square, which in the thick of night was dark and quiet and tomblike. Elias and I quietly slipped around to the servants' entrance and, according to plan, met Bessie at eleven o'clock. She stared at Elias with some confusion (while he stared at her with some delight), but let us in just the same.

"All's asleep," she said quietly. "What's this gentleman for?"

"Bessie," I whispered, "you're a charming lass, and your beauty is not lost on me, but I am here to look at Mr. Bloathwait's study. I don't want to take anything, just to look about. If you'd like, you can follow us and raise the alarm if we do anything you don't like."

"Mr. Bloathwait's study?" Her voice became unnervingly shrill.

"Here's a half crown for you," I said, slipping a coin into her hand. "There will be another when we're done if you agree to look the other way."

She eyed the coin in her hand, her hurt feelings squeezed out by the money's heft. "All right," she said slowly. "But I don't want nothing to do with you. You go on your way, and if they catch you, I won't say I ever saw you here."

It wasn't quite what I had wanted, but it would have to do. So I told her that if we had to depart in a hurry, I'd send her the other half crown in the morning. The bargain thus struck, we made our way to the study.

This room, which had been dark even during the daytime, took upon itself a new feeling of evil now, as we cast shadows within the narrow space of the chamber, which seemed to wrap about us like an enormous coffin. I moved toward the desk, lighting a few candles along the way, but the dim light of too-few flames created a feeling of more rather than less menace.

While I attempted to make conditions bearable for our invasive search, Elias wandered about the room, examining books upon the shelves and touching Bloathwait's artifacts.

"Come here," I hissed. "I don't know how much time we have, and I want to quit this felony as quickly as we can." I gathered some candles about Bloathwait's great desk, and began to scan the daunting mounds of documents spread across the surface as though the wind had blown them there.

Elias joined me at the desk and lifted up a piece of paper at random. Bloathwait's hand was cramped and difficult to read. It would be no easy thing to scan through these writings.

He held the page to the candle, as though threatening it with flame would force it to yield forth its secrets. "What are we looking for?" Elias asked.

"I cannot say, but there was something he wished to hide. Seek out anything having to do with my father or the South Sea Company or Michael Balfour."

We both began leafing through the papers, doing our best not to misplace anything from its original order. There was so much on the desk, and its organization so chaotic, that I could not care if Bloathwait discovered his papers had been searched. So long as he could not prove it had been done by me, I was content.

"You haven't told me what your widow looks like," Elias said, as he ran his finger along a line of gnarled prose.

"Pay attention to your work," I muttered, though in truth I took some comfort from the sound of his voice. We were engaged upon a tense business; my eyes darted to each shifting shadow upon the wall, and my body stiffened with each creak of the house.

Elias understood my rebuke to mean nothing. "I can concentrate and discuss widows simultaneously. I do it all the time while performing surgery. So tell me, is she a charming Jewess, with olive skin and dark hair and pretty eyes?"

"Yes, she is," I told him, trying not to grin. "She's quite lovely."

"I should not expect any less of you, Weaver. You've always had a good eye in your own way." He handed me a piece of paper on which there were notes about some loan venture of the Bank, but I could not see how it might be of value.

"Are you thinking matrimony?" he asked impishly, moving to a stack of papers bound together with a thick string. He carefully worked out the knot and began to glance at the pages. "Have you begun to consider starting a home, circumcising some young ones?"

"I know not why my fondness for this woman so amuses you," I said churlishly. "You fall in love three times a fortnight."

"Which makes me immune to mockery, then, does it not? Everyone expects me to fall in love. But you, the stony, stout, fighting Israelite—that's another matter."

I held up my hand. I heard creaking from somewhere—like footsteps. We both remained motionless in the flickering candlelight for some minutes, listening only to the sound of our own breathing and the ticking of Bloathwait's great clock. What should we do if Bloathwait were to stroll in, candle in one hand, dressing gown wrapped about his enormous form? He might laugh, send us away, mock us—or he might commit us to the magistrate and use his mighty influence to see us hang for housebreaking. Possibility after possibility ran though my mind, scorn and haughtiness and sinister laughter, or prison and suffering and the scaffold. I fingered the handle of my hangar, and then my pistol. Elias watched me do so; he knew what I was about. I would kill Bloathwait, I would go upon the road, leave London and never return. I would not face trial for this adventure of mine, nor could I think of permitting Elias to know the horrors of prison. I resolved myself to do what I believed necessary.

The noise did not come again, and after a few moments in which I could not quite believe my own conviction that the danger had passed, I signaled that we should resume.

"I wonder about you," Elias said, trying once more to lighten my mood—and his own. "All this spending time among your coreligionists. Are you thinking of returning to the fold? Moving to Dukes Place and becoming an elder at the synagogue? Growing a beard and such?"

"And what if I should?" The idea of returning to Dukes Place had crossed my mind, not as a resolution, but as a question—what should it be like to live there, to be one Jew among many rather than to be the one Jew that my acquaintances knew?

"I can only hope that when you find the path of abstemious devotion, you do not entirely forget the friends of your debauched youth."

"You might consider converting to our faith," I said. "I suppose the operation may prove painful—but I have no specific memory of being uncomfortable."

"Look at this." He waved a piece of paper before me. "It's Henry Upshaw. He owes me ten shillings, and he's dealing with Bloathwait for two hundred pounds."

"Stop looking for gossip," I told him. "We mustn't stay here longer than we need to."

We had been there perhaps two hours, and we were both growing anxious, wondering how foolish an idea this had been, when a piece of paper caught my eye—not because of anything written upon it, but because it looked familiar. It had the same kind of torn corner that I had seen on the document Bloathwait had attempted to hide from me.

Picking it up carefully, I saw written at the top "S. S. Co.?" My heart rate quickened. Underneath he had written "forge?" and under that "warning Lienzo." Did he mean that he had received a warning from my father, that he had given a warning to my father, or even that he took my father's death as a warning?

A little farther down the page he had written "Rochester," and then, under that, "S. S. Co. Contact—Virgil Cowper."

I called Elias over and showed it to him.

"Could these be notes that he took after your meeting?" he asked.

"I never mentioned Rochester to him," I said. "And I have no idea who Virgil Cowper is, so even if these are notes he took later, it shows that he knows something he's not telling me."

"But these could just be his speculations. They don't prove anything."

"True enough, but at least we have a name we didn't have before. Virgil Cowper. I suspect he's someone at the South Sea Company, and he may be able to tell us something."

I took out a piece of paper and wrote down the name, and then continued looking through the piles. Elias by now had grown bored, and began looking through Bloathwait's bound notes upon the bookshelves, but all he found there were incomprehensible pages of names and numbers and dates.

We worked together in silence once more, both of us exhilarated by the find. We were not wasting our time. I do not believe, however, that Elias was capable of periods of prolonged silence.

"You never answered my question," he said at last. "Would you marry this widow if she would have you?"

Although Elias sought mostly to rail at me, there was something else in his voice—a kind of sadness, and a kind of excitement, too, as though he were on the brink of something wonderful and altering.

"She would never have me," I said at last. "So there is no answering the question."

"I think you have answered it," he said gently.

I escaped further probing by discovering a draft of a letter, made out to a name I could not decipher. I should have overlooked it completely, but a name in the middle of the page caught my eye. "Sarmento proves himself to be an idiot, but more on that later." It was the only mention of my uncle's man that I could find. The reference made me smile, and for some reason it gave me a curious pleasure to know that he and I agreed on Sarmento's character.

My reflection was halted by the sound of footsteps coming down the hall. We both quickly rushed to replace all the papers and blow out candles. But our frenzy halted when we saw Bessie come dashing through the door, her skirt lifted to aid her running.

"Mr. Bloathwait's awake," she breathed. "His gout roused him. I'm to be fixing him a dish of chocolate, and then he aims to come down. So give me my half crown, and then off with you."

I slipped her the coin as Elias finished dousing the lights. I could only hope that enough time elapsed before Bloathwait made his way in here that whoever lit them again would not notice the wax to be soft and warm.

Bessie quietly led us through the maze of hallways to the servants' entrance. "Don't be coming back here," she said to me, "unless you have something else on your mind. I've no time for the intrigues of you men of business. I don't much care for such things."

She curtsied and closed the door, and Elias and I scrambled into the street. It was late, and I took out my pistol so that anyone passing by would think twice before setting upon us.

"Was it a successful venture?" Elias asked.

"I think so," I said. "We know that Bloathwait has some knowledge of the South Sea forgeries, and that he had some kind of idea about my father in relation to it. And we have this name, this Virgil Cowper. I tell you, Elias, I have a good feeling about tonight. I think the information we've taken of Bloathwait will prove most useful to us."

I could not tell if Elias disagreed or merely wished to return to his room and sleep.

NINETEEN

I AIMED TO MAKE my way to South Sea House the next afternoon, but I first wished to visit my uncle and report to him of my adventures with Bloathwait. I was not yet certain that I wanted to tell him what I had seen of Sarmento, but I grew tired of playing these cat-and-mouse games. For the nonce I would inform him that the Bank of England director had made it clear that he had some interest in the inquiry.

I confess that my desire to meet with my uncle was in some way augmented by a desire to see Miriam once again. I wondered how the matter of the twenty-five pounds she borrowed of me would sit between us. A loan of necessity such as this could produce a discomfort, and I was determined to do all in power to keep such a thing from happening.

The irony of my interest in Miriam amused me; had I known more of Aaron's pretty widow, perhaps I would have contemplated a reconciliation long before. And yet, even as I sang a little drinking ditty to myself as I walked, I wondered about my intentions. Despite the world's opinion of widows, I could not think myself such a cad as to attempt to encroach upon the virtue of a woman who was very nearly a relation, and living under the protection of my uncle, too. Yet what could a man such as myself offer? I who scraped together, at the very most, a few hundred pounds each year, had nothing for Miriam.

As I approached my uncle's house, coming on to Berry Street from Grey Hound Alley, I was shocked out of my reverie by an ungainly beggar man, who materialized with jarring suddenness. He was a Tudesco Jew— as we Iberian Jews called our coreligionists from Eastern Europe—

perhaps of middle years, though he looked ageless in that way of men who are undernourished and oppressed with labors and hardships. My readers may not even realize that there are different categories of Jews, but we separate ourselves based on our culture of origin. Here in England, those of us of Iberian descent were the first to return in the last century and until recently outnumbered our Tudesco cousins. Because of the opportunities our exiled forebears found among the Dutch, most Jewish businessmen and brokers in England are Iberian. The Tudescos are frequently persecuted and harassed in their native lands, and when they come here they find themselves without skills or trades, and thus the largest number of beggars and old-clothes men about the streets are of Eastern European origin. These distinctions are not etched in stone, though, for there are rich Tudescos, such as Adelman, and there is no shortage of poor among the Iberian Jews.

I should like to say that I formed no prejudice against the Tudescos simply because I thought their appearance and language strange, but the truth is that I found such men as this peddler an embarrassment—I believed them to cast our people in a shockingly bad light, and I felt ashamed of their poverty and ignorance and helplessness. This man's bones jutted out of his parchmentlike skin, and his black, foreign garments hung upon him as though he had simply draped bedclothes across his body. He wore his beard long, in the fashion of his countrymen, and a conspicuous skullcap spread over his head, with stringy locks creeping from beneath. As he stood there, a foolish smile upon his face, asking me in poor English if I wished to purchase a penknife or a pencil or a shoelace, I was overcome with a desire, intense and surprising, to strike him down, to destroy him, to make him disappear. I believed at that moment that it was these men, whose looks and manners were repulsive to Englishmen, who were responsible for the difficulties other Jews suffered in England. Were it not for this buffoon, who gave the English something to gawk at, I would not have been so humiliated in Sir Owen's club. Indeed, I should not find so many obstacles in my path that block me from learning what had happened to my father. But even this was a lie, I told myself, for I knew that the truth was that this peddler did not make the English hate us—he merely gave their hatred a focus. He was an outcast, he was strange to look at, his speech abused the language, and he could never blend into London society—not even as a foreigner blends in. This man made me hate myself for what I was, and made me wish to strike out at him. I understood this passion for what it was; I knew that I hated him for reasons that related not at all to him, so I hurried off, hoping to make him and the feelings he engendered in me fade away.

Yet as I rushed, I heard him call to me. "Mister!" he shouted. "I know who you are."

This claim only fueled my anger, for what could I, the son of one of London's prominent Jewish families—and this was a title that I rarely claimed—have to do with a beggar such as he? I clenched my fists and turned to face him.

"I know you," he said again, pointing at me. "You." He shook his head, unable to summon the words. "You this, yes?" He balled his hands into fists and brought them up level to his nose before he pantomimed some quick jabs. "You the great man, the Lion of Judah, yes?" He took a few steps forward and nodded vigorously, his beard swinging back and forth like a crazed and hairy pendulum. He barked a little laugh, as though his ignorance of the English tongue suddenly amused him. Then, placing one of his hands upon his heart, he reached down to his tray of trinkets and held something forth. "Please," he said. "From me."

As he held out an hourglass in the palm of his bony hand, I understood that, while I saw him as what I hated about myself, he saw me as something in which he could take pride. It is a terrible thing to come to so humbling a realization, for in an instant a man sees himself as petty and illiberal and weak. And so I took the hourglass from him and dropped a shilling upon his tray, rushing away as I did so. I knew a shilling to be an enormous amount of money to the Tudesco, but he chased after me, holding the coin. "No, no, no," he repeated nearly endlessly. "You take from me. Please."

I turned to face him. I saw that one hand was once again pressed to his heart, the other held out the coin. "Please," he said again.

I took the coin from his hand and then dropped it in his tray. Before he could react I put a hand to my own heart. "Please."

We exchanged brief nods, expressing a communion I did not entirely understand, and then I hurried off in the direction of King Street.

I walked quickly, hoping to remove the encounter with the peddler from my mind, and when my uncle's house came in sight, I nearly trotted. The servant Isaac opened the door only after I had knocked several times, and even then he attempted to block my entrance by maneuvering his withered frame before me. "Mr. Lienzo is not in," he said sharply. "He is at the warehouse. You can see him there."

He sounded clipped, perhaps a bit frightened. "Is something wrong, Isaac?"

"No," he said rapidly. "But your uncle is not here."

He attempted to close the door, but I pushed against it. "Is Mrs. Miriam about?"

Isaac's face changed dramatically upon the mention of her name, and on an impulse I forced my way past him and into the foyer, from where I could hear voices, raised as if shouting. One of them was clearly Miriam's.

"What happens in there?"

"Mrs. Miriam, she is having an argument," he said, as though offering precisely the information I needed to ease my confusion.

"With whom?" I demanded. But at that very moment the withdrawing-room door opened and Noah Sarmento emerged, his face bearing a scowl something grimmer than his usual. He paused for a moment, visibly astonished to see the two of us standing in close proximity to their quarrel.

"What do you want, Weaver?" he asked me, as if I had just barged into his own home.

"This is where my family lives," I said with what I admit was a bellicose inflection.

"And for a sufficient quantity of silver, you now care about your family," he snapped. He grabbed his hat from Isaac, who had produced it without my notice, and stepped out of the already open door. Isaac closed it as Miriam emerged from the withdrawing room. She opened her mouth to speak to Isaac, but stopped upon seeing me.

I can only presume that she found some irony in my presence there, for she smiled slightly to herself. "Good afternoon, Cousin," she said. "Would you care for some tea?"

I told her I would enjoy it very much, and we retreated into the withdrawing room, where we waited for the maid to bring us the tea things.

Miriam was still heated from her argument with Sarmento, and her olive skin had enough of the red mixed in to make her eyes glow like emeralds. On this day she wore a particularly striking shade of royal blue, which I speculated was a favorite color with her.

She was disordered, I could see that quite clearly, but she tried hard to mask her mood with smiles and pleasantries. After a few moments of asking me about the weather and how I had entertained myself since last we met, she produced a dazzling Chinese fan and began to wave it at herself somewhat violently.

"Well," I breathed. At least, I thought, the difficulties with Sarmento made the matter of the money I'd lent seem less pressing. I had thought to engage her in idle chatter for a while, but I soon decided I should get nowhere with a woman like Miriam if I pretended to a frivolousness I surely did not possess. "Is Mr. Sarmento causing you any difficulties with which I can assist you?"

She set aside her fan. "Yes," Miriam said. "I should like you to beat him soundly."

"Do you mean at cards? Billiards, perhaps?"

We might have been discussing the opera for all her face revealed. "I would prefer cudgels."

"I think Mr. Sarmento would hold his own nicely in a battle," I said absently.

"Not against you, surely."

I stiffened a bit at this. Miriam flirted with me, quite obviously so. She had not failed to observe that I found her attractive, and I thought to myself that I would be wise to keep my wits about me. I could not allow myself to forget that she had been in an argument that her servant had been at pains to conceal from me. Whatever I was to this family, I was not yet trusted. "No," I said, looking about the room. "Not against me. And against you, Miriam, he fared poorly as well. You have quite knocked him out of the ring."

"I hope I have done so permanently," she said acidly.

The maid wheeled in the tea things, and Miriam sent her off with a wave of her hand. In that time I chose to speak bluntly to Miriam, for I had nothing to lose by doing so. "Will you tell me about your quarrel with Mr. Sarmento?" I asked, as she poured me a dish of tea.

She smiled. "Among the English, it is considered impolite to be so blunt."

"I have lived among them, but I do not observe all of their customs."

"So I see," she said, handing me my drink. I had not been quick enough to ask Miriam not to put sugar in my dish, so I accepted the sweetened mixture.

"Mr. Sarmento came to request my permission to speak to Mr. Lienzo for my hand," she continued. "It was a shockingly awkward thing, I can assure you, and I am unaccustomed to being confronted so boldly. Like you, Mr. Sarmento might better learn the English customs."

"What happened?" I kept my voice quiet, casual, disinterested.

"Mr. Sarmento said that he had a mind to speak to Mr. Lienzo and that he wished to inform me in advance. I told him that I had no knowledge of any business he might have with Mr. Lienzo. He accused me of being overly mannered, and said that I knew well what business he had. Seeing that I grew unacceptably warm, I corrected myself by saying he had no business that could possibly interest me. He became quite angry and said that it was foolish of me not to seek to marry him. Some other words were exchanged along the same topic—some rather loud words, I believe. Then he left, which you saw."

"Surely my uncle will not condone his behavior. Will you tell him?"

She was silent for a moment. "I do not think so. Sarmento has a promising future in the trade, you know, and my father-in-law quite depends upon him. I think my feelings toward him were made entirely clear, and so long as he bothers me no further, I see no reason to be petty."

"You are perhaps more generous than I would advise, but I admire your spirit," I told her. I sipped my sweet tea and wished it were something stronger. "Do you trust Mr. Sarmento? What I mean to say is, he works for my uncle, but he seems to have his own dealings upon the Exchange."

She set down her cup of tea and stared at me. "What do you know of his dealings?" Her face had grown stiff and inanimate.

"I have been spending a great deal of time in 'Change Alley, and I have seen him there, conducting affairs of which I know nothing."

Miriam smiled in a way that unnerved me. "Your uncle employs Mr. Sarmento, he does not own him. It is no uncommon thing for a man in Mr. Sarmento's position to pursue his own affairs as he has the opportunity."

"Why did Isaac wish to keep this quarrel from my ears?" I asked. I think I had been wondering this in my mind, and I had not meant to speak it.

If the question surprised Miriam, she answered with composure. "Isaac is a good servant. He does not wish to allow family business to become public. A quarrel in a private room between two unmarried people can be interpreted in many ways, especially by malicious tongues."

"True enough," I agreed with some embarrassment, stinging a bit from Miriam's exclusion of her wayward cousin from the family business.

She said nothing, and I shifted uncomfortably in the silence. I believe Miriam took some small pleasure at having me upon the rack, and smiled sweetly at me for some minutes before speaking. "Have you come on a social call, or do you have business with Mr. Lienzo?"

For reasons I cannot explain, this question put me at my ease. I settled comfortably into my chair. "Rather a bit of both, I think."

"I hope more the former than the latter," she said, smiling. "And if you have come to be sociable, then perhaps you would like to take a walk with me," she suggested. "I long to examine some of the goods at the market, and I would welcome your company."

I could hardly refuse the offer, so I silently determined to postpone my visit to South Sea House until the next morning. Miriam disappeared to ready herself, and after perhaps a quarter of an hour she reentered the room with an unexpected slowness, as though she were a child called forth for punishment. She held in her hand an envelope.

"There is a matter I must discuss, Mr. Weaver. I know not how to account for the generosity you showed in sending me so enormous a sum, and I do not wish to insult you, but considering the accompanying note, I believe there has been some small error. Your letter suggested that I had made a request of you. I cannot say how you made this error. Though I admit I am none the most sufficient in money, I am afraid I cannot accept a gift that is clearly not intended for me."

She handed me the envelope, which I absently dropped into my pocket. "Do you mean to say," I began incredulously, "that you sent me no note requesting this amount?"

"I fear I know not of what you speak." She looked down to conceal the blush that spread along her face and neck. "I sent no note."

I had been dealing with thieves and felons too long not to know when someone unpracticed in the art ineptly attempted a lie. Miriam now had reasons for not wishing to accept the money of me, and I would not press her to say why, or act as though I misbelieved her.

"I am greatly sorry to have caused such an embarrassment. I fear some prankster must have played a little joke upon us. We shall say no more of it."

Miriam smiled with gratitude and told me she wished to visit the market at Petticoat Lane, but by the time Miriam and I arrived it was late for the market, and much of the best of the perishables had been taken. Consequently, the market was not bursting with activity—yet it was far from empty. Around us was a busy crowd, principally of Jewish women, who strolled from vendor to vendor, examining the wares. Around us the hawkers shouted at us in Spanish, Portuguese, English, and even the language of the Tudescos—a curious mixture of Hebrew and German.

Miriam had, I was beginning to learn, a sense of purpose about her that ordered the chaos of the marketplace. She took her time, strolling from one stall to the next, examining this piece of linen or that of silk. Many of the merchants—mostly men of middle years who found themselves seduced by Miriam's beauty—called out to her as she passed. She offered a bow to each, but stopped only where she wished to examine goods.

"Mr. Lienzo prefers that when I make purchases, I buy all I can here," she explained to me. "He likes that the money should remain among our people."

"He is a conscientious man," I observed.

She said nothing at first, but there was a look of mischief in her eyes. "Too conscientious, I sometimes think. It is certainly possible to be overly nice in one's dedication to his community, don't you agree? If we are to be accepted in England, surely we must learn to act as the English do."

"We shall never be accepted here," I said with a conviction that surprised me. I did not think of myself as having strong feelings on this subject, but when she asked, I found these words flowed freely: "This is not our country. We shall never be English and our children will never be English. If we convert and join the Church of England, then our descendants shall always be known as the Jews who converted. We are what we are."

Miriam let out a little laugh—as though I had said something witty. "For an apostate, you are certainly very concerned about these matters, Cousin."

"Perhaps apostasy is but an opportunity to consider what is otherwise impossible to see," I said with a shrug.

A vendor called to Miriam in Portuguese, wanting her to examine his collection of household trinkets, but she waved him off and shouted a few friendly words in his tongue. "You are probably right," she said to me. "But even so, I think Mr. Lienzo could be a bit more"—she paused to consider her words—"a bit more English in his ways, I think. There is no need for him to wear that beard. No one else does. It only makes him look backward."

"I disagree," I said. "I think it shows he is his own man."

"You are your own man," Miriam observed, "and you wear no beard."

I laughed. "There are many ways to show one's independence."

Miriam stopped again and fingered a roll of India cloth. She held it up to the light for a moment and then to her own skin. It was a bright aqua blue—just the sort of color I knew her to admire.

"It look very nice for you," the stall-keeper told her eagerly.

"Thank you, Mr. Henriques," she said absently. "But I'm afraid I can ill afford it."

"I take you credit," he said eagerly.

Miriam looked at me for an instant. Perhaps owing to the nature of her original, and now-disavowed, request, she had no wish to have me see her take goods upon credit. She politely thanked the man and moved on.

"Do you ever wonder what I do with my time?" she asked me abruptly.

"I'm not sure what you mean," I said. Indeed I did wonder, but only in the way a man does when he finds a woman attractive. The thought of her doing anything—sewing or playing upon the harpsichord or practicing French—struck me as utterly charming.

"Do you wonder what I do to keep myself occupied?"

"I suppose it is like the life of any woman of means," I stammered, feeling somewhat foolish. "You take lessons in order to become accomplished in music and painting and languages. You learn to dance. You make social visits. You read."

"Only those books that are acceptable for young ladies, of course," Miriam said as we avoided a group of children who ran through the market paying no attention to the people or things with which they collided.

"Of course," I agreed.

"I think you have a superior understanding of the typical day of a woman of means," she said. "What is a typical day like for you, Benjamin?"

I almost stopped walking. "How do you mean?" I asked foolishly.

"In a typical day, what do you do? Surely it cannot be such a difficult question. I have asked Mr. Lienzo about his affairs, and he has given me a rather dull answer having to do with shipments and ledgers and letter-writing. I wonder if your life is less dull."

"I don't find it dull," I told her cautiously.

"Then perhaps you could tell me about it."

I could hardly do any such thing. How could my uncle ever forgive me if I told his daughter tales of beating upon prigs and hauling impecunious gentlemen to prison for their debts? "You understand that my business is to help people who require a man to find things for them," I began slowly, "sometimes people and sometimes goods. That is what I spend my time doing—finding things." I was rather delighted with the ambiguous way I had found to describe my activities.

She laughed. "I was hoping you would describe this process more fully. But if you feel the topic is too indelicate to discuss with a young woman, I quite understand." A devilish smile crossed her lips. "We may talk about something else instead. Tell me—do you have plans to marry?"

I could not imagine how she had summoned the courage to ask me so improper a thing, and yet she had—and boldly too. She knew she was being indecorous, and she cared not a whit. Indeed, she took some pleasure in violating the strictest rules of polite behavior in my company. I wondered if I should take this as a sign of her favor or of her belief that I was such a ruffian that I would know no better.

"There are women I, shall we say, admire," I told her. "But I have no marriage plans at the moment."

"I see." She continued to smile, taking pleasure in my discomfort. "It must be a fine thing to be a man and to go wherever you so please."

"It is a fine thing," I said, thrilled to think so quickly of a gallant reply, "but in the end, we only go wherever the women we admire please, so perhaps we have not the freedom you imagine."

"I hope you will marry well, Cousin." Her voice seemed carefully regulated. "Marry into money. That is my advice."

The words were out of my mouth before I could stop them. "Advice your late husband took."

"Yes," she agreed. "But I hope you will take better care of your wife's fortune than Aaron did of mine. I suppose he did not choose to be lost at sea, but he might have chosen not to take my independence with him. And anyone who would try to take away what little liberties I have—would he not be a villain?"

I was not sure I understood her. "Do you mean Mr. Sarmento?"

Miriam appeared prepared to respond, but then changed her mind. "I am done here," she explained. "We may return home. I know you have business to attend to." We began to walk toward Houndsditch. "Perhaps you could take me to the theatre one night," she suggested.

My heart leapt at the suggestion. "I should like nothing better. Do you believe my uncle would approve of your attending the theatre with me?"

"He may not relish the idea," she explained, "but he has permitted it in the past, provided I had protection against the dangers of that place. I believe your protection would be adequate."

"I would certainly never let any harm befall you."

"I am delighted to hear it," she said.

We were not at all far from my uncle's house, just turning upon Shoemaker Lane, when I noticed a large crowd at the end of the street. Perhaps twenty people gathered in a semicircle, hooting and laughing with what sounded to my ears like malice. I cautiously measured the composition of the crowd, which I saw to be mean and lowly.

"Miriam," I said deliberately, "you must get to safety." There was a milliner's shop not one hundred feet from us on the High Street. "Go into that shop and remain there. If there is a manservant, send him for the constable."

She screwed her face into a look of exasperation. "Surely you do not think me incapable—"

"Now!" I commanded through clenched teeth. "Get to that shop. I shall come for you in a moment." I watched her turn away and head toward the High Street.

No citizen of London requires that I speak of the danger of the crowds of this great metropolis. There was no saying when a mob would form, but once it did, it could rain violence and terror as sure as any storm, and it could dissipate just as quickly. I had seen riots begin over almost nothing at all, such as the apprehension of a pickpocket. I had once witnessed a mob form to guard a fellow caught nabbing a watch. I cannot say why or how it began, but as it awaited the constable, the crowd began to grow violent with the fellow, tossing him back and forth as though he were a dead dog at the Lord Mayor's Show. Out of anger and rage and frustration, this fellow struck back, laying one of his tormentors upon the ground with a mighty blow to the jaw. In retaliation, the mob jumped upon him, and someone—whose only motivation was the thrill of the act itself—found a loose piece of brick and threw it into the window of a glazier's shop. Under these fragile conditions, the noise was as a spark to dry kindling. Men and women were grabbed and beaten at random. A house was set afire. A little boy was trampled, nearly to death. Yet, within a half an hour, the mob was gone, like a wave of locusts, leaving nothing in its wake. Even the pickpocket had disappeared.

Having been witness to London riots, I knew to approach this crowd with caution, for anything at all might inflame it. As I grew closer, I could hear applause and shrill laughter, and I saw that the circle of rioters surrounded the old Tudesco who had given me the hourglass. A large man with a shaved head, punctuated with a bushy and drooping mustache of a dazzling orange color, stood holding the old man by his beard. He appeared to be a laborer of some sort—his clothing was cheap wool, torn and stained, showing dirt and muscle though the rips in the fabric. As I moved forward, the laborer pulled hard on the old man's beard, and the Tudesco staggered, held from the ground only by the force of the hand upon his whiskers.

"Stop!" I shouted as I pushed my way through the crowd. I could taste in the air their hatred and violence and rage. Day after day of hard and underpaid labor had left them hungry for a poor sod upon whom to exact revenge. These people might live in a different world from the men of Sir Owen's club, but they heard the same stories. Jews corrupted the nation, taking wealth away from Englishmen, attempting to turn a Protestant country into a Jewish one. I had been told of this manner of attack, but I had never before witnessed one. Not like this. I knew these people would not think kindly of my interference, and I concentrated on hiding my fear. "Let him go," I said to the laborer with the mustache. "If there has been a crime, send someone to fetch the constable."

This mustachioed man complied with the first part of my command. With a malicious grin he opened his hand and the old man fell to the ground. I could see he was conscious and not terribly hurt, but he lay still as though dead. Perhaps that was what he had learned to do in Poland or Russia or Germany, or whatever barbaric nation he had fled for the safety of Britain.

"No need to get a constable," the rude laborer told me. "We know 'ow to 'andle a thievin' Jew."

"What did this man do?" I demanded.

" 'E crucified Our Lord!" the mustache shouted to the crowd, who rewarded him with cheers and laughter. Several people shouted for me to get out of the way, but both the mustache and I ignored them. "And be-sides that," the ruffian continued in a much-softened voice, " 'e tried to pick me pocket, 'e did."

"Do you have witnesses?"

"Aye," he said, again in his mountebank voice, "these good people. They saw it all."

Again, laughter and cheering, now joined by shouts calling for the Jew to be tarred and feathered, crucified, have his nose slit, and, inexplicably, to be circumcised.

I held up my hand to silence the crowd, hoping my performance of au-thority would have some sway with them. It seemed to for a moment. "Hold with your rough music, friends," I said. "If there is justice to be done, I'll not stand in your way. But let me hear what the peddler says."

I reached down and helped the man to his feet. He looked around, his eyes hard and bloodshot. I suppose I expected him to stand with quivering lips, like a child trying not to cry, but he only looked like a man out in the cold with insufficient clothing, braced against the elements, knowing he could do naught but endure them.

"Tell me the truth, old fellow," I said. "I shall do my best to see that it goes as easy as possible with you. Did you try to pick this man's pocket?"

He turned to me and began to speak excitedly in a language I did not understand. It took me a moment to realize that he spoke Hebrew, but with the strangest accent I had ever heard. True, had he spoken it with an orator's clarity, I should have had some trouble understanding him, but in his frantic speech I managed to fix upon a few words: *"Lo lekachtie devar."* I did not take a thing.

He saw that I could not easily understand him, and stopped speaking in the ancient language, again reverting to gesture. He once more put his hand upon his heart. "I take nothing," he said.

His denial could not have surprised me. What else would he say? In my heart I knew that there was at least the possibility that he had committed the crime. Because he was a kindly old man did not mean that he could not have attempted to pick a pocket. I cannot say it was the way he spoke or the look in his eyes or the desperately earnest way he held his body that convinced me—not so much as it was my desire to protect him from this senseless mob—but I believed him as I would have believed him had he told me that the sun shone above.

"This man," I announced in the most commanding voice I could muster, "says he tried to steal nothing. What we have here is a simple mis-understanding. So go about your business, and I shall see that he goes about his."

The crowd was still, and for a moment I thought that I had triumphed, but I saw that the matter was now a contest, not between man and mind-less throng, but between two men.

"It's you that'll be about yer business," the mustache told me in a shrill if commanding voice. "Or we can take care of two as easy as one."

He began moving toward me, and I knew that it was time to set aside my more gentle nature. I took from my pocket a loaded pistol, and with a strained gesture I pulled back the hammer with my thumb. "Disperse," I said, "before someone gets himself hurt." I backed up a bit, grabbing the old man's arm and pulling him with me.

The crowd moved forward, as if they were all one being controlled by a single will. The tone of the confrontation now changed dramatically. They were not angry or enraged anymore—they struck me instead as brute beasts that, once set upon a certain course, had not the capacity to alter that course.

"You can't fire upon us all," the mustache said with a forced sneer. It was incumbent upon him to be brave, as the gun was aimed at his chest.

"True enough, but someone must die first, and I suspect it shall be you. And once I discharge this pistol I still have this hangar at my side. You'll win in the end; I've no doubt of it. The mob shall have the old peddler. These is no question of who shall win the battle, only the number of ca-sualties."

The mustache was quiet for a moment and then told the old man that he should consider himself warned. He then turned on his heel and, grumbling loudly about the enslavement of the Englishman in his own country, he turned away. In a moment the crowd disbanded as though they had all just awoken from dreams, and I stood alone with the Tudesco, who cast a glazed stare upon me.

"I thank you," he said quietly. He sucked in his breath in an effort to calm himself, but I could see that he shook violently and was on the verge of tears. "You give my life." Scattered about his feet, his trinkets looked to me like a child's playthings overturned by a petulant temper.

I shook my head, denying his words and the swell of passions I held at bay. "They would not have killed you. They would only have roughed you up a bit."

He shook his head. "No. You give my life."

With quiet dignity he stooped to collect his goods. Overcome with sadness, I dropped some silver in his tray—I don't know how much, it might have reckoned in shillings or pounds—and turned toward the milliner's shop to find Miriam, but as I turned she stood directly behind me.

It was hard to read her face. She might have been horrified at the violence she had been witness to, impressed by my response to it, relieved that no real harm had been done.

"Why are you not in the shop?" I snapped. Perhaps I responded too strongly, but my sense of perspective had abandoned me.

She let out a little laugh, which she used to hide her embarrassment. "I thought this would be my last opportunity to see the Lion of Judah fight."

My heart was still pounding from the encounter with the mob, and I had to concentrate to keep from growing furious. "Miriam, I cannot take you with me to the theatre or anywhere else unless I can be certain that you will listen to me should there be a threat."

"I am sorry, Benjamin." She nodded solemnly, perhaps for the first time thinking seriously on the danger. "You are quite right. Next time I shall listen. I promise."

"I should hope there will be no next time."

When I turned back to the old man, he had gathered up his things and begun to hurry along to whatever decrepit hovel he called home, where he would try to forget what had happened.

"His kind are used to far worse," Miriam said. "And they're not used to being pulled from the flames. Your friend will remember this as a good day."

Unsure how to respond, I told her it was dangerous to linger. We headed away from the crowd and I saw her home to safety.

Once I had discharged myself of her, I remembered the envelope in which she had returned the money she claimed not to have asked of me. I marveled at its lightness, for it could hardly contain even one of the coins I had sent her. I tore it open and discovered a negotiable Bank of England note for the amount of twenty-five pounds.

I folded the note and put it into my purse, but I could not help but wonder. Why did she not merely return the silver I had given her? And if she had so little money, as she had claimed, how did she obtain this note?

Twenty

I WAS VERY SHAKEN by my encounters that day, and the hour had grown too late for business, so instead of visiting South Sea House, I took to wandering. I walked, with no particular destination in mind, avoiding the gauntlet of beggars as I passed London Wall and the Bedlam Hospital, where the insane were locked away, and where I feared I might be driven if I did not soon discover more about these strange dealings.

I stopped into a tavern and took myself a mug of ale, ate some cold meat, and passed an hour or two by conversing with the friendly tapman, who recollected me from my days as a pugilist. When I stepped outside into the smoky air of the late afternoon, I realized that I was upon Fore Street, but very close to Moor Lane, where Nahum Bryce, once my father's printer, kept his shop. Cheered by the thought that I might indeed put my time to good use, I walked briskly to Moor Lane and found the shop at the sign of the three turtles.

During the height of the day sunlight would flood this spacious shop, but now, in the approaching dusk, candles had been struck throughout, making it bright enough to read comfortably. The shop was long and a bit narrow, the walls almost entirely lined with volumes, and in the back stood a spiral stairway that rose to a second level of bookshelves. I was nearly overwhelmed by the scents of leather and wax and flowers, for there was a great abundance of tulips in vases near where the clerk stood behind his counter.

I passed by a few browsers—an old gentleman and a pleasing girl of about seventeen with an older lady I took to be her mother—and I approached the clerk. He was a boy of perhaps fifteen or so, probably an apprentice, and I could see that anything I might say to him should be vastly less interesting than watching the young lady leaf through an octavo.

"Is Mr. Nahum Bryce within?"

The boy startled himself out of his befuddlement and told me he would return shortly.

In a few moments a plump woman of middle years—never quite pretty, but perhaps she had once been attractive in a sturdy sense—emerged from the back, a pile of manuscripts in one hand. She set them down and turned to me with a kind of polite and proper smile. She wore black—a widow's attire, and her hair was neatly hidden under a modest, perhaps oversized, bonnet.

"May I be of some assistance?" she asked.

"I wished to speak with Mr. Nahum Bryce," I began.

"Mr. Bryce was taken from us a little more than a year ago," she said with an awkward half-smile. "I am Mrs. Bryce."

I bowed at her politely. "I am sorry to hear of it, madam. I cannot claim to have known your husband, but I am saddened all the same."

"You are very kind," she told me.

I informed her that I desired a private word with her, so we retreated to one of the far corners of the shop, all but invisible to anyone who did not go into the nook just past the clerk's station. "I am interested, madam, in knowing if you have been approached at any time in recent months by a Mr. Samuel Lienzo, who might have wished to publish a pamphlet."

Mrs. Bryce furrowed her brow. "Mr. Lienzo, you say? I haven't heard that name in some time."

"So you know of him?" I asked eagerly.

She nodded. "Oh yes. My husband published a few things by him some time back, as I recall. But nothing in recent years, you know. Mr. Bryce found his writing a bit somber—all that Bank of England and Parliamentary measures. He preferred to keep things lighter."

"But you have recently published works that concern Exchange Alley. What of 'Change Alley Laid Open, which I noted on the title page you published just this year?"

She laughed softly. "Yes, that's true. But that kind of harangue against stock-jobbery, you know, always sells quite well. Mr. Lienzo, now he sought to publish serious material, and Mr. Bryce had little stomach for that. He preferred much more entertaining matters. Novels and plays and delightful histories. After I undertook the burden of managing this shop, I tried my hand at that political nonsense, but it never earned me much for my trouble. It's no surprise to me that my husband abandoned it."

"Do you have any idea," I inquired, "whom Mr. Lienzo might have sought for a publisher?"

"Yes." She nodded gravely. "I know he had dealings with Christopher Hodge, who kept his shop just near here on Grub Street. But as for that unfortunate"—she began, but I did not permit her to continue, for as we had been speaking a dashing young gentleman began to descend the spiral stairway assisting a beautiful young lady. I am infrequently so struck by beauty that I allow it to interfere with my business, but this case was rather different, for the lady in question was Miriam.

I could hardly contain my emotions at seeing her twice in a single day, but I understood at once that I was not to step forward and express my delight. She had changed her clothing, and was now dressed in a charming gown of green with an ivory stomacher and a white petticoat with black spots. She wore a handsome bonnet upon her head, one that matched her gown, and she appeared like the neat and respectable London ladies she so admired. Her companion was something of a dashing spark, dressed in a velvet outer coat flaring widely at the knees, with wide gold buttons and ample gold lace. His wig, long and dark, bespoke knowledge of the finest peruke-makers, and a muslin cravat about his neck set off his sharply angled, handsome, and pale face to advantage.

Miriam was in the company of a wealthy gentleman.

I knew that we could not be seen from where we stood, so I pointed to the gentleman and interrupted Mrs. Bryce. "Gad," I swore, though keeping my tone low. "I believe I know that gentleman. Unless I am mistaken, I attended the same college at Oxford as he. But for the life of me I cannot remember how he is called."

"That, sir, is Mr. Philip Deloney," Mrs. Bryce said.

I snapped my fingers. "The very name. Does he come here often?"

"Mr. Deloney is not much of a reader, I fear, but he is wont to use my shop as a discreet meeting place with his young ladies, and he will buy several volumes, chosen at random, I believe, from time to time in order to earn my silence."

"Ah, that Deloney was always something of a rake. Does he bring many ladies here?"

"I should have thought it a great number when I was a young lady.

Now that I am a widow, it doesn't seem so very many. Perhaps for a gentleman of his stripe, he brings too few." Mrs. Bryce let out a quiet laugh. "I think he's very handsome," she said in a whisper.

"Oh, I believe he would tell you that much himself, madam," I noted as Deloney escorted Miriam from the shop. I turned to Mrs. Bryce. "Thank you for your help. But I must dash off now and renew the acquaintance." I bowed briefly and walked to the door.

I was pleased to see that the two of them had stepped sufficiently away from the shop that I might avoid detection. Deloney kissed Miriam's hand and uttered some words I was too distant to hear and then assisted her into a hackney. He watched as it rode off, and then headed toward Fore Street. I kept pace behind him, watching as he secured a coach for himself.

I was determined to learn more of this gentleman, so when the hackney pulled from the curb, I dashed off, putting the pressure on my stronger leg as I began my sprint, that I might reach the coach without doing too much injury to myself. The street was good and full, so it was none too difficult to overtake the coach. Making as little noise as I could, I jumped upon the back.

As I clung to the bouncing hackney, it occurred to me briefly to wonder why exactly I did what I did. Certainly I had developed a fondness for Miriam, but the fondness hardly warranted such drastic action. I could only think that the matter of my father's death had somehow infected all the other concerns of my life—everything seemed urgent. Even so, I cannot claim that it was my inquiry that occupied my thoughts as I dashed after the fiend who had dared to kiss Miriam's hand. All that mattered to me, in that instant, was learning who he was and what hold he had over a woman whose heart I wished for myself.

I easily held on to the coach, for in the years after my boxing injury one of my many disreputable employments had been working as a footman—or I should say, pretending to be a footman—with a wealthy family in Bath. I had planned to insinuate myself into the household, and then, come the earliest opportunity, rob it most mercilessly. But I soon learned that it is one thing to take from anonymous strangers, quite another to take the jewelry from a pleasant lady one had been escorting about town for a month. So I had settled for obtaining an intimacy with the eldest daughter and then disappearing one night, taking only a few pounds for my most immediate needs.

My familiarity with riding upon the back of a carriage left me dexterous enough to deal with the coachman when he looked backward to see me clinging there. Pressing my head against the back so I would not lose my hat, I reached with my free hand into my purse and came up with a shilling, which I showed to the driver. I then put a finger to my lips to indicate silence. He held up two fingers which indicated he wished for two shillings. I, in return, held up three, to let him know that I should be grateful for his looking the other way. With a smile that told me that he would say nothing even if put to torture, the coachman rode on.

The coach made its way toward the vicinity of the Royal Exchange, and then west on Cheapside, until I thought that our destination was prayer at St. Paul's Cathedral. But Mr. Deloney had a much more dissolute intent, for his destination was that notorious place known as White's Chocolate House, the most fashionable place for gaming in the city.

White's was located in a pleasing enough structure on St. James's Street, near the Covent Garden Market. I had never been inside, for my gaming days were long behind me; I had set them aside when I set aside my less honest methods of earning my bread. White's had not been the place of mode in my younger days, and I had not sought it out since my return to the city.

When the hackney stopped, I jumped off and slid into the shadows as Deloney paid the coachman and went inside. I then emerged and, true to my promise, gave the man three shillings and reminded him that he had never seen me. He touched his cap and rode off.

Dusk had almost entirely given way to darkness, and I stood upon the street wondering what I should do once I entered. I knew so little of this place, and I did not want to make my presence there obvious. It was the abode of the wealthy and the fashionable and the privileged, and, while I was not afraid of such men, I did not know that I would be best served by barging in and nosing my way around until I found the man I sought.

The dark streets were far from abandoned; folk walked about me on the road in the near distance, including the vast number of jades who haunted this part of town, and I should have been more cautious than I was, for as I stood there, foolishly gaping, I felt the sharp poke of a blade pressed against my back.

It had not been pressed too hard—it had perhaps broken the skin a little, but no more. From its feel I thought it to be a hangar, not a knife. That meant more distance between the tip of the blade and the hand that held it. Such a distance worked in my favor.

I remained motionless for a lengthy second until I heard the culprit say, "Give me yer purse, and I won't 'urt ye none."

I could hear by his voice that he was but a lad—no more than twelve or thirteen, and though I could not turn my head to see him, I believed myself to be more than a match for the young rogue, who could possess little knowledge of a weapon he had certainly stolen. I took a quick step forward and to my right, and then, to confuse him, spun widely to my left. While he jabbed into the empty air where I had stood, I grabbed his wrist hard and squeezed until the hangar, old and rusty, slipped from his grasp and bounced upon the ground. Keeping my eye upon him, I picked up his weapon, and then twisted his arm behind him and forced him face-first against a wall.

As I had moved the boy, I noticed that a pair of gentlemen looked up at my proceedings with uncommon interest, but I could pay them no attention now. I turned my attention to this little thief, who was, as I had suspected, quite young. He was also thin, poorly dressed, and the owner of a surprisingly unpleasant odor. "You want something from my purse, do you?" I asked.

I admit that his courage impressed me. "Aye. What 'ave ye?"

I let go, took a step back, and reached into my purse. "Here's a tuppence," I said. "I want you to run an errand for me. If you do it right, I'll give you a shilling."

He turned around slowly. "A'right then, sir. Let's see the money."

Now one of the two gentlemen began to shout at me. "You're not going to let him run off, are you?"

"If you were so interested in his apprehension, why did you not assist me?" I spat back.

"I wasn't interested in his apprehension, but in your apprehending him. *That's* what I wagered."

"Don't whine about it," his friend snickered. "You've lost, Harry. Now pay up."

Such are the sort of men one encounters in front of White's Chocolate House.

I turned from these gamblers to the boy, to whom I gave Elias's address and a brief message and sent him off, hoping he would return in the expectation of a shilling rather than settle for his tuppence. I expected Elias would be at home, as I believed that his recent celebratory expedition would have left him financially unable to enjoy many late nights for a week or so. While my thieving errand boy was gone, I kept a watchful eye upon the door to be certain that Mr. Deloney did not depart, and I kept an eye on my surroundings as well, unwilling to be taken as a cull a second time. It seemed to me an interminable wait as I paced back and forth upon St. James's Street, watching, as with each moment of increasing darkness the strollers of Covent Garden became more vicious and desperate in appearance. At last, within the hour, Elias appeared, the boy on his tail.

"Where's me shilling?" the young thief demanded.

"And mine?" Elias echoed. "I deserve something for this imposition."

I tossed the boy his shilling.

"What about me 'angar?" he asked.

"You will only use it to perpetrate more robberies, and with your skills, you should soon perish at the end of a rope."

"It beats perishin' of 'unger," he told me petulantly.

"Fair enough," I agreed, and tossed him his weapon. It was an easy toss, but he missed and chased it as it bounced upon the roadway.

I turned to Elias. "I'd like to take a turn about White's, and I can think of no better companion than you for such an expedition."

He clapped his hands together like a child. "That's splendid news. I'm sure you know that one must have money to enjoy White's," Elias assured me. "Or let me rephrase that," he said with a grin. "One most likely has money, but I believe *two* require it."

"I shall pay your way," I assured him.

"It is my pleasure to serve you, Weaver. Allow me to introduce you to London's foremost gaming academy."

I paid the small entrance fee for the two of us, and we thus entered into the strange world of London wagering. Places such as White's, with their desperation and joy and suspense, are but miniatures of 'Change Alley, and indeed as much can be won, or, more likely, lost, at a card table in a single evening than in an entire season of stock-jobbing.

Though it was early in the evening, White's was already quite full of pleasure seekers who huddled about large tables strewn through the room, playing at faro or ombre or simpler card games, rolling the hazard dice across tables, or any of a variety of house ventures that I could not fathom. The room smelled thick of tobacco and strong beer and sweaty clothing, and boomed with conversations too loud and too cheerful, occasionally punctuated by cries of glee or groans of wretchedness. Handsome young women, who I suspect may have had other duties, served a variety of drinks to the patrons, but among them I saw none of the chocolate of which this business's name bespoke. And what stood before me was only the main room of White's. I knew there were small rooms all about me for private gatherings, high-stakes games, and rendezvous with ladies.

"Now," Elias said to me, "what new adventure of yours brings you to this place? I do not believe you are hard on your luck and wish to raise a few guineas."

I chose to say nothing to Elias about Miriam. I had no interest in hearing any more of his observations on widows and pretty Jewesses, so I merely told him I had followed a suspicious gentleman to this place.

"And what is this man that he made you suspicious?"

"I didn't like his look," I replied impatiently as I scanned the room.

"That will leave you following half of London," Elias muttered, none too pleased with my evasion. "Well," he said, "perhaps this is my good fortune as your philosophy master, for there is no better place for you to see the laws of probability better displayed than in a gaming house."

"If such laws are so apprehensible, why do so many men lose?"

"Because they are fools and know no better. Or, like me, they are ruled by their passions rather than their minds. And yet we have tools to beat the odds. It is astonishing to me, you know, this new world of philosophy in which we live. For the first time since the Creation itself we are truly learning how to think about what we see." He paused for a moment. "How best to demonstrate?" he wondered aloud.

He then excused himself for a moment, which was all it took for him to find a gentleman willing to engage in a simple game of chance with us. He was a hollow-cheeked fellow of indeterminate age, who slouched at a small table, large enough only for four men. His arm guarded a pewter mug of punch as though one of us might attempt to rip it from his protection.

"This gentleman has agreed to play with us," Elias told me. He then turned to our friend. "What return will you give on a simple coin toss?"

"Fifty percent," the man droned, "betting a pound." He sipped his punch.

"Very good. Give me a pound, Weaver."

A pound! He was daring enough with my money, but I had no wish to argue in front of this stranger. Reluctantly, I gave him the coin.

"Now, our friend here is going to toss the coin into the air, and you must guess, before it lands, if it be heads or tails."

Before I had a chance to object, the coin was in the air, and I called heads. It landed in the dealer's hand, but Elias gestured for him to hold off uncovering it. "What do you think were your chances of being right?"

"One in two, I should think."

"Precisely." He nodded to the gamester, who revealed that I had guessed correctly, thus winning ten shillings. With a slowness that revealed his reluctance, he opened his purse and counted out the ten coins.

"Now we do it again," Elias announced.

He signaled the man to toss the coin once more, and I again called it heads. I was right once more.

Elias grinned, as though his wisdom were responsible for my luck. "You have guessed heads twice in a row. Do your chances diminish if you were right the first time?"

"Of course not."

"So you have the same chance of getting a thousand throws right if you guess heads every time?"

"I believe I understand. That the chances of heads coming up every time are smaller than the chances of both heads and tails coming up. But in the end, the coin has only two sides, and each toss must be a matter of one in two. Though I suspect that the more one tosses the coin, the greater the chances of the two sides coming down in the same number."

"Quite right," he said. "Now, let us take your money and turn to cards. We shall play the same game, only guess whether the card be black or red." Elias removed from his coat a deck of cards, which he shuffled, fanned, and presented to me.

Our companion pulled a card and asked me my opinion; I told him red. He turned the first card over, and it was indeed red. With a look of disgust, he handed over the ten shillings.

"Great gad, Weaver. You're the luckiest man who ever lived."

"I'll say so," our friend told us. He bowed and disappeared into the crowd.

Elias wistfully watched him depart. "Oh, rabbit it! But I suppose he has taught us what we need to know. Now let me ask you, can you continue to bet upon red as you might upon heads?"

I considered this for a moment. "There is no limit but chance to the number of times a card might turn up, but there is only a particular number of red or black cards in a deck."

"Precisely." Elias nodded, clearly pleased with my answer. "There was a time, and not so very long ago, that even an experienced cardplayer would always think of the chances as one in two, no matter what the deck had produced so far. But we have learned to think differently, to calculate possibilities. If two black cards have already been produced, the chances are slightly less than one in two. If you have produced twenty black cards and five red cards, the chances are now significantly greater on each turn of producing a red card. To me this idea is obvious, but two hundred years ago, it would not have occurred to anyone—not a living man, you understand. It does not even now occur to most gamesters, but it must occur to you, Weaver, if you are to outsmart whoever has committed these crimes, for guessing the motivation of your fellowman is no different from guessing the face of a coin or card. You must only determine what is likely and act upon that supposition."

"In the meantime, I must catch up with that gentleman." I spotted Deloney at one of the gaming tables. He had a look of no great joy on his face, and I could only assume that the cards had not been turning up as he might like. "That's the man I seek." I pointed.

"The devil," Elias breathed. "Why, that's Philip Deloney."

"You know him?"

"Of course. He's the sort of man who makes a point of showing himself at all the most fashionable events, and by coincidence, so am I. He has attempted to interest me in projects from time to time—I recall he had one for building a series of canals to connect the metropolis to the rest of the island, but I never overly much trusted his wares."

"He must sell dubious projects indeed if you would not bite," I observed.

"It's the man, you know. Never buy from someone who cannot manage his own affairs, for how could he, of all people, have discovered a likely project?"

"Perhaps you could introduce me," I suggested.

"I shall require a few shillings."

"Whatever for?"

"To keep myself occupied while you converse with your suspicious wastrel."

I handed Elias my winnings, and he then led me over to Deloney, whose face was now red with anguish. It took a few moments for Elias to secure his attention, but at last Deloney looked over in his direction, and Elias rewarded him with a bow.

"Mr. Deloney. I trust the cards are treating you well."

"You trust badly, Gordon," he grunted. "I am cursed this evening."

"Allow me," Elias continued, paying no attention to Deloney's mood, "to introduce my friend, Mr. Benjamin Weaver."

Deloney muttered something by way of greeting, and then turned to me again. "Are you not that buck I've seen in the ring?"

I bowed. "That was some years ago, but I did spend time as a pugilist."

"You've cleaned yourself up now, haven't you? Turned gentleman, I see. Now, perhaps you'd like to do me a favor and beat this fellow into submission." Deloney gestured to a diminutive and ashen man of advancing years who stood with a deck of cards in hand. They played some sort of game I did not know; it involved Deloney's guessing the numerical value of a certain number of cards. And guessing rather badly, if his opinion was any measure.

"Say, Gordon—" He turned to Elias; but Elias had already slipped off to a backgammon table, where he insinuated himself with a group of young sparks. "Well"—Deloney turned to me—"you wouldn't have an extra guinea upon you?"

"Your luck is about to turn, then?"

"It is. I would consider a loan of one guinea between gentlemen to be of the greatest service, and I should be pleased to pay you back at any time after this evening."

I smirked only a little at his sudden decision to think of me as a fellow-*gentleman*, but I showed him nothing of my thoughts, and with affected good cheer handed him the guinea. Deloney's face betrayed some surprise, even suspicion at the ease with which I gave up the coin, but he took it all the same and set it down upon the table.

The dealer began to lay out cards, and Deloney gave orders to indicate that he either wished another one or wished the dealer to reshuffle. I cannot say I understood the game, but I understood the look upon his face as the dealer slapped a king down upon the pile and collected the guinea.

Deloney shrugged and began to walk away from the table, but he spoke to me as he did so, indicating that he wished me to follow suit. "That's the difficulty with playing these high-stakes games—one rarely plans on it, you know, and doesn't bring enough of the ready to cover the expenses. I believe you will agree, Mr. Weaver, that a loan of two guineas is hardly more of an imposition than a loan of one, and should you feel kind enough to advance me this sum, it should be my great honor to buy you a glass of punch."

I could see there was no talking to this man without surrendering the coin. I handed over my last guinea, afraid to calculate the small sum I had remaining. He smiled, held it in his hand as though to gauge the weight, and then called to a passing strumpet for two glasses of punch.

"I think of myself as something of a physiognomist," he said, "and I can see that you are a man of honor. Give me your hand, sir. I am glad to have made this acquaintance."

I shook his hand. "As am I. For as you yourself noted, I am rather new to the world of fashion, and should welcome the experience of a man such as yourself, who, I can tell from one look, is vastly familiar with such things."

"You pay me too much of a compliment. But I do enjoy spending my time in places such as White's. It is such a wonderful entertainment, even when one loses."

"If I may be so indelicate, you must have at your disposal a vast sum in order to lose at a place such as this."

He bowed again. "I flatter myself that I am sufficient."

"I suppose I too am sufficient," I ventured, "but a man must always strive to be better. Yet I no longer wish to labor for my money. You know, Mr. Deloney, what I should like more than anything else is to find myself a pretty lass that comes with as pretty a fortune."

Deloney smiled. "You are a well-enough-looking man. I see no reason that you should not be able to find such a lass."

"Ah, but fathers and such. Always wanting their daughters to marry into money. And while I am comfortable, I assure you, I am by no means in a position of opulence."

"Widows," Deloney announced. "Widows are the very thing. They are in command of their own fortunes, you know. And they are not bound by the strictest bonds of virtue as are young ladies with their fathers. Though I have broken some of those shackles, I assure you."

He laughed heartily, showing me a mouth full of teeth that I wished to see scattered about the floor. Was it for this scoundrel that Miriam had asked to borrow money of me—that she might support his gaming? The thought was too humiliating to yield anything but rage, yet I wished to learn more of Deloney, so I laughed along with this man I wanted only to pummel.

Just then our lass returned with our two glasses of punch. She curtsied deeply, that we might enjoy a better view of her bosoms, which jutted forth from her bodice. Deloney was so transfixed by the sight that he did not even flinch when she announced that the punch cost a shilling a glass. He handed her the guinea, which she clutched in her long, charming fingers.

"If you allow me to keep this coin," she cooed, "I shall make it worth your while."

Deloney reached out and stroked her chin with his knuckles. "I'll take the coins, my sweet, but I shall seek you out before I leave, and perhaps we may reach an understanding."

She giggled as though Deloney had displayed unprecedented wit, and then reluctantly handed over the remaining nineteen shillings.

I took a sip and watched her disappear though the crowd. The punch might have been overpriced, but they poured rum generously, and it felt hot and comforting as it went down. A few such glasses and any man might cheerfully mortgage his house for an extra hand of whist.

Deloney drank deep of his punch and grinned at nothing I could discern.

"Widows," I said, in the hopes of continuing my line of inquiry. "Have you such a widow at your disposal now?" I kept my voice controlled and even.

"Several, I promise you. Several. I have just come from extracting funds of one of them. So very pretty and so very gullible. She's a charming Jessica whom I have made to believe I should liberate from her Shylock." He paused. "As I recall, you are yourself a member of that ancient race of Hebrews, are you not? I hope you take no offense at the conquest of your women."

I managed a hearty enough laugh. "Only so long as you don't object to my conquest of your Christian ladies."

He joined me in my laughter. "Oh, there are more than enough of those for everyone." He gulped at his punch. "I have devised the most absolutely clever method in the world to convince her to hand over to me enormously pleasing sums of money."

I could not contain my disappointment when he paused. "You must tell me," I proceeded.

"I can't let the secret out to just anyone. Yet, you have trusted me. Perhaps it is only fair."

Elias then picked the most damnable moment to interrupt me, with none other than Sir Owen Nettleton as his companion. "Look here, Weaver. I have found a mutual acquaintance."

The baronet clapped Elias upon the back. "I so rarely get to see him when he isn't taking my blood," Sir Owen said to me, and then turning, he saw my companion. "Ah, Mr. Deloney."

Deloney only bowed, but his face grew pallid and his lip quivery. "Sir Owen. Always a delight to see you, sir." He drank his remaining punch— half a glass, and enough, I would have thought, to fell a man twice his size—in a single gulp and turned to me. "May I know where you lodge, sir, so I know where I may pay my respects?"

I handed him my card, and he bowed and departed.

"I don't think it my place to dictate your companions," Sir Owen said, "but I hope you do not put too much stock in that man."

"I have just met him tonight. How do you know him, sir?"

"He frequents White's and some other gaming houses I have been known to visit. And he is avoided by all, for he owes every gentleman in this city money. Either from his pernicious *borrowing*, though I insult the very term by aligning it with him, or by his false projecting."

"False projecting?" Elias asked. "Not merely inept projecting?"

"Oh, I think with Deloney there is nothing but guile—harvesting chickens from cows, or turning the Thames into a great pork pie. Deloney invents them and sells shares for ten pounds or twenty and then runs off, leaving his victims with a pretty piece of paper for their trouble."

"Hmm. I have lent him two guineas," I said meekly.

Sir Owen laughed. "He owes me ten times that, which is why he scurried away like a rodent. You will never see that money again, I can assure you, but be thankful you escaped so cheap."

"Where does he reside?" I inquired.

Sir Owen laughed again. "I hardly know where such a man might live. In the kennel drains is where he belongs. If you wish to beat your money out of him, I shall offer you 10 percent of mine if you can get it. But I think you are wasting your time. That money is gone and never to return."

I made some further conversation with Sir Owen, who then excused himself to go chase the very serving lass who had offered her services to Deloney. Elias suggested that I lend him more money for play, but unwilling to extend myself any further, I told him I thought we should both go home to bed.

TWENTY-ONE

AT A TIME OF the morning that was far too early for social calls and concerns of society, London's financial center was already thick with activity. The sky was as yet cloudless, and the day bright, so I shielded my eyes as I stepped out of the coach. I lingered for a moment from my elevated position and marveled at the street, a sea of wigs, as men rushed from this shop to that, from one coffeehouse to another, from the Bank to the vendor upon the street who hawked discounted lottery tickets.

South Sea House on Threadneedle Street, near Bishopsgate, was an enormous building, and struck me with its carved marble and life-sized portraits that decorated the lobby as an institution steeped in tradition. One would hardly suspect from its façade that the Company was less than ten years old and that its purpose—trade with the South American coast—had never been realized. There was something about the way people scurried through the lobby, the anxious, suspicious hurry in their walk, that made South Sea House little more than an adjunct of Jonathan's Coffeehouse—that is, an extension of the Royal Exchange itself—and the men who conducted business there simply another order of stock-jobber. If stock-jobbing was but financial villainy, as so many had argued, then this was certainly one of the great breeding grounds of corruption in the Kingdom.

No doubt part of the hivelike buzz of South Sea House arose from the Company's sense of urgency. This was an organization, as Mr. Adelman had told me, on the verge of striking a momentous bargain within the ministry—a bargain that I now understood would involve the exchange of millions of pounds. Millions of pounds—who could imagine such sums? This bargain would certainly be opposed by the Bank of England, whose even more auspicious building stood less than a quarter-hour's walk from here. I did not know if I would find the answers to the mysteries of my father's death in South Sea House, but I felt to some small degree emboldened by the name I had taken from Mr. Bloathwait's desk: Virgil Cowper. I had not an inkling who Virgil Cowper was nor how he might offer me any assistance, but I repeated his name over and over again in my head, as though it were a little prayer or a song to ward off evil.

I stood for some minutes considering my course as the business of South Sea House flowed about me like some great river of pecuniary interest. At last I looked for someone to direct me, but as I did so I noted a scurvy-looking fellow making his way through the front doors and toward the back of the lobby. There was no particular reason for him to draw my attention, only that he was large and ugly and his clothing was none the best. By pure coincidence our eyes met, and we both looked upon each other for the most fleeing of moments; in that instant I knew him to be the very man who had set upon me on Cecil Street when I had been pursued by the mad hackney coachman.

We paused for a moment, he and I, and stared across this swell of people, neither of us knowing what came next. I could not simply grab him, he was too far away, and I suppose he wondered if he could successfully elude me. He had nothing to fear in the eyes of the law, for what could I do? I could hardly bring him before a magistrate, as I had no second witness to corroborate my testimony. I could, however, beat him mercilessly, and if he knew who I was, he knew I should not hesitate to do so. I thought, just for an instant, for time moved slowly as we stared at each other, of the fear I had felt that night as I believed myself to know what my father had felt just before the hooves of horses trampled upon him, and I yearned to hurt this miscreant. And so, with a sudden resolve, I made my move, and rudely shoving other visitors aside, I dashed forward.

He was far closer to the door than I, and he too had been poised to flee. The thief, most certainly accustomed to evading constables and watchmen upon the patrol, moved quickly and gracefully, evading the men around us. The crowds of South Sea House, who had come to buy and sell, invest and exchange, hardly cared for two men who pursued each other madly across the lobby, and I hardly cared for them, trying to keep my eye upon my prey as a hunting beast attempts to fix his sights upon one creature in the herd.

He reached the door, and I was hard upon him, but I slipped while climbing up the marble stairs, and collided with a portly gentleman just as I threw open the doors to see where this knave had run. When I looked around me, I could see no sign of him. I thought for a moment of asking other travelers upon the street if they had noted a large, ill-formed ruffian, but in London mine was a useless question, for where was there not a man of that description? I therefore abandoned all hope of catching him and returned to South Sea House.

The presence of this man here only served to give credit to Elias's claims that one of the chartered companies was behind these crimes, for what business would a man who had attacked me on a deserted street have at a place like this—unless the company employed him for some nefarious purpose? By returning to South Sea House, I quite possibly ventured into the very heart of villainy, into the lair of the people who had murdered two men and who had attempted my life as well. Feeling the grip upon my hangar—more for comfort than because I believed I would need to draw it—I returned to the lobby of this great institution that sought to rival the Bank of England.

I thus proceeded up a flight of stairs and asked a gentleman who appeared to do business in the building if there was an office where I might find one Virgil Cowper. He mumbled that he toiled in the office dealing in stock-holder records, and then directed me up yet another flight. There I found a cramped room where some dozen or so clerks were at work with some business I could not divine. Each desk was weighted down with enormous, if orderly, piles of paper, and I watched as the clerks took pieces, made some markings upon them, annotated ledger books, replaced the papers in another pile, and then started anew. I asked the scribe nearest to the door where I might find a Mr. Cowper, and he gestured to a desk toward the back.

I could not imagine what an interview with Cowper might yield, but I invested this man with no small importance. I had discovered his name, and I had followed his trail here. I had followed Elias's advice and taken probabilities into account, and they, in turn, had led me to a man whose connection with Bloathwait I hoped to learn.

I had all but forgotten my brief pursuit of the ruffian as I approached

Cowper. He was a man of about forty years, haggard by his look, for the skin was loose about his face, and his hands were rough, callused, and stained with ink. A suit of clothes—gray and austere—made his grayish-yellow complexion and beveined eyes seem all the more cadaverous; nevertheless, he had an intelligent look about him and possessed something in his face that spoke of a kind of earnest ambition, but he also seemed a man whose youthful promise had yielded nothing but the feelings of failure that come with the advance of age. It is this moment in life, when the bounty of the future becomes the drudgery of the present, that all men fear, myself included, and for that reason I immediately felt a sympathy for this man.

"I beg a few moments of your time, sir," I said, "it is upon a matter of business."

I am told that it grows more common for clerks in places such as a trading company to think of themselves as dedicated to that company, but such was not the case in 1719, I assure you. A clerk at the South Sea Company would gladly use whatever access and influence his position afforded in order to turn a few pounds for himself, and I aimed to take advantage of that predilection.

"Business, you say?" Mr. Cowper said softly. "I am always game for business. Please describe the nature of this business."

I handed him my card, which he glanced at quickly and then put away.

"It is of a private nature," I said quietly.

"Then let us take a walk," he said. He stood up and led me down the stairway to the lobby. I began to explain my interests, but he held up a hand to stop my speech. "Not yet, sir."

When we reached the lobby, he began a walk directly across to the far wall. "We may talk here in some privacy, provided we continue to travel back and forth. That way no man may listen in to our conversation without making himself conspicuous."

I nodded at his sage precaution, at first thinking it was Mr. Cowper's own idea, but I soon noticed that a dozen or so pairs or small groups of men did as we did, moving back and forth, each group upon its own trajectory, like billiard balls rolling at an easy pace.

"Now what is it I may do for you, sir?" he inquired with a polished obsequiousness.

What, indeed? I had so rejoiced at the idea of tracking this man to the source, of following my guesses and the trail of probability, that I had not thought on what I might do with Mr. Cowper once I found him. I could presume from the notes I had discovered upon Bloathwait's desk that this man had some knowledge of the forgeries, but I could not even be sure of that. I did know, however, that he worked in the records office, and therefore would have access to useful information.

"Do you have access to stock-holder records?" I inquired.

"Such as they are," Cowper said, still keeping his voice quiet. "I fear this Company is none the best at organizing its archives."

"I should very much like," I said cautiously, "to learn if some particular people subscribed to Company stock."

Cowper stroked his chin. "This may prove difficult. The more recent the record, however, the greater the chance it can be found. For older records, I can promise you nothing."

Cowper's willingness to undertake this talk told me that he was certainly into something, I need only learn what. "I believe what I search for should be no more than a year old. I wish to know if two men I shall name held South Sea issues. If so, I wish to know in what amounts, when they were bought, and if they were again sold. Is that something you can do?"

He smiled. "I believe I can be of service to you. It shall take some time—a week perhaps. But it can certainly be done."

"And what shall I pay you for your services?"

Cowper thought about this for a moment, as we nearly collided with a pair of enormously fat men involved in a conference far more jolly than ours. They laughed so hard that they were nearly oblivious to where they walked.

"I believe five guineas per name shall answer it."

I began to regret the bargain, for his price was so high I could hardly even think that I might lower it to something reasonable. Finally we settled upon eight guineas for both names—still an exorbitant price.

Cowper and I had just concluded our business when I spotted, or I should say, I was spotted by, Nathan Adelman, who came down the stairs with his eyes affixed to me. Cowper hurriedly completed our farewell and disappeared into the throng while I awaited Adelman.

"Good day to you, sir." I nodded.

"I see there is no dissuading you from wasting your time," Adelman said blandly. He remained upon the first stair, that he might look me in the eye without straining. "Well, if you are going to be poking about, I suppose I may as well keep you from doing any harm. I shall take my dinner now," he said, "perhaps you can join me at the chophouse across the way. Their pork is most excellent," he said with a pointed look, as though challenging me to eat forbidden meat.

We walked down Bishopsgate and then to Leadenhall Street, where the chophouse stood near the Green Market. We silently agreed to a truce of civility, and our conversation as we walked rested upon trivial matters: the pleasantness of the recent weather, the excitement of the new theatrical season, and the increase of business upon the Exchange.

He led me to a crowded, smoky hall that offered overcooked chops of meat and stale mugs of ale for a shilling. We took ourselves a table, and Adelman called out for two plates. Within minutes a boy delivered two servings of a greasy mixture of chops, buttered cabbage, and pale yellowish bread—a dyed and chalky coarse bread, not true white bread made of refined flour.

"Tell me how your inquiry proceeds?" Adelman asked, as he turned to dragging a chunk of chalk-bread through the grease of his chop.

This was by no means the first time someone had placed pork before me, and I had not much scrupled to eat it since I had run away from home. Nevertheless, there was something so distressing about Adelman's need to devour pig flesh before my eyes that made the thought utterly distasteful to me. "It proceeds apace, I believe." I dipped a piece of bread into the grease and then set it back down.

Adelman laughed, his mouth full of food. "I am pleased to hear it. I trust the clerks at South Sea House are giving you their full cooperation."

"Would that all of South Sea House gave me its full cooperation."

Adelman continued to dig at his food. "You have yet to ask of me anything I can provide."

"You have made it clear that you would provide me with nothing."

He glanced at me. "No taste for pork, eh? I thought you more modern than that." He shook his head and smiled. "Your foolishness about diet is much like the foolishness of your inquiry. I had hoped to dissuade you from a course born of tribal ignorance, but if I cannot prevent your inquiry, I hope to limit the damage it does this Kingdom."

I thought it a bit obvious; he wished to lead me astray, and any information I received of Adelman I would have to scrutinize with care. "Very well, then," I said, ready to test his new spirit. "What can you tell me of Perceval Bloathwait?"

Adelman set down his fork. "Bloathwait? What concern is he of yours?"

"I believe my father was a concern of his. And," I added, hoping to incite some response, "he has made it clear that he wishes to aid me in my inquiry."

Adelman made a sound of disgust. "He wishes to aid you so long as he might cast aspersions upon South Sea House. Allow me to tell you a fine story, Mr. Weaver. As you may recall, four years ago, when the Pretender made his most violent attempt to invade this island and retake the throne for the House of Stuart, there were at one point rumors that the Pretender's carriage was on its way to London. You may also recollect, sir, the panic caused by this rumor—the idea that the Pretender should feel safe to enter the city as its monarch made many a man believe that the war had already been all but lost and King George would flee. In reality, the rebellion had already been quite stopped in Scotland, but these rumors were not simply fed by mania and fear, for an entourage, including a carriage bearing the insignia of the Pretender, was discovered on the London road."

"I fail to see what this has to do with me."

"No doubt," Adelman said. "But you will. When news of the Pretender's advance on London reached 'Change Alley, stock prices plummeted. Every man with large investments in the funds sold out for fear that if the Pretender succeeded in his attempt to replace King George, then the funds would be worth nothing. Now, I do not wish to suggest that every man who bought during this crisis was a villain. There were many patriots, myself included, who had faith in His Majesty's ability to withstand an invasion. But Mr. Bloathwait bought tremendously, and he made an inestimable fortune when the invasion was revealed to be a hoax and the stock prices normalized."

"Your idea of villainy is rather changeable," I observed. "You say you also bought when the prices fell. Is he a blackguard because he bought more than you?"

"No, he is a blackguard because he orchestrated the panic," Adelman said, taking a bite of chop. "Bloathwait hired the coaches, had them appear as the Pretender and his men, and sat back and awaited the collapse of the markets. It was a very clever plan, and it made a man who was only comfortable into a man who is now very wealthy indeed."

I betrayed no disgust, hoping my lack of concern would prompt Adelman to reveal even more. "It seems rather like Mr. d'Arblay's false lottery scare," I noted blandly.

"The difference is one of scale, I suppose. Mr. d'Arblay threatened to ruin a few investors' plans. Mr. Bloathwait threatened to ruin an entire nation. I admit I feel some bitterness because when the newspapers excoriate stock-jobbers they have a habit of looking to me, but I am merely a man of business who sees opportunity in serving my nation. Bloathwait is your true villainous stock-jobber. He would, and did, send the entire nation's finances into chaos to give himself an advantage upon the Exchange. Now, you must decide if you wish to trust such a man."

"What is it you wish of me, Mr. Adelman?"

"Only to give you some advice. Continue your inquiry, Mr. Weaver. It is spoken of in the coffeehouses now, but not as much as it might be. I say continue, and continue as boldly and as loudly as you dare. Then you may sit back, and like your friend Mr. Bloathwait, watch the prices in 'Change Alley fall, and when they do so, you may buy great quantities. With any luck, the damage you do will last but a short while, and you will find yourself a rich man."

"What know you," I began, unimpressed by his speech, "of forged South Sea issues?"

Like a creature from Ovid, Mr. Adelman was suddenly transformed. He sprang forth and grabbed me by the arm, hissing in the most hideous and barely audible voice, "You must never speak of such a thing again. You know not the damage you can do. Those words are like a magic incantation that, if uttered too loudly in the wrong place, can destroy the Kingdom."

Adelman relaxed somewhat. He returned to his seat. "Forgive my excitement, but there are things of which you know nothing. I cannot sit by and watch you destroy the good we have done."

"You talk of serving the nation, but you are no different from Bloathwait, who attempts to serve his own profits. I must believe that these things, which I shall do you the courtesy of not mentioning again, exist. I shall continue to pursue that line of inquiry, so you may as well tell me what you know."

"It is but a vicious rumor," Adelman said, after ruminating for a moment, "started by Bloathwait. A hoax, like his Pretender's carriage. For all I know he produced some false stock and circulated it to give his story credit, but I promise you, it is but a ruse to ruin the credit of this Company, and you, Mr. Weaver, are but a tool of those who would bring about such a ruin."

"What if I told you that my father believed in the existence of such false stock—that he believed that a factor within South Sea House produced it?"

"I would say that you have been most horribly deceived. Your father was too perspicacious a jobber to believe such a false rumor."

I waited a moment, hoping to unnerve Adelman. "I am in possession of evidence," I said at last. I chose not to clarify if I had evidence of the false stock or my father's belief in it.

"What manner of evidence?" Adelman's face now grew crimson beneath his white wig.

"I shall only say that it is evidence that has quite convinced me." I overstated my conviction in my father's pamphlet—for all I knew, it was but hyperbolic rhetoric—but I believed I had an advantage over Adelman and I wished to use it for all it was worth.

"What have you?" he demanded. "A false issue?" He spoke those words so quietly he did little more than move his lips. "If that is what you have, let me promise that what you have is a base forgery. Such a thing could never have come from South Sea House—if you have anything it is only designed to make you believe it to be something it is not, something it cannot be."

"A forgery of a forgery?" I almost laughed. "A feint within a feint? How very charming. This stock-jobbery is as much the devil as its enemies say."

"Name your price for this 'evidence' of yours. Do not for a moment believe that I think what you have is proof of anything, but if I have to pay to keep rumors from circulating, I shall do so."

I hope I shall not disillusion my reader if I say that, for an instant at any rate, I wondered what my price might be. What loyalty had I to my father that I should turn away a sum of money to do what I had done for so many years—forget him. What could Adelman mean when he said I might name my price? A thousand pounds? Ten thousand? Might it not be wise to clarify his meaning before rejecting this offer?

It is always something of a disappointment for me when I learn that I have not the stomach for such villainy or calculation as might be in my best interest. And perhaps to overcompensate for this war that raged inside me, I assumed a stance of indignation. "My price? My price is knowing who killed my father and Balfour—and why. There is no other price."

"Damn you, sir." He threw his utensils hard upon the table.

I admit I enjoyed this moment of power, and I saw no reason not to indulge myself. "Damn me, you say? Would you care to damn me at dawn tomorrow morning at Hyde Park?"

Adelman's face lost its redness and now matched the color of his wig. "I assure you, sir, I never duel. It is a barbaric practice, and one practiced only by equals. You should be ashamed to have even suggested such a thing."

"Dueling is dangerous," I agreed. "But insulting a man to his face, Mr. Adelman, is also a dangerous practice. I tell you, I grow tired of your attempts to dissuade me from my course. I shall not be dissuaded. I shall not be bought out. This inquiry will cease, sir, when it reaches its conclusion, and not a moment sooner. If I have to expose the South Sea Company, the Bank of England, or anyone else who has had a hand in these deaths, I shall not hesitate to do so."

I stood up and glared down at this great man, who, perhaps for the first time in many years, knew not how to respond. "If you wish to discuss this matter further, you know where you may find me, and I am always ready to receive your commands."

I turned and departed, full of self-satisfaction; I felt—for the first time since I had begun this search for the truth behind my father's death—that I might possess some small measure of strength.

I LOOKED FORWARD TO returning to my lodgings, for I had found my encounter with Adelman to be surprisingly tiring. My hopes of removing my boots and taking a drink were dashed, however, when I noticed my landlady waiting to greet me at the front door. The look on her face told me I would not be resting soon. I saw that she was anxious and tired, but had I been less tired myself I would surely have seen the signifiers of fear in her sunken eyes and pale complexion.

"There are some men to see you in the parlor, Mr. Weaver," she told me in a shaky voice.

"Some men," I muttered. "Pray, not some Christian gentlemen, Mrs.

Garrison? Shall I assume that the Hindoo Rajah and his entourage have stopped by to honor me with a visit?"

She pressed her hands together in a gesture of supplication. "They are in the parlor."

Much raced through my mind in the few seconds it took to storm into the room. Had the constable come to arrest me for the murder of Jemmy? As I walked through the door I saw five men, dressed reasonably well, but their malicious eyes gave the lie to the cuts of their clothing and the niceness of their wigs. Three of them sat on the sofa, their legs spread out in an air of comfortable disrespect. Two stood behind the sofa, one of them toying recklessly with Mrs. Garrison's China vase. The other man fingered a bulge in his coat pocket that I knew could only be a pistol.

They were not the constable's men.

"Ah," the man with the vase said. He placed it down hard, perhaps hoping to see a crack wind its way up from the base. "At last the great Mr. Weaver shows himself. You've kept us here all day, you have. That's something of an incivility, don'cha think, me spark?"

Mrs. Garrison had not followed me in, but she remained in the hall that she might listen to what transpired.

I could not imagine who they might be, but their presence intrigued me. I understood that I might be in grave danger, but I also believed that I was very close to learning much about the deaths into which I inquired.

"If you have business," I said sternly, "speak it. Otherwise you can get out."

"Listen to 'im," one of the men on the sofa said. " 'E thinks 'e can tell us what to do."

"Mr. Weaver," the leader said, "we've come to take you for a visit. Our employer has invited you to come see him. And to make sure you don't get lost along the way, he's asked us to bring you over ourselves."

"And who is your employer?"

"You'll find out in due course," the leader said. "You just cooperate, and you won't get hurt. We've got enough men here, and pistols too, to keep a man like yourself from giving us any trouble."

Behind me Mrs. Garrison let out a shriek. I turned to her quickly. "Do not be alarmed," I said. "Have these men done you any harm?"

She shook her head.

"Then they shan't." I turned to the leader. "Let us go." Alone, perhaps, I might have attempted to extricate myself from the situation more forcefully, but I could not risk the safety of Mrs. Garrison. She was an unpleasant woman to be sure, but I knew my duty too well to engage in an altercation that might bring her harm.

" 'E's quite the gallant," one of them noted as they ushered me out in front of Mrs. Garrison's house. Seeing a coach waiting, I walked toward it at a brisk pace, anxious to have the adventure ended. A small crowd had gathered to watch this odd procession, and I thought to myself that at least while others looked on I should have little to fear. But even as this thought passed through my mind, I felt from behind me a sudden sharp blow to the back of my skull. The pain consumed my every sensation. I have taken no small number of blows to my head in my time in the ring, but it is one thing to feel a man's fist against your face, quite another to be struck from behind with a solid object. The pain was, in a disorienting way, quite literally unbelievable—blunt and stabbing, hot and cold all at once. I thought to myself, *That cannot be—it cannot hurt that much.*

Without taking time to consider, I reached to grab the spot that hurt so implausibly. I should have known better than to render myself vulnerable, for another of the men took advantage of the opening and struck me hard in the stomach. My chest constricted as I struggled for air. As I doubled over, I felt another blow, this one in the small of my back, which knocked me to the ground.

I thought that if only I could catch my breath I might rise up and pummel these men, but I was no sooner upon the ground than I was struck again in the face and side, and before I could resist I felt my arms pulled behind me and bound with a cord. Just before a cloth was slipped over my head, I looked up and saw the faces in the crowd that watched me beaten before my own lodgings. Not one of them stepped forward to help, and I found myself attempting to commit each face to memory that I might return and beat everyone who had watched my misfortune with such cowardly indifference. I heard someone say that he would go for the constable, but that I knew would do me little service.

Abruptly I was pulled to my feet and pushed against the side of the coach; what felt like a dozen hands were upon me, roughly searching for weapons. My pistol, my hangar, and my knives were removed, and I was shoved into the carriage, where I collapsed into my seat.

I struggled futilely against my bonds, not because I believed I could escape them, but because I could not endure the idea of these men believing me entirely conquered. I soon grew tired of thrashing about like an unhooked trout; there was little good I might accomplish, and I had no desire to bring more beatings upon myself. Thus biding my time, attempting to persuade myself into feeling no agony, I felt the wheels begin to roll, and I vowed that I would have vengeance for this anger and humiliation before the sun set that night.

TWENTY-TWO

I SAT SILENT and brooding, taut with anger and pain, as the chaise rode on for I know not how long. My abductors spoke not a word, and in the silence and darkness I contemplated who might have orchestrated this attack. I could not but suspect the South Sea Company, but would the architects of a villainous conspiracy that had secretly taken the lives of two men be so sloppy as to attempt a violent abduction before a crowd of onlookers? But if it was not the South Sea, then who would wish to abuse me so, and for what purpose?

At last we stopped, and I was led out to walk a short distance. I heard a door open and felt a pair of hands pushing me into a building. Within a few seconds the hood upon my head was removed, and I could see I had entered a gaudily decorated house. The walls were adorned with classical-inspired imagery that suggested less the virtues of Plutarch than the excesses of the *Satyricon* of Petronius Arbiter. I shall not ask my reader to blush by describing the attitudes of the plaster statues and the painted figures of this chamber.

The men about me held themselves like children whose sure punishment only awaited the return of a parent. They watched me warily, though my arms were still firmly bound behind me.

I was brought to a drawing room and instructed to sit. The men withdrew somewhat, but did not leave. Next I felt a person approach from behind and cut loose the cord that tied my hands. At once I almost jumped up, but I decided to survey the scene quietly before taking any action. The room bore furnishings of the Eastern vogue, with Chinese-style vases and

Oriental decorations upon the wall hangings. A painting, offset with a thick frame of gold, depicted a coronation scene among the Turks. I tried to take in as much as I could, not knowing what could be important, for I knew that the man who had summoned me was to be my enemy for some time to come. Presuming he let me live.

The man who had freed my arms turned to face me, and I saw that it was the Great Man himself who walked, or I should say, limped toward me to shake my hand. Though Jonathan Wild was ten years older than myself, he had a youthful glow about him. His broad face would have struck an uncritical man as unaffectedly jolly, but I had too recently tasted of his tricks to see it as anything but villainous.

Following immediately upon Wild's footsteps was his man, Abraham Mendes, who stood impassively. He showed no sign that he recalled our brief dialogue outside the Bevis Marks synagogue. His task, I believed, was to cast menacing looks at anything that moved—the fact that he knew me changed his behavior not at all.

"Mr. Weaver, I'm so glad to meet you again." Wild grabbed my hand and shook it in a powerful and constricting grip, as though he wished to convey meaning even in so small a gesture. "I really must apologize for the unconscionable way you have been treated by these men. I asked them to treat you with courtesy, but I think your reputation must have intimidated them, and they reverted to their rude ways."

Since he had greeted me in the Bedford Arms tavern, I had anticipated that I would sooner or later meet up with Wild, but I still could not imagine what he hoped to gain from this adventure. Why had I been beaten, if only to take my revenge on my attackers? Why had I been blindfolded, when the entire world knew that Jonathan Wild resides in a spacious house he had only recently bought in the Great Old Bailey?

Wild ordered the men out of the room and sat in a hard-looking chair with enormous arms. Mendes stepped around and stood behind him, glaring at me with a coldness I found chilling. I could not understand how Mendes could so easily make himself into two people—the violent henchman and the affable fellow-Jew.

"Again," Wild said quietly, "I apologize for this misunderstanding, and I hope we will be able to recover from this debacle. Might I get you a glass to calm your spirits?" He limped toward a decanter set upon a table in the middle of the room, having every intention of pouring my wine himself rather than have a servant perform this task.

"I should welcome a glass of wine." I slowly shifted my battered body, attempting to find a comfortable position. This conversation, I told myself, was much like a battle within the ring. I would have to force myself to ignore my pain, to keep my wits about me though my body urged me to surrender.

Wild poured the wine, handed it to me with the greatest deference, and then returned to his chair. "We have so many things to discuss. It astonishes one, does it not, to think that we do not have the opportunity to speak to each other more often."

I took a sip and found that the wine did calm my spirits to a small degree. I straightened myself out, ignored the throbbing in my head, and met Wild's villainous gaze. "I find there is little left that astonishes me, Mr. Wild, and much that tries my patience. You may not have intended to treat me ill, but I have been ill-treated and my disposition is not entirely amicable, so if you have business, I would have you state it."

"Very well, Mr. Weaver. I too am a man pressed for time." He sat down. "I would so like for us to have an understanding, because it would be so easy for us to become adversaries. After all, we are in the same business, and I fear that since I have made such a success of the thief-taking trade, there is little left for you. Yet I think there are ample opportunities in collecting debts, protecting gentlemen, and even uncovering the truths behind terrible crimes—such as the one committed against your father."

"What do you know of the matter?" I asked, wishing to sound relaxed.

He shook his head, as if at the foolishness of my question. "I assure you, sir, that there is very little that happens in this town of which I do not know."

"Then you may tell me who killed my father," I replied.

"Alas"—he shook his head—"that is one bit of information that has eluded me."

"Perhaps, then, the scope of your information is not so broad as you would like me to believe."

He narrowed his eyes in disapproval. "You must not be so hasty, sir. But I have heard of your haste, and of your temper too. Tell me, Mr. Weaver, is it true that when you were younger and rode upon the highway, taking from others the wealth you wanted for yourself, that you were a great favorite among the gentle sex? I have heard it said that you were known by the name of Gentleman Ben and that you were loved by the ladies even as they handed you their rings and jewels. Once you had to discourage the daughter of a wealthy merchant who wished to ride away with you."

I should not have been surprised that he knew such things. I had indeed taken a false name when I rode upon the highway, and as there would be men about town who knew me from those days, it was inevitable that Wild should learn of my past. For my part, I had never even spoken of those days since setting up my business in London. There were some secrets I kept even from Elias. "I am not interested in discussing the improprieties of my youth."

He showed me another grin. "There is nothing to shame you in your past. I heard that once, when a fellow-adventurer threatened to become too rough with a lady whose wealth you desired, you turned and fired your pistol directly into his face, killing him on the spot."

I felt at least some relief in his repetition of this rumor that had followed me for some years—not because I was pleased that these stories were assigned to me, but it proved that Wild heard only the same false stories that had circulated for years. His information had limitations. "The pistol misfired," I said slowly. "No one was hurt, and the man you speak of later hanged at Tyburn for his crimes."

"I only hope you turned him in yourself—procured a nice reward. I think it a shame to see enemies hang and receive no other compensation than the satisfaction of watching them dangle."

I studied his face, hoping for some sign of what he was about. But I could read nothing into his unctuous smile. "I fear the crux of your discourse eludes me, sir."

"Ah, my point. My point, sir, is that I wish to discuss the matter of this inquiry into your father's death."

"Shall I guess?" I asked tartly. "You wish to see me discontinue the inquiry."

Wild laughed, as a benevolent patron laughs at the foolishness of his charges. "No, Mr. Weaver. Just the opposite, in fact. I wish to make certain you proceed apace."

I sat patiently to await his explanation.

"I wish to keep you out of a business that I claim for myself," Wild continued. "The public approves of me heartily, and I have no desire to compete with you for the trade. Since thief-taking is so unpleasant a business I am sure you wish to find other avenues of employment. Thus I am to see that your investigation into the matter of these deaths is successful, for I believe that such a conclusion would open new opportunities for you, and we would no longer find ourselves competitors." He looked at me in the most challenging manner imaginable. "You will note that I have not let this unfortunate business with Kate Cole trouble me."

I took a drink of wine. "So much the better," I said, affecting indifference. In truth, his oily speech only exacerbated the pain in my head, and I wished to say nothing that might extend our conversation.

"Yes, it is too bad about Jemmy," Wild continued cheerfully. "Not too bad that he's dead, for I could not trust the fellow and would have 'peached him myself soon enough. It is a shame that I shall receive no money for his death, but I shall see money of Kate, and that's all one to me. You might have wondered if I would feel ill will toward you for stepping into my business as you did, but I can assure you that I hold no grudge. I promise that your name will never be raised at Kate's trial."

"I am pleased to hear that," I muttered. I cannot say that I was surprised by Wild's intention to let Kate swing, but the coldness of his resolve unsettled me. Did he believe himself to be charming or terrifying?

"Yes, I thought you might be pleased," he continued. "Now, shall we return to your more pressing problem? I do want to be of service."

"I shall not stop you." Wild surely could not believe that I should be fooled by his bombastic claims of fellowship—I saw not what I had to gain by pretending to be more foolish than he might hope. "Frankly, Mr. Wild, I don't believe you, and I should be utterly astonished if you expected me to believe you. Perhaps you can simply tell me what it is you want, and then I may return to my lodgings to heal myself of this meeting."

He placed a hand upon his breast. "You wound me, sir." He froze in this position, and then appeared to change his mind. "No, you do not. Of course you do not wound me; when I have been telling you of my plans to let Kate swing, there is no reason for you to see me as anything but a schemer—which I am, and a devilish good one, too. The truth is that I have reasons of my own for wishing to see you succeed in your inquiry— for uncovering the truth behind these murders. My business thrives upon the plague of thieves in this city, but murder is another matter altogether. A murder is something I never condone. It is quite bad for my business. If a man finds his watch missing, that is one thing, but when wealthy merchants are plotted against, it is something else."

"Then why did you wait for me to begin an inquiry? If these murders distressed you so, why not manage the affair yourself?"

"Because until you began your inquiry, no one believed they were murders. As long as the public is content, I am content. But I assure you, Weaver, that having stirred up public sentiment about these deaths, if you now fail to resolve the matter, it is bad for both of us."

"What rot!" I could not help but laugh, though the motion hurt both my ribs and my head.

Wild laughed with me. "You will have to accept it. My motives are my own. I wish you to succeed, but if you do not wish to succeed, you may ignore my advice and my assistance. There is no better-informed man in the city, and I may have knowledge that could aid you. Feel free to ask me anything, sir. Anything at all."

I considered this offer. "Where can I find Bertie Fenn, the man who ran down my father?"

Wild held out his hands to signify his helplessness. "I do not know where you can find him, but I have heard that he works for a man named Martin Rochester, who is something of a criminal mind in his own right. Not a man to trifle with, from what I hear."

"I have heard this name of Rochester for some time. It seems the entire world knows of him, but no one knows him. It is indeed enigmatic."

"Yes, you are on an enigmatic course, are you not?"

"Then if you wish to aid me, you can clear up some of the enigmas rather than add to them. Tell me everything you know about Rochester—his business, where he lives, whom else he employs."

Wild only shrugged. "Alas, Rochester is a very secretive man. I know not where he works nor whom he employs—other than Fenn, that is. I am simply a thief-taker, sir, and cannot begin to fathom the world of stock-jobbers such as Rochester. These stock-jobbers are the very devil. They turn everything upside down. There is no sorting out of one's business around them."

I sighed. These endless railleries against stock-jobbers frustrated me—not because I wished to defend them, not because these condemnations insulted my father's memory, but because these words were upon every man's lips and proved worse than empty and useless.

"You do not really have any information for me then? For a man who knows of everything, you share remarkably little." I started to rise, and even this slight motion caused Mendes to shift the weight upon his feet.

Wild held up a staying hand, I could not say at which of us. "Perhaps

I do not have precisely the information you desire. Yet I hear things, and I should like to share with you some of the things I have heard."

I made no effort to disguise my skepticism. "By all means." I settled back into my chair.

"It is my understanding that Rochester arranged for the death of your father as well as Michael Balfour. I do not know why, but I do know that he employed Bertie Fenn. Further, sir, it is my understanding that Mr. Rochester has some connection with the South Sea Company. I believe you will have to look to the Company to find the truth behind these murders."

"How is it," I asked, "that so many men point me in the direction of the South Sea Company but can then tell me no more?"

Wild looked at me with something like surprise. "I cannot speak for other men."

"What is your affiliation with Perceval Bloathwait?" I demanded.

"Bloathwait?" I had either genuinely surprised him or he was a superb actor. "The Bank of England director? What dealings should I have with him?"

"That is precisely what I wish to determine."

"None. I suspect I never shall, unless he should find his pocket picked one day or the other."

"Then tell me how you know these things about the Company," I said.

"Men are undone in whispers, you know. A prig tells me a piece, a whore tells me another piece. I put all these pieces together. Sometimes I can ask no more than I am told."

I thought hard on what else I might ask. I could not begin to guess at Wild's motives, but if he wished to aid me, for the nonce I would take his information. "What do you know of a man named Noah Sarmento?" I asked. Wild might deny dealings with Bloathwait, but if my uncle's clerk was a villain of some description, then Wild might know of him.

His face was a blank. "I cannot say I know of him."

"Very well. You had your men beat me and drag me here in order to give me your friendly encouragement. Do I understand that correctly, Mr. Wild?"

"Really, Weaver, I have apologized about that. I have told you all I know of Rochester and the South Sea involvement. You must do some of this work yourself."

"Then I shall get to it." I began to rise. "Thank you for your time, Mr. Wild," I said sourly, as I attempted to steady myself. I did not wish to give Wild the satisfaction of seeing me in any way incapacitated. "I cannot say how much faith I can place in your promise, but I can assure you that this meeting has been illuminating for me."

"I am delighted to hear that. You know, Mr. Weaver, my offer still stands—if you wish to find employment with me, there is always room for a man of your stripe."

"Your offer is as tempting to me today as the day you first made it, sir."

"Ah, then. One more thing I wish to bring up. It's about this Kate Cole matter. I could not but detect some squeamishness on your part when I mentioned her hanging day. I suppose you are one of those unfortunates crippled with sentiment—such a nasty condition. It occurs to me that if the idea of her hanging distresses you, I might choose to spare her the rope."

"And in exchange?" I asked.

"In exchange," he said, "you will owe me a favor. One of my choice, that I may call upon when I choose."

I believed that he could arrange to spare her life. A man like Wild would have precisely the influence to abort the trial, just as he would have the power to see her hang should he choose to do so. Yet I wondered what price he would extract for clearing my conscience. What would it mean to be in Wild's debt—to have no say in how that debt might be paid? I thought about this offer in terms of probability, in terms of risk and reward, in terms of Wild's efforts to speculate on lives as though he jobbed people themselves upon some felonious exchange. In the end, and it is a decision I have come to regret in many ways, I placed my fear of Wild's power over my concern for Kate's life. I said nothing and watched the images of a hanged Kate play themselves out before my mind's eye and told myself that, should Kate's life end in this way, I could endure the guilt.

I chose not to honor Wild with a response to his offer, so he continued speaking. "Very well, then. Shall I have Mr. Mendes return you to your lodgings?"

I glanced at my old acquaintance, who had hardly moved since his arrival in the room. "Yes," I said, making sure to betray nothing of my feelings. "I think I'd like that."

. . .

MENDES AND I SAT in the coach in silence for a few moments. Finally he turned to me. "You will understand if I do not return your arms until we reach your home."

"If I wished to harm you, Mr. Mendes, I would not require weaponry. Tell me," I said, changing my tone dramatically, "do you enjoy working for Wild, being treated like his mameluke?"

Mendes laughed. "My employment with Mr. Wild has served me well."

I thought on this for a moment, attempting to concentrate, though the jarring movements of the hackney aggravated my too-recent wounds. "Come now, Mendes. Let us be honest with each other. It may well be that Wild is an easy master, but he is a master all the same. No matter the trust he may put in you, you must remain for him always a Hebrew, and nothing more."

"I hardly know what you mean," Mendes said. "For Wild, any man is but the sum of what he does. I am no different. While I serve him well, he treats me well."

"We, however, are of the same neighborhood," I continued. "I ask you now to think of that commonality and tell me the truth of these matters."

"The truth?" Mendes stared.

"Yes. I know you and I have never been great friends, but we have a common bond. You continue to associate yourself with the Jews of Dukes Place—more than I do. You attend services at the synagogue, and I admire your desire to maintain a connection with our people. Can you not look at that commonality and find it within you to be honest with me?"

"Perhaps it is you who should be honest with me, sir. What is it that motivates you?"

"Me? Why, I wish to find the man who killed my father. No difficult motivation, that."

"Except you never cared a fig for your father while he was alive. I, however, saw him quite regularly about the neighborhood, while you feared to set foot within our quarter."

I could hardly answer these charges, which I knew were only too just. I told myself that his words meant nothing, that Mendes knew nothing of how my father treated me, that a man of his spirit could have taken it no more than I. But I could not quite believe my own thoughts, perhaps because when I left, I left not out of anger or indignation or the justice of my cause—I left with my father's stolen money in my pocket.

We rode in silence until the hackney now stumbled to a halt. "We are arrived, Mr. Weaver." He handed me my daggers, hangar, and pistol, and wished that I might use them in the best of health. "I hope you meet great success in your inquiry," Mendes said as I stepped out of the hackney. "Mr. Wild does as well. That may be difficult for you to believe just now, but I promise you it is so."

My legs shook a bit as I touched the cobbled street, and the daylight in my eyes, after the dark of the hackney, made me feel like a drunkard just roused from last night's stupor. As I limped toward Mrs. Garrison's front door I thought of all the information I had obtained that day, and wondered why I felt no closer to knowing anything at all.

TWENTY-THREE

I FOUND WILD'S MANEUVERINGS rough and barbaric, but for all his clumsiness, I could not see his game. There was no shortage of men pushing me toward the South Sea Company, and to suspect that they all conspired in this together was to say that my uncle was part of this conspiracy. That possibility filled me with dread, but in light of the information I had obtained, it was one I could not entirely dismiss. Why had my uncle wished to keep me clear of Bloathwait, whose involvement in these matters grew evident? Did Sarmento deal with Bloathwait with or without my uncle's knowledge? And why did my uncle maintain a friendship with Adelman, a man so important to the South Sea Company, if it appeared that the Company's hand in my father's death was undeniable?

For the nonce, no question plagued me more than Wild's interest. I could not imagine how a dandified pickpocket like Wild stood to gain from exposing the Company. Despite his claims about the importance of punishing murder, my success in these matters would perhaps be the greatest threat to Wild's concerns, for many a man in London, as Sir Owen had shown by example, would pay more to have an honest man return his goods than pay a more moderate fee to the thief that took them in the first place. I could only conclude two probable explanations for Wild's behavior: either he aimed somehow, through all his maneuverings, to remove me from his way; or, for reasons I could not yet guess, the South Sea Company was so dangerous to him that he would risk my injuring him in the future in order to expose the Company now. I could not even speculate on what the Company could have to do with an oily fiend like Wild, but if he did fear the South Sea, why did he not give me more information with which to do the Company harm?

Quite exhausted and hurting from the blows I'd taken of Wild's men, I entered Mrs. Garrison's house, now prepared at last to sleep. I could not say with any truthfulness that the pain had subsided much; if anything, it ached more acutely, though the sting of it had passed. I believed that I could tell from past experience when an injury was serious or no, and while I knew I should be in discomfort for some days ahead, I did not believe myself in any danger. I would think through these matters properly once I had rested, but rest was not to prove so easy to obtain. Mrs. Garrison awaited me in the hall, her hands red from her incessant wringing.

"Mr. Weaver, sir, are you unharmed?" She appeared something like concerned, even, I would venture, glad to see me, but I knew too well the meaning of her clucking her tongue. I had heard it many a time and often when my rent was past due.

"Yes, Mrs. Garrison," I said with a soft voice, doing my best to put her at ease. She would not soon forget the horror of having those villainous men in her home. "There was no cause for alarm. These were some foolish men, but utterly harmless."

"I am glad you are well," she said. "I thought they had hurt you quite grievously." There was a pause.

"You wish to add something, madam?"

"Mr. Weaver, I cannot have ruffians coming into my home. This is a respectable house I run, sir. I have looked the other way, with your being a Hebrew and such, sir. Many's the folk who would not do so," she added hastily. "But I can't have these ruffians, armed with swords and guns and the Lord only knows what manner of weapons, come into my house and threaten me and frighten me and the servants, sir."

"I quite understand, Mrs. Garrison," I said soothingly. "It shan't happen again. It was all an unfortunate misunderstanding that could have happened to any gentleman."

"Any gentleman?" she asked. "Begging your pardon, sir, I am afraid I misbelieve you." She paused. "Mr. Weaver, I must ask you to leave. I must. I cannot have such men in here to frighten me like to death and to do what mischief I know not to me and to my tenants. I'll need you gone before sundown, Mr. Weaver."

"Before sundown?" I almost shouted. "I quite understand your concern, Mrs. Garrison, and I do not resent it, but before sundown is hardly reasonable. I shall not have time to search for other lodgings. I might remind you that I am paid through the end of the quarter."

"I'll return your money. You needn't worry on that score. But I must insist upon your departure, sir." She stood there, continuing to wring her hands. I suppose I could have either charmed or frightened her into changing her mind, but I could not deny that my adventures had placed her in jeopardy. I had no great love for my landlady, but I should have been enraged had she been harmed by any enemy of mine. What she asked of me was an inconvenience, not an impossibility, and the right thing to do would be to comply.

"Very well, madam," I said. "I shall not cause you further grief."

She sighed with relief. "Thank you, Mr. Weaver. I *am* sorry to have to do this."

I thought this might be the beginning of a protracted apology, and I held up my hand. "Enough, Mrs. Garrison. I quite understand. You must do justice to yourself."

"Thank you, sir. Oh, and Mr. Weaver, sir, I think I should only tell you that there is another gentleman waiting for you upstairs. I told him I didn't know if you wanted anyone up there and that there was no knowing when you was to be back, but he took me no mind and—"

Without another word I turned and ran upstairs as best I could, reaching, as I moved, for the pistol I had only recently replaced into my coat pocket. There was no way of knowing who it could be. Perhaps Wild's deception had not yet run its full course. Perhaps now I was to contend with the South Sea Company or even an agent of Bloathwait's. I stood outside my door for a moment, my pistol held high, and with a fluid movement, I pushed the door open and stepped forward boldly, aiming my firearm at the figure who sat facing me.

"You've had a lively day, then?" Elias said calmly. "The old bird's been having seizures. I mollified her a bit by taking some of her blood. Shall I send a bill to Mr. Balfour?" Elias paused. "You can put that pistol down, you know."

I did as he suggested and threw myself into my armchair. "There's no condition unbettered by the loss of blood," I mumbled. "It's a wonder men who have their limbs lopped off don't stand healthier than we who still have all ours attached."

"You laugh," Elias said cheerfully, "but were I to bleed you now, you'd soon discover a vast improvement in your disposition. Shall you tell me what happened? You look dreadful."

I briefly recounted my adventure with Wild, trying not to omit any detail that might be of value. Elias's jaw hung open as he listened. "This is an impenetrable turn. Why should Wild wish to set you against the South Sea Company? What could a trading company be to a man like Wild?"

I shook my head, suddenly quite thirsty. I wished that I kept something such as drinking water around my rooms, but that was a luxury I rarely indulged in. "I don't know." I sighed such that my ribs ached. "He mentioned counterfeiting, but if Wild were involved in a scheme to falsify stock, why would he point me to the Company? My inquiry would only risk exposing the scheme."

Elias nodded thoughtfully. "Maybe he wishes to put you off the Company?"

I could not follow his thinking, and my eyes became unfocused.

"Wild is devious," Elias continued. "What if he tells you to look to the Company because he knows you mistrust him? Perhaps he claims the Company as his enemy precisely because it is his ally."

I closed my eyes. "It is a strange business, but I cannot believe that even if the Company were ruthless enough to involve itself in the murder of two prominent businessmen, it would be so reckless as to risk dealings with Wild. These men may be villains, but they are not fools."

"I have known several and found them as subject to buffoonery as men in any profession."

"If Wild were connected with the Company, why should he expose himself now? Why should he involve me? Surely it is a risk to call upon me. I cannot see what he or the South Sea Company or Bloathwait or anyone else has to gain by handing me these minute pieces of information and asking me to proceed from them. If anything, such actions suggest that they do not work together—that each individual who provides me with information accounts at least one of the others as his enemy. I cannot claim to understand it all, Elias, but if this is an inquiry of probability rather than fact, I believe it likely that whoever killed my father and Balfour has other enemies, and that all of those enemies are attempting to use this inquiry to serve their own aims."

"Perhaps these men were part of a cabal that has broken down. Perhaps the different elements have gone off in their own direction to man-age their own affairs as they see best. I cannot say. What did you learn from your visit at the South Sea House?"

I told Elias about my encounter with the clerk, Cowper. "Until I hear what he has learned, I do not know that we can advance on that front. I wonder if it is not time for me to pay a visit to Mr. Balfour. After all, he is my employer. I ought to keep him informed."

"Selectively, I should think," Elias said.

"Oh, I quite agree. No one is above suspicion, Elias, and Balfour is a strange fish indeed. Perhaps if I apply a bit of pressure we shall see a crack in his edifice."

"Splendid."

"In the meantime, I have more immediate concerns, such as where I shall sleep tonight. Mrs. Garrison has sent me packing over the small mat-ter of Wild's ruffians forcing their way into her parlor."

"That's a nasty bit of news, isn't it? Where shall you go?"

"Perhaps I'll impose on my uncle for a while—until I have the time to search for a place. He has shown himself in favor of families helping one another out." I said nothing to Elias about the uneasiness I had about my uncle. I can hardly explain why I found the very idea of villainy within my own family most embarrassing, but if my uncle had been less than forth-right with me, what better way to uncover his deception than by moving in with him?

Elias then inspected the wounds inflicted by Wild's soldiers, all the while indicating that my recovery would be speeded by the removal of a small quantity of my blood, but I would not have it. When he had finished his ministrations, I screwed up my resolve to face my pain and set off in search of my uncle. I found him at his warehouse, reviewing some ledgers in his closet, and I approached him with trepidation as I made my request, fearing that he would suspect me of taking advantage of his good nature. Such was not the case.

"You will have Aaron's room," he said after a moment of considera-tion. He then looked down at his ledgers, suggesting our business was complete.

"Thank you, Uncle," I said after a moment.

He raised his eyes from his book. "I shall see you tonight, then."

So, having had my favor granted in the style of a punishment meted out, I returned to Mrs. Garrison's to put my effects in order, collect those things I could not wait upon her servant sending, and make my way out of her house.

This final departure took far longer than I had anticipated, and its taste was more bitter than I could have imagined. I suppose I had been foolish for not taking better care of it, for not locking it within a strongbox, or hiding it, or disguising its nature. Simply sliding it within a pile of papers on my writing desk had seemed sufficient, but I was proved wrong indeed. It was, therefore, with a kind of ignominious shame that I went forth to the generosity of my uncle's lodgings to inform him that my father's pamphlet, perhaps the most convincing evidence that his death had been orchestrated by the powers of 'Change Alley, had disappeared from my possession.

TWENTY-FOUR

I SAT IN MY uncle's study staring at the mug of mulled wine that stood steaming on the table beside me. I had already moved most of my things to the room that I had been given on the second floor. I had already thought about my location strategically; Miriam's room was located on the third floor, so while I had no cause to walk by her door, she had cause to walk by mine. I had only to wonder precisely how aggressive a widow she was.

In the meantime, my mind focused more upon the events of the day. Isaac had made the wine too hot, and in his efforts to handle the hot pewter, my uncle had already spilled a healthy amount on his austere brown coat. He hardly seemed to care, however, just as he hardly seemed to care that I had lost our only copy of *A Conspiracy of Paper.* "It would be better if we still had it," he had said with a shrug, "but these men, they killed your father to keep him silent. If you escape with only having it stolen, perhaps that is not so very terrible."

It had taken a great deal of courage, and two glasses of scalding wine, for me to confess the loss to my uncle. It was a confession that had hurt, for I felt that I had failed in my responsibility to my family, and this failure tasted far too much like the time I had run away from my father. But Uncle Miguel had only clucked in concern, asked me about my injuries, and uttered a blessing to thank God that I had not been further injured. I tried to put myself in his place, to imagine how he should feel, and I in no way could understand why he cared not about the loss of the manuscript. I wished that I could banish the suspicions conjured by his composed spirits, but I could only think that it no longer mattered to him if I found my father's killer—if it had ever mattered.

He sat across from me, eyeing me with concern as his fingers cautiously probed the hot silver handle of his mug. "I fear," he said, "that this inquiry of yours grows too dangerous."

The pain throughout my body had begun to subside into a dull ache. My legs and my neck were both stiff, and my head pounded horribly. "I can hardly stop now," I said, hoping to draw him out. "Does not this violence confirm our suspicions?"

"This family has suffered too many losses," he said as he shook his head. "I cannot look quietly on while you are threatened as well."

"I don't understand. You wanted this inquiry. Has something happened to make you change your mind? Has Mr. Adelman convinced you?"

He laughed. "Adelman," he said, as though the name were enough to explain his mirth. "You think me so easily persuaded by Adelman?"

"I could not say," I mumbled. I thought about what Sarmento had told me—that my father hated Adelman. And I thought about how my uncle welcomed him at his table for Sabbath dinner. "We cannot just walk away from something because it is dangerous, Uncle."

"That is precisely why we should walk away. Because it is dangerous. But"—he held a hand in the air—"you know your business more than I. I would not presume to tell you how to proceed or how to take care for your own safety. I merely wished to say, Benjamin, that I will not have you press on, put yourself in harm's way, on my account."

I could longer remain silent. "Why do you maintain a friendship with Adelman, a man who was my father's enemy?"

He thought to laugh, but held his laughter back, as though it would offend me. Perhaps it would have. "Who told you he and your father were enemies?" He did not pause for an answer. "Mr. Adelman and I have had dealings since he arrived on this island. Your father cared not much for his involvement with the Company, it is true, and he was a man who could little trouble himself to conceal his feelings, but they were not enemies. Merely cool acquaintances."

Perhaps I had misunderstood my uncle. Perhaps he did only wish to see me stay clear of danger. My uncle, unlike my father, was not a coward, but I knew him to be cautious, to guard his position in the community with care, to wish always to say the right thing before the watchful eyes of our Christian neighbors. His concern made me feel ungenerous for doubting him.

Intending to change the topic, I cleared my throat and took a gulp of wine, which had cooled enough that it was pleasingly hot. "Would you object if I wished to escort Miriam to the theatre?"

He shifted uneasily in his chair. "I am not certain that the theatre is the best place for a woman such as Miriam. Perhaps some other social event," he suggested.

"You are very protective of her," I observed.

"She has grown up in this house since she was hardly more than a child, and she married my own son. I feel I have a great responsibility toward her."

"A responsibility to keep her from the theatre?"

"To keep her from harm," he corrected. "You know the sort of elements that haunt the theatre, Benjamin. And you know what a delicate thing a lady's reputation is. To be seen simply talking with the wrong man can ruin her forever. You would not want that, I'm sure."

"Of course not," I said nervously. Uncle Miguel's eyes hung upon every change in my face.

"I shall be direct with you, Benjamin. I notice that you have developed a certain fondness for Miriam. I have not inquired of the matter with her, but I believe she may have it within her to feel the same. You know that she has other suitors, but I do not believe she cares for any of them, and as I say, I wish for her happiness. But I am not such a fool as to send her off in a love match with a man who cannot do her justice."

"I see." I nodded, wishing nothing so much as that this conversation had never happened.

"It would be inappropriate to consider you as a suitor in your current state, but there are always options. You may know that I still have need of an agent in the Levant, and since Aaron's death, I have not found a suitable substitute. You would have to travel a great deal, but there are many opportunities to earn a substantial fortune for both yourself and your family. And, as I'm sure you know, Miriam has one hundred a year settled on her, which should provide an initial level of comfort in establishing a household."

"Miriam has a hundred a year?" I nearly blurted out. While it might be difficult to maintain a luxurious household upon such an amount, for a woman who had no concerns of food or rent, it was an enormous sum. I could not think why Miriam had needed to borrow money, nor why she had tried to deny that she ever made the request. "Does she receive this money now?" I asked.

"Of course. She receives quarterly payments. She received the last one only a few weeks ago. Why do you ask?"

Why did I ask, indeed. "Your offer is very generous, Uncle." I took another drink of my wine and pushed myself to my feet, feeling the ache as I did so. "I do not wish you to think me insensible to what you propose. But I know that I am not the right man to be your Turkey merchant. And though the prize you offer is an estimable one, it shall do me little good if I am so far away."

My uncle stood as well, and placed a hand gently upon my shoulder. "I am perhaps not the most observant man, Benjamin, but I do notice some things. Miriam chose not to travel with Aaron for certain reasons. I am not sure she would feel the same way about you. In any case, I hope you will consider what I offer you. It stands whether you marry or no. I should very much like to see you within the family trade."

I bowed at my uncle, even as I condemned myself for the formal politeness I offered in return for his generous warmth. But I had no wish to live and trade amongst a pack of turbaned Turks, and I had less of a desire to slip so easily into the role of my dead cousin.

THE NEXT DAY I awoke to find myself stiff from the beating I had taken of Wild's men, and the area around my right eye was purple and swollen. My uncle had already left for the warehouse by the time I came downstairs, so I sat at the breakfast table with the two ladies of the house. My aunt inquired if I had taken to fighting in the ring again. Miriam stared at me with a kind of horror.

After breakfast I followed Miriam to the parlor, where she had begun leafing through the newspapers. I could not but feel that there was a coolness in her demeanor, and I suppose there was in mine. I knew that I had no right to resent her for having a lover, but I resented her all the same. I think I wanted her to behave somehow to make my resentment disappear or to make it grow. I knew only that I cared for her and that her intrigue with a man I knew to be a rascal tormented me.

"You are to be part of the family in earnest now," she said to me.

"My uncle has graciously permitted me to stay here during a difficult period."

She turned a page. "He is a generous man, then."

I stared at her. "Have I somehow offended you, Miriam?"

She looked up at me. "You know something of the social politenesses. Have you?"

Had she somehow learned about my following Deloney? If she had, would she dare confront me? I could hardly think so. "I cannot think that I have, madam."

"Then," she said, "it is likely you have not."

I had no mind to play these games with her. "If you decide otherwise," I said, "I can only hope that you will inform me of my transgression so that I may make amends."

"You are too good," she said, and looked back at her paper.

I had too much to do to press on, so I simply bowed and departed. I believed the hour was sufficiently seasonable, so I quit the house and made my way to Balfour's lodgings, but I was told by his landlady that he no longer resided there. "The gentleman is now lodged with his mother," she said. "I thought I knew his type, and I was sure I would have to call the bailiff were I ever to see the rent from the likes of him. But he gives me all what he owes me not three days ago and bids me pack up his things and send them to his mother, he says. And that's what I done."

I retrieved Balfour's new address and thanked her for her time. I then hired a chair to his mother's town house on the Tottenham Court Road. The footman had me cool my heels for well over an hour in a neatly decorated parlor before Balfour whirled into the room, looking about for something or another, which at last he placed in his pocket before turning to address me. He had, I noted, already made an appointment with a tailor, for he had traded his fine but worn suit of clothes for something much finer and newer. He wore a brownish outer coat with a burgundy waistcoat beneath, lined about the sleeve with ample gold stuff. His shirt was of the finest and cleanest white silk, and even his wig—much in the style of his old wig—was quite full, well proportioned, and properly groomed. Balfour was a new man, and he had the clothing to bespeak his newness.

"What do you want?" he asked, as though he had not known I was there and had not noticed me until that moment. He proceeded to a bookshelf, where he pretended to busy himself by searching out a volume.

"And how dare you come here with that mark upon your face, looking like a brawling street ruffian."

I thought I should like to show him how a brawling street ruffian behaved, but I concentrated on the matter at hand. "I am come to report on my progress."

He tapped his foot, but did not turn to face me. "How dreadfully dull. Did I not ask you to stay away from here?"

"If you would prefer, we may retire to a coffeehouse to continue our business."

"*Business*, is it?" He turned around to look at me, his face screwed into an expression of superior scorn—practiced for many hours before the mirror, no doubt. "That is unaccountably presumptuous, don't you think? And why should we have *business* together, may I ask?"

"You did engage my services, Mr. Balfour," I said, careful to keep my tone even.

Balfour snorted. "I suppose I did such a preposterous thing, didn't I? Well, I repent of it now. Mother and I have mended our rift, and I need no longer trouble myself with sordid matters of stock-jobbers and Jews."

He looked about quickly, anxious to find a definitive word to end our conversation, but I was not willing to let him go so easily. I could not say why he wished to dispose of the matter, or even that I cared, but I did think that he might have information I could use. "Tell me," I began, as though we had been having a pleasant conversation all along, "do you know if your father had any dealings with the South Sea Company?"

"I cannot say I know or care," he told me impatiently. "I really must demand—"

I chose not to let him demand. "Mr. Balfour, I am now absolutely convinced that my father was murdered, but I have found no evidence connecting his death to your father's. If you wish to uncover the truth of this matter, then I shall need your cooperation at the very least."

"My father was a silly sod," he said. "An overreaching merchant, and nothing more. No one would bother himself to kill him. It's time for you to depart, Weaver."

I rose slowly. "You are no longer interested in recovering the funds you believe stolen of your father?"

"It always comes down to money with your people, does it not, Weaver? Tell me, have you heard about the little Jew fellow who tumbled to his death from the balcony of the theatre at Drury Lane? The manager kindly presented the poor, grieving mother with a bag of silver to show his regret. 'But, sir,' the Jewess said, 'you must also give me a half shilling, for little Isaac saw only half the show, so he should have half the price of his ticket refunded.' " He burst out laughing, but it was a forced laugh. I stood impassive.

Balfour studied me for a moment and then walked to the door. "Like any other tradesman, you may submit your bill for the work you have performed. Now, I am sure you will excuse me, as I have an appointment to keep."

I wondered how far I could push Balfour and what I would gain should I choose to continue pushing him. His rapprochement with his mother had clearly terminated any desire he had to learn of his father's death. Was I now but an embarrassment to him? A reminder of a few dreadful months when his future was in the balance? Or had he learned something he did not wish me to know? Perhaps the connection between his father and mine was not as friendly as I had once suspected. Balfour was weak; his independence was gone, and his wealth rested in the hands of a mother for whom he cared little—a mother, I could only assume, who would torture Balfour as the price for his regained wealth. I saw I had little to lose by attempting to make him yield.

"I care nothing for any petty discomforts my inquiry brings you. And I should also remind you, sir, that I look into a matter of murder, and if you have any information that might aid my inquiry, you must offer it. If not here, or in the private place of your own choosing, then perhaps in one of His Majesty's courts."

Balfour studied me, and in a moment of strength that I had not been sure he possessed, he chose to disregard my warning. "Get out of my house, Weaver. I have no more business with you."

"Very well." I rose and tucked my hat under my arm. "I see I shall find no cooperation from you. That is your choice, but I can assure you that I am now independently interested in the death of your father, and I intend to continue my inquiry."

"Frankly, Weaver, you may go to the deuce for all I care. What I require is that you stay out of my way."

I smiled and stepped forward until I stood close to him—too close for his comfort. I stared, hovering over his frame. "And how do you propose to stop me, Mr. Balfour, if I should choose to do otherwise?"

Balfour stammered as he struggled to speak. "I promise you, this rudeness shall not again be tolerated." He took a hasty step backward and struck the wall abruptly, frightening himself. "You think yourself the only man in London who knows how to defend himself? Do you think that because it would be beneath a gentleman's honor to call you out to a duel that there are no means left to dispose of a wretch like you? Try my patience no longer, Jew. Get out."

"You will hear from me again," I said, as I placed my hat upon my head. "The moment I have more questions for you."

I left Balfour standing in mute amazement, clutching his hands and certainly thanking the powers of the universe that our altercation had been without witness. For my part, I could not easily forgive this rodent who had set me upon so dangerous a course only to lose interest and obstruct my path. My anger with Balfour was so profound that I knew I should be distracted all day if I did not strike out at him, so on the way home I visited a bailiff to whom I was unknown. Assuming a false name, I swore out an arrest warrant for Balfour for the amount of fifty pounds. Nothing would come of the arrest—it would be thrown out of the courts immediately—but I took great pleasure in thinking of his confusion when spirited away from a public place by some ruffian, locked in a sponging house where he would remain until a lawyer could be procured to make the entire matter disappear.

IN PERPETRATING MY TRICKERY upon Balfour I was not aware that I was participating in a bit of irony set up for me by fate. As I walked the streets, attempting to divine the meaning behind Balfour's rudeness, I noticed that there was a fellow some twenty feet back working to keep apace with me. When I first noticed him, I was not certain that he truly followed, so I increased my pace, dodging hastily between a woman pushing a cart of vegetables and an oyster woman crying her wares. From the peripheries of my vision I saw this fellow struggling to keep me in sight. My pursuer was shockingly tall, perhaps six feet and a half, and monstrous thin as well. His clothes were adequate and neat, like those of a respectable tradesman or lower servant, and his face had been recently shaved. In truth he appeared nothing like the sort of miscreant that Wild engaged in his employ, but the cove followed me for some reason, and, with my late-night encounter with the hackney coach still fresh in my mind, I would believe him as dangerous until he proved otherwise.

Keeping him at a distance as best I could, I slipped into an alley that I knew to have no other point of egress. It made its way straight for some hundred feet or so, and then with a sharp turn, ended another twenty feet on. The alley was a filthy affair, as people in the surrounding houses here emptied their privy stools from the windows above. Rats squeaked noisily as I quickly trotted my way through the filth, which clung about my boots and stockings. I concentrated on my goal; I pretended that I smelled nothing. I had no care for disgust, for the piles of excrement and pools of piss would serve as an effective ally, provided my pursuer's stomach turned while mine remained calm.

And so it worked, for he entered the alley slowly, his own thin leather shoes providing not nearly the protection of my sturdier boots. I heard him as he trudged onward, cursing quietly as he waded toward me. Having passed the bend, I could not see him, but I listened to each slow, painful, repulsed step. I heard him slip, a splash, and then a volley of muttered oaths. If he had anything like the knowledge I had of the Covent Garden streets, he knew the alley to be a blind one and that he must find me cornered in the end. And so he moved on, suppressing a gag, startling at rats, wincing at the cold of his submerged feet. At last he rounded the darkened corner, and unable to see, he took a few steps forward, which was precisely what I had been waiting for.

I jumped down from the narrow walls above where I had lodged myself, and where this fellow had passed directly under me without noticing my presence. As I landed directly behind him, filth splattering the two of us, I pulled my pistol from my waistcoat and pointed it square in the fellow's face.

"Now, my shitten friend," I said with a sneer, "you will tell me who you are and why you follow me, or you will rot here unnoticed until the rains wash all away."

He moved to drop to his knees, but soon thought better of it, and instead staggered to and fro, holding his hands together in supplication. "Don't kill me, Mr. Weaver, sir. It's my first time, it is, and I only want to do right."

Taken aback, but still cautious, I asked who he was and why he followed me.

"I work for Justice Duncombe, sir. The justice of the peace, he is. He's sent me to fetch you. It's me first time for that, sir, as a constable."

"And what does the justice want with me?" I asked, still waving the pistol in his face, though now more absently than maliciously.

"He wants you before his court, he does," the poor constable sputtered, tears in his eyes. "You're under arrest, you are."

JUSTICE JOHN DUNCOMBE was something of an anomaly in London's corrupt legal system. He was a trading justice, to be sure, and would sell a verdict for even a slight consideration rather than pass an opportunity to augment his income. Yet if there was no bribe to be lost he did not, like so many other trading justices, shirk his responsibilities or rule with arbitrary cruelty. Rather, unfettered by the bonds of corruption, he chose to pursue true justice vigorously and often wisely. It was said of John Duncombe that the corruption of justice was his business, but the pursuit of justice was his pleasure.

I could not say if it was for business or pleasure that Duncombe had brought me into his rooms on Great Hart Street. I waited in anticipation, along with the constable, both of us attracting looks of derision from whores and pickpockets, until Duncombe called us before his bench.

He held his court in a largish space attached to his own lodgings upstairs. Perhaps previous tenants had once used the room for balls or other such entertainment, but now it merely housed only the most wretched of the London streets. The judge sat behind his imposing desk toward one end of the room, surrounded by his constables and clerks and servants. His desk was covered with a pile of documents, a few legal books strewn about, and a large bottle of port wine, from which he frequently refilled his glass. At the height of the afternoon, such as it was, the court was not full of the most wretched that could expect to pass through its doors. Duncombe's custom was to handle first thing in the morning the nightly crop of prostitutes, the drunkards, the late-night mischief-makers, housebreakers, footpads, and the other criminals rounded up by the night watch.

During the day, a judge like Duncombe would attend to business held over from these criminals—such as reviewing the case of a vagrant he had committed to a few weeks of labor in Bridewell—or he would take depositions or review matters of somewhat larger consequence as they trickled in before him.

Duncombe was an aging, jowl-heavy man, with small eyes and an enormous bewarted nose. He remained in possession of only a small number of teeth, and his face collapsed grotesquely about the mouth area, giving him a look of an empty satchel dangling below a yellowing wig. I watched, but could not hear as he spoke to a woman who stood before him. She was young, filthy from the kennel of the streets, and her clothes did little more than cover the most delicate secrets of her female anatomy. Duncombe asked her questions with a stony face. She replied with sobs. Finally the justice made a pronouncement of some sort, and the woman fell to her knees and thanked God loudly. One of the constables came by and helped her to her feet and led her out as she praised Duncombe wholeheartedly. I hoped her happiness boded well for me.

"Mr. Benjamin Weaver?" he pronounced my name loudly so that his voice would carry. Duncombe scanned the courtroom until his eyes landed on me. He refused to establish any intimacy with me, though he knew me well; I frequented his court as a witness when I brought forth prigs I apprehended and visited him with some regularity to obtain warrants and to procure a constable for arrests, but Duncombe cared not much for thief-takers, and he believed I must be as dishonest as most of that trade.

"Step forward," he intoned. "But not too much forward, if you please."

I approached the bench and attempted to ignore the laughter around me.

"How came you to be so befouled?" he asked me. "You have frequented this court, but I believe this is the first time you have done so while covered with kennel water."

"As I walked down the street, your honor, I found that I was pursued by a strange man. Not knowing him to be an officer of this court, I thought my life in danger. I sought shelter in an alleyway, which was, unfortunately, notable only for its filth."

He regarded me gravely. "Do you always run from strangers, Mr. Weaver?"

"This is London, your honor. Who that wishes to stay alive does not run from strangers?"

Those who had heard my retort laughed with appreciation. Even the judge smirked a bit.

"I call you here in the matter regarding one Kate Cole, who is to stand trial in two weeks' time for the crime of murder. Your name has been implicated in this case, and I have been asked to take your deposition."

I believe my appearance betrayed nothing of my shock, but I felt as though I had been once again struck from behind by Wild's ruffians. I like to think that I put my life as a criminal behind me in part because I could not condone the immorality of a criminal life. While that is true to some extent, it is no doubt equally true that as a thief-taker I did not expose myself to the haphazard rulings of the legal system. I mean no disrespect to the gentlemen of the bench, but it is no secret that our system of justice, praised throughout Europe for its severity and its swiftness, is a terrible and fearful thing, and no man, guilty or innocent, wishes to stand before it.

Thus my fear was well justified. Had I never in my life heard of Kate Cole nor knew the slightest thing of what the judge spoke, it would in no way guarantee I would not wind up dangling at the end of a rope at Tyburn Tree. I knew I would have to proceed slowly and carefully. "I have nothing to depose," I said, trying hard to look tired and confused. "I have no knowledge of this matter." It was a ticklish business, and while I did not like perjuring myself before the law, I felt I had no choice. To tell the truth in this matter would be to compromise Sir Owen's anonymity, which I had promised to protect. All I could do for the nonce was to attempt to gain more time.

"You have never heard of Kate Cole?" the judge asked skeptically.

"Never," I said.

"That rather saves me some time, then, doesn't it?"

And it was then that I knew that this was a financial matter, not a juridical one. Duncombe would not have dropped the deposition so quickly were it justice instead of silver he chased. I took this development ill; if Duncombe was being paid to involve me in this, then any bribe I might offer, and that he would accept, would do me little good. It was the rule of trading justices to take bribes from all parties but to favor the most powerful. I was no match for Wild in this regard.

"I shall indicate that you deny all knowledge of this person and her crimes," Duncombe said. "However, you must be informed that her trial is to take place at the Old Bailey in exactly two weeks' time, and that you must be prepared to be called as a witness for the defense. You are not to leave London between now and that time, for this court might have need of you again. Do you understand, Mr. Weaver?"

I nodded. "I believe I understand quite clearly, your honor."

"Then it is my advice that you bathe."

With that Duncombe dismissed me, and after offering a sympathetic clap on the shoulder of my miserable constable, I left the justice's offices with a feeling of dejection. In my mind I could see myself standing before the bar at Kate Cole's murder trial. And while I was willing to lie before someone such as Duncombe, I did not feel willing to perjure myself at a murder trial in the Old Bailey. Should it come to that, I would be forced to tell the truth, and I was therefore obliged to let Sir Owen know what turn events had taken.

Duncombe had said that I was to be a witness for the defense. That meant that it was not Wild, but Kate, who had offered my name, for there was no reason why Wild would want to see a woman defended whose conviction would yield him forty pounds. Yet I could not fathom how Kate could have learned of my name, or if she had, what she had to gain by involving me without first seeking me out. She surely understood that I was anxious to keep my name out of her trial and would have gone to great lengths to do just that. It was possible that Wild had indeed thrown my name into the matter in order to play me against Kate. Was it his hope that he could hang Kate and ruin my reputation with a single stroke? I could not even begin to guess. Elias had advised that I inquire into these matters using probability, not facts, but for probability there needed at least to be logic, and here I could find none.

TWENTY-FIVE

O NCE I HAD cleaned myself and dressed, doing what I could to avoid too much attention from the servants at my uncle's house, I sent a message to Sir Owen asking him to meet me at a local alehouse. He sent back a reply, and within a few hours I sat facing him over a comforting mug.

Sir Owen, however, did not look comforted. Gone was the avuncular warmth I had recognized from our earlier meetings. His tight-lipped scowl bespoke agitated nerves, and he looked at the door several times each minute.

"This is an unpleasant business," Sir Owen said. "You promised me to keep my name out of this affair, Weaver." He absently ran a finger over the handle of his mug.

I was still quite stiff, but I attempted to affect the air of a man relaxed and in command. I had often learned that, like a player upon the stage, the way I held my body could affect the emotions of those to whom I spoke. "I promised to do all I could, and I intend to keep that promise, but I cannot lie before the court, or I could very well face murder charges myself. Sir Owen, this matter has grown larger than either of us had anticipated, and I believe that the prudent course is now to prepare for the possibility that I may have to mention your name in court. I am certain that with the proper preparation you can ensure that no serious damage—"

"Your job is to protect those who hire you," he grumbled, without looking up. "You must do what it takes. Is it more money you want?"

"Really, Sir Owen, you shock me with these accusations. I have served you as best I could at every turn."

"I wonder," he said absently, "how do you explain this woman's sudden ability to name you in this matter? You told me that she had no knowledge of who you were or where to find you." He sat upright and drank hard from his mug.

"That is true," I said, "but it seems that Wild has found out, and I cannot but assume that Wild is behind this mischief."

"Wild," he spat. "He will see us all undone. I was a fool to trust you in this, Weaver. You are, if you will forgive me for saying so, a short-tempered Jew who thinks with his fists. Had you not shot anyone, none of this would have happened."

I had no patience for Sir Owen's sudden unpleasant and accusatory mood. He had been jolly enough when I had shot Jemmy down in the street—so long as the shooting never need trouble his quiet. "It is true that had no one been killed there would be no need for a murder trial, but one might add that had you not been careless with your papers none of this might have happened."

I had thought to anger him, unbalance him perhaps, but my accusation only served to make Sir Owen believe in his own authority. He straightened out in his chair, and he regarded me with cold eyes. "You forget yourself," he said quietly. "You have brought far too much trouble upon your head, and mine as well, by sneaking about where you have no business. How do we know that it is not the South Sea that is behind this sudden turn with the whore? The Company would certainly like to see you silenced in any way possible. All this sneaking about, looking to see who killed your father. Could it not wait until the business with the whore was done?"

I was about to speak when I stopped myself and thought on what Sir Owen had said. "How do you know of that matter?" I asked in a calm voice, hoping to reveal nothing.

I watched Sir Owen carefully for any sign of confusion, but he exhibited nothing but exasperation. "Who in London does not know that you are poking about into Balfour's self-murder? It is no secret that you are stirring up trouble for the South Sea Company, and I heartily fear that you are stirring up trouble for me at the same time. What kind of a man are you, anyway, to keep your father's name a secret? We sat among men of parts talking about Lienzo and you never said a word. Did you wish to embarrass me in my own club, Weaver? Is that what you are about?"

"If you are embarrassed," I said calmly, "it is your own doing."

Sir Owen clenched his teeth. "You are an irresponsible rascal to involve me in your sordid matters. I wish you had kept me out of it, for they will surely drag me into the gutter beside you."

As Sir Owen grew increasingly belligerent, I thought it best to let him rant, ignoring his unkind observations about Jews in general and me in particular until he quite wore himself out. Finally he assumed a more reasonable posture. "I shall speak to men I know who are not without some small influence. Perhaps I can do something to keep you from being summoned at this trial. In the meantime, you must give me your word that should you be summoned, you will not speak my name or in any way connect me to your shooting that man."

"Sir Owen," I said in a calm, quiet voice, "we must do what we can to see that it does not come to that, but I cannot make that promise. I shall hold my tongue as long as I can safely do so. I do not know that your name will never be asked of me. The court may not consider it of importance on whose behalf I sought out Kate. But if forced to speak in whose name I acted that night, I shall not be able to refuse. Is there no way to inform your wife-to-be, Miss Decker, of some small notion of your past—just enough to steel her against any unpleasant rumors she may encounter?"

I chose the wrong thing to say. Sir Owen's fist clenched and his jaw tightened. He stared at me in disbelief for what seemed like ages. "What would you know of a refined lady's sensibilities?" he sputtered. "You know nothing more than whores and gutter rubbish."

Perhaps I should have been more sensitive to a man in his position, but I could not find it in my heart to feel sympathy with Sir Owen's accusatory tone. I had done all I could do and more in his service. His expectation that I swing at Tyburn to show my loyalty was hardly just, and his accusations about the women in my life inappropriate, to say the least. "Is there not," I asked calmly, "something in your gospels about only the sinless casting stones, Sir Owen?"

He stared full at me. "We have nothing more to discuss," he said, and hastily departed.

. . .

SIR OWEN'S PANIC left me confused, but not entirely dejected. He was, after all, on the verge of a public embarrassment—one that could jeopardize his upcoming marriage—and I felt that he was right in suggesting that I was in no small part to blame. I was more concerned with how this unfortunate chain of activity had been set into motion and what I could do to set it right. I thought it logical that Jonathan Wild had been the man to bring me into Kate Cole's business, but again the question remained why. Sir Owen had suggested that it might be the Company itself that had tossed me, and the baronet along with me, into harm's way, and that was a possibility I could not ignore.

I believed there was but one person who could explain these matters to my satisfaction, and so once again I made my way to Newgate prison to speak to Kate Cole.

After I passed through the terrible Newgate portal, and in exchange for a few coins, the warder led me to the Press Yard, where Kate's room lay. The turnkey there explained to me that Kate had asked to take no visitors, but that was a request a few shillings soon dispensed with.

The room itself was surprisingly pleasant—it had a reasonably comfortable-looking bed, a few sitting chairs, a table, a writing desk, and a wardrobe. A small window allowed for a modicum of light to trickle in, but not enough to render the room sufficiently bright—even in full daylight—and a superfluity of cheap tallow candles cast streaks of black soot against the wall. Scattered about the room were empty flagons and tankards, pieces of half-eaten joints of meat, and stale crusts of white bread. Kate had been living well off her remittance.

If, however, she had been making the purchases of a gentlewoman, she knew not how to live as one. She wore new clothes—no doubt procured from the money I left her—but they were horribly soiled with food and drink, wrinkled as though she had slept in them, and smelled distractingly filthy. The lice she had acquired during her nightmarish hours on the Common Side of the prison had stayed with her, and they fairly crawled about her skin like anxious pedestrians on a busy street.

Kate showed no small amount of displeasure at seeing me in her doorway. She greeted me with a scowl of broken teeth and promptly turned away, unwilling to look me in the face.

The turnkey appeared at the threshold. "Will ye be wantin' anything, then?" he asked.

"A bottle of wine," Kate hissed. " 'E's paying for it." She pointed to me. He politely shut the door.

"Now, Kate," I began, taking one of her wooden chairs and turning it to face her, "is this any way to treat your benefactor?" I sat down and awaited her reply, gently pushing away with my foot an uncovered chamber pot.

"I've nothing to say to ya." She pouted like a child.

"I cannot imagine why you are angry with me. Have I not set you up in ease and taken you out of harm's way?"

Kate looked up slowly. "Ya 'aven't taken me out of the gallows' way, nor Wild's neither. So if that's what ya 'ere about, ya kin be damned, for I 'adn't a choice, ya see."

"What precisely are you saying to me, Kate?"

"That it was Wild, it was. It was 'im that 'ad me 'peach ya. I weren't to say nothing, but Wild, first 'e said as ya was to see me 'ang, but when I told 'im it weren't true, 'e then told me that *'e* would see me 'ang and that 'e 'ad more pull with the judge, 'e did, than ever ya did. So that's what 'appened an' ya kin do with it what ya will."

I was silent for a moment, attempting to put it all in perspective. Kate was breathing hard, as though that speech had taken all her energy. I suppose part of it had been rehearsed—she had to know I would pay her this visit.

It was at least some small progress to learn that it was Wild who had involved me in Kate's case. It did not mean that Wild was behind the murders of Balfour and my father, but it did mean that he had been far less than honest when he asserted that he was willing to suffer me as a rival so long as I went after the South Sea Company.

There were simply too many unrelated pieces of information for me to sort it all out, perhaps because my sorting method was flawed; Elias *had* chastised me for thinking of each element of the inquiry separately. How, then, might I consider the relationships between the disparate elements?

I was here to speak to Kate about Wild, but perhaps I should speak to her about something else, for there was still one enigma at the center of my inquiry—Martin Rochester. He had supposedly hired the man who ran down my father, and it seemed as though every man in 'Change Alley knew something of him. But it was Wild's assertions about Rochester that most interested me, for the great thief-taker had been determined to convince me of Rochester's villainy while at the same time providing me with no useful information. Now, here I was with Kate—Kate who knew at least something of Wild's business and who had no love for her master. Perhaps I could learn from her what share of these crimes belonged to Rochester.

The turnkey returned and provided us with a bottle of wine. He demanded the outrageous price of six shillings, which I paid because it was more convenient to do so than to debate the matter.

Kate grabbed the bottle from my hand, uncorked it, and took a long swig. After wiping her mouth with the back of her hand she looked at me, certainly debating whether or not to offer me any. I suppose she considered that she had done me too much harm to make amends with small gestures, so she kept the wine for herself.

I let her take another drink before I spoke. "Do you know a man named Martin Rochester?"

"Ooh," she screeched like a rat pressed beneath a boot, "now it's Martin Roch'ster that's in it, eh? Well I'll not be put upon by the like of 'im. 'E's caused me enough trouble, 'e 'as."

"Then you know him?" I asked anxiously. I felt my heart should burst with excitement. Could it be that I had finally found someone who was willing to admit to more than a vague familiarity with this enigmatic man?

"Oh, I know 'im all right, I do," Kate said indolently. " 'E's as mis'ble a bastard as Wild, and twice as smart 'e is, too. What's Roch'ster got on this?"

I could not believe my luck. I was astonished that Kate should speak of her acquaintance with this man so casually. "I don't know," I said truthfully. "But I grow convinced that if I can find him, I can make both of our lives easier. What can you tell me about him?"

Kate opened her mouth, indeed she began to make some noises, but she caught herself, and her lips spread into a carnivorous smirk. "Ya still ain't told me what Roch'ster is to ya."

"What is he to you?" I demanded. "What do you know of him?"

"I know 'im well, I do. Very well indeed."

"You've met him, then?" I asked. "Do you know where he can be found?"

"Oh, I met 'im, sure. But 'e can't be found if 'e don't wan'cha finding 'im, I kin tell ya as much. That's 'is stock an' trade, it is. 'E's an 'ard one."

"Can you tell me anything that might make it easier for me to find him?"

She shook her head. "Only that ya'd better find 'im before 'e finds ya."

"Can you describe him to me?"

"Oh, I reckon I could."

"Then please do."

Kate looked at me with a gleam in her eye. I could see she had an idea she thought remarkably clever. "Why don't we say I'll do that after I'm set free?" She flashed a wine-stained grin at me.

"I am willing to pay for any information that will help me find Rochester."

"I'll wager yer willin' to pay, but while yer willin' to pay, I'm rottin' in jail, ain't I? Ya keep tellin' me what ya want, but if I give ya everythin' that ya want then I don't got nothin', and I'm sure to be carted off to Tyburn. So from now on, ya just think about all the things ya want of me, and I'll be 'appy to 'and 'em over once I walk outta Newgate."

"Kate," I said, feeling my body clench with anger, "I don't think you understand how important this is." I thought about Wild's interest in my inquiry, and his efforts to drag me into Kate's trial. There had to be some link between these two matters, but I knew not what it was. Rochester was the elusive figure behind my father's death, and he had some connection with Wild. I believed that if only I could learn more of it, I would understand many of the mysteries that plagued me.

Kate, however, showed no interest in my concerns. "I care nothin' for yer troubles, and I know full well that it's Wild what's be'ind mine. And I know there's nothin' with Wild and Roch'ster, so there's nothin' ya can say or do to Roch'ster to 'elp me."

I attempted to reason with her for near another quarter hour, but she would not budge. I thought of evicting her from the cell I had provided, but that could do me no good. So I left her, determined to try again and determined to think of something that would offer me the leverage to make her speak.

THE NEXT DAY I received a message to meet Virgil Cowper at Jonathan's. I arrived a quarter of an hour before our planned meeting time, but found him at a table by himself, huddled over a dish of coffee.

"What have you found?" I asked, sitting across from him.

He hardly even looked at me. "There is no evidence that Samuel Lienzo ever subscribed to any South Sea issues."

I cannot claim this information greatly surprised me. Considering what I knew of my father's stance about the Company and the Bank of England, I should be surprised to learn he had been a stock-holder.

"However," he continued, "Mr. Balfour is another case altogether. He had owned stock worth more than twenty thousand pounds."

I knew not how successful a businessman Balfour had been, but twenty thousand pounds was an astronomical amount to invest in but a single fund. And if that fund should prove ruined, I should think nearly any investor should prove ruined too.

"You said *had* owned," I thought aloud. "He did not own, then, at the time of his death?"

"I cannot comment on the time of his death, but the records show that Mr. Balfour bought his stock near two years ago and sold it again fourteen months later—about ten months ago. The stock rose not insignificantly in that time, and he made himself a handsome profit."

If Balfour had sold his stock ten months ago, then his transaction with the South Sea Company had come and gone ten months before his death. How, then, could his supposed self-murder be linked to the Company?

"To whom did he sell?" I inquired.

"Why, he sold back to the Company, sir," Cowper cheerfully informed me.

That was hard luck, for had he sold to another individual, I could trace that person. Once again the trail ended with the Company, and once again, I could think of no next step.

"I did come across another name," Cowper then informed me. He smiled crookedly, like a thief upon the street offering to sell a costly handkerchief cheap.

"Another name?"

"Yes. Related to one of the names you gave me."

"And what name is that?"

He ran his index finger along the bridge of his nose. "It will cost you another five pounds."

"And what if this name means nothing to me?"

"Then you have wasted your five pounds, I should think."

I shook my head, but I counted out the coins all the same.

Cowper quickly pocketed them. "The name I came across is also Lienzo. Miriam Lienzo—address listed as Broad Court, Dukes Place."

I worked my jaw over nothing. "That is the only Lienzo you found?"

"The only one."

I could not even take the time to consider what it meant that Miriam owned South Sea stock. With Cowper here, I needed to be sure about my father and Balfour.

"Is there another possibility?" I inquired. "About the other name, Samuel Lienzo?"

"What sort of possibility?" He affected a laugh and then stared without interest at his coffee.

I thought on how I could word my idea. "That he thought he had stock when he did not."

"I'm sure I do not understand you," Cowper said. He moved to drink from the dish, but he could not bring himself to place it to his lips.

"Then let me be more precise. Is there a possibility that he owned forged South Sea issues?"

"There is no possibility," he said hastily. "Now, if you will excuse me." He began to stand.

I was not prepared to let him depart. I reached out, grabbed his shoulder, and forced him back down. Perhaps I did so a bit too roughly. He grimaced with discomfort as I shoved him onto his bench. "Do not toy with me, Mr. Cowper. What do you know?"

He sighed and pretended to be unimpressed with my bellicose manner. "There have been rumors around South Sea House, but nothing specific. Please, Mr. Weaver, I could lose my position for even speculating that such things might exist. I wish to speak no more about it. Do you not understand the risks I take by telling you as much as I have?"

"Do you know anything of a Mr. Martin Rochester?" I demanded.

His face now turned bright red. "I told you, sir, that I would not discuss the matter."

I rejoiced inwardly, for Cowper had just inadvertently given me far more information than I could have hoped for: in his mind, it seemed, forged stock and Martin Rochester were related concerns. "What amount could entice you to change your mind?"

"Not any amount." He stood up and made his way from the coffee-house.

I sat there for some moments, staring at the pulse of the crowd around me, uncertain of how to proceed. Could the South Sea Company have killed old Balfour to regain its twenty thousand pounds? Clearly not, for I now had learned that he had sold the stock back to the Company itself. More than that, if their dealings were as massive as my uncle suggested, measured in the millions, then twenty thousand pounds were as nothing to so grand an institution. Could it be that there was something else here—something I had overlooked? What if their motivation was not the money, but the ruin itself? I had assumed all along that old Balfour had been killed for money while my father had been killed for another reason—a reason related to the theft of old Balfour's estate. Now it appeared that those assumptions were wrong—or at the very least dubious.

My thoughts were then interrupted by one of the house boys who came through crying out the name of a gentleman for whom he had a message. I bethought myself of a wonderful idea, and immediately called for a paper and pen and wrote out a brief note. I then summoned the boy over and slipped a few pence into his hand.

"Call out for this in a quarter of an hour," I told him. "If no one claims it, tear it up."

"Certainly, Mr. Weaver." He flashed a silly grin and began to trot off.

I grabbed his arm. Not hard, but just enough to make him stop. "How do you know my name?" I asked, freeing him from my grip. I had no wish to make him feel threatened.

"You're a famous person, sir," he announced, pleased with his knowledge. "A boxer, sir."

"Are you not a little young to have seen me fight?" I inquired, half to myself.

"I never saw you fight, but I heard about you. And then you was pointed out to me."

My face betrayed nothing. "Who pointed me out?"

"Mr. Nathan Adelman, sir. He asked me to let him know if I saw you. Though he had no message for you." His voice trailed off, for the first time, I think, suspecting that Adelman might not have wished him to say anything to me. He covered up the damage he had done by showing me another grin.

I gave him a few more pence. "For your trouble," I said, hoping my money would dissuade him from thinking too hard on his blunder.

The boy ran off, giving me some time to think of what he had said.

Adelman wished to know if I made my way to Jonathan's. I could not suppose there was anything too sinister in that. One thing I had come to believe was that Adelman told the truth when he said that even men who had nothing to hide would wish to impede my inquiry. I knew not if Bloathwait's suspicions, like my father's, of false South Sea stock were true or not, but I did know that even the rumor of it would be horribly damaging to the Company—so much so that Virgil Cowper had been afraid even to listen to talk of such a thing.

In a quarter of an hour, as promised, the boy reappeared, ringing his bell loudly. "Mr. Martin Rochester," he bellowed. "Message for Mr. Martin Rochester."

I thought it something of a stroke of brilliance on my part. I had no expectation that Rochester would be here, that he would reveal himself so easily—he had done far too much to keep himself hidden for that, but I thought this display might shake something loose. And I was correct.

I cannot say that all conversation stopped. Indeed, many conversations continued oblivious to the boy's cry. But some stopped. I watched as men deep in argument ceased speaking in mid-sentence and looked up, mouths still open like befuddled cattle. I saw men whispering, men scratching their heads, men scanning the room, looking to see if anyone answered the call. The boy strolled through the room and could not have received more attention if he had been the finest actress of the stage, come to strut naked through a gentleman's club.

The boy made a complete pass, and then shrugged and returned to his duties. Slowly, the jobbers who had been disturbed by my experiment returned to their other interests, but within a few minutes I saw a man stand and begin to walk after the boy.

It was Miriam's lover, Philip Deloney.

I watched him exchange a few words with the boy and then leave. I stood up and walked over to the boy, who was busy collecting dirtied dishes from tables.

"Did that man say what he wanted?"

"He wanted to know who sent that message, Mr. Weaver."

"And what did you tell him?"

"I told him you did, sir."

I laughed softly. Why not tell him? "What did he say?"

"He asked to see it, but I told him I'd already torn it to bits, just like you said."

I could not fault the boy his honesty. I thanked him and made my way out of Jonathan's.

A strong wind struck me as I opened the door and headed into the Alley. What interest could Deloney have with Martin Rochester? Was it simply coincidence that he had an intimacy with Miriam and also involved himself with the man I believed responsible for my father's death? I could not answer that question with any certainty. But I knew that I could no longer consider my interest in my cousin Miriam a distraction from my work. I could no longer doubt that her lover somehow had a connection to the death of my father.

I WANDERED UNTIL I was close to Grub Street, where the bookseller, Mrs. Nahum Bryce, had told me I should find the shop belonging to Christopher Hodge, who had published my father's pamphlets. At Grub Street I stepped into a public house to inquire the location of Hodge's business, but the tapman there only shook his head.

"Shop's gone, it is," he said. "An' Hodge went with it. Fire, it was— terrible one what killed him and pretty badly scorched a couple of 'prentice boys with 'im. Coulda been much worse, I reckon, but at least it happened when he'd given most everyone a night off."

"A fire," I repeated. "When?"

The tapman looked up, trying to recall. "I'm thinking three, four months now," he speculated.

I thanked him and made my way to Moor Lane, where I once again called upon Mr. Bryce's widow. She emerged from the back of his shop, a quiver in the corners of her mouth betraying some small amusement upon seeing me again. I requested a private audience, and she escorted me through the back to a small parlor of sorts, where I sat upon an aging and somewhat threadbare settee. She took an armchair across from me and instructed one of the apprentices to bring us tea.

"How may I be of service to you, sir?" Mrs. Bryce asked me.

"I wish to inquire of some information you gave me that I found most odd. You see, I find it very strange that you would advise me to seek out a Mr. Christopher Hodge of Grub Street when Mr. Hodge's shop, along with Mr. Hodge, appears to have burned down some months ago."

Mrs. Bryce's mouth opened and closed several times, as she attempted to form some thought. "You astonish me," she began at last. "And it pains me, sir, for you to believe that I should in some way deceive you. Were I a man, I might call you out for such an error; as I am a woman, I must understand that you do not know me, and any insult you offer me is an insult to a person you think me to be—a person who does not exist."

"I stand ready to offer you my apology if I have in some way misjudged you."

"I never seek an apology, I assure you. Only that you should not be convinced of a falsehood. As I recall, sir, when you inquired of the publisher of Mr. Lienzo's pamphlets, I mentioned Christopher Hodge, for he had, indeed, sent to press some writings of Mr. Lienzo's. I know much about Mr. Hodge's doings, for he was a great friend of my husband's and of mine. Indeed, after Mr. Bryce's death, Mr. Hodge provided me with a great deal of assistance in running this business. I was not ignorant of his death, for it touched upon me very deeply. But as to my failing to inform you of Kit Hodge's passing, I need only remind you that you interrupted my narrative to ask me about Mr. Deloney, and you then abruptly rushed off. If I omitted any details you may have sought, you must consider that the fault rests with you, sir, for having departed in such a haste."

I stood and bowed. "You are just in your censure, Mrs. Bryce. I have been hasty." I returned to my seat.

"It is no matter. As I say, I only wished for matters to be clear in your mind. Although," she said, and I could see from the grin she attempted to suppress, that she was perhaps about to say something that might amuse her, "I find this accusation of deception most interesting. For it occurs to me that Mr. Deloney returned to my store just yesterday, and I asked him if he had been contacted by you, sir. When I told him your name, he assured me that he had never gone to school with you, and he then abused you with some names I shall never repeat. So, you see, sir, from my point of view, it appears very much as though you have been deceiving me."

I could do nothing but laugh, and heartily too. I rose again to my feet and bowed at Mrs. Bryce. "You have corrected me, madam, and I thank you."

She only returned her charming widow's smile. "I must say your response astonishes me. And I should very much like to hear more why you felt compelled to deceive me on the score of your relationship with Mr. Deloney."

"Mrs. Bryce," I began, "I shall be honest with you, but I hope you will forgive me if I am circumspect as well. I have been hired to determine if there was something other than accidental in the death of Samuel Lienzo, and I have come to suspect that there may indeed be, and that his death may be related to information he had obtained—information he wished to publish in a pamphlet. I held, and lost, a manuscript copy of the pamphlet, and I wished to know if Mr. Lienzo had attempted to publish a copy of it before his death. If I was deceptive, or if I suspected you of deception, it is only because this inquiry has imparted upon me the need to be both discreet and suspicious."

Mrs. Bryce gasped. "Do you mean to say," she began, "that you think Mr. Deloney is somehow involved in all of this?"

I had no desire to speak of my suspicions, so I only told the bookseller that my suspicion of Mr. Deloney had proved misguided.

"The fire that burned down Mr. Hodge's shop," I pressed on. "As you knew him, I cannot but wonder if you were in any way suspicious of this blaze."

Mrs. Bryce shook her head. "I was not. As much as his death pained me, we cannot look for intent in all disasters. I thought nothing more of it than its sadness. Do you mean to suggest, sir, that you believe his shop was burned and he was murdered in order to prevent the publication of Lienzo's pamphlet? Why, the very notion is fantastical."

"I should have thought much the same," I told her, "until very recently. I do not say I believe these allegations to be true, madam, but I believe them to be at least possible."

"I suppose the first step must be to determine whether he had the pamphlet in his possession at the time the shop burned. As it happens, I took over his affairs after his death. He had stipulated as much in his will. Most of his materials were destroyed, but some of his record books remain. If you'd like, we can look through these."

I thanked Mrs. Bryce and together we went to her study, where she presented to me a half-dozen volumes of ledger books that smelled of charring and mildew. Hodge had written in them in a dense but legible hand, and for the second time in a very short period I found myself feeling uneasy at studying the scribblings of a man whose life had been, in all probability, taken from him. Together we pored over the books for two hours, drinking tea as Mrs. Bryce explained to me notations and talked about particular works—if they had done well or poorly, if her husband had liked them or not. Finally, after we had been forced to strike several candles against the growing darkness, Mrs. Bryce found a line in one of the books: "Lienzo—conspiracy/paper."

I stared at it. "It seems compelling evidence," I said quietly.

Mrs. Bryce took her time responding. "It doesn't prove anyone killed Mr. Hodge," she said at last, "but all the same, I would appreciate it if you no longer frequented my shop."

Twenty-six

WHEN I RETURNED to my uncle's house I found that old Isaac, the servant, awaited my return with a large package just delivered for me.

"Who is it from?" I asked Isaac.

He shook his head. "The boy who brought it wouldn't say, sir. He gave it to me, held out his hand for a coin, and left without answering any questions."

I hesitated for a moment, for I found something frightening in secret messages, and I did not like the idea of the players in this game seeking me out in my uncle's home.

While I inspected the box, Miriam entered the room and greeted me casually. The look on my face gave her pause, however. "Does something trouble you?" I felt uncomfortable under the heat of her gaze upon my bruised eye, but at least she seemed to have forgotten her earlier coolness, and that was perhaps enough for me.

I showed her the bundle. She merely shrugged. "Open it," she said.

I sucked in my breath and began to untie the packaging. Miriam looked on curiously as I opened it and found inside the most remarkable contents. It was a costume and a ticket to a masquerade ball to be held that evening at the Haymarket. A note affixed to the invitation read:

Sir,

You are encouraged to attend this ball of Mr. Heidegger's tonight, where many of the questions you seek will be answered. In a place where all are disguised, one may feel free to speak openly. I look forward to our meeting in a place where I hope to prove myself,

A friend.

Miriam attempted to read the note, but I quickly folded it and hid it from her view.

"How intriguing," Miriam noted. "It's rather like a romance."

"Rather too much like one," I noted as I removed the costume. Perhaps this secret contact hoped to throw suspicion off me by casting me in the most obvious light, for the costume provided was that of a Tudesco peddler. The clothes were tattered robes accompanied by a floppy hat and a collection of inconsequential trinkets affixed to a tray. The mask covered the top of my face only, with eye-holes over two tiny, evil-looking eyes perched above a grotesquely huge false nose. Below and above the mask were ample quantities of false red hair to make an unruly cover over my own hair as well as to disguise the bottom of my face with an impenetrable thicket of false beard.

"Someone," I noted, "has a grotesque sense of humor."

"Does that help you determine who sent the costume?"

"Not particularly," I mused, "unless it was my friend Elias."

"Will you go?" Miriam asked me. She sounded excited, as though she found the idea of this intrigue thrilling—and like a romance, without any true risk of danger.

"Oh, I should think so," I said.

But I did not wish to go according to the terms of my anonymous patron. I therefore sent for Elias, who was kind enough to exit himself from a rehearsal of his play to attend me at Broad Court.

Miriam and I sat in the parlor, though she hardly spoke to me. I remained in contemplation while she read a book of verse. Several times I believed she had been upon the cusp of speaking to me, but she held herself back. I wished she would tell me what was upon her mind, but my own thoughts were so occupied with the matter at hand that I could hardly think of how to frame my question. So I said nothing until Isaac brought Elias into the room. I could see from the look upon his face that he was poised to produce some quip at the expense of my people, but he held his tongue upon seeing Miriam, whose beauty stopped him in midbreath.

"Weaver," he said, "I see you have been wise in not speaking of your cousin's loveliness, for such treasures must be kept in secret, lest they be stolen." He bowed deeply to Miriam.

"But he has not kept you a secret, sir," Miriam replied, "for he has told me of his great and trusted friend Elias, on whom he depends more than any man alive."

Elias bowed again, beaming with pride.

Miriam grinned with pleasure. "He has also told me that his great friend is a libertine who will tell any lie that he might undo innocence."

"Good God, Weaver!"

She laughed. "Perhaps he said no such thing, and I merely draw my own conclusions."

"Madam, you misunderstand me," Elias began desperately.

"Elias," I snapped, "we have urgent business, and time is not our ally."

A waggish smile washed over Elias's face. "What has developed, my less-than-jovial Jew?"

Under the circumstances I thought it best that Miriam leave the room; she knew nothing of these matters, and I had no wish to introduce her to my intrigues.

Once Miriam left, I showed Elias the note and invitation. "What know you of these balls?"

"You cannot be serious," he said. "Heidegger's masquerades are the very pink of the fashion. I should be ashamed of myself if I did not attend them regularly. Only the most fashionable sort can count on procuring an invitation." With that he produced a pair of tickets from his pocketbook. "I shall attend tonight, accompanied by Miss Lucy Daston, an ambitious young lady with a small but nevertheless crucial role in a comedy soon to take Drury Lane by surprise."

"You will indeed be there," I said with a smile, "but instead of a beautiful actress, I think you would have a far superior time escorting a more manful companion." I grinned at him. "And I have the very costume for you." I showed him the disguise that came with the invitation.

Elias stared in horror. "Gad, Weaver, surely you mock me. Can you expect me to give up my evening with fair Lucy in order to wander about Heidegger's dressed as a bearded mendicant? I shall never get this close to such a beauty again; it seems as though every time I take a liking to an actress she disappears, only to become one of Jonathan Wild's whores. And you do not seem to understand the effect my failure to bed this wench will have on my constitution."

I placed an arm about his shoulder. "I must say I am delighted with you. You come here with a ticket and, I am confident, a costume I might borrow. I think we shall have a splendid time."

Elias picked up the costume and stared at the mask. "It is true that Lucy lacks your wit," he said mournfully, "but I must say that you are a devilish harsh companion. I have no other friends who ask me to do such things."

"And that is why you spend your time with me." I grinned.

"Will your uncle reward me for my efforts when we capture the murderous fiend?"

"I am certain. If you were not already to be rich of the proceeds of your play, your help in this matter would make you a rich man."

"Splendid!" Elias chirped. "Now, let us talk about this widow cousin of yours."

MASQUERADES, AS MY READER will know well, were at the very height of their popularity at the time of this history, but until one has actually attended such a gathering, its precise nature cannot be imagined fully. Think of a large, gorgeously decorated space, exquisite music playing, delectable foods passed about in abundance, and hundreds of the most absurdly dressed men and women intermixing freely. Anonymity made women bold and men bolder, and the hiding of one's face left one free to expose parts of one's mind and body normally left concealed in public.

To complement the disguise of the costume, no one spoke in his true voice, but obscured it with the masquerade squeak. Thus, to envision the assembly, think only of the Haymarket full of shrill and squawking Pans and milkmaids, devils and shepherdesses, and of course countless black, hooded dominos—the ideal costume for men who enjoyed the hunt of the masquerade but lacked the imagination, desire, or sense of humor to dress as a goatherd, harlequin, friar, or any of the characters in vogue. While the string band played delightful tunes from Italy, these identical blackened figures—enshrouded in shapeless robes, faces covered with masks that hid the visage above the nose—moved about the room as wolves circling a wounded hart.

In such a black disguise I, too, moved about. I had originally thought to borrow Elias's costume—with an appropriate sense of self, my friend had planned on attending dressed as Jove, and we traveled to his lodgings, where I found that the Olympian's robes fit too snug upon me, so we set out to procure a masquerade domino.

Elias took me to a tailor with whom he was friendly—that is to say, he currently owed him no money—and whose shop was well known to masqueraders. Even as we entered we saw a pair of gentlemen purchasing dominos. And as we engaged upon the errand, I made an effort to inform Elias of all I had recently discovered—most distressingly, the news that old Balfour had once owned twenty thousand pounds' worth of South Sea stock.

"No wonder he was ruined," he said, as I slipped a black domino over me and adjusted the hood. "To lose so much. Inconceivable."

I put the mask upon my face, and looked in the mirror. I looked like a great black apparition. "But according to my man at South Sea House, Balfour sold the stock long before his death."

Elias fiddled with the sleeves in his fastidious way. "Could your man not inform you to whom he sold?"

"He sold to no one," I said, as I slipped the domino off. "He sold back to the Company."

I stepped forward from the secluded area to purchase the costume. Elias had grown red in the face, as though he could not stand to breathe. I knew he wished to tell me something in private, but he had to wait until I had paid for my costume and the tailor had wrapped it for me. After these excruciating minutes had passed, we stepped out in the street, and afforded privacy by noise and distraction, Elias let forth a long breath.

"Have you no idea how that sounds, Weaver? You cannot just sell back to the Company. Stock is not a trinket that you can return to the shop."

"If Cowper wished to sell me misinformation, would he not have sold me believable misinformation?"

"You did believe it," he pointed out, pushing his way past a slow-moving gathering of old ladies. "But I take your point. Perhaps what he wished was to make you suspicious."

"I shall go mad," I announced, "if I must always suspect people of telling me lies so that I shall know they are lying. What ever happened to telling a man lies he meant a man to believe?"

"The problem with you, Weaver," Elias announced, "is that you are too invested in the values of the past."

After dining and taking a bottle of wine, we arrived at the masquerade, and I spent much of the evening drifting about, sometimes speaking to Elias, but mainly keeping my distance, so that it would not be obvious that the begging Jew was with me—or even that he had come with help should he need it. I was nevertheless shocked when, near enough to Elias to hear his conversation, yet inconspicuously acquiring a drink of wine from a serving boy, I saw a woman with a stunning shape, dressed as some Roman goddess or other, approach Elias, and from behind her mask, which entirely obscured her face, squeaked, "Do you know me?"

When Elias squeaked the same response in reply, the goddess said, "I should think I do, Cousin. I must say, your costume is the talk of the ball."

Unable to contain myself, I stepped forward and grabbed her by her arm. "Good Lord, Miriam," I whispered in my own voice. "What is it you do here?"

It took her but a moment to sort out the confusion. "You surprise me," she said, peering from one side of my hood to the other, as if to find some fissure that should allow her to see my face. "Why did you give away so original a costume?"

I ignored the question. "Is my uncle aware that you attend such events?" I asked evenly.

She laughed it off, though I could see I had insulted her. "Oh, he works late at his warehouse tonight, you know. And Mrs. Lienzo is always asleep long before I must leave the house."

"Have you eaten the food?" I asked her.

Her eyes sparkled underneath her mask. "You are certainly preposterous, Benjamin. What do you care if I keep the dietary laws? They are nothing to you."

"You must go home," I said. "This ball is no place for a lady."

"No place for a lady? Every fashionable lady in town is in attendance."

Elias leaned forward, sticking his enormous orange false beard between us. "She's got you there, Weaver."

The string band struck up with a sprightly tune, and shocking myself as much as Miriam, I set a hand upon my cousin's elbow, and without so much as asking for her permission, I guided her to the dance floor. I astonished myself, I say, because I was no accomplished dancer—indeed, even as I approached the dozens of couples, already turning about the floor with absolute grace, my throat tightened with apprehension. This business of dancing belonged to the genteel, not to a man of action such as myself. I hoped to show Miriam that I was not without some polite skills, but I feared I would show her the very reverse.

I comforted myself with the thought that I did have some experience behind me. When I had fought under Mr. Yardley's protection, he insisted that his boxers take dancing lessons, for he believed that from dancing one learned a kind of agility that invariably served even the most powerful man in the ring. "The strongest country blockhead you find," he had said, "even if he could tear you in half, shall never be able to touch you if you can but cut capers 'round him."

I could not be certain of Miriam's response to my rather abrupt decision to serve as her partner, for her mask covered almost all of her face, but her lips parted with surprise, and speechlessly we commenced our movements about the floor. I felt a bit lumbering and oafish, and I could tell that Miriam struggled not to stumble upon my graceless motions, but she nevertheless followed my lead, and if I was any judge of these things, enjoyed herself somewhat.

"You know," she said at last, a grin suspended beneath her mask, "that I am already engaged to a dancing partner for this night. You have committed a great social affront."

"We shall see if he challenges me," I grumbled, attempting to maintain my balance. "Who is this dancing partner of yours?" I asked after a moment, though I knew the answer full well.

"Is that your concern, Cousin?"

"I think it is."

"I thought you wished to dance with me so we might have a gay time. Do you plan to spoil that by playing the father with me?"

"I would never choose to spoil a gay time," I said, nearly colliding with a plump lady of Arabia, "but is it not my responsibility as a man and a kinsman to look after your well-being?"

"My being has never been more well," she assured me. "It is a rare thing I am allowed to put to use the dancing skills. And what could be more delightful than the variety of the masquerade?"

I pressed onward, knowing I should spoil this dance by doing so. "Do you not risk your honor, as well as your family's, by coming here without my uncle's knowledge, consorting with men he knows not who?"

Miriam's jaw tightened. She had wished to make banter, to play the free woman unconcerned with what the world thinks, and I was determined to shatter this illusion. I had angered her, but I truly feared for her reputation. From what Elias told me of this Deloney rascal she consorted with, I could not even be certain that her honor remained unbesieged. I suspected that Deloney was somewhere at the ball, and I heartily wished that he should confront me for dancing with his partner. In this way I should show Miriam that a man such as myself should protect her with honor, and the pretty talk of a spark was but a bubble.

At last she spoke. "Would you lecture me on disobedience? You left your family, almost forever, when you were younger than I. You believed yourself capable of choosing your own way in the world. You would deny me that same choice?"

I found her so perplexing it was all I could do to continue the dance. "You are being absurd. You are a lady, and cannot assume that the avenues open to a man are open to you. A man may do many things, take many risks, that a lady must never even consider. It is monstrous strange that you should even think of taking the same liberties I did."

"So because more liberties are denied me, I should presume to take for myself even fewer?" Miriam pushed away, breaking from the dance floor in the midst of the minuet. Her anger sparked the interest of the crowd, and as I rushed after her, I did all I could to obscure our exit from the gathering. Ignoring the knot of tension that twisted in my stomach, I caught up to her as she hurried along, her Roman goddess robes rustling as she went, and led her through a maze of men identically dressed in black dominos. We emerged close to one of the large punch bowls, and by that point some other reveler had certainly behaved either badly or comically enough to create a new diversion, freeing us from the ignominy of public spectacle.

"Miriam," I began, uncertain what to say after that. Her eyes, behind her mask, looked away, but I pressed onward. "Miriam, surely you understand that I am only concerned for your safety."

Her eyes softened as she began to relent. "I understand your motivations entirely, but I do not think that you understand mine. Do you not know what a masquerade ball means to a woman? I can be bold and forward and coquettish, or masculine and learned in my ideas—and no one knows who I am. My reputation will not suffer. Where else could I go to indulge these freedoms and hope to escape with my name unblemished?"

I could not but see the reason of her argument, but I had no wish to admit as much. Fortunately my response was cut short by the arrival of a gentleman dressed in a Venetian-style costume, featuring a birdlike mask with an elongated beak, and a suit of varicolored robes. "Miriam?" he asked in the masquerade squeak.

Miriam remained motionless, uncertain how to respond. So I spoke for her. "The lady is occupied at present," I told this man in a clipped tone. Neither the mask nor the squeak concealed him from me. I recognized him as Deloney, though he surely did not recognize me.

"I say!" he exclaimed in his natural voice. "You are a rude enough fellow behind that mask, but I'll wager that if I could see your face you would not be so free with your insults."

I took a step forward and leaned toward him, clutching the beak of his mask in my hand. "Why, you know me, Deloney," I whispered. "My name is Benjamin Weaver, and I am available to answer your commands at any time. I trust you will repay my loan before you call me to a duel. One would not want to fight with a debt of honor upon his conscience."

He staggered backward, as though my challenge had been an actual violence upon him. I could hardly feel comforted by Miriam's having this weakling for an escort. "Come," I said to her. "I shall put you in a hackney and send you home."

She cast a glance at this fellow, whose bird mask now hung in shame, but they exchanged no words. We exited the Haymarket, and I directed a footman to procure for us a hackney, and while he did so we stood in silence until the coach rode up and the footman we had sent jumped off.

Miriam walked toward the door, and then turned to me. "I had come hoping to feel emboldened, but I only feel shamed."

I shook my head. "The next time you wish for an adventure, I hope you will come speak to me. We shall arrange something that you will find delightful but will involve no unnecessary intrigues."

I thought for a moment that I had won her over—that she understood and respected my concern—but when she looked up, I saw none of these things. Only anger.

"You misunderstand my shame. I would have liked to have trusted you," she said. "I would have liked to believe you cared something of my safety and my reputation."

I shook my head. I could not understand her, and I could not even understand my confusion. I thought hard on what I had said, what I had done. I had given her reasons to think me bold and overbearing, but not untrustworthy. "What do you say?"

"I know what you are about," she said, just above a whisper. Through her mask I saw voluptuous tears welling in her eyes. "I know why you are in Mr. Lienzo's house, and I know the nature of your inquiry. Is he so jealous of the insurance money from Aaron's lost ship—money he has refused to give me, though it is in truth, if not in law, mine? Ruin me if you wish, and collect your little reward for doing it. I cannot pretend any longer to find you anything but a villain." With that she rushed into her coach and ordered the driver to ride.

I did not even think to chase after her. I stood still in a kind of foolish stupor, wondering what I had said and done, wondering what her words could mean.

I could indulge in this wonderment only a short while, for I had left Elias, dressed as he was in his Jew costume, awaiting someone who believed he was me. I pushed Miriam from my thoughts and rushed back in.

Elias had not been molested in my absence. I found him tolerably well, if a bit overly jolly, taking refreshment at the punch bowl.

"Ah, there you are," he chirped. "I don't think I was aware of what a truly terrible dancer you are, but I believe I like your cousin. She's a girl of some spirit."

"That is the trouble," I muttered and separated from him again, hoping that whoever had invited me to the ball would make himself known soon. I had grown weary of costumes and dances.

Elias ventured into a crowd of nymphs, but I was careful never to let my friend out of my sight. While I found myself disgusted with the gawking and laughing of the other masqueraders as they pointed to his costume with delight, I could not but be grateful the disguise was as conspicuous as it was, for it was never long out of my view. Elias very much enjoyed the notoriety the Jewish peddler costume afforded him, and danced companionably with an assortment of Chloes, Phyllises, Phoebes, and Dorindas. For my part I kept my distance, concerned only to watch Elias and those in his vicinity. Aiming to keep myself unoccupied, I was astonished to discover how many ladies approached me with an inquisitive squeak, asking if they knew me. And while I have certainly been guilty of vanity in my days, it was hard to take pride of one's appearance when dressed in a formless black robe and a mask that covered all of one's face. Nevertheless, these masked ladies were aggressive, and I found that responding to the "Do I know you?" introduction with "I do not believe so, madam," only produced further unwelcome conversation. I soon discovered that "Certainly not!" did my business admirably, and I was free to watch Elias's feet, as well as his hands, roam nimbly about the dance floor.

The night wore on, and the hall began to thin out, and I soon wondered if our enemies had somehow detected our ruse, or if our allies had been too frightened to make the connection they had thought to make. Then, as I watched Elias bow a farewell to a striking sultana, I saw four domino-clad men approach him and, after a moment of discussion, beckon him to join them. I must say that while Elias was somewhat unsuited in constitution for combat between men of grit, he knew to keep his head about him, and he demonstrated an implicit trust in my vigilance. Without straining his neck to see if I observed what transpired, Elias nodded to the men and followed along.

I was dismayed to see that they escorted him with two behind and two before, for it would make it hard for me to get to Elias should the confrontation turn vicious. Nevertheless, as inconspicuously as I could, I followed along. They led him out of the ballroom and into a hallway. Hanging back, I turned the corner to see that they were already gone, but I surmised that they had taken a staircase, which I then quietly, though with stealth, ascended. Within a moment I was not far behind these men as they spiraled upward in silence. I, too, had to be entirely silent, for if they but looked down they would see me in pursuit.

At what I believed to be the uppermost floor they removed themselves down a dark hallway. A few candles flickered, producing a confusing maze of darkness and shadow. I struggled to proceed quietly while keeping up with the rapidly advancing men ahead of me, all but invisible in the poorly lit halls. But if the dominos were indistinguishable from the shadows, Elias's red beard glowed dimly in the candlelight.

Finally they stopped in a room at the end of the hallway. Thinking themselves alone, they did not bother to close the door, and I remained unobserved just outside.

The men in dominos circled around Elias. "We've a message for you," one of them said, in a familiar-sounding country accent.

"From whom?" Elias asked. I smiled at his mangled imitation of my voice.

The one who had spoken before took a step closer to Elias. "From them what wants yer to mind yer own business," he said. And with a fluid motion he picked up a thick, rounded stick that leaned against the wall and pushed the blunt end hard into Elias's stomach.

My good friend collapsed like a cut sail, but his helplessness deterred the villains not at all. Soon they had sticks in their hands, and before I could reach Elias they had begun to beat mercilessly about his back and sides. I suppose they believed him to be Benjamin Weaver and felt they must incapacitate the experienced pugilist before he could respond. I cared not a fig, however, and only saw that my friend whose safety I had jeopardized was suffering prodigiously.

I threw off my mask, for the time to forsake disguise was upon me. Before my presence was even detected I had grabbed one of the larger scoundrels by the back of his neck and shoved him face-first into the exposed brick of the wall. This blow took care of him effectively, but now the three remaining men realized their error and hesitantly faced me with their sticks at the ready.

"Who sent you?" I demanded.

"Those you've made angry," one of them said. Perhaps seeing me prepared for combat, with their companion insensible and bleeding upon the floor, they were hesitant to take me on. And I knew this hesitation gave me as much of an advantage as I could expect of three armed men. I was, as always, armed myself. I had no hangar about me, for a sword would have been difficult to carry under the costume, but I had my pistol by my side. Yet, with one shot, and three adversaries, I thought it foolish to brandish the firearm, and I always believed that the pistol was the weapon of last resort. I also had no desire to kill anyone if I could avoid doing so. With the case against Kate Cole to be tried in a matter of weeks, I wished more than anything to remain out of the public eye.

I crouched down quickly and grabbed the stick belonging to the man I had felled, keeping my eyes on my assailants at all times. This movement dissolved the surprise of my manifestation and, in an effort to take back the advantage, one of the men took his stick and hit the groaning Elias hard about the knee. I fear I was as predictable as he had hoped, and stepped in to stop further beating. With my stick raised in my left hand, I threw a hard punch with my right to the man's head, and it connected most satisfyingly, but I soon felt the harsh blows of heavy wood about my back. These blows preyed upon a weakness caused by Jonathan Wild's men, and I went black for a moment. In my confusion, I lost my stick, but recovered my senses before I hit the ground. Holding out a hand to the wall to steady myself, I saw that the man I had hit sat on the floor, rubbing his skull, and that he had let go of his weapon.

With an abrupt jerk, I grabbed his stick and swung it wildly at the two remaining rascals. I succeeded in scattering them away from Elias, but I soon realized my mistake; before, they had been close together, and I might have struck one quickly and then evened the odds. Instead they now had the advantage, for one could hit me from behind while the other took me on directly.

I shifted my position, hoping to place myself in a corner, for while it would give me no chance to exit, it would limit my enemies' paths of approach. This I did, and saw that I faced more danger than I had realized, for the man I had struck was now on his feet, and in the light of the moon from the window behind him, I saw that he held a pistol aimed toward me.

"Drop the cudgel, Jew," he spat, "or you're pig meat for sure."

This man clearly misunderstood me if he thought this tack would prove persuasive. With the stick still in my left hand, I reached into my costume for my own pistol, which I pulled out in a fluid motion. In the dark of the room I could see the villain's firearm flash, and, acting upon pure animal instinct, I fired my own. It was not an irrational action, but I saw immediately that it had been unnecessary, for his pistol had misfired and burst into flame in his hand. He let out a scream, as much of anger as of pain, and dropped the gun just as the ball from mine struck him slightly below the shoulder, forcing him backward, as though he had been tackled. The weight of the blow pressed him hard against the window, and he penetrated the fragile and, I suspect, already cracked glass. I could not see what happened, but as I turned to face my other enemies I heard him shriek with terror as he slid down the roof and dropped to the ground no small distance below.

When I turned, I saw that my attackers had fled, leaving behind the man I had rendered unconscious. I thought to pursue them, but I knew my first duty was Elias, who lay on the floor motionless. I grabbed one of the only candles from a sconce and held it to Elias's face. I could see no visible breaks in the skin, and he was clearly breathing, if in a hoarse and labored manner. I turned him over to see that his eyes were open and he winced in pain. "Phlebotomize me," he whispered with a sickly grin. "But first, catch those scoundrels."

I trusted in Elias's knowledge as a surgeon, and indeed his womanish valor, not to send me away if his life was in any real danger, so I grabbed a cudgel and flew down the stairs, finding no evidence of my attackers.

Outside, a crowd had gathered about the body of the man who had fallen, and I forced my way through to see if he were still alive. He was not. He lay, his face to one side, blood trickling from his mouth as well as from the wound I had inflicted upon him. In the attitude of death his looks were quite changed, but I knew the man. I recognized him. It was he who had attacked me on Cecil Street late at night, and it was he who had fled from me at South Sea House.

I was sorry to have killed him. Not quite true, perhaps. My heart raced and my blood pounded through my veins, and I felt no remorse and no guilt. However, I was sorry that he had not lived long enough to answer some questions before expiring. My task now, I knew, was to find his companions and make them speak or to meet the same fate as their friend.

My plans were thwarted by the arrival of the constables. They were as much a pair of blackguards as ever performed the task of justice in this town. I knew them both from Duncombe's court, but never took either when I ventured upon an arrest, for they were known villains who delighted only in random violence. One was a fat, squat fellow with a hideous purplish rash all about his face. The other was a less-disgusting creature—a normal-enough-looking man, I suppose, but for his narrow eyes, slitted just enough to reveal his cruelty.

"Does anyone know who shot this man?" the fat one shouted.

"Aye." A man stepped forward. He wore no costume, but I knew from his voice that he was one of the men who had attacked me. He pointed in my direction. "There's the man," he said in the same tone he might use to ask an oyster woman for a tuppence' worth. "I saw it all, and I'll swear before the justice. It was cold-blooded murder, it was."

"See that you do swear it before the judge," I spat, as the constables approached me. "I'll enjoy watching you hang." I was too angry to do much but spit curses. There was nothing to be gained by running from the constables, for my attackers knew my name, and I would be apprehended in the end. I have a witness, I thought, who will clear this matter in but an instant. But it then occurred to me that I knew not where this man's remaining conspirators were, and that Elias lay defenseless upstairs. I started to move forward, but two constables grabbed me from behind. "You'll go nowhere," the cruel-looking one said.

I struggled against the grip of the two men. I felt certain I could break away if I could but invoke the sum of my strength, but I was tired and dejected, and I feared for my friend, who could, even at that moment, be having his throat slit while he lay helpless. My weakened struggles only angered the men who contained me, and they forced my arms back into the most uncomfortable of positions. I scanned the crowd, as if for help, searching for someone who might speak in my behalf. As I searched, I saw none other than Noah Sarmento, who stood far back in the crowd, watching me coldly with his hollow eyes. Our gazes met for an instant, and in my moment of panic it did not occur to me to wonder what he did there, only that he was an employee of my uncle's and he would surely help me. Instead he turned away from me, his face betraying a hardened kind of shame.

The man who had attacked me was standing and talking with one of the constables, elaborating upon his slander. "That man is the villain here," I said, gesturing with my head toward my accuser, "and my witness is injured above and may fall victim to this man's companion. I pray that if you will not free me, you will bring help to my friend on the upper floor."

Murders have a curious effect on crowds. No one in the mob, you understand, has any particular desire to help—only the wish to see something truly terrible, something horrendous enough to make all the other men in the alehouse crowd around for the tale. So the revelation that there was yet another victim to be found sent the bulk of the crowd streaming into the building. I hoped their presence would be enough to protect Elias.

"Does anyone know who this man is?" one of the constables asked the remaining stragglers as he gestured toward the dead man.

"No," said my accuser nervously, as though to speak definitively for the dozen or so people who looked on. "No one knows him."

"I know him," a voice spoke up. An older man shuffled forward. He held himself erect only with an old walking cane, chipped and cracked and looking as though it was ready to collapse under the man's weight. "Aye, he's the miserable blackguard what's ruined me niece," he said. "He's a thief and pickpocket, he is, and I'm not sorry to see him there with all his life gone from 'im."

"What's his name?" the constable asked.

"Don't nobody know his name," my accuser interrupted. He glared viciously at the old man. "Pay no heed to what this old one has to say. He ain't right in his head, he ain't."

"You're the one who's not right," the old man spat back. "I can't say I've ever seen you before in me life."

"What's his name?" the constable again asked the old man.

"Why that miserable shitten sod is Bertie Fenn, it is."

And as the constables took me away, and as I fretted anxiously for the safety of Elias, I took no small satisfaction in the knowledge that I had just killed the man who had run down my father.

Twenty-seven

Once again I found myself facing Justice John Duncombe, and once again it was in the matter of a murder—a fact not lost on the judge. For such a serious crime, Duncombe would sometimes convene his court in the middle of the night. Murderers were tricky villains and were wont to escape, and when murderers escaped, trading justices faced more scrutiny than they liked.

Word of my adventures had already begun to spread through the streets, and the judge's rooms, while by no means full with its usual number of spectators, held about a dozen onlookers—a sufficient audience for a midnight performance.

The judge studied me with his foggy and bloodshot gaze. His face was covered with the stubble of his thick beard, and his wig sat upon his head askew. The dark bags under his eyes suggested that he had not slept well, and I could not imagine he was pleased to be dragged from his bed at so late an hour to tend to the matter of a murderer he had himself set free so recently.

"I see I treated you with far too much leniency last time you appeared before my bench," he intoned, as his skin flapped around his toothless mouth. "I shall not make the same mistake twice."

If Duncombe was anxious to commit me to Newgate promptly that he might return to bed, then what appeared much like a desire to see justice served goaded him to follow correct procedures.

"I am told," he said to the court, "that there are eyewitnesses who saw this man kill the deceased. Will such witnesses step forward?"

A moment of silence passed before I heard a familiar voice shout, "I am a witness."

I felt an inexpressible relief when I saw Elias push his way through the spectators and, with steps unsteady and halting, make his way toward the bench. The stiffness of his movements bespoke his pain, and he looked haggard, not to mention absurd, for he still wore the robes of a Jew beggar, but with the mask removed he exposed his shaved and unwigged head before the world. His face had been spared any injury, but I winced to see him clutch at his side in pain.

"The dead man was one of a group of four men who attacked me without provocation," Elias began in a tremulous voice. "This man, Benjamin Weaver, came to my rescue, and in the course of his efforts to save my life, one of my attackers fired a pistol. In order to defend himself, Mr. Weaver did the same, and the man you found paid the price of his villainy."

A murmur spread throughout the court. I heard my name repeated, as well as details of Elias's account. I sensed already that public opinion was with me, but I knew that the crowd's desire to see me freed would have no effect on a man like Duncombe.

"The constable tells me he took of you a pistol that had been fired," the judge said, "so that much has been confirmed. Yet at the scene of the crime there was another man who said the killing was intentional murder, is that not true?"

"It is, your honor," the constable said.

"That man was one of my attackers," Elias said. "He was lying."

"And why did these men attack you, sir?" Duncombe asked.

Elias was silent for a moment. He found himself faced with a powerful dilemma—did he tell all he knew and expose our inquiry before the court, perhaps before our enemies, or did he remain as taciturn as possible, hoping a mere trickle of truths would spare me?

"I do not know why these men attacked me," Elias said at last. "I would hardly be the first man in London to be attacked by strangers. I assume they wanted my money."

"Were demands made for your money?" The judge pressed on. He stared hard at Elias, his face molded into a practiced mask of penetration.

"There was no time," Elias explained. "Soon after these men forced me to follow them, Mr. Weaver attempted to assist me."

"I see. And are you already acquainted with Mr. Weaver?"

Elias paused for an instant. "Yes, he and I are friends. I can only presume that he witnessed these men attack me and intervened with the intent of freeing me."

"And where did this attack take place?"

"At Mr. Heidegger's masquerade at the Haymarket."

"So I gathered from your attire. Are you to tell me that these four men attacked you in the midst of a masquerade ball, sir?"

"They led me away from the ball, upstairs where I would be defenseless."

"And you followed these men, whom you did not know?"

"They claimed to have important information to tell me," Elias said hesitantly. It sounded like a question.

"And explain to me again how Mr. Weaver appeared in this exchange?"

"Mr. Weaver, who is my friend, was presumably suspicious and followed me. Once the men set upon me, he stepped in to aid me."

"Very commendable," the judge said. "And rather convenient, I should think. Are there any other witnesses to this affair?" he asked. He received no answer but the murmurs of the crowd.

"And what do you have to add, Mr. Weaver?"

It would have been pointless to mention that the man I had shot had killed my father—hardly the sort of information that would exonerate me. I believed that Elias's story might prove as effective as any. However, I did not have much hope that Duncombe would grant me freedom. I had killed a man under mysterious circumstances. A trial would be inevitable unless I could say something to make the judge more sympathetic. I could not even hope my uncle would be able to bribe him if I had been bound over for trial. Once a prisoner was committed to Newgate, the matter was quite out of Duncombe's hands. I would have to bribe him before his ruling in order to sway his opinion, and Duncombe, it was well known, did not accept credit.

"I only acted to assist Mr. Gordon," I explained. "When I saw that his safety, perhaps his very life, was endangered, I behaved as I think any friend, indeed, any man, would have done. While I regret the loss of life, I think you will agree that London is a dangerous city, and it should be very hard if a man were prohibited from protecting himself and his friends from the criminals that roam the streets and even, as in this case, force themselves into fashionable gatherings."

My testimony had won over the crowd, if not Duncombe. The spectators burst out in applause and a smattering of "huzzahs," which the judge silenced by slamming his gavel against his desk. "Thank you for that impassioned speech, which I assure you has affected me not at all. It is not my place to judge of your innocence or guilt—merely of whether or not the facts before me deserve further examination. Considering the corroborating evidence of your associate, there can be no ambiguity in the question of whether or not you were under attack. And while I do not encourage the use of deadly force, it should be very strange if I were to begin placing men on trial for protecting their own safety or the safety of other innocents. I shall therefore release you, sir, with the understanding that if further evidence comes to light, you may be brought back for questioning."

The crowd let out a cheer, and I, flooded with a mixture of confusion and relief, went immediately to Elias to check on his condition.

"I am uncomfortable," he said, "and should enjoy a few days of rest, but I don't believe any of the damage was either serious or permanent."

I clapped him warmly on the shoulder. "I am sorry so much harm should have come to you, for you were following my plan."

"I presume you will find some way to make it up to me," he said with an affected petulance.

I grinned, pleased that Elias was uninjured in the main and held no grudge.

"And I presume this reward you have in mind will in some way involve your cousin."

"The moment you are circumcised," I told Elias, "she will be yours."

"You people do conduct a grueling business," he sighed. "But tell me, how is it that the judge ruled in our favor? It seemed to me that the evidence of our case was but poor, and by your own admission you had shot the fellow. I feared to see you bound over for trial."

I shook my head at the puzzle. The only explanation was that someone had paid for the judge's verdict, but I could not imagine who had provided Duncombe with sufficient funds for him to turn free a possible murderer—a dangerous act, for a judge might bring many difficulties upon his head for winking at so serious a crime. However, this was a case well disputed, and if forced to justify himself before any of his patrons, Duncombe could argue easily that he ruled for self-defense. But Duncombe's strategy did not help me understand who could have provided the funds—or, for that matter, to what end. "I can only presume that some unknown friend, or perhaps even an unknown enemy, intervened on my behalf," I told Elias, as I considered the matter aloud.

"Enemy? Why should an enemy wish to offer such generous aid?"

"Perhaps it would be worse for us to stand trial and speak what we know than for us to walk the streets where we may again fall victim to their machinations."

"You are a comforting friend, Weaver."

It turned out that Elias and I did not have long to wonder about the identity of our benefactor. As we exited the judge's house into the chill of the night I saw an opulent coach parked immediately in front, and as the door opened I witnessed no other than Mr. Perceval Bloathwait, the Bank of England director, step forward.

"I believe you owe me a favor, Mr. Weaver," Bloathwait said in his dull voice. "Had my enemies at the South Sea arrived here first, they would certainly have paid heavily to keep you held over for trial. Not that they would have permitted a trial—no doubt too dangerous to allow a man like you to tell what he knows in a public forum. Once in Newgate you would certainly have been more susceptible to a variety of misadventures—gaol fever, fights with other prisoners, and so forth; I should never have seen you alive again."

"An idea that no doubt filled you with horror," I said skeptically. Bloathwait had aided me only to further his own plans, and I could not quite bring myself to feel anything like gratitude.

"As you know, I want you to get to the heart of this matter. I believe you must be getting close, for your enemies are growing significantly bolder. Well done."

I opened my mouth to respond, but my injured friend Elias forced his way past me to greet Bloathwait and bow at him profusely. "It is a great pleasure to see you once again, sir. It has been far too long since I have had the honor to serve you."

Bloathwait stared at Elias's costume. "Do you know this vagabond, Weaver?"

I tried to suppress a smile. "This gentleman is Mr. Elias Gordon," I said, "who was injured tonight performing a service for me. I believe he once had the opportunity to perform a service for you as well. Something of a medical matter, if I am not mistaken."

Bloathwait waved his hand in the air. "You are that Irish surgeon who fawned over me one night in the theatre."

"Just so," Elias agreed with surprising obsequiousness. I had once seen him covertly administer a triple dose of laxative to a gentleman who had made the mistake of calling him an Irishman, but for a man of Bloathwait's wealth, Elias bore up under what he perceived as an insult.

Bloathwait turned back to me. "I hope you will use this freedom I've purchased."

"I appreciate your assistance," I said dryly, "yet I feel that you know more than you are letting on, Mr. Bloathwait, and I do not much enjoy being so toyed with."

"I know only that the South Sea Company is somehow involved and, in ways I do not understand, so is that rascal Jonathan Wild. But I know little more."

"What of Martin Rochester?" I asked.

"Yes, there is Rochester, is there not? Such goes without saying."

I could barely contain my fury. Why would no one tell me anything of this phantom? "Have you any idea where I can find him?" I asked.

Bloathwait stared at me. "Where you can find Rochester? I see I have overestimated you, Weaver. I should have thought you would have reasoned that out by now."

"Reasoned what out?" I own I snapped rather than spoke.

Bloathwait's small mouth curled into a smile. "There is no such man as Martin Rochester."

I felt like a man who suddenly awakens in a strange place, knowing not where he is or how he has arrived there. How could there be no Martin Rochester? For what had I been searching? I concentrated to gather in my passions and form these questions. "Every man upon the Exchange has heard of him. How can there be no Martin Rochester?"

"He is a mere apparition of a stock-jobber," Bloathwait explained in his grand manner. "He is a shield under which another man or men do business. If you want to learn who killed your father, you do not need to find Martin Rochester; you need to learn who he is."

I needed some time to consider this revelation. It explained why no one knew him, certainly. But how could this apparition do business with so many and still remain unknown? "Gad," I mumbled to myself, "how very wretched."

I noticed that Elias had stopped simpering. "This is the villainy of which I have warned you," he said. "Our very enemy is constructed of paper. The crime is paper and the criminal is paper. Only the victims are real."

I could not share Elias's philosophical horror. I still believed there were such things as questions with answers, and I wished very much to believe that any veil of deceit, no matter how cleverly placed, might be torn away.

"A man of paper," I said aloud. "Do you have any idea of his real identity?"

Bloathwait shook his head. "He could be one man or he could be an entire club. I cringe to see that you have been wasting your time seeking out a flesh-and-blood man when you could have been endeavoring to get to the bottom of this matter. I should see if I might sell you back to the judge for all you are apparently worth."

"Regardless of who this man is," Elias said, "should we not know more of *what* he is? What is his connection to the South Sea Company?"

Bloathwait flashed us a scowl. "You have not even learned so much as that?"

I thought on what Cowper had said; I had asked him of Rochester hard on the heels of my asking about the stock forgery. *I told you, sir, that I would not discuss the matter.* I could draw only one probable conclusion. "Rochester is the purveyor of false stock," I said to Bloathwait.

He stared at me and nodded very slowly. "You may yet serve," he said.

I ignored his reserved praise. Did he think me a dog he might pat upon the head?

"You know where you may call upon me should you require anything further," Bloathwait said. He then entered his carriage, and his horses slowly trotted off, leaving me and Elias perhaps more confused than ever.

ELIAS MET WITH ME the next morning. The hesitation in his walk suggested that pain still hindered his movements, but he appeared otherwise quite well. He informed me that he had pressing business at the theatre, but he was happy to lend me such time as he had. We sat in my uncle's parlor, sipping tea, trying not to think of the disasters we had narrowly escaped the previous night.

"I cannot think of how to continue," I said. "There are so many men involved, and I have so many suspicions. I know not how to sort it out, who to visit, nor what questions to ask."

Elias laughed. "I believe you have struck upon the problems of conspiracies. There are men who wish to keep you from uncovering the truth about this particular matter, but there are others who are only privately villainous and have their own little truths to hide. When you confront a conspiracy it becomes monstrous hard to distinguish between wretched villainy and ordinary, common lies."

I nodded. "Last night Bloathwait confirmed my suspicion that Rochester, whoever he might be, is the vendor of the false stock. Several men have suggested that it was Rochester who had my father run down, which would certainly make sense if my father threatened the false-stock trade. It is therefore likely that Rochester is responsible for the various assaults upon my person, and indeed now your person."

"Soundly argued," Elias agreed.

"We further know that Rochester will go to seemingly any length to stay hidden, but our greatest chance of concluding this inquiry is in bringing Rochester to light. If we cannot locate him, as indeed it seems we cannot, perhaps we can locate his other victims."

Elias clapped his hands. "I believe you may be on the verge of striking a very sound blow."

I smiled. "Is it not probable that we might find some of his enemies— the holders of false stock, or those who have had violent dealings with him? When I attempted to deliver my false message at Jonathan's, many a man looked up when the boy cried out the name of Rochester."

"I hardly think you can question every broker upon the 'Change," Elias observed.

"Not the brokers, but what about his buyers? As you say, the ones who have no idea that they have been wronged. They are the ones, Elias, because not knowing they have been wronged, they know not that they have something to fear." My heart began to race. I saw at last a solution. "We must find them. They will lead me to Rochester."

I could not tell if Elias was more excited by the idea or by my enthusiasm. "Good Gad, Weaver. That look upon your face is one of inspiration. I hardly know you any longer."

I told him of my idea, and Elias helped me work out the details. We then traveled to the offices of the *Daily Advertiser*, and placed the following advertisement:

To Any and All Persons
Who have bought stock from, or sold stock to,
Mr. Martin Rochester
You are asked to attend
Mr. Kent's Coffeehouse, in *Peter Street*, near *Bloomsbury Square*
this *Thursday* between the hours of noon and three,
at which time you will receive compensation
for your time

After conducting our business, we returned to the street to make our way home. Elias and I both covered our noses with handkerchiefs as we passed a pauper pushing a cart of spoiled mutton. "It is an audacious stroke," I mumbled, as we hurried past this foulness.

"Rather," Elias agreed, "but I believe it cannot fail. Your enemies, sir, know who you are and what you are about. They have been able to make you come to them, and they have been able to find you. Now you, sir, must expose their weaknesses. This rascal Rochester has gone to great lengths to protect his identity, but no one can be so careful as to be undetectable. He has made mistakes, and we shall find them soon enough."

"It cannot but be otherwise," I agreed, fired by the thrill of decisive action. "I suspect this false identity of his was never meant to withstand the degree of scrutiny we shall unleash upon him."

Elias nodded. "You begin to understand the theory of probability," he said. "From the general necessity of the existence of victims, you will find the particular of the villain."

"If only we still had my father's pamphlet." I could not easily estimate the loss of that document. "If we still had it in hand, I imagine we might have done some pushing here and there with a very powerful tool."

"I believe you did," Elias pointed out. "Is that not why the document was stolen?"

He was quite correct. I would have to learn to think more as he did if I was to outwit these villains.

THE IDEA OF THE advertisement filled me with a glowing pleasure in my own ingenuity, and I longed to inform my uncle of what I had done. The door to my uncle's study sat ajar, and I approached in the hope of finding him unoccupied, but I soon saw my mistake. Several voices came from within, and I should have turned away, thinking only to return at a more convenient time, but I discovered something that sat ill with me. One of the men who spoke was Noah Sarmento, and while I had no love for the man, I could feel no surprise to find him in my uncle's presence. No, it was a second voice that struck me, for it belonged to none other than Abraham Mendes, Jonathan Wild's man.

I quickly retreated—too quickly, for I heard hardly more than a word or two of their conversation, but I dared not linger where I might be caught spying so boldly upon my own kinsman.

Instead I walked outside and waited upon the street, pacing up and down for the better part of an hour until I saw Sarmento and Mendes leave the house together. Perhaps I should say they left simultaneously, for there was nothing cooperative, or even congenial, about the way these two men acted with each other. They merely departed from the same place at the same time.

I stepped forward before they could part, however. "Ho, gentlemen," I said with affected gaiety. "How good to see you both. Especially you, Mr. Mendes, emerging so unexpectedly from my uncle's house."

"What do you want, Weaver?" Sarmento asked sourly.

"And you," I continued, now driven by nothing but bluster. "You, my good friend, Mr. Sarmento. I have hardly seen you since—when was it now?—ah, yes. It was after the masquerade where you lurked in the crowd just after a failed effort to assassinate my person. How do you do, sir?"

Sarmento clucked disgustedly, as though I had mentioned something ribald in polite company. "I neither understand you nor wish to," he said, "nor shall I spend any more time with a man who speaks nonsensical stuff." He spun sharply and affected to walk off with dignity, but he repeatedly turned to see if I pursued, and did not stop straining his neck until he rounded the corner and disappeared from sight.

I thought to give chase, but Mendes went nowhere, as though he dared me to inquire into his business. I had no doubt I should be able to break Sarmento at the time of my choosing, but Mendes was quite another matter.

"I am pleased to see you in so fine a mood, sir," he said to me. "I hope your inquiry treats you well."

"Yes," I said, though my good spirits had now dissipated. "At this moment I inquire into a very curious matter indeed. I inquire into your presence in my uncle's house."

"Nothing simpler," he told me. "I had a matter of business to resolve."

"But the details, Mr. Mendes, the details. What matter of business might that be?"

"Merely some fashionable cloth that Mr. Lienzo found upon his hands and that a sometimes too-zealous government would not let him easily dispose of. He entrusted me with these goods some months ago, and having found a buyer, I only wished to pay your uncle what he was owed."

"And Sarmento's role in all of this?"

"He is your uncle's factor. You know that. He was with your uncle when I arrived. Surely," he added with a grin, "you do not suspect your uncle of some mischief, do you? I should hate to see you break with him as you broke with your father."

I stiffened at these words, which I knew he meant most provocatively. "I should be careful, sir. Do you in truth wish to test whether or no I am a match for you?"

"I meant no challenge," he told me, in a voice of oily mock-conciliation. "I speak only out of concern. You see, I, who have lived many years in this neighborhood, saw the pain your father felt at having lost his son to the plague of pride. Both his and yours, I believe."

I opened my mouth to respond, but I could think of nothing to say, and he proceeded apace. "Shall I tell you a story of your father, sir? I think you might find it most interesting."

I stood silent, hardly able to guess what he would say.

"Not more than two or three days before the accident that took his life, he called upon me in my home and offered me a handsome sum of money to perform a task for him."

He wished to make me ask, and so I did. "What task?"

"One I thought strange, I promise you. He wished me to deliver a message."

"A message," I repeated. I could hardly hide my confusion.

"Yes. I thought it most incomprehensible, and with every effort to avoid appearing to put on airs, I told Mr. Lienzo that I thought it somewhat beneath my station to deliver messages. He appeared embarrassed, and he explained to me that he feared someone might intend him harm. He thought a man of my stripe might be able to deliver the message both safely and inconspicuously."

This story hurt far more than I would have anticipated. Mendes had been hired to perform a task that I might have done had my father and I been upon speaking terms. My father had needed a man upon whose strength and courage he could depend, and he had not called upon me—perhaps he had not even thought to call upon me. If he had, I wondered, how should I have responded?

"I brought the message to its recipient," Mendes continued, "who was, at that time, at Garraway's Coffeehouse in 'Change Alley. The man opened the note and muttered only, 'Damme, the Company and Lienzo in the same day.' Do you know who this recipient was?"

I fixed my gaze hard upon him.

"Why, the very man you asked Mr. Wild about. Perceval Bloathwait."

I licked my lips, which were now quite dry. "Did Mr. Bloathwait have a reply?" I asked.

Mendes nodded, strangely pleased with himself. "Mr. Bloathwait asked me to tell your father that he thanked him for the honor he did him by sharing this information, and that he should keep it to himself until he, Bloathwait that is, had a chance to reflect upon it."

"Wild denied any knowledge of Bloathwait—now you tell me this story. Am I to believe that you defy Wild? More likely, this conversation between Jews is all part of his plan."

Mendes only smiled. "So many puzzles. If only you had attended more to your studies as a boy, you might now have the intelligence to make some order out of chaos. Good day, sir." He tipped his hat and walked off.

I stood for a moment, contemplating what he had told me. My father had sought out some contact with Bloathwait—the very man I had spied meeting secretly with Sarmento. Now my uncle meets with Sarmento and Mendes together. What could it mean?

I would wait no longer to learn. I reentered the house and walked boldly into my uncle's study. He sat at his desk, reviewing some papers, and smiled broadly as I walked in.

"Good day, Benjamin," he said cheerfully. "What news?"

"I thought you might tell me," I began in a voice I hardly tried to modulate. "We might begin with your business with Mr. Mendes."

"Mendes," he repeated. "I have told you of my business with him. He merely wished to pay me for some cambrics which he had sold for me." His keen eyes determinedly measured my expression.

"I know not why you would conduct business with such a man," I said.

"Perhaps not," he replied, his voice showing just a hint of hardness. "But it is not your place to understand my affairs, is it?"

"I believe it is," I retorted. "I am engaged in an inquiry which involves the mysterious dealings of your brother. It has led me to form suspicions of Mendes's master. I believe that I am within my rights when I express my concern."

My uncle arose from his chair to meet my gaze upon my level. "I do not disagree," he said carefully. "But I should prefer you do so in a less accusatory tone. What is it you wish to say to me, Benjamin? That I am involved in some sort of scheme with Jonathan Wild into tricking you into doing—I cannot even imagine what? I urge you to recall who I am."

I sat down, controlling my passions and having no desire to inflame my uncle's. Perhaps he was right. He had a long-standing business with Mendes. I could hardly ask him to suspend it because I liked neither him nor his master. "I believe I spoke hastily," I said at last. "I never meant to suggest anything about your conduct, Uncle. It is merely that I know not whom to trust, and I mistrust almost everyone—particularly those associated with Jonathan Wild. It troubles me greatly to see you with Mendes. You may believe you simply engage in some old business, but I should be surprised to believe that he does not have more on his mind."

My uncle relented as well. He sat down and allowed himself to soften. "I know you wish only to uncover the truth behind these deaths," he said. "I delight in your dedication, but we must not forget that while we try to do justice for the dead, we must remain among the living. I cannot discontinue my affairs because of this inquiry."

"I would not suggest you do." I sighed. "But Wild, Uncle. I do not believe you fully understand how dangerous he is."

"I am certain in matters of theft and suchlike he is dangerous indeed," my uncle said complacently. "But this is a matter of textiles. Your mind is set upon a conspiratorial path, Benjamin. Now everything appears suspicious to you."

I thought on this for a moment. Elias had observed that the danger of inquiring into conspiracy is that all manner of misdeeds seem equally implicit. It was surely conceivable that I made too much of my uncle's business with Mendes.

"I have never had any dealings with Wild," he continued. "And I have always known Mr. Mendes to behave honorably. I understand your concern, but I could hardly refuse to allow him to pay me what he owes me because you mislike the man. But if you prefer, I shall engage him for no more business until this matter is resolved."

"I would be most appreciative."

"Very well, then," he said cheerfully. "I am glad we resolved this business. I know you did not intend to be overly harsh, but you have worked far too hard upon this matter. I know you do not wish to abandon your inquiry, but you might set it aside for a few days and allow your thoughts to clear."

I nodded. Maybe he was right, I thought. A few days' rest might do me some good, but whether they did or no, I thought, I should have little choice, for I could not think of how to proceed until I found out what my advertisement might yield.

Believing the tension had passed, my uncle arose and poured us both a glass of port, which I sipped with some pleasure. I had finished nearly half of it before I realized that I had said nothing about my business at the *Daily Advertiser* and that I had no intention of doing so. It was not that I misbelieved my uncle when he described his dealings with Mendes, but I was not sure I precisely believed him either. He could be the victim of deception as much as any man, and his insistence upon conducting his affairs as he saw fit could blind him to certain truths.

I spoke cheerfully with my uncle, and I enjoyed his conversation, but I declined to inform him of many things: of my suspicions of Sarmento, of Miriam's wayward and inexplicable behavior, of the attempt upon my life, of the advertisement I had placed, and now of Mendes's revelation of my father's communication with Bloathwait. I did not wish to believe that my uncle's behavior stemmed from anything more than a lifetime of having his own way indulged, but for the nonce my silence felt disturbingly wise.

I LIVED UPON THE rack until the next Thursday, when I should see who appeared to respond to the advertisement I had placed. I could ill think of how to occupy my time in this inquiry, and I had no desire to accept new business. Instead I spent my time brooding incessantly over what I already knew and watching the swelling about my face subside. I took notes and made lists and drew diagrams—all of which helped me to understand better the complexity of my search, and none of which, I feared, brought me any closer to a solution.

I chastised myself viciously for not having fully read, fully understood, my father's pamphlet while I had the chance. I convinced myself all the answers had been therein contained, but even if that were not so, it did contain the words of my father, speaking, if only indirectly, upon the matter of his own death. Now it was lost to me.

At Elias's invitation I passed one of my free mornings at the theatre at Drury Lane, where I found myself almost entirely distracted. While I watched one scene of Elias's comedy rehearsed perhaps fifteen times until I felt I could have played each part myself, I found it witty and cleverly acted. Elias strutted about the stage as though he were the theatre manager himself, suggesting to the players different poses and different deliveries. When I was leaving, he gave me a copy of the play, which I later read and found strangely delightful.

I spent that afternoon with my Aunt Sophia, attending her on her social calls and meeting other prominent Iberian Jewesses of Dukes Place. Some of these women were quite young and quite unmarried, and as I spent these stressful hours attempting to make myself understood in Portuguese, I could not but wonder if my aunt was trying to settle me in marriage.

In an effort not to let my investigation run cold in this period of waiting, I visited Perceval Bloathwait's town house on several occasions, but each time his servant denied me. I left several messages for the Bank of England director, but I received no replies. I greatly wished to know more of this message that Mendes had told me my father had sent to his old adversary, but Bloathwait, it would seem, had decided to have no more to do with me.

I ruminated on how to remedy that situation while I kept myself busy in more mundane tasks: news of my move to Dukes Place had circulated, and a few men made their way to my new home to ask for my help. So I distracted myself by finding a few debtors while I awaited what I hoped, and hoped correctly, would be a fruitful return of our advertisement.

My relations with Miriam had continued to be cool, especially after her inexplicable accusation at the masquerade. I attempted on several occasions to speak with her, but she always assiduously avoided me. One day, after a silent breakfast with her and my aunt, I followed her from the table and into the parlor.

"Miriam," I began, "tell me why you are angry with me. I do not understand how I have betrayed you." The only explanation I had summoned was that she was angry that I had discovered her relationship with Deloney, but as I had not circulated the information or used it to harm her, that knowledge could hardly stand as a betrayal.

"I have nothing to say to you," she announced, and began to depart.

I grabbed her by the wrist—as gently as I could. "You must speak to me. I have searched my memories for something I did that may have hurt you, but I can think of nothing."

"Do not attempt to deceive me." She tore her arm from me, but did not move away. "I know why you are here in this house, and I know the nature of your inquiry. Are a few guineas from your uncle—or is it perhaps Mr. Adelman?—worth having established a false intimacy with me? I thought you had returned to your family for some greater purpose than to expose it."

She ran out of the room; I might perhaps have followed her if I had been able to formulate some idea of what to say. I could think of no reasons or explanations, and I wondered if I should ever understand. I could not have known then that my next conversation with Miriam would clarify far more than the reasons for her anger with me.

AT LAST THURSDAY was upon me. The weather had turned significantly cooler, and in the crisp morning air that smelled of impending snow, I made my way to Kent's Coffeehouse. I arrived an hour earlier than the advertisement indicated that I might establish myself before anyone came to call. I let the servants know who I was, and I sat down with the papers to busy myself until I should be called for, but I found myself too distracted to read with any absorption. I must say that the events at the masquerade had left me apprehensive, for I saw that there was nothing these villains would not do to protect themselves, and there was certainly something reckless about my publishing my defiance of them in the *Daily Advertiser.* Yet I knew that Elias was right, for if I followed up only on the evidence that they had left behind, they would know my thoughts even before I did. Here, at least, was something they had not anticipated.

Every few minutes I looked up to see if someone sought me out, and on one of those occasions I noticed a grim gentleman at another table. He held a paper before him, but it was obvious that he did not read it. Although this man dressed neatly, there was something about the way he wore his wig, the way his coat hung upon his shoulders, and, most strikingly, the fact that he wore thick leather gloves inside the coffeehouse, that made him conspicuous and strange. I felt certain that if I were to remove his wig and look square into his face, I would see someone I had encountered before.

Feeling bold, and perhaps overly animated by a bit too much of Mr. Kent's coffee, I approached the table and sat down, and as I did so, I knew the man at once. I recognized the hard, cruel, stupid look, as well as the left eye that sat useless in a sea of yellowish rot. For his part, he knew not how to respond to my direct assault and pretended to continue with his reading.

"How is your hand, Mr. Arnold?" I asked. He no longer appeared the same ruffian from whom I had so violently retrieved Sir Owen's amorous letters. He had cleaned himself up considerably, but the mark of villainy still stained him thoroughly. I was certain he felt no small amount of fear of me, and his fear was not misplaced. We both knew that the violence I had once visited upon him I would not hesitate to repeat.

I sought in my mind to recall if it had been the right or the left hand I had stabbed, for that was the hand I wished to grab. Arnold, however, took advantage of my moment of contemplation, leapt to his feet, tossed a chair at me to slow me down, and ran out the front door. I followed, only a few seconds behind him, but those few seconds were sufficient for him to take the advantage. When I emerged onto the street he was nowhere in sight. With little to lose, I picked a direction and ran, hoping that fortune would favor my search, but such was not the case, and after a quarter of an hour of fruitless searching I abandoned the cause and returned to the coffeehouse.

It was well that I had engaged in that frustrating encounter with Mr. Arnold, for when I returned, winded and looking all askew, I saw the coffee girl in conversation with a young lady, and I overheard her conversation just enough to learn that she was describing my appearance. Had this young lady entered the coffeehouse and seen me in waiting, she would certainly have departed before I knew she had been there, but now I stood, breathing deeply, absently dusting off my coat, while our eyes made contact.

Miriam had come in response to my advertisement.

Twenty-eight

In a strange mirroring of my motions, Miriam began to wipe her hands upon the hoops of her gown. She looked at me. She looked at the door. She could hardly hope to escape, but the thought, as absurd thoughts do in moments of confusion, surely crossed her mind.

I asked the girl for a private room and a bottle of wine, and we retired into a small and neat closet that offered little more than a few oldish chairs scattered around a table. It was a room of business, and I appreciated that. From the wall, crudely rendered portraits of Queen Anne and Charles II stared at us; there was no mistaking Mr. Kent's Tory politics.

Miriam sat stiffly in her chair. I poured a glass of wine and set it in front of her. She wrapped her delicate hands around the glass but neither lifted it nor tasted the wine. "I did not expect to see you here, Cousin," she said quietly, not meeting my eye.

I proved myself less shy than Miriam about the drinking of wine. After taking a long sip, I sat down and tried to decide if it was more comfortable to look at her or away from her. "What is your connection to Rochester?" I said at last. I had hoped to moderate my tone, to sound relaxed, concerned, simply curious. It came out as an accusation.

She let go of her glass and met my gaze. She had the frightened and outraged look of a parish beggar. "What business have you speaking to me thus? I have responded to your notice in the paper. I do not believe that to be a crime."

"But I assure you murder is a crime, and a very serious one, and it is in connection to murder that I seek Mr. Rochester."

She gasped. She moved to stand up, but then sat again. Her eyes darted about the room in search of something that would comfort her, but she could find nothing. "Murder?" she breathed at last. "What can you mean?"

"I shall withhold nothing from you, Miriam, but you must tell me what you know of Rochester."

She shook her head slowly, and I watched her spotted green bonnet sway with her movements. "I know so little of him. I bought—that is to say, I had some funds bought through him. That's all." She now drank of her wine, and drank vigorously, too.

"South Sea funds," I said.

She nodded.

"How did you buy these funds? It is very important you tell me everything. Did you meet him, correspond with him, talk with a servant of his? I must know."

"There's so little," she said. Her fingernails gently scratched on the roughhewn surface of the table. "I—I had no contact with him myself. I had someone who dealt with him for me."

"Philip Deloney."

"Yes, it's been clear to me for some time that you know we . . ." Her voice trailed off.

"That you are lovers, yes. And that he is some kind of petty gamester and jobber."

"He has bought and sold at Jonathan's for me," she explained quietly. "I have so little money, and I needed to try to secure more that I might afford to establish a household of my own."

I could not but laugh. Elias should have been delighted to hear about this odd commingling of hearts and money, of romance being bought and sold upon the 'Change. Miriam looked at me in puzzlement, and I shook off my mirth, for it was a kind of panicked laughter.

"What is the nature of Deloney's relationship with Rochester?"

"I know that it is a distant one. Philip has been searching for him and unable to find him."

"And why has he been searching? Indeed, why are you looking here today?"

"Philip arranged to have Rochester buy South Sea stock in my name. In his name as well."

"But why? You have a connection, albeit a strange one, with Adelman. Surely you did not need a third party to secure you stock."

"Mr. Deloney told me that Rochester could get stock at a discount—fifteen, even twenty points below market. I know from Mr. Adelman that the stock is soon to rise, so with the discount, I thought I could secure enough money to move from your uncle's house. But Philip grew tired of waiting, and needed to convert his stock to ready cash. The agreement was that we were not to attempt to convert the stock for a year from the time of purchase—something having to do with the way in which we received the discount—but Philip wanted silver. He tried seeking out Rochester to find out how he might go about the conversion, and I know not the nature of the correspondence, but I do know that it agitated him severely. He would hardly speak to me of it, only to say that the stock was now but dross. So when I saw the advertisement in the paper, I thought I might learn more."

"Do you own—that is to say—possess your South Sea stock?"

Miriam nodded. "Certainly."

I pressed my hands together. "I have hardly heard such good news."

"Good news? Why should my stock prove good news for you?"

"Take me to the stock, and I'll show you."

We left the coffeehouse in a hurry, after telling the girl there to collect the names of anyone else who came in search of me. We returned to the house at Broad Court, and Miriam invited me into her dressing room, where she removed a gold filigree box containing a large pile of thick parchment paper. I first looked at the thinner documents—projecting shares, mainly for the construction of two new bridges across the Thames. I had seen Elias deceived with his projects often enough to recognize mere stuff when I saw it.

"I believe Mr. Deloney has fooled you with these. They are but empty promises."

"Fooled me?" Miriam stared at them. "Then where has the money gone?"

"To the hazard table, I presume." I found myself asking the question that I had not thought to articulate. "Is it for this thief that you wished to borrow twenty-five pounds of me?"

"I had given him all I had of my remittance, and I had promised him future remittances," she said quietly. "I was worth less than nothing after purchasing these." Miriam's hand trembled as she then produced the South Sea issues. These were an impressive set of documents, written on the finest parchment in the finest hand. They bespoke their authenticity to all who would but take a moment to glance in their direction.

Nevertheless, I was entirely convinced that they were false.

I knew that Rochester sold false stock, and I knew that Deloney had dealings with Rochester. The inexplicable *discount* that Miriam received only confirmed my suspicion.

From what little I knew of the price of shares, I could see why Miriam was so short of ready money. She had spent five or six hundred pounds on issues not worth five or six farthings. It pained me to tell her that she had destroyed her savings. "I believe these stocks are but forgeries," I said softly.

She took them from me and stared at them. I could see her thoughts. They looked so very real. She had been a fool to believe those project shares, but these—these looked official, embossed, approved. "You are mistaken," she said at last. "If they were forgeries, I would not have received a dividend payment, as I did last quarter."

I felt a kind of cold terror. I slowly lowered myself onto Miriam's divan and attempted to understand what I had heard. A dividend payment! Then the stocks were not false, and if she had bought them of Rochester, then perhaps Rochester sold only true stock. After all, Virgil Cowper, the South Sea clerk, had told me he had seen Miriam's name in the South Sea records. I clenched my fists and attempted to understand what Miriam's dividend payment might mean—and how it might not mean what I most feared: that Rochester was no villain and that I had been mistaken all along.

I reached out and took the papers back from Miriam. My eyes wandered all about the parchment, looking for something I knew not what, some kind of evidence of their falseness, as though I would recognize such a thing were it right before my eyes. I feared my ignorance had led me to this moment—to this revelation of my foolishness. Elias's probability had yielded nothing but failure.

Miriam took the issues from me again and replaced them in her box. "How can they be false?" she asked, unaware that her information had devastated me. "I would think that if they were forgeries should not a stock-jobber such as your father have seen their falseness at once?"

I pulled myself out of my misery. "My father? He saw these?"

"Yes. He happened to pass by one afternoon when I had them out of the box. I suppose I was daydreaming, thinking about the house I might rent when I sold them. He asked to look at them, and I dared not refuse. I asked him to tell no one, that I wished to keep my speculation a secret, and I hoped he would understand."

"What did he say?"

"He was very strange. He gave me a kind of knowing look, as though we shared a secret, and said that I might depend upon his silence. I will admit he surprised me because I feared he should tell your uncle about the secret just for the pleasure of doing so." She lowered her eyes, feeling some sudden shame at having insulted my father. "I'm sorry," she said.

I would have none of it. Had she told me my father had revealed himself a secret Mohammedan I should hardly have cared. Instead I grabbed her hand and smothered it with kisses. In the hours to come I would think back and laugh at myself, for in that moment I hardly thought of Miriam as a beautiful woman, but as a beautiful bearer of news. My father had *seen* the stocks. And if I had not studied his pamphlet, if I had not read enough of it to even remember it well, I had read enough to understand the nature of Miriam's stock, and how it was that she had received dividends.

More to the point, I understood now that I had not been a fool and that Elias's philosophy had served me well—better than I could have imagined.

Miriam pulled her hand from me, but she only just managed to stifle a burst of genuine amusement. "You are either mad or the most changeable man in the world. Regardless, I should thank you to cease drooling upon my hand."

"I beg your pardon, madam," I almost shouted. "But you have given me the very news I needed, and I am most grateful."

"But what is it? Can there be some connection between this stock and your father? What could he have—" She stopped. The blood drained from her face and her mouth slowly slid open into an expression of understanding and horror. "Your search for Mr. Rochester. It's about your father, isn't it? Mr. Sarmento was wrong."

It only then occurred to me that she did not know. I had been so deep within my own inquiry that I thought its nature obvious to all. But

Miriam had not known—and she had wondered what my uncle and I spoke about in his study, and she had wondered why I had moved into the house.

I nodded, for I now understood Miriam's odd behavior had been based upon groundless speculation—her own failed exercise in probability. "Aye. You thought I inquired into a different matter, didn't you? Sarmento told you something. That is why you were angry. You thought I inquired into you—your money, your intimacy with Deloney."

She sat down slowly upon a divan and slowly lifted a hand to her mouth. "How could Philip have been involved with something so hideous?"

"That is what I must find out. He may have been in league with Rochester to deceive you, and I don't know how many others. Perhaps he was deceived himself and never meant any harm."

"But how could he have been deceived? He himself falsified stocks." She gestured at the shares of the absurd projects she held. "I knew they were false when I bought them. It was only five pounds now and again, and I could not bear to embarrass him by refusing."

"You can see these South Sea holdings are of a superior quality. Perhaps the biter was bit. But we cannot take the time to concern ourselves with Deloney. Not now. Our first concern must be to take these shares to South Sea House."

Miriam put a hand to her mouth. "Surely that is dangerous. If they know we have false stock, will they not act against us?"

"They know we have not falsified this stock ourselves. I believe they have suspicions about Rochester and his forgeries, but until now I have had no proof that these falsifications exist. And I believe they will pay you handsomely for them, for they wish to suppress all evidence of their existence."

"Would it not be better to try to sell the stock than to risk bringing it to South Sea House?"

I shook my head. "We dare not hold on to these issues. The sooner you remove them from your hands and turn them into ready money, the safer you will be. I believe I may have endangered you, Miriam, and this household, for the entire world now knows that I seek the truth behind Samuel Lienzo's death, and the world now knows that Samuel Lienzo was my father. Whoever forged the stock may know some of it is in the name of Miriam Lienzo. We must be rid of it at once."

I allowed Miriam to hold two of the issues, and put the rest upon my person. We then went to the street and procured a hackney to take us to the Exchange.

"You are uncomfortable," I said, as we approached Threadneedle Street.

Her hands trembled slightly. "I fear something terrible will happen in there," she said. "That I am to lose everything. You have told me so little."

"You have done nothing wrong, Miriam. You were cheated, and it happens that in this matter I believe some very wealthy men may be willing to pay for you to keep this cheat to yourself. I have my own interests to pursue in South Sea House, but I am committed to assisting you."

She nodded, I think more resigned than comforted. And so we made our way into the building. I gently guided Miriam to the office I had previously visited and there I asked to speak to Mr. Cowper, but one of the clerks in the office told me that Cowper had not been in the office in some days. "It's almost a week since I've seen him," he muttered. "Strange. He used to come to work so regular."

"Then I should like to speak to someone else on a matter of the most urgent business."

"What business is that?" His haughtiness told me he liked not my voice. So much the better.

"That of forged South Sea Stock." I handed the clerk one of Miriam's issues.

I might have stabbed this clerk through the heart for the reaction my pronouncement generated. Clerks let go their pens in mid-sentence. A pile of ledgers fell to the floor. The man to whom I spoke pushed back his chair, producing a tortured squeal of leg against floor.

He rose and studied the paper. "Oh, this," he said with a nervous laugh. "Of course. That error is one that, you know . . ." He cleared his throat. "I shall return in a moment," he added abruptly and ran into the hall.

We stood there for some minutes, the South Sea men staring upon us, until this first clerk returned and told us to follow him.

The clerk began to walk at such an absurd pace that Miriam had a difficult time keeping up with him. The loose folds of her gown flapped about her like wings. He stopped several times, some fifteen paces ahead of us, to wave us on, as he led us down the hall and up two flights of stairs, where he ushered us into a private office—a room with a large table in the center and several windows overlooking the street. Advising us to cool our heels, he slammed the door as he departed.

Miriam stared at me. "What will happen?" she began in a tremulous voice.

"Do not be frightened," I told her, though I was perhaps a bit frightened myself. "This matter, I believe, proceeds beautifully. We have their attention. We have the advantage. They may try to frighten us, Miriam, but you will need to be equal to their harsh words. And rest assured that I shall allow no harm to come to you."

I fear my words did more to frighten than to comfort. Miriam turned pale, lowered herself slowly into a chair and quickly began to flutter her fan. I affected a calm pose, but faced the door, preparing myself for anything. It was hardly conceivable that the South Sea Company would attempt violence upon me in their own building, but I could no longer rule out any possibility.

"You must remember," I began, hoping to offer her comfort, "that it is you who have this company at a disadvantage. They may wish to convince you otherwise, but never forget that they will do anything to obtain your silence." Indeed, I feared that to be true.

We waited for well over an hour, and with each moment I could see Miriam grow more concerned. She spoke occasionally to suggest that they had certainly forgotten about us or that we might simply leave, but I would not hear of it. "I cannot believe that they could be so rude as to lock us in this room and then ignore us. Perhaps we should not bear this indignity. Let us go at once."

I shook my head. "It is too late for that. We cannot put things as they were. It is better to have this confrontation now, while the advantage of surprise remains with us."

My words were poorly chosen, for Miriam began to fidget with nervousness, picking at a loose thread upon the sleeve of her gown until I feared the entire garment should unravel.

At last the door swung open hard, and a fat, ruddy-faced man of late years burst through, waving Miriam's issue above his head. He wore a dark and thick periwig that set off a grublike complexion. "Who has brought this here?" he demanded. He slammed the door behind him and then slapped the paper down hard upon the table.

Miriam winced as though struck. It was no doubt precisely what this villain intended.

"The issue belongs to this lady," I said. "And who are you, sir?"

"Who I am is none of your concern, Weaver. What I am concerned with is this brazen attempt to compromise the South Sea Company and the integrity of the nation's wealth. Did you believe," he asked, looking directly into Miriam's eyes, "that you could pass off this rubbish in South Sea House—that we would not know this for a forgery? We know you have more of these, you scurvy slut. Where are they?"

Miriam rose to her feet, and I thought she should slap him—and I cannot quite recollect why I prevented this worthy woman from administering a well-deserved punishment. But interfere I did.

"You rascal," I exclaimed, abruptly stepping between the two. "How dare you speak to a lady in that manner? Were you more than a bloated pudding I would kick you in your arse right here. You cannot believe that this lady is the author of that forgery. Were your problems no more than a single canny widow, you would be fortunate indeed. I cannot think what you hope to accomplish by insulting a lady, to whom I think you owe far more courtesy, and I know you do not expect me to allow a lady under my protection to endure this treatment."

"Don't attempt to deceive me with your street-ruffian's lies," the man bellowed, almost directly in my face. "This woman is guilty of a forgery, and it is my intention to prosecute in a court of law." This was a chilling threat. There could be no doubt that the Company could arrange for a conviction if it desired to see her hang.

Miriam turned to me. She was a strong woman, but I could see this threat had frightened her. Her eyes had grown moist and her fingers tremulous. "You said we were in no danger," she began.

"Do not concern yourself," I told her quietly. "He would not dare prosecute you."

"I see that you are this trollop's accomplice, Weaver. She had better concern herself, and so had you. Can you believe that a company, so nearly watched by the King, and among whose directors is the Prince of Wales himself, would let itself fall victim to an insult of this magnitude?"

"There is no question that the Company has fallen victim to the insult," I replied, "regardless of who its patrons are. What is at issue is who has insulted whom. You know very well, sir, that Mrs. Lienzo has nothing to do with the forgery."

"As for you, Weaver," he snapped, "I dismiss the idea that you have had anything but the most villainous motives in this crime, and I shall not rest until I see you hanged!"

"I know not your name," I said in response, "and I know not what title you pretend to, but I know what you are in truth, and it is I who shall see you pay the price for murder."

"*I* pay a price for murder? Surely you are mad! It is you who have committed murder, as I have been at great pains to learn. Did you think that you, who have been so publicly our enemy, should escape our notice? I know that you have been introduced to His Majesty's case against Kate Cole, and I know of your involvement in the death of that blackguard. This company is committed to seeing you stand trial."

I was stunned. I could not believe that this man could make so bold a pronouncement. I felt that it was a confession of connections, but I could not guess of what connections precisely. Did this mean that the Company was in league with Wild? That the Company had as good as confessed to being behind my father's death? I could not sort it out. I was a trapped animal, and I had to restrain myself from jumping upon this man and beating him bloody.

Miriam looked on mutely. Her face was as that of a child whose parents bicker before her. I wished she had not been made to feel so threatened, but there was nothing to be done for it now.

"You have taken a misstep," I said to the South Sea man, "in making me your enemy."

He laughed aloud, and my rage increased, for I knew that I had nothing to threaten him with but the violence of the moment. But then a thought came to my mind. "If you want to silence me, I suggest you do it here and now. All your talk is but a bubble, for I assure you the moment I leave this building I shall inform the world of these forged issues."

"Perhaps we are being hasty." I had not seen Nathan Adelman enter the room, but he stood in the doorway, looking mildly amused. "Perhaps Mrs. Lienzo is but a victim and not a villain."

I knew instantly their game; Adelman was to play the part of the compassionate man. Miriam breathed a sigh of relief, but I knew she was too clever to be fooled for more than an instant.

"Keep out of this, Adelman," the other man said, "you know not of what you speak."

"I think I do. Miriam, you merely want these stocks turned to cash, do you not?"

She nodded slowly.

"I see clearly that you have been swindled, and I shall tell you what we shall do. The Company is prepared to offer you three hundred pounds for these shares. Shall that satisfy the matter?"

I saw that Miriam, in her ignorance, was prepared to accept this meager offer. I would have none of it. "Adelman," I spat, "why are you playing us for the fools that we are not? You know well that if this were valid stock it would sell for more than twice that on the open market."

"You have learned a thing or two about the funds, Weaver. I am pleased to see that you are your father's son after all. Yes, South Sea stock is now selling at over two hundred, but these are not valid stock—they are merely worth the value of printed paper, which is to say, nearly nothing. Three hundred pounds in exchange for nearly nothing is a good bargain, I think."

"What both Miriam and I have is worth far more than that," I said, "for now we have proof that counterfeit South Sea stock is in circulation. What will that do to its worth on the market when the word is spread, Adelman? Your efforts to eclipse the Bank shall come to a sudden halt. Do not think to try any of your Company tricks with us, for we have prepared ourselves by placing samples of this forged stock in a half-dozen different locations," I lied hurriedly. "Should we fail to retrieve them before a time we have determined, our factors shall make them public. You cannot threaten to harm us or to destroy these issues without seeing your Company utterly undone."

Miriam and I glanced at each other and nodded, as though this lie had been practiced all along. I delighted in seeing her hold herself in an attitude of authority—arms crossed, bosom thrust forward, chin held high. She knew that the balance of power had shifted.

Adelman's companion nearly spat at the image of our complaisance. "Do you dare to threaten the South Sea Company?" he barked.

"No more so than this Company has threatened us. Let me make you a counteroffer. This woman will sign a paper swearing never to reveal her knowledge of forged stock, and submit to you all forged issues she possesses. She will do this in exchange for five thousand pounds."

Miriam had not so much composure that she did not let out a gasp at the mention of that sum—an amount surely beyond what she dreamed of ever having at her disposal; she did not understand that an opulent fortune for her was but a pittance for a company that in months to come would offer a gift of millions of pounds to the government in exchange for the right to do business.

"Five thousand pounds? Are you mad, sir?" the gruff fellow barked.

Adelman, however, played the more diplomatic role, and I saw immediately that he was relieved to have escaped so cheap. "Very well, Weaver. Miriam, will you agree to sign a document? If you forfeit, then you will be considered to be in default of your agreement and you will owe the Company five thousand pounds, for which I can assure you we shall prosecute."

The lady had regained her composure. "I accept your terms," she said calmly, though I believed ready to sing with relief and excitement.

"Now," Adelman said to Miriam, "would you wait outside for a moment while we conclude our business with Mr. Weaver?"

No sooner was she out of the room than the unpleasant man began to shout at me in an animated fashion. "You must believe you are beyond our grasp to have challenged us thus, Weaver, but let me assure you that this Company can destroy you."

"As you destroyed my father, Michael Balfour, and Christopher Hodge, the bookseller?"

"Nonsense," Adelman said, waving a hand about the air. "You cannot believe that the Company orchestrated these crimes. The very notion is absurd."

I believed him right, but I would not avert my gaze. "Then who did?"

"Why, I should think you would know that by now," he said casually. "Martin Rochester."

I suspected they were testing me, attempting to learn what I knew. "And who is Rochester?"

"That," Adelman said, "we are as anxious to learn as you. We only know that it is a pseudonym used by a clumsy purveyor of false stock. He is but an insignificant forger who has fooled a small number of people—women such as Mrs. Lienzo, who know nothing of the Exchange."

"That is a lie," I said. "Rochester is more than an insignificant forger, and I shall wager that he has fooled more than a small number of white-gloved ladies." Miriam had received dividends, which could only mean that someone had helped Rochester to falsify records as well as stock. When my father saw her issues, he understood at once what they signi- fied. *This forgery can only have been perpetrated with the cooperation of certain elements within South Sea House itself,* he had written. *The Company is as a piece of meat, rotted and crawling with maggots.* "Tell me," I said with a grin. "What has become of Mr. Virgil Cowper?"

"We hardly keep track of our clerks," the South Sea man barked with unexpected venom. "I care nothing for your foolish questions."

"So what is it you want of me? What further threats do you offer? Need I fear more violence and theft that you can keep your secret?"

Adelman and his companion exchanged glances, but it was Adelman who spoke. "You have correctly surmised that we wish to keep the matter of the stock quiet, but we shall not threaten you. And I know nothing of matters of violence and theft."

"You would impose on me to believe that you did not attempt, in any way, to suppress a pamphlet written by my father that would have ex- posed the existence of the forged stock?"

They exchanged looks once again. "Until this moment," Adelman said, "I did not know your father intended to write such a pamphlet. I can- not believe he would have been so reckless. If you have come across such a thing, I suspect it is yet another forgery."

I did not know if I should even credit the possibility. The manuscript had looked to me to be written in my father's hand, and I should think that my uncle would have recognized a forgery, but my enemies were cer- tainly expert forgers. Still, it was no forged fire that had killed Christopher Hodge, my father's printer; and it was no forged thief who had taken the only copy of the manuscript from my room. Someone was desperate to hide all traces of this document.

"There is ample evidence that tells me the pamphlet was real," I an- nounced.

"That evidence has been planted," Adelman said wearily, "to deceive you."

I shook my head. I would not believe it. "And you have nothing more to tell me that will help me find who killed my father?"

"We are not here to help you, Weaver," the unpleasant man spat.

Adelman held up his hand to silence his companion. "I fear not, Mr.

Weaver. Except to assure you that our enemies have been using you. I suspect the hand of the Bank of England."

"That is rot," I hissed. I had been engaged in this business far too long in order to believe that I had been led astray from the first. Nevertheless, I could not quite banish Adelman's words, and they filled me with anger at myself and him and almost anyone whose name came to mind.

"I warned you of this, you may recall," Adelman continued. "We sat in Jonathan's and I told you that you could not see yourself in the maze, but the game-masters would see you and lead you astray. And so it has happened. Everything you have worked so hard to discover is a lie."

"Nonsense!" I proclaimed, hoping to silence their lies with the force of my conviction. "I have discovered that the South Sea Company has been violated by forgeries, and that is not a lie. I have discovered that this Rochester, who certainly killed my father, is behind these forgeries."

"It is more than likely that this Rochester shadow, while a blackguard, has nothing to do with your father," Adelman said softly. "Our enemies only wished you to think otherwise that you might expose this forgery to the public."

"I shall not have it," I said adamantly, as though by summoning a force of will I could dispel these ideas. I wanted to grab Adelman by the throat and squeeze until he admitted the truth. I suppose I wanted to believe that the truth was precisely that accessible.

"You may choose to believe what you wish, but if you seek the answer to your father's death, you cannot but know that you have been led astray. Do not grow angry with yourself; our enemies are clever and wealthy—and they surely are *our* enemies, for they have sought to do us both wrong. And after all, did you ever really believe that the South Sea Company, so in need of the approval of the public and of Parliament in order to transact our business, would engage in activities of so despicable and villainous a nature, to associate ourselves with murder—*murder*, Mr. Weaver—at the risk of losing business that would serve the nation and enrich our directors?"

I had no answer. I could not make myself credit his words, but I could think of nothing to refute them.

Adelman saw the expression upon my face, and believed me defeated. "And so, Mr. Weaver, this is where we find ourselves. You are not to be the Company's ally, but that does not mean you are to be its enemy. Should you have further questions, you may call upon me. I do not wish you to make any more scenes or perpetuate these dangerous lies. You have been an effective agent for Mr. Bloathwait and the Bank of England. If by being more open with you we can make you less dangerous to our reputation, then we shall do so."

He opened the door. "I bid you a good day, sir."

TWENTY-NINE

MIRIAM COULD NOT have been more delighted with her prize, but I had difficulty sharing in her joy. I allowed her to thank me for my help, and I placed her in a hackney and then retired to a tavern to think on my situation. If I had learned anything since beginning my inquiry, it was that these men of finance were skilled in the arts of deception, but I now found myself so deep within their illusions that I could no longer be sure what was real and what was mere fiction. Did the men of the South Sea Company lie boldly to my face to obscure their crimes, or was I a victim of Bloathwait's machinations to destroy a rival company? And if Bloathwait had been willing to deceive me in order to help ruin the South Sea, was it possible that he had been willing to kill my father, Balfour, and Christopher Hodge? With millions of pounds in the balance for the company that serviced the government's loans, was it unthinkable that the Bank of England would commit these crimes in pursuit of such profits? I had believed as much of the South Sea Company. And if my enemy were the Bank and not the Company, then was my pursuit of Rochester misguided all along?

I attempted to drive the doubts from my mind by entering once more into the thick of the inquiry. I returned to Kent's to discover if anyone else had come by in response to the advertisement and there received two names and addresses. Neither proved of any use—merely parasites who attempted to extort money from me by pretending to information they did not possess. After leaving the second house, I thought hard on my next move. I could not simply go back to my uncle's; I could not remain still. I found the nearest alehouse, and drank quickly as I thought hard.

I had to find Rochester, or find that which called himself Rochester. I knew of but two people I believed could point me toward this person or persons, and Jonathan Wild I dare not trust, so I would make the other tell me what I wanted to know. Without bothering to finish my ale, I rose to my feet and departed for Newgate once again to interview Kate Cole.

I could offer her nothing to make her help me, and I blush to own that I did not entirely dismiss the use of violence to convince Kate to cooperate. Perhaps the idea was not fully formed, but I believed that I would not leave her cell until she told me all she knew of Martin Rochester.

When I reached Newgate, I marched toward Kate's cell and banged with violent intent upon her door. Nothing, no evasion on her part, would prevent me from learning what I wished to know.

When the door opened, I found myself facing a plump fellow with narrow, slitlike eyes and a mouth stained with rich red wine. For a moment I felt some embarrassment at barging so rudely into Kate's closet when she had a guest, but this was no time for good breeding. I ignored the fellow and pushed hard upon the door, which opened to reveal not Kate, wallowing like a sow in her filth, but a woman as plump as the man and a pair of plump children, all gathered around a little table, eating their afternoon meal.

My embarrassment returned. There was no mistaking that this closet was Kate's. "Where is the woman who resided here?" I asked, some conciliation creeping into my voice.

"No idea," the man replied, and observing that my business was concluded, he slammed shut the door.

It was not yet time for a session at the Old Bailey, so she could not have been brought to trial. Had she sold her room for more ready cash?

"Where's Kate Cole?" I demanded of the first turnkey I could find. "I must see her."

" 'Fraid yer can't see 'er," the turnkey told me, "or even if yer could, she couldn't see yer. What with 'er being dead and all."

"Dead," I sputtered. I felt, I don't know what—faint, perhaps. I felt that death was all around me. That my enemies knew everything I knew— they anticipated my plans before I even thought of them. "Of what is she dead?"

"Of 'anging by 'er neck."

"But there was no trial yet," I argued.

"Yer just don't get it, do yer? She 'anged 'erself in 'er fancy cell, she did."

"Self-murder?" I judged it inconceivable that someone like Kate would be capable of the despair required to contemplate self-murder. And even if she were, would she not wait to see the results of her trial before abandoning hope? "You are certain it is self-murder?"

"That's what the coroner said it is."

My mind raced to ask the questions that would allow me to know who had done this. "And did she have any visitors immediately prior to her death?"

"Not as I know of."

"Is there someone else who would know?" I snapped. "Another turnkey perhaps?"

"Not as I know of."

I placed a shilling in his hand. "Do you know now?"

"No," he said, "but thank ye for yer generosity."

THERE WERE NOW four murders. Kate Cole had not hanged herself; if I were to think on what was probable, I could only believe that Kate Cole would rather have lived to spit in the eye of the hangman than to take her own life. No, Kate had been caught in the same web that had caught my father, Michael Balfour, and Christopher Hodge, the bookseller. I now understood more clearly than I ever had that Elias was right. The new finance had produced an unstoppable power on a scale that I could not even comprehend. I had been searching for a man, or perhaps a cabal of men, who sat somewhere plotting out evil deeds, executing them, perhaps with a chilling callousness. Now I no longer believed that one man or even one group of men were responsible. There were too many connections, too many avenues of villainy. Too many men had too much power and knowledge, but none could be made to answer for their crimes because they hid themselves in endless mazes of deceit and fiction. It was, as my father had written, a conspiracy of paper that allowed these men to prosper. They inscribed their fictions upon banknotes, which the world read and believed.

My stomach was empty, and I felt quite lightheaded, so I stopped into a tavern to take some refreshment. When I sat, however, I found myself in no mind for food, so I called for a mug of a thick ale. And then perhaps I called for another. I suppose by the time I had my fourth mug of ale, all on an empty stomach, I had turned from dejected to morose. I now contemplated the sorrow of not being ten years younger than I was, of having brought about the death of Kate Cole, of having shot Jemmy, of having turned my back on my family. In such a mood I at last returned to my uncle's house on Broad Court. I settled comfortably in the dark of the parlor, conveniently close to a bottle of Madeira, of which I partook as I tried once more to understand all I had seen.

I sat in the dark I don't know how long, but the sound of someone descending the stairs shattered my stupor. I had been in my trade and on the more dangerous side of the law too long not to recognize the sound of someone walking with the hope of making no noise, so I set my glass down upon the table and slowly pushed myself to my feet. Once at the doorway, which afforded me a fair view of the staircase, I saw Miriam creeping down the stairs. She wore a greatcoat over her gown, and she had all pulled up past her ankles so she could take each step with quiet care.

I held myself back until she moved past the parlor and then to the front of the house, which she skillfully—and I could only assume that she was not without practice—maneuvered noiselessly and then stepped out into the courtyard.

I waited only a moment before following, and saw that she entered a hackney that was a few yards past the entrance of my uncle's house.

The hackney began to roll down the street, and I then sprinted after it, making my way as best I could upon an injured leg, and, as I had done once before when following Deloney, I leapt onto the back of the coach. In the cover of the London darkness, I hardly needed to pay the coachman for my ride, so I crouched low that he would not see me, and held on as the carriage rode in the direction of Spitalfields. I hoped it would not be a long ride, for I had not the protection of an outer coat, and I grew cold quickly.

The hackney soon stopped on Princes Street, and Miriam hurried into a public house. At least, I noted with some relief, it had the looks of a respectable place, but I could still hardly check my concern. I waited a moment, rubbed my hands together for warmth, and then entered, keeping close to the door in case Miriam was still in full sight. She was not. Here was a cozy sort of place with a warm fireplace and a collection of middling tradesmen, and some ladies too, scattered about the tables. I saw nothing of Miriam, so I approached the tapman, gave him a coin, and learned that she had met a gentleman in a room on the second floor.

I climbed the stairs and found the room the tapman had specified. The door was closed, but it was also none the sturdiest, so I knew that even if it were locked, I should have little difficulty making my way inside. I pressed my ear to the door, and I heard voices, but I could little tell their disposition. Another door opened, and I stepped away, that I might now look like a madman, but I think I attempted this masquerade unsuccessfully, for the gentleman who emerged down the hall cast me the most suspicious look as he squeezed past me and descended the stairs.

I could hardly endure the thought of standing here all night, lurking in the halls while patrons cast me suspicious looks, so I formed a strategy. That is to say, I turned the doorknob, and finding it yielded to my pressure, I opened the door.

Miriam and Deloney stood facing each other at a small distance. I cannot say how pleased I was to see that they were both red with anger and not, as I had feared, tangled in a lovers' embrace. Both stopped speaking as I entered the room and closed the door behind me.

"Weaver," Deloney spat. "What is this outrage?"

"What are you doing here?" Miriam stammered.

I could not stand to see her uneasy, but could stand even less to think that whatever conflict they had might eventually resolve itself, so sowed some bitter seeds for Deloney. "You *did* ask me to wait a quarter of an hour before entering, did you not?" I asked Miriam. "Have I come too soon?"

Miriam knew not how to respond to my ruse, but she hardly had to.

"What do you mean by this?" Deloney demanded of her. "You so little trusted me that you felt the need to bring in this ruffian. I cannot endure this."

"You cannot endure?" I moved forward, and Miriam stepped out of my way. I saw at once that her rupture with Deloney was complete, for she did nothing to stop me or temper my approach. "What is it that you cannot endure, Deloney? The thought of having tricked this woman out of her money or that of having done business with a murderer?"

"A murderer?" he demanded. "You had better choose your words with care, sir, lest you know my wrath."

"If I could gather together all the gentlemen of this city who would welcome the chance to know your wrath, they could hardly fit in the opera house, sir. What fear I of so hollow a promise as your wrath? I shall brook no prevarication. I must know at once the nature of your dealings with Martin Rochester."

"I've never heard of anyone named—"

I could scarce comprehend that he would lie thus, and the effrontery of it—the way in which he presumed me so easily deceived—filled me with outrage. I grabbed him by his coat collar and pushed him hard against the wall. From behind my back, I could hear Miriam begin to utter a protest and then stifle herself.

"I know you have had dealings with him. You will tell me about them."

He held out his hands submissively, and I could see in his downcast gaze that he had no more fight in him. "I arranged to buy stock from him. Nothing more."

I released my grip and took a step back, but I remained close enough to make him feel the threat of my presence. Proximity, I have learned, is often as effective as violence. "How did you conduct your business with him?"

"He would never meet with me, but he contacted me one day by letter, saying he knew of my interest in raising money upon the 'Change."

"Your false projects," I said.

"Projects, yes. He told me he could sell me South Sea stock discounted. I needed only arrange the sales and send him the money, and he would provide the stock."

"And to whom did you sell besides Miriam?"

He shook his head. "No one."

"And why have you been seeking him out? Why did you follow the messenger when I sent the note for Rochester?"

"I bought some shares myself. I then began to suspect there was something wrong. I was motivated at first by my desire to acquire the stock cheap, but I then began to wonder how he could have ordered the matter. When I tried to contact him, he had disappeared."

"Very well. You will take me to see those shares now." If I could lay my hands upon more false issues, I thought, then I might have some leverage with the South Sea Company. But I saw at once that I could never hope to acquire any forged stock from Deloney.

"There are circumstances that make that difficult." He gritted his teeth as though the ineptitude of his lie caused him pain. But why would he lie? Because he had no wish to surrender his stock? No, for by now he knew it was false. There was only one answer that seemed within the limits of probability.

"You never bought any of the stock yourself." I spoke it like a statement of fact.

He shook his head, half relieved, half shamed to have the truth aired. "No, I never did."

Miriam stared at him, but he refused to meet her gaze. I guessed that he had lied to her, told her that he had invested heavily in order to convince her to do the same.

"You said you sold to no one but Miriam," I observed. "How so? If this scheme was so profitable, why did you not exploit it further?"

"I had trouble finding buyers," Deloney said haltingly.

"Of course." I now understood clearly. I was not the only man to think on what was probable. "Your false projects had made your name a mockery to any man with a substantial amount to invest. You could find no investors, and your failed efforts no doubt injured Rochester's plans—for men would begin to talk about the discounted stock as one more of your petty projects. Once Rochester learned of your reputation for false projects, he knew an association with you could only injure his schemes, and he severed all connections with you."

That Deloney did not disagree told me I had guessed correctly.

"You knew the stock was false when you sold it to Miriam, did you not?" I announced, testing my theory by speaking it aloud. "You knew it was as false as those foolish projects that you concocted at your own escritoire. Miriam gave you six hundred pounds, even though you were aware that she needed this money in order to establish her own household."

Deloney tried to move backward, but there was nowhere to go. "She could have sold the stocks herself. The fact that they were false did not undo their value."

I leaned closer to him. "Martin Rochester killed my father, and he killed a woman I had sought to protect. If you know something of who he is or where I might find him, you had better tell me now. If you hold back any information, I swear to you that I shall seek my vengeance upon you as ruthlessly as I do upon him."

"I tell you I don't know," he almost squealed. "If I knew how to find him, would I have been chasing after messenger boys at Jonathan's?"

It was true that Deloney had been desperate to find Rochester and had no more idea how to do so than I did. There was nothing more to be gained from this man. It was only my desire to assert my manhood before Miriam that made me humiliate him once more. I took a step back, drew my hangar, and pointed the blade to his throat. "Return to me the two guineas I lent you in good faith."

I saw at once that he opened his mouth to utter a lie, but he checked it. With trembling hands he reached into his purse and procured the coins, which, with great difficulty, he set upon the table.

I sheathed my weapon. "Go. And do not let me, or anyone of my family, see you no more."

Deloney dared not even look at Miriam, but as though his legs had turned into puddings, he walked toward the door, opened it, and was gone.

I closed the door and turned to Miriam. She had seated herself, and she had buried her face in her hands. At first I thought she wept, but I suppose she sensed my gaze upon her and she looked up at me. Her face showed confusion, anger, perhaps even shame, but she shed no tears.

I pulled a chair over to her. "Why did you come here tonight?" I asked as gently as I could.

"What business have you to demand that of me?" she snapped, but she soon decided her anger was misplaced. She took a breath and straightened her posture. "I wanted to know the truth. I wanted to learn what you wished to learn—if he had deceived me knowingly, if he had been in league with this Rochester. I suppose I should not have learned the truth had you not arrived."

"It is the nature of a man like Deloney to lie. He is naught but deception and foolish greed."

Miriam, to my dismay, understood the insult I had intended, but she did not bristle at it. "Please understand, Benjamin, that when you are trapped, when a person is trapped, any escape seems so much like a good one. I know it was foolish of me to trust him, but our association gave me pleasure, made me feel free. I had command over something in my life."

"Would you have felt free had he lodged his child in your belly?" I asked pointedly.

Miriam gasped. Her head snapped back. "How dare you make such an accusation?"

"I accuse you of nothing, but I am not unfamiliar with the ways of such men as Deloney."

"Or of widows such as myself?" she demanded.

"I apologize," I said, though my words dropped from my mouth with leaden thickness. "It is no place of mine to dictate your behavior. Soon you will be your own mistress, and you will be able to make any decisions you see fit." The thought sat with me rather ill, however, for I had little faith, based on the decision I had seen, that Miriam would prove skillful at managing her affairs.

Miriam raised her eyebrows slightly. She appeared to sense my thoughts. "You need not worry about me selling my little fortune to the first gentleman who comes along. I am not interested in marrying any such grasping fools. I do not suppose the man I should like to marry exists."

I took a deep breath. "Perhaps the man you seek is one who knows both the ways of our people and the ways of the English. Someone who can help guide you into English society while protecting you from its evils and excesses." My heart raced in the silence that followed my speech.

Miriam looked nervously at her hands. "I cannot imagine where I might find such a man," she said quickly, "and I cannot believe you can tell me."

"I can," I said softly, "for he sits before you." I own that my voice trembled as I spoke.

She stared at me as though it had never occurred to her that I would say such a thing, though I had flattered myself that I had only said as much as she expected. She rose to her feet, attempting to order her thoughts. At last she stood and offered me a nervous smile. "I think it best that we both pretend this conversation never took place. We should return to your uncle's house."

I stood and faced her manfully. "Miriam, if I have offended you—"

She met my gaze with more boldness and assurance than I would have expected. "Offense is not important," she told me, her voice hardly more than a whisper. I listened to her words, but my eye fixed upon the sweet smile of her lips. "You must know that I like you prodigiously. I admire you, and I think you a very worthy man, but you cannot imagine for an instant that I could learn to endure what you offer. At South Sea House, they spoke of a man you had killed, and here tonight you spoke of a woman who died under your protection. You removed your blade and held it to Philip's throat as though you had done so a thousand times, and as though you could kill him and think nothing of it." She could not meet my gaze. "I am not the woman for you, Benjamin."

I could say nothing. There were no words with which I could counter this too-just complaint. We had been born of the same station, but my decisions had placed me far below this woman. I had made my own way, and because I could not undo what I had done, I could only act in accordance with the life I had chosen.

I leaned toward Miriam and kissed her gently upon the lips.

The moment dazzled me. She did not move—either away from me or toward me—but she closed her eyes and kissed me back. I smelled nothing but the dizzy mingling of her sweet breath and her floral perfume. I had never kissed a woman such as she—a woman of wealth and station and intelligence and wit. It was a kiss that made me hungry for more.

I pressed forward, and in doing so broke the spell. Miriam opened her eyes and pulled away from me, backing up only a few small steps, but enough to impose a wall of awkward space between us. I know not how long we stood there, saying nothing, I looking upon her, she upon me. I heard only the sound of footsteps in the hall and my own deep breathing.

"My uncle has offered me a position," I said. "I could trade in the Levant. I could be something other than a man you fear. If I made a mistake when I left my father's house, I can right that error."

Miriam let out a slight gasp—almost inaudible, and sounding as though she had choked upon the air. Her eyes moistened; they clouded over like windows in a rainstorm. She blinked and blinked, trying to make her tears disappear, but the tears betrayed her and trickled down her face. "It cannot be." She shook her head only slightly. "I do not wish to marry Aaron once more. I could not bear to see you try to become him for my sake. I should only hate myself." She wiped at the tears with her fingers. "I should come to hate you too." She attempted a smile, but it failed her, and instead she turned from me and opened the door.

I could not call after her. I could not move to hold her back. I had no argument with which to refute what she said. I had only the passions of my heart, and I knew that for the world, and for Miriam, these were not enough. I watched her descend the stairs and hand the tapman a coin to procure her a hackney.

With nothing else to do, I rang the bell and called for a bottle of wine, which I used to wash away the taste of Miriam's lips.

THE NEXT MORNING my head and heart ached with equal urgency, but such pain only made me wish for distractions.

I made my way once more to Bloathwait's town house, determined this time I would speak with him whether he would or no. I waited at the door for several minutes before his scruffy servant appeared. He glanced at me, by now familiar with a face he had denied a half-dozen times. "Mr. Bloathwait is not in," he said.

"Did not Mr. Bloathwait inform you that he was always to be in for me?" I inquired, as I pushed past him. "I think you will find yourself to be glad I did not take your denial to heart."

I moved forward at a steady and only slightly hurried pace, but this servant rushed to move before me and block my path. I would have none of it, and shoved him aside, this time with a small measure of violence, knocking him slightly against the wall. I suffered no more interference and made my way to Bloathwait's study. I knocked once and then opened the door to find the man at his desk with his shaved head exposed. His wig hung on a hook behind him, and his pale and beveined head bobbed up and down as he wrote furiously upon a piece of paper.

"Weaver." He looked up, and then returned to his writing. "Forced your way in, did you?"

"Yes," I said. I reached his desk and stood there, not taking a seat.

Bloathwait looked up once more, and this time he set aside his quill. "You'll not get far if you allow servants and little men to block your path. I hope you didn't hurt poor Andrew too much, but if you had to, do not trouble yourself about it."

"Do you mean to say," I nearly stammered, "that you had your servant deny me in the expectation that I would force my way in to see you?"

"Not the expectation, but certainly the hope. I make it my business to know what sort of men I'm dealing with. Now, please stop standing before me. You look as eager as a hunting dog. Sit down and tell me what you have to say for yourself."

A little stunned, I sat down. "You have not been entirely honest with me, Mr. Bloathwait," I began.

He shrugged.

I took that as permission to continue. "It has come to my attention that before he died, my father sent some sort of message to you. I wish to know the content of that message. I also wish to know why you withheld this contact from me."

Bloathwait's tiny mouth pouted. I could not say if he smiled or frowned. "How did you learn of the message?"

"From the messenger."

He nodded. "The note contained some information that he believed could do a great injury to the South Sea Company. He proposed we set aside our differences in order to bring this information to light."

"The information being the existence of forged South Sea issues?"

"Of course."

I dug my fingernails into my palms. "You knew of the forged stock from the beginning, but you said nothing to me. You offered to share with me any knowledge you might have, and yet you kept this from me. Why?"

Bloathwait merely smiled. "I thought it in my best interest to do so."

"Mr. Bloathwait, I have only recently had a very distressing encounter at South Sea House, where their agents sought to convince me that any suspicions I might have of that Company are fabricated by their enemies: the Bank of England, and no doubt you in particular. I find their claims very disturbing, sir, and your reluctance to share information with me makes their claims even more disturbing. So, again, I must ask you about your reluctance to share information with me."

"I admit I was not entirely forthright with you, Mr. Weaver. I told you that I would give you any information to aid in your inquiry. Such was clearly not the case. You have found me out. I have given you what information I have wanted you to have and no more."

"But why?" I demanded. "Do you want the South Sea Company exposed or no?"

"Oh, I do. I do indeed. But in my own way, sir. On my own schedule."

I was silent for a moment as I considered the consequences of using violence against a man of Bloathwait's stature. "I wish to see the message you received of my father."

"I am afraid that is not possible. I have destroyed it."

"Then I wish for you to tell me, as nearly as you can recall, what it said."

He showed me a tight-lipped smile. "Your question suggests that you have your own suspicions of what it said. Perhaps you should tell me."

I sucked in a breath of air. "I believe," I said, attempting to keep my voice from wavering, "that there is only one reason why my father would have contacted you after so many years—after all the unpleasantness that passed between you. He believed himself to be in some danger, and he sought your help because those who threatened him were the enemies of the Bank of England. Thus by helping you he might have secured his own protection."

"Very clever. You have guessed the nature of the message precisely."

"And what assistance did you offer?" I breathed.

"Alas," Bloathwait said, his face a mockery of contrition, "I had scarcely time to contemplate the import of your father's message before his horrific fate befell him."

I rose to my feet. I understood that I had as much information as I would receive of Bloathwait, and I believed I understood why he told me what he did and told me no more. I turned then to exit the room, but I briefly stopped myself and looked back. "I am most curious," I said, "about the nature of your relationship with Mr. Sarmento."

Bloathwait let out another laugh. "Sarmento." He said the name as though it were the first word of a poem. He then picked up his pen. "My relationship with Sarmento is much like my relationship with you, sir." He stared at me for a moment before continuing. "That is to say, he does what I wish of him. Good day to you."

Bloathwait returned to writing, and I walked from his study knowing that I would need to do so immediately if I was to escape without harming him.

THIRTY

I**T WAS** F**RIDAY AFTERNOON,** and my uncle had returned from his warehouse early. I met him in the parlor and joined him in a glass of Madeira. The wine helped calm me after my meeting with Bloathwait, and it also gave me courage to ask my uncle uncomfortable questions. He had been kind to me, given me a home, offered me funds, and aided my inquiry. But I still did not know that I could trust him, nor understand why he kept information from me, or even what his motives were.

"Before he died," I began, "my father contacted Bloathwait. Did you know that, sir?"

I looked him straight in his eye, for if he wished to lie to me, I would make that lie as difficult as I might. I watched his face, and I saw his discomfort. He shifted his eyes, as though to move them away, but I kept my gaze clenched. I would not free him from my scrutiny.

He said nothing.

"You knew," I said.

He nodded.

"You knew what Bloathwait had been to him, to my family. You saw this notorious villain at my father's funeral. And yet you said nothing to me. I must know why."

My uncle took a long time to respond. "Benjamin," he began, "you are used to saying what you wish, to being afraid of no one. In the world in which you live, you have no one to fear. That is not true for me. My home, my business, everything I have—it can all be taken away if I anger the wrong men. Were you to come into business with me, you would find yourself a rich man, but you would also understand the dangers of being a rich Jew in this country. We cannot own property, we cannot engage in certain kinds of business. For centuries they have herded us into dealing with their money for them, and they have hated us for doing what they permitted."

"But what have you to fear?"

"Everything. I am no more dishonest than any other English merchant. I bring in a few contraband cloths from France, I sometimes sell them through sullied channels. It is what a man must do, but any public exposure of my dealings would prove a danger to this family and to our community here." He let out a sigh. "I said nothing about Bloathwait because I feared his anger."

He could not quite look at me. I hardly knew how to respond. "But," I said at last, "you told me you wished me to learn the truth about my father's death."

"I did," he said anxiously. "I do. Benjamin, Mr. Bloathwait did not have your father killed, but I know what kind of a man he is—vengeful, single-minded. I wanted nothing so much as that you should stay away from him, to find out who did this without crossing his path."

"And what about Adelman? Do you not speak ill of him because you fear him as well?"

"I must be careful of these men. Surely you see that. Yet I must do justice for Samuel, too. I know you must think me a coward, but I must balance myself like a ropedancer. I want only what is right, and I shall do what I can to see that Samuel's killers are punished. If I must appear to you and all the world a coward to do so, then so be it. I know no other way."

There was a strange dignity in his cowardice that I could not deny. My uncle was not someone I could strive to be like, but I believed I understood him.

"Between us, then," I said, "for I believe you know you can trust me. What do you think of Adelman? Of the South Sea Company?"

He shook his head. "I no longer know. Once I thought Adelman was a man of honor, but these schemes of his seem to preclude all honor. Tell me what you think."

"What I think? I think that Adelman wishes me to believe that all of this villainy is a hoax perpetrated by Bloathwait. I believe that Bloathwait tells me only what he wishes me to know so that I shall investigate the South Sea further."

"Because the inquiry itself, not necessarily the truth, injures the Company?"

"Precisely. Bloathwait has been arranging that I obtain just enough information to keep me interested. I would not be surprised if the pamphlet you gave me was a forgery."

"It was no forgery," my uncle assured me. "I know Samuel's hand."

"Let me ask you something else," I pressed on, hoping that by involving him I might make him feel more at ease. "Sarmento—did you know that he has dealings with Bloathwait?"

My uncle laughed. "Of course. The world knows that. Bloathwait has hired him to keep an eye on Adelman, but Sarmento is so very poor at subtlety, one would need to be a fool not to see it."

"Then why does Bloathwait continue to employ his services?"

"Because," he said with a grin, "if Adelman is watching Sarmento watching him, then perhaps he is not watching someone else. Even if Bloathwait has no one else, Sarmento, for all his ineptitude, is a reminder of Bloathwait's presence."

We both sipped at our wine and said nothing for some long minutes. I could not guess what my uncle felt. I suppose I could hardly guess what I felt.

"How will you feel if this inquiry comes to nothing?" he asked. "If you never discover who did these things, or even if they were done?"

"A man must fail sometimes," I said. "And my enemies here are formidable. I would not choose to fail, but if I do, I must not despair."

"Have you given any more thought to my offer?" he asked quietly.

I considered how to respond for some time. My uncle, as near as I could tell, had acquitted himself of all villainy in the matter of the conspiracy surrounding my father's death. He had not sufficiently acquitted himself in the matter of Miriam's fortune, so I pressed him.

"Let us say that I took you up on your offer, Uncle, and that I married Miriam. What if something were to happen to me? What should become of Miriam?"

My uncle braced himself. It had simply been a question, but it made him think of the loss of his son. Perhaps I had been in error even to suggest such a thing.

"I understand why you might have such a concern. It is only right of you to think of such things, but Miriam has always been welcome in my home."

"But should she not be sufficient in herself? And what of you? If you were to lose a ship full of goods, surely that would prove disastrous to your finances."

"It would prove disastrous in many ways, but not to my finances. I always insure my shipments against such damages that in the event of tragedy, as much as one suffers, one does not suffer ruin." He set down his wine. "You wish to know what happened to Miriam's fortune." There was a coolness in his voice I had not heard since he and I had set upon this inquiry. "You wish to know how many coins shall land in your pocket should you marry her."

"No," I said quickly. "You misunderstand me. I am sorry I did not pay you the courtesy of being plain. I wish to know what happened to Miriam's money for her sake, not for mine."

"For her sake?" he asked. "Why, I have it. It shall be hers again should she remarry."

"And should she not?"

He laughed. "Then, I shall hold it for her for as long as she resides in my house. Should she remain unmarried at the time of my death, I have arranged that it should be held in trust."

"But why do you not give it to her?" I asked.

He shook his head. "The money is no longer truly hers, except in spirit. Aaron invested in the trade, and when his ship was lost, I received the payment of the insurance. It becomes so hard to tell whose money belongs to whom. But Miriam shall never want for anything as long as she stays in my protection or marries a man of whom I approve."

"And what if she does not wish your protection," I continued, "or wishes to marry a man of whom you do not approve?"

"Do you think I have been sinister, Benjamin? That I have robbed the wife of my own son for the benefit of a few thousand pounds?" To my relief there was no indignation in his voice. He believed himself so free of ill motives that he could not take such suspicions seriously.

I took it seriously, however. For he was guilty, but not of malice. "I do not believe you have taken anything with ill intent," I said. "I believe you have presumed to speak for Miriam."

"And now you do?" Now his voice grew hot again. I had touched upon something.

"I would never do so," I said, "but I feared you would not listen to her words. I thought perhaps you might listen to mine."

"It is foolish for her to want such a thing," my uncle told me. "Miriam has lived in my home for a very long time," he said. "If I have done anything she has not liked, I have done it in the name of her greater good."

"How can you decide such a thing for Miriam?" I asked. "Have you never consulted with her?"

"It is foolishness to consult with women in these matters," he replied. "You saw that I withheld Miriam's money and you thought I did so out of greed? I am shocked, Benjamin. Perhaps now you will accuse me of being illiberal, but I have seen women bring estates to ruin many a time, and I only wish to preserve for Miriam a fortune that should be hers and her children's. Left to her own devices, she would squander her money upon gowns and equipages and expensive entertainments. Women cannot be entrusted with these matters."

I shook my head. I felt as though he had surely never met his daughter-in-law to say such things about her. "Some women may be thus, but surely not Miriam."

He laughed softly. "When you have your own wife, your own children, we may again have this conversation." He rose and left the room. I could hardly tell if he had dismissed me or yielded.

MY UNCLE ASKED NOTHING of me, for he had promised he would ask nothing, but I understood that he would have preferred for me to suspend my inquiry for the Sabbath. I did so in order to show respect for his house and also because I needed some time to consider all that had happened. He said nothing to me of our conversation about Miriam, and I said nothing to him. I had not the heart to bring up a matter of conflict with him. Not yet, at least. It was strange for me to think that I had come into my uncle's house in the hopes that he would be the man that my father had never been. I suppose I had expected too much of him—that is to say, I had expected he would think like me on all accounts. I took some comfort, however, in the knowledge that he withheld money from Miriam not out of villainy but out of a prejudice against her sex.

For our Friday-night meal, my uncle wisely chose to invite neither Adelman or Sarmento, but he did invite a neighboring family—a married couple of about my uncle and aunt's age and their son and his wife. I was pleased for the company, for it was a much-needed distraction and the presence of the women relieved me of the uncomfortable burden of attempting conversation with Miriam.

After prayer at the synagogue the next day, I once again found myself in conversation with Abraham Mendes. It was so strange to me that this man who appeared nothing but a mindless ruffian when with his master, Jonathan Wild, could prove himself socially competent in other circumstances. To my surprise, I felt something like pleasure when I saw him approach.

Mendes and I exchanged the traditional Sabbath greeting. He inquired after the health of my family, and then turned his attention to me. "How does your inquiry progress, if I may ask?"

"Does it not violate the law of God to discuss such matters on the Sabbath?" I inquired.

"It does," he agreed, "but so does theft, so I think it best not to pick over our sins."

"The inquiry goes badly," I muttered. "And even if you care not about disturbing the Lord, you might care about disturbing me. I am in no mood to discuss the matter."

"Very well." He smiled. "But if you like, I might mention your difficulties to Mr. Wild. Perhaps he might offer some assistance."

"You will do nothing of the kind. Mendes, I am not entirely convinced of the scope of your villainy, but I have no uncertainty about your master. You will please not mention my name to him."

Mendes bowed and departed.

Once back at my uncle's house, I again found myself avoiding Miriam. She and I had gone to great lengths to elude one another since our unfortunate conversation. On Saturday, after synagogue, Miriam announced she had a headache and spent the rest of the day in her room. I cannot claim I was anything but relieved.

That night, as I climbed the stairs, I found her hovering in the hall, just outside her door. She was waiting for me.

"Benjamin," she said softly. My uncle and aunt were asleep one flight upward. Our voices would carry if we were not careful.

I could not think if I should take a step toward her or away. It seemed foolish to remain still, but for the moment it was easier than making a decision.

"There's something I want to say to you," she whispered, almost inaudibly.

I moved forward, hand outstretched. She backed up a step. "It's about your father."

This pronouncement stopped me in my tracks. My limbs tingled. I had been through too much not to be terrified by that pronouncement. "What is it?"

"There is something I want to say—something I think you should hear. Your father—" She paused, pressed her lips together, and sucked in air through her nose like a sailor filling his lungs before diving into the sea. "Your father was not a nice man."

I almost laughed—indeed I should have cackled if I had not been so confused. "I believe I knew that."

She bit her lip. "You don't understand. You told me once that you feel guilt, you feel remorse, you feel as though you have made mistakes. Maybe you should feel those things; maybe you did err horribly when you ran away and even more so when you didn't return. But that does not mean you were in the wrong—at least not entirely. You may blame yourself if you wish, but you must blame him, too."

I shook my head over and over again, only partially aware that I was doing so.

"Your father knew where you were. He had only to read the papers to see where you fought. He could have gone to you, and he didn't. He didn't because he knew not how to be kind. I have seen him with your brother, and he was no warmer to José than he was with you—only more satisfied. Your memories of him are not a fabrication—they are the truth. Perhaps the qualities that made him a good businessman made him a poor father. But I think . . ." Her voice trailed off for a moment. "You have too many regrets," she said. "More than you ought."

Her words left me as though frozen. I felt such a torrent of emotions I could not sort one out from another.

"I wish us to be friends, Benjamin," she said after a moment, perhaps weary of my silence. "Do you understand that?"

I nodded dumbly.

"Then tomorrow we may speak as we used to." She smiled so sweetly, so shyly, I thought my heart should burst. And then she climbed up the stairs and left me in the hall, where I remained until I heard a clock chime below, and then I staggered to my room like a drunkard.

IT WAS JUST AFTER one in the afternoon when I reached Sir Owen's house, and I was pleasantly surprised to find that he was awake, fully dressed, and ready to see me within a quarter hour of my arrival. Far from the harsh man I had encountered the last time I had seen him, he now appeared for all the world his old self.

"Weaver," he shouted with some pleasure as he walked into his drawing room. "So good to see you. What can I do for you? A glass of something?"

"No, thank you, Sir Owen," I said as he poured himself a port. I was too agitated, too confused, I thought, even to swallow.

"I have learned that Scottish surgeon of yours, Gordon, is to dazzle the Theatre Royal, Drury Lane, with a new comedy. I never miss a new comedy, you know—and if it is written by a man who has cured me of the clap, so much the better. Please tell him that I shall be there for the first night."

"I think he should like it better if you were there for the author's benefit night," I said with reflexive warmth. If I was to gain anything with Sir Owen, he could not know my state of mind.

He laughed. "Well, if it is a worthwhile endeavor, I shall return for the third night. I always believe in supporting the authors' benefits, you know. It is the least one can do for a good play."

"He will be gratified to hear that." I was quiet for a moment, and Sir Owen joined in the silence and contented himself with twirling his morning port about his glass. "I have come with some news that I thought you should know of," I continued. "It would appear that Kate Cole has been murdered."

"Murdered!" He nearly dropped his wineglass. "Gad, sir, I have heard she hanged herself." He began to set his port down and then changed his mind and took a long drink.

That he had heard anything at all astonished me. "Then you know of it?"

"Oh yes, oh yes," he said. He finished his glass and poured himself another. "You are sure, now? No? Well, you see, the matter of her trial was something that touched on me very nearly, and, as you know, I am not without some connections. I received a message from a friend I know not unconnected with the governor of Newgate prison; he told me of her death. He clearly indicated that the woman had hanged herself. I am astonished to hear you speak of murder."

"In truth, I but suspect she was murdered," I admitted, "because of another matter that concerns me."

"What is this other matter?" he asked. "This business with your father? How should it involve this woman?"

"It is hard to say," I said. "I can hardly piece it together, for there are so many players."

Sir Owen squinted. "Is there any way I can assist you? You know I am not without connections, and if I can provide you with any service at all, you need but ask me."

I could not help but be disgusted with such a friend as Sir Owen, who had been pleased to sacrifice me when there was some small danger to his reputation, but now that he had nothing to lose, he was eager to show his influence. "You are certainly kind." I thought on this for a moment. That Sir Owen's character was flawed was perhaps not sufficient reason not to take advantage of his connections. "I do not wish to involve you, for I have come to learn that it is a dangerous matter, but there is one thing you might be able to help me with, and indeed, it would be an enormous help. Have you ever heard the name of Martin Rochester?"

"Rochester," he repeated. He took a moment to think on the name. "I have heard of him, I believe, but I know not who he is. Perhaps a name I have heard in the gambling houses?" He screwed up his eyes and then took a drink. "Is he connected with this whore's death?"

"Yes," I said. "I believe Rochester had her killed because she could identify him. You see, I have come to learn that Rochester is but a pseudonym, and that he is behind some shocking acts. If I can find out who he is, then I can discover the truth behind the crimes into which I inquire."

Sir Owen sipped his port. "Should that be so very difficult?"

"Rochester is clever, and he has both friends and enemies who cover his tracks for him. It is one thing to use a false name as a matter of convenience, but with Rochester it seems something else entirely. He has created a false self," I said, reasoning this matter out as I spoke, "a representation of a jobber, much like paper money is a representation of silver."

"Sounds a rather tricky business," he said cheerfully. "I cannot tell you how relieved I am to have this unpleasantness with the whore behind me, Weaver, and I wish I could show you my appreciation. Perhaps if you told me more of what you know about this Rochester, it might help. One meets and hears of so many men, it is hard to keep them all clear in one's mind."

I wasn't sure how much I wanted to tell Sir Owen. "I cannot imagine what kind of contact you could have had with him," I said at last. "He is a corrupt jobber who has probably had some dealings with the South Sea Company."

Sir Owen appeared to make a connection. He screwed up his face and rolled his eyes toward the ceiling. "And all of this has some relationship to that matter with Balfour and your father?"

"Yes."

He leaned forward. "May I ask how this Rochester fits in?"

"I know not," I said cautiously. "I can only say that his name is frequently mentioned in connection with these deaths, and until I meet him and speak to him, I shall know no more."

"As he appears to be such a villain, I can only wish you luck. Although perhaps it is he who needs the luck, for I have come to have nothing but respect, sir, for your skills in these matters."

"You are too kind," I said with a formal bow.

Sir Owen then snapped his fingers and looked at me excitedly. "Gad, I just recalled something. As you know, your inquiry into these deaths is being talked about all over town. Needless to say, I was interested whenever I heard the business discussed, for our fates have been of late so nearly connected. And now that I think on it, it was in one of these conversations that I heard Rochester's name mentioned. I cannot quite think of the context, for I am not now even certain that I had heard the name before. But some fellow I did not know was speaking of him, and the deuce if I can remember what it is he said, but he mentioned him in connection with another. It was a Jew named—oh, what was it now—Sardino? Salmono, perhaps? Something rather fishy, I believe."

"Sarmento?" I said quietly.

He snapped his fingers. "The very name! I wish I could say more, but by Gad it is all I can recall. I hope that is of some assistance."

"So do I," I said, and politely made my exit.

. . .

IT WAS NOT A task to which I looked forward, but I knew it had to be done. So I made a trip to Sarmento's lodgings off Thames Street, almost in the shadow of St. Paul's. He took rooms in a pleasant enough, if plain, house an inconvenient distance from my uncle's warehouse.

When his landlady showed me into the sitting room, I saw that there was someone already waiting—I presumed for another lodger, for it was a cleric of the Church of England. He was a youngish fellow, apparently not long out of school, for he had the enthusiastic air of a man who had recently taken orders. I had not been without some contact with church-men in my day, though I had normally found them to be either bland, empty men or more of the wild sort who considered religion not at all ex-cept when their duties absolutely demanded it. In either case, I had often thought that the Church of England produced a system that encouraged its clerics to think of their positions much as clerks in stores thought of theirs—as a way to make money and little else.

"Good morning, sir," he said with a wide, happy smile.

I bade him good morning and took a seat. He reached into his pocket and produced a watch, quickly noting the time. "I have been awaiting Mr. Sarmento for some time now," he said. "I know not when he will step down."

"You await Mr. Sarmento?" I asked with clear astonishment.

I realized that it was a rude way to speak, but it was intentional—not because I have any particular dislike of priests, but because I wished to goad the man into saying more than he might have otherwise. The cleric, however, took my rudeness in his stride. "He is a dear acquaintance of mine and a good student." He smiled. "I have been encouraging him to write his memoirs. I find conversion stories most inspirational."

I felt myself reeling with astonishment. "I am quite certain I do not understand you. Do you mean to say Mr. Sarmento is a convert?"

The priest reddened. "Oh, my goodness. I hope I have not spoken out of turn. I did not know that his acquaintances were unaware he had been a Jew. Please do not hold this against him." He leaned forward and lowered his voice, as though sharing a secret. "I can assure you his conversion is entirely sincere, and it is my experience that converts are always the most devout Christians, for they must think about their religion in ways that the rest of us need not."

I must admit I was stunned, perhaps even horrified. It was one thing to be a Jew lax in observance, such as myself, but even a man as negligent as Adelman was not bold enough to consider conversion seriously. My Christian readers will perhaps not understand that among your denominations—the Anglican and the Papist and the Presbyterian and the Dissenters—are all Britons alike, but to be a Jew is to be a member of a nation as well as a religion. To convert is to deny one's self in a way I found utterly shocking. It was to say not *I shall be this no longer*, but rather *I have never been this*. At that moment I believed Sarmento capable of anything. "When did this conversion take place?" I asked, forcing a polite smile upon my lips.

"Not more than six months ago, I am sure," he explained happily. "But Mr. Sarmento had been coming to me for instruction long before that. Like many of his tribe, he was hesitant to cast aside his old superstitions. These things often take a great deal of time."

I did not know what this meant, and I had little time to think on it, for Sarmento entered the room. He stood in the door and stared at the two of us, saying nothing, attempting to assess what damage had been done. Finally he turned to me. "Weaver, what do you do here?"

"I have come to speak to you on a matter of business, sir." I could not help taking pleasure in his confusion. "But if you wish to speak first with your confessor . . ."

Sarmento's mouth opened, and then closed. He knew the advantage was mine, and he hated me for it. Perhaps he hated the cleric as well. "Mr. Norbert," he said at last, "I do not wish to be rude, but I must speak to Mr. Weaver in private."

The priest appeared immune to insult, though he may have felt some discomfort at having spoken of what he now knew should have been kept a secret. He smiled and stood, collecting his hat. "I shall return at a time more convenient, sir." He offered us both a bow and was gone.

I had not stirred from my chair. Sarmento remained standing. I enjoyed the feeling of power his distress gave me. "I did not know you to be a member of the Church of England," I said in a relaxed and easy voice. "What thinks my uncle of this?"

Sarmento clenched and unclenched his fists. "You have me at a disadvantage, Weaver. You are correct to assume your uncle does not know. I do not think he would understand, but I have found a home in the Church, and I need not feel judged by you, who adhere to no religion at all."

"I remember quite clearly," I mused, "that you accused me of speaking too much like an Englishman. 'We do not speak thus,' you said to me. A mere deception to confuse me?"

"Just so," he said blandly.

"I am interested to have settled that you are comfortable deceiving others. Please understand that I did not come here to discuss religion with you, sir. I care not for what you believe nor whom you worship, though I do care of your playing games with my uncle's confidence." He attempted to interrupt me, no doubt to say something insulting, but I would not have it. "I came to learn why you were in that crowd the other night, sir, outside the masquerade ball."

"For what reason," he snapped, "should I answer any of your impertinent questions?"

"Because," I said as I stood to face him, "I wish to know whether or not you have played some role in the murder of my father."

His face turned ashen. He took a step back as though I had slapped him. He looked much like a puppet at a Smithfield droll—his mouth opened and closed without making a sound and his eyes grew absurdly large. Finally he began to sputter, "Surely you don't think . . . you cannot mean that . . ." Then something in him clicked like the gears of a machine. "What reason could I possibly have to kill Samuel Lienzo?"

"Then what were you doing in the crowd outside the Haymarket?" I demanded.

"If you suspect everyone in that crowd," he stammered, "then you will have much work to do speaking to all of them. And what has that crowd to do with your father's death?"

"It's not the crowd that concerns me," I said harshly. "I suspect you."

"I think much of this Kingdom would be shocked to learn that it is a Jewish belief that any man who would become a Christian would commit a murder."

"Do not play the Jew-hater with me, sir." I felt myself redden. "I know that rhetoric far too well to be intimidated by it, particularly when it comes from the mouth of one such as you. What were you doing there, Sarmento?"

"What do you think I was doing there? I was looking for Miriam. I knew she was placing herself at risk with that rake, and I was merely there to make sure he tried nothing that would dishonor her. It was happenstance that I became separated from her and came upon the crowd surrounding the man you felt inclined to kill. I saw you had been seized by the constables, but it would have done no good for me to step forward. I could hardly have vouched for your character, when I think so little of it."

"Are you certain that is the only reason you were at the Haymarket that night?"

"Of course I am certain. Don't be irritating."

"Your presence there had nothing to do with my inquiry?"

"Damn your inquiry, Weaver. I care not whether it is your inquiry into the South Sea or into Miriam's money. Why can you not mind your own affairs?"

I then understood his agitation. "Miriam told you that she believed me to be inquiring into her finances."

"Quite so," he said proudly, as though he did not understand the words, "it was I who told her that your business with your uncle was to discover what had happened to her money."

"Why did you tell her that?"

"Because I believed it to be true. The stories about you and the South Sea Company and such had not yet begun to circulate about the 'Change. I could imagine no other reason for your uncle to welcome you back."

"Why do you follow Miriam, Sarmento? Is it not clear that she cares nothing for you? Do you really believe that you can win her?"

"It is none of your concern, I promise you, for she will never consent to a marriage with a ruffian like you. And to win her, I only need her to give me one more chance."

"One more chance at what?"

Sarmento opened his mouth to speak, but stopped himself. A heavy blush began to spread across his face like a ruddy shadow.

"One more chance at what?" I repeated.

"To get her money back." He nearly shouted. "She'd been asking me to manage her investments, and I did well at first. But I made some foolish moves."

"How much did you lose?"

He shook his head. "More than a hundred pounds." He let out a long, almost comic sigh. "After that she had me relinquish all control over her funds. One foolish move, one stupid mistake, and 'Change Alley un-manned me in a single day. She entrusted her money to Deloney. I tried to warn her that he was a profligate rogue, but she would not listen."

"She listened to me," I told him. "I've exposed Deloney."

Sarmento gasped. "Then where is her money now? Perhaps I can re-claim it."

"Her money isn't the same thing as her heart. You seem to forget that."

Sarmento laughed. "You may believe what you wish."

I waved my hand in dismissal. I had not come here to learn of Sarmento's feelings for Miriam. "I have more important business with you—and that is your connection to Martin Rochester."

"Rochester?" he asked. "What have I to do with him?"

"What do you know of him?" I demanded, raising my voice and taking a step forward.

Sarmento was clearly shaken. "I know nothing of him, Weaver. He's a jobber. I've heard his name, and that is all. He and I have had no dealings."

I did not misbelieve him. Sarmento was an unpleasant man, but he was a transparent one. I did not believe he could lie to me on this matter and convince me. I took a few steps back to indicate that I would not harm him.

"I came here because a man I know told me he had overheard you speaking of me in connection with Rochester," I told him.

A strange look of pleasure spread upon Sarmento's face, as though he had been waiting all along to tell me what he now had to say. "I believe I might have mentioned your name. There was some betting to be done—whether you would survive your inquiry. A gentleman offered to bet that you would be dead before the end of December. I put down fifty pounds that you would yet live."

This news truly astonished me. "I am gratified by your confidence," I told him blankly.

"Don't be. I was merely handling the odds as I have been taught to in 'Change Alley. You see, it is a perfect bet, Weaver. Either way, I win something."

"Tell me," I said as I opened his door, "for I really wish to understand. I have lived among the Christians for ten years now, but I have never felt compelled to become one of them. What is it that has driven you to do so?"

"You have lived among them," he said as he turned to leave the drawing room. "I should like to do the same."

THIRTY-ONE

I SPENT THE REST of the day and most of the next attempting to determine my next move. I found that I could theorize no more. Thus, on Monday night, I changed into some worn and tattered clothes, for I had no wish that evening to look the gentleman. I had the misfortune to pass my aunt as I left the house, and she looked at me so disparagingly that I could only smile and tell her I would explain later. My destination was the Laughing Negro in Wapping, where I had not set foot since retrieving Sir Owen's letters from Quilt Arnold.

After Adelman had attempted to convince me that I had been deceived about the South Sea Company, I felt that I could no longer know anything for certain, and I began to worry that I had been relying too much on my own abilities to make sense of information of which no sense could be made. I therefore took a detour on my way to pay a visit to Elias on the chance that he might be at home. Though it was early, especially for a man of Elias's tastes, he was not only in, but undressed and ready for bed. The rigors of preparing his play for the stage had nearly exhausted him, but he assured me he was eager to learn more about my progress. In his nightdress and cap, he invited me into his rooms, where we shared a bottle of claret.

"I have read your comedy," I told him, "and found it utterly delightful."

His face fairly glowed with pride. "Thank you, Weaver. I trust your opinion considerably."

"I have no doubt that it shall be a success," I said.

He smiled with pleasure, refilled my glass, and asked which parts I liked in particular. We spent some time discussing *The Unsuspecting Lover,* and then Elias asked me again of my inquiry. I explained to him all that had happened of late, including my business with Miriam, the encounter at South Sea House, the death of Kate Cole, and even my confrontation with Sarmento.

Elias listened closely to each detail. "I am astonished," he said, once I had finished my narrative. "This story exposes the deceptive villainy of the new finance. Each step you take makes you disbelieve that you had ever taken the previous one."

"There are very few things I know for certain now. The South Sea Company may indeed be my enemy, or Bloathwait may have been manipulating me all along. Wild may be planning to murder me, or he may simply be looking to profit from my inquiry. Rochester may be his partner or his enemy. And with Kate dead, I can think of no sure way to get closer to Rochester."

"And what do you do now?" Elias studied my face with a particular attention. From the way he stared I thought he wished to gauge something medical about me.

"I shall return to the Laughing Negro," I said. "I shall seek out Wild's man to see what I may learn of him."

"Why do you seek out Wild's man? Are we not convinced that Rochester is our villain?"

"I do not believe that Wild is a prime mover in this villainy, but he has shown more than a common interest in my business, and I should be astonished if he does not withhold from me some useful information—not because he is involved with these murders, but because it is some advantage to him that I should continue my inquiry."

Elias rubbed his nose quizzically. "How can you be certain that Wild has had no share in the murders? Indeed, since we know his name to be a false one, must we not consider that Rochester might *be* Wild? After all, who would be better equipped to engage in so dangerous an affair as the purveyance of false South Sea stock?"

I nodded. "I had thought on that, certainly, but I do not believe what you suggest is at all probable. Wild encouraged my inquiry. He set me upon the South Sea Company. Even if we assume that he gave me erroneous or incomplete information, we cannot dismiss the simple fact that he did not try to stop me. We speak of Jonathan Wild, do not forget. It would have been no difficult thing for him to have me arrested, or even killed."

"No," Elias observed, "he merely had you beaten upon the street."

Elias's observation was one to which I had given a great deal of thought. "Why would Wild have me beaten in public and then try to charm me in private?" I asked, half to myself, half to my friend. "He told me that his men defied his orders, but his men know full well the consequence of disobliging their master."

"I understand you," Elias muttered. "He wished for the world to see his men assault you."

"I think so," I agreed. "And why? Perhaps because he fears Rochester. He wishes to keep me upon my course, but he wishes for the world to believe that he and I are at odds."

"If he fears telling you what he knows—if your possession of that knowledge would make it clear to Rochester that you had obtained it of Wild—we must assume that Wild knows things that no one else knows."

"And that," I announced, "is why I seek out Wild's man, Quilt Arnold—the man who spied upon me at Kent's Coffeehouse when I awaited a response to our advertisement. If I can learn why Wild sent Arnold there, I may be closer to learning more of Wild's involvement, and that may take me closer to Rochester."

Elias smiled. "You have truly learned to think like a philosopher."

I swirled my wine about in my cup. "Perhaps. I promise you I shall not forget to think like a pugilist when I find Arnold. I grow tired of this matter, Elias. I must resolve it soon."

"I heartily endorse your sentiments," he told me, rubbing his injured knee.

"I only hope I *can* resolve it. Your philosophy has allowed me to come this far, but I cannot see how it can take me farther. Perhaps if I were more of a philosopher I would have concluded this unpleasantness long ago."

Elias looked down for a moment. He appeared to me to be nervous, agitated. "Weaver, our friendship frequently involves a great deal of raillery—too much, I think. When you fought in the ring, you were the best fighter this island had ever seen. I must have had the sixth sense of a Highland seer to have bet against you that day, for only a fool would have done so. As a pugilist, you turned a sport that was the province of mindless animals into an art. And when you set your mind to thief-taking, you turned something that had been the province of criminals and petty minds into an art as well. If philosophy no longer yields results, perhaps it is not because you have reached your limit to understanding philosophy. I think it far more probable that philosophy has done what philosophy can do, and you would be wise to trust your instincts as a fighter and a thief-taker."

My face burned with pleasure as I listened to Elias's sentiments. He did not often speak thus, and his doing so made me determined. "My instincts tell me to find anyone whom I believe to have information and beat that information from him."

Elias smiled. "Trust your instincts."

BUOYED BY HIS COMMENTS, I left my friend's lodgings and traveled to the Laughing Negro. I sat at a table in the back that gave me a good view of the door, and I snuffed the candles around me to obscure my face should Arnold look in my direction before I should look in his. There was, however, no sign of him; I had to fend off the advances of several whores and gamblers, and soon I heard whispers about the foul sod who sat in the corner, not drinking enough to satisfy the barkeeper.

By eleven o'clock it was clear to me that Arnold was not to come in, so I paid my reckoning and stepped outside. I was not ten feet away from the door before I saw a shadow rushing from the darkness toward me. Perhaps I was too eager for violence, for I drew my hangar and ran it through someone's shoulder before I realized that my assailants were but a few boys out to knock me down for my money. They had no connection with murders or Wild or the South Sea Company. This was no conspiracy, just London after nightfall. I wiped my sword blade as I laughed upon my own panic, and I somehow managed to make my way from that place without further incident.

IN THE DAYTIME Bawdy Moll's is but a dank place of sleepy drunks and whispering prigs, but at night it becomes something else entirely. It was so full of sweaty and sickly bodies that I could barely press my way inside, and the air was thick with the stink of vomit and urine and tobacco. I could not call Moll's crowd merrymakers, for no one came to a gin house to make merry; they came to forget and to recast misery into senselessness. They pretended they took some pleasure in it, however, and I could hear a hundred conversations, the shrill and nervous laughter of women, the breaking of glass, and somewhere in the back a player scraped a bow across an untuned fiddle.

I pushed through the crowd, as my boots sloshed in things I did not care to think of, and I felt countless fingers of undetectable origin explore my body, but I held secure my sword, my pistol, and my purse, and I made it to the bar without any serious damage. There I found Bawdy Moll cheerfully dispensing gin by the pint and collecting her pennies with equal delight.

"Ben," she shouted as she saw me. "I 'ardly expected to see ye 'ere at a time like this. 'Avin' a bad time are ye? Well, I've the cure for it, and it comes a penny a pint."

I was in no mood for Moll's banter. I was in a foul temper, and the stench of sewage from the Fleet Ditch was particularly rancid that night. "What," I said as quietly as I could, "know you of a man called Quilt Arnold?"

Moll screwed up her face in displeasure; I watched her face paint crack like the earth in the summer sun. "Ye know better than to come 'ere on a busy night and ask me suchlike questions. I can't have me customers thinkin' they'll be 'peached in me place."

I slipped Moll a guinea. I had not the time to equivocate with smaller coins. "It is a matter of the utmost importance, Moll, or I should not bother you."

She held the coin in her hand, feeling the weight of the gold. It had a power no paper or banknote could ever match. Her objection vanished.

"Quilt's a no-good blackguard, but he ain't the murderin' type what I can tell. Stands close to Wild, 'e does, and does the great man's bidding. Least 'e used to. 'E also run with that whore ye asked me for last week: Kate Cole, what 'ung 'erself in Newgate."

"Do you know where I can find him?"

She did. At least she knew of a few likely places, not one near the other, unfortunately. I surreptitiously slid her another guinea; I had violated the trust we had by making my inquiries before a crowd, and I was more than willing to pay the price to keep Moll happy.

I inspected two more places that night, but I caught no sign of Arnold, and growing tired and despondent I returned home to sleep. I began the search anew the next day, and was fortunate enough to catch him around noon, eating his dinner in a tavern Moll had told me to be a favorite day-time haunt of his. He sat at a table, shoving spoonfuls of watery gruel into his face, caring little of his bad aim or the effects it had upon his attire. Across from him sat a sickly whore, hideously in need of nourishment, who was so thin I feared she might expire as I looked on. She stared at Arnold's food, but he shared none of it with her.

I carefully kept myself from Arnold's sight as I hired a private room on the first floor. The tapman blankly accepted an extra shilling in exchange for paying no mind to what happened next. I approached Arnold from be-hind and kicked out his chair from under him. He fell hard, and much of his meal followed him. His companion cried out while I compounded Arnold's surprise by stomping hard on his left hand, which was sloppily wrapped with a filthy bandage. He let out a howl—shrill and desperate. His whore clapped a hand over her mouth and stifled her own scream. I grabbed the stunned Arnold under his armpits and dragged him down the hall and threw him into the room I had hired. I closed the door and locked it, placing the key in my coat. The room was perfect: dark, small, and poorly lit through a window too small to admit thieves, and thus too small to allow Arnold's escape.

His one good eye bugged in terror, but he said nothing. I had seen once before that he was not at heart the ruffian he pretended to be, and I knew his kind too well not to know how to get him feeling talkative. For good measure, and because I felt little other than anger, I picked him up and threw him hard against the wall. Too hard, I fear, for his head hit the brick, and his good eye rolled back into his skull as he collapsed upon the floor.

I returned to the bar, locking the door behind me, and bought two pints of small beer. The whore, I noticed, was now at another man's table, and she paid me no attention. The barkeeper showed me nothing but terse indifference—something just shy of politeness. I made a note to myself to return to this place, for I liked its way of conducting business.

I reentered the room and threw one of the pints of beer into Arnold's face. He stirred like a man awakened from a pleasing slumber. "Oh, Christ." He used his hand to wipe the ale from his eye.

"I hope I shall not have to kill you," I said. "I even hope I might avoid inflicting much more pain upon you, but you had better be very coopera-tive if we are to realize these hopes."

He rubbed at his good eye until I began to fear he should pluck it out. "I knew you was trouble," he mumbled.

"You are a keen observer," I said. "Let's start with a simple question. Why were you at Kent's Coffeehouse when I came in response to my advertisement?"

"I was just having a dish o' coffee," he said meekly.

I would have to be creative if he did not become more forthcoming, but for the time being, a good stomp upon his injured hand proved the fastest way of assuring him I would have no nonsense. The bandage was now covered with fresh blood and a kind of brownish liquid I did not care to consider at length. "You will lose that hand I think," I said, "and perhaps your life if you don't have that looked at. But you may not live long enough for the rot to advance. So perhaps you will tell me what it was you were doing at Kent's?"

"Let me go," he said with a whimper. "This is me last chance. Wild, 'e used to trust me. Now 'e's got that Jew Mendes doing me work. I need to make things right." His face turned a sickly shade, and I feared he would lose consciousness.

"What were you doing there?" I repeated.

"Wild sent me," he told me at last. Then he vomited, making no effort to avoid soiling himself.

I felt no surprise to learn that Wild was behind it, but I still needed to understand Wild's interest in my inquiry. "Why?" I continued. "What did Wild tell you to do?"

"To watch you, 'e said." He was gasping for breath as he spoke. "To let 'im know if anyone bothered you."

It was not an answer I had anticipated. "What? Are you telling me that Wild sent you to tell him if I was attacked?"

Arnold attempted to move farther away from me. He crawled toward the corner. "Aye, I swear it. 'E wanted to know if you was bothered. And 'e wanted to see who it was what showed up to see you. He said I should see if I recognized 'em, and if not, to let 'im know what they looked like. But 'e said not to let you see me, and so when you did, I got scared and run off."

"Who did he expect to show up?" I barked.

"I don't know. 'E didn't say."

"Who killed Michael Balfour and Samuel Lienzo?"

I thought a direct approach worked best for a man in Arnold's state. At first he only groaned and said "Oh, Christ," again, but I moved toward his hand, and he came around. "It was Rochester," he said at last. "Martin Rochester done it."

I fought the swell of frustration. "And who is Martin Rochester?"

He looked up at me with an equal mixture of supplication and incredulousness. "Rochester is Rochester. What kind of question is that?"

"Does he have another name?"

He shook his head. "Not what I know."

"I find it hard to believe that this man broke into Michael Balfour's home and staged a false hanging himself. Who helped him?"

I knew he didn't want to tell me, and he stared at me in such a way as to implore that I did not force him, but my look told him I cared nothing for him and I would as soon kill him myself as wait for Rochester to do it in revenge. " 'E's got 'is boys. Bertie Fenn, who I reckon you know about what with your killing 'im and all. Then 'e's got three more—Kit Mann, Fat Billy, who ain't fat, so don't let the name fool you, and a third cove whose name I don't know, but 'e's got red hair. I keep my distance from all of 'em, except as what I see 'em once in a while, but I don't have no truck with them, and I ain't got nothin' to do with these killings."

"Where can I find these men?"

Arnold let out a string of public houses, taverns, and gin houses where they might be, but because he didn't know the men well, he said he was only guessing.

I looked down at him—broken, beaten, and miserable. It was the second time I had left him so. I suppose, I thought to myself, he deserves no better. He is Wild's man, and he plays his part in this villainy, yet I could not but feel some sympathy for a man so totally shattered.

I threw a few shillings on the floor before him and bade him come see me if he ever wished to serve a better master than Wild. I had no expectation that he would abandon the Thief-Taker General, and he never did do so, but I believed that by making the offer I would appear a greater man than I was.

I FOUND THE MEN before nightfall in a disreputable tavern near Covent Garden Market. They sat together, drinking and shouting incomprehensibly at one another in a language that was half impenetrable country accent and half drunken slur. I suppose I must have been fatigued, for I let them see me first. I had gone around the back to look at the various tables, when I heard a commotion of chairs overturning and saw three men running toward the door. I had looked at them when I first walked in and thought them only drinking men of the lower orders. Only once they had seen me and scrambled to their feet did I know them. I recognized one of them quite clearly, for he was the man who had denounced me outside the masquerade in the Haymarket.

Two of them got away, but one was slow, and I managed to tackle him, though I felt my age when I did so, for the old wound in my leg sent a pain shooting up to my hip. Nevertheless, I had a grip on the fellow, whose head knocked hard upon the dirt floor as I threw him down.

I had been in enough of these places to expect a crowd to gather around me, which it did, but to believe myself immune from interference—and indeed I was. I thus felt free to go about my business. Having banged his head sufficiently to obtain his full attention, I thought it time to begin. "What's your name?"

"Billy, sir," he gasped in the pathetic way of a begging street urchin. Indeed, he looked young, perhaps not more than seventeen, but his youthful appearance might have been owing to his extremely light and small form.

"Fat Billy?" I asked.

He nodded.

"Fat Billy," I said, "you will answer my questions or your new nickname is going to be 'Breathing Billy,' and I assure you your new name will be every bit as ironic as the old." My threat only confounded him, so I placed a hand hard over his throat and squeezed just a little—not enough to prevent him from speaking, but enough that he would understand my meaning. "What is Martin Rochester's real name?"

"I don't know, sir, I swear," he rasped. His eyes bugged, and he looked to me like a fish, but I knew not if he feared me or the consequence of answering my question.

"What does he look like?" I tightened the pressure just a little.

"We never seen 'im. We get messages from 'im. Kit does. And 'e sends us money, but we ain't never seen 'im. Maybe Kit 'as. I don't know. We ain't supposed to talk about 'im at all."

I eased my grip a bit. "Did you kill Michael Balfour?"

He said nothing. He only stared up at me, terrified. A thin stream of blood trickled from his nose. I suppose my more delicate readers may grow weary of these descriptions of violence, but I know they will understand that these means were unavoidable in dealing with this species of man. Thus, let us suffice to say that there were cracking noises and a bit of screaming as well, and Fat Billy then felt comfortable telling me that, yes, he had indeed taken Michael Balfour's life with the help of his three friends. They arranged to get the servants drunk and, with the potential witnesses off drinking or pursuing other pleasures, they had dragged Balfour into the stable, where they forced him into a noose and hanged him. The servants, I could only guess, feared the discovery of the unwitting role they had played and chose to remain silent.

What I wished more than anything else, as I sat atop him with my hand upon his throat, was to ask him if he had played any role in the murder of my father. Fenn was dead, but how did I know that Fat Billy had not participated? I tightened my grasp even as I thought on the question, but I knew I had not the time to indulge that particular revenge. Fat Billy's friends might return, perhaps with help, and there was much I needed to know before they did.

"Did you steal anything?" I demanded.

"Nothing!" he exclaimed indignantly, as though outraged that I would ask so insulting a question. He would drag a man from his home and hang him, but he would not steal from him.

"You were not to search for anything. Stock issues?"

He tried to shake his head under my grasp. "We didn't have nothing to do with those."

He appeared to know about them, however. "Who was supposed to take the stock?"

He tried to shake his head again. "I wasn't supposed to 'ear about it. Don't want trouble."

"Fat Billy, it occurs to me that you are in trouble right now."

He must have agreed, because he gave me the name. Had Fat Billy delayed but an instant, he could have withheld his information, for just as our conversation ended, his two friends reappeared at the door, pistols in hand. There was some screaming of women, and men too, and a great deal of running for the door, which struck me as illogical, for the men with the guns were at the door. I grabbed Fat Billy and hoisted up his limp body to use him as a shield. I did not know if his friends would hesitate to shoot him, but I believed that even his slight frame would slow the lead.

I followed the momentum of the crowd, which forced the men away from the door, and angled my way around as well, until there was an instant when there was no one between me and Fat Billy and, ten feet away, the two other ruffians, pistols loaded and ready to fire. With a mighty thrust that sent pain shooting up my leg, I hurled Billy into them, knocking them off balance, but not down. I then took my chance while I had it and ran out of the tavern, where I managed to lose the villains in the crowd that had gathered outside to bemoan and delight in the carnage.

I HAD NO DIFFICULTY breaking into the house—I'd pillaged so many houses in my past that to do so now, on the side of justice rather than theft, gave me nothing but delight. This house was something larger than any I'd forced my way into before; there were four floors, and many rooms that my quarry might sleep in, so I had to maneuver my way about, avoiding servants who moved through the halls like shadowy figures, brandishing candles that seemed designed to hunt me out.

The first bedroom I slipped into was clearly not his. It was already occupied, and when I saw the silhouette of the old woman in the dark, heard her muttering in her sleep, I made my way out and tried another. I looked in four more rooms before I found another sleeping closet, this one empty, but I recognized a coat hung on a hook by the door. I sat down to wait, hoping that he was not out carousing all night, that he had not decided to travel from London. I was ready, and the sooner he returned, the sooner I would feel some measure of justice.

I had in my pocket the half-minute hourglass that the Tudesco beggar had given me. It had occurred to me to take it along just before I had departed my uncle's house. I liked the idea that the Tudesco's gift might serve me in some way, and I supposed if I ever saw him again, and could tell him how I had put his hourglass to use, he should be most pleased.

I turned it over time and again as I waited in the dark in his room. The chair I sat in was shockingly hard and uncomfortable, and my leg and hip ached prodigiously, but I suffered it all, for I knew that now I was close to understanding everything. After Fat Billy had spoken of the stolen stocks and told me who removed them of old Balfour's property, I had felt only the joy of success. It took some time for the real import of this information to occur to me. Before I had known for certain that there were counterfeit stocks; now I knew for certain that old Balfour had been killed for them. I may not have understood the motives of all the players in my drama, but

I was not sure I any longer needed to. Balfour and my father had been killed because they wished to tell the world of the false stocks. All I required now was the true name of Rochester.

Each minute in the blackness of his closet dragged on interminably, but the confidence that I knew what I was doing, that I no longer wandered aimlessly, gave me a resilient kind of patience. I turned over my hourglass. I watched the sands trickle out and I turned it again.

It was not too late, almost eleven, before he came in. I heard the creaking of the stairs and hissing of his feet as he lazily dragged them upward. There were a few words muttered I know not whether to a servant or himself and then the slow, clumsy turning of the doorknob. He held out a candle in one hand and lit a lamp that rested on a table by the door. Now a soft, orange glow filled the room, and when he turned around, Balfour saw me in his chair, pistol pointed directly at him.

"Lock the door and step forward," I said calmly.

He opened his mouth to speak, to express some outrage or another, but in the dim light of his candle he saw at once that he dare not. I had a practiced expression for him—cold, hard, merciless. He locked the door and turned to me.

"I have wondered sometimes, Balfour, that if a man were a blockhead, let us say the greatest blockhead who ever lived, would he know of his own idiocy, or would he be too much a fool even to sense that he was deficient? I believe you can answer that question for me."

A pistol raised upon him and a murderous look in my eye had silenced him, but he could not bear my insult. "Weaver, I cannot claim to guess what you think you are doing, but I suggest you take these outrages no further."

The hourglass sat on a table by my chair. Not taking my eyes off Balfour, I turned it over with my left hand. "You have half a minute," I said coolly, "to give me the true name of Martin Rochester, or I shall shoot you. You know me too well, I think, to wonder even for an instant if I mean what I say."

I had anticipated he would not be a strong man, but I had not expected that his weakness would prove so very complete. He collapsed to his knees as though his feet and shins had simply disappeared. He opened his mouth to beg for mercy, but said nothing.

I would show him no mercy. He would receive no sign from me that his panic would grant him any leniency. The hourglass ran down. I pulled back the hammer on my pistol and prepared my eyes for the powder's burst into flame.

He gagged, trying to speak through his terror. I suppose that somewhere, on some level I ignored, I sympathized with him. I think we all have had dreams in which something terrible has happened and we try to scream, but we can produce no sound. Balfour acted out this terror. He heaved, like a man attempting to expel a piece of bone from his throat, and at last he opened his mouth wide and released a mighty bellow with all the force of his lungs. "I don't know!"

His cry seemed to harness all of the power of his previous attempts to speak. We both sat in silence for some time, shocked at the force of his scream and with the silence that followed. Perhaps it was because he had gotten these first words out, and perhaps it was because his thirty seconds had expired and he was not dead yet. I could hardly even guess why, but his tongue at last loosened. "I don't know who he is," he said in a quiet voice. "I swear it. No one does."

"But you stole your father's South Sea issues for him." It was not a question.

His head hung loose, like the limp skull of a skeleton I had seen once at Bartholomew Fair. "How did you know?" he asked quietly.

"Who else could have?" I preferred to make him believe that I had reasoned it out rather than explain that I had beaten the information out of a young weakling. "If they were missing from the estate, someone had to have taken them. Who was in a better position than you? After all, unless the issues were transferred to another owner, they were of no value, and they couldn't be transferred, could they? They were counterfeit, so no one would want them other than those who would wish to destroy them— that is, Rochester or the South Sea Company. I simply presumed that it was Rochester's hand behind their theft. He then used his man inside the Company to alter the records so as to make it appear that your father had sold his holdings long before his death."

Balfour anticipated my question. "He sent me a banknote by messenger: one hundred pounds if I would agree to do it. Another three hundred when he received the issues. My father was already dead, and I had no idea they had been planning on killing him before it happened. After they'd killed him, there was nothing to be done. I never stood the chance of seeing a penny from him otherwise, so why should I not have taken advantage of this opportunity?" As he spoke, I believe that Balfour began to convince himself with his own excuses. I could see his face begin to change from the hollow countenance of shame to the hopeful expression of a man who believes he is on the verge of absolution.

"When you consider the matter, I did nothing wrong."

"Nothing but aid the men who killed your father," I said. "But I wish to return to the matter of your idiocy for a moment. You see, Balfour, I have no trouble believing that you had no actual hand in your father's death, for I believe you too much of a coward for such a thing."

I cannot say how much I enjoyed this insult. He bristled at this accusation of cowardice, but he could hardly argue that indeed he was a stout enough man to commit patricide.

"I believe you knave enough to profit from your father's death and to aid his murderer," I continued. "What I do not understand is why you should ask me to find the man who killed your father. You asked me in particular to look into his missing issues. Unless I am mistaken, you hired me to expose *you*. Why should you do such a thing?"

"Because," he spat, angered at my effrontery, "I never believed you could learn as much as you did. I thought myself safe."

"That doesn't explain why, Balfour. *Why?*"

"Damn you, Weaver, for a filthy Jew. I won't answer your questions. I merely have to call out for my servants to open this door and drag you before the magistrate."

"You've already called out and your servants did not hear you. These handsome town houses are so finely built, you know—all thick stone walls and heavy doors."

"Then I shall wait you out. I do not believe you will shoot me. I shall remain here for as long as you, and I dare say, your arm will grow tired before I grow weary of sitting."

I smiled and dropped my pistol into my pocket. "You are quite right, sir. I shall not shoot you. The pistol merely makes a dramatic point. I shall tell you what I *am* willing to do, however. I am willing to break each of your fingers, sir—to ask you the same question each time I break a finger. You will have ten chances before I finish with your hands. I shan't mess with the toes—the pain is too slight—but there are numerous objects in this room with sufficient strength to smash a foot. A knee too, I suppose. And let us suppose I break all I can think of to break and you still do not tell me what I wish to know, there remains only your skull. You will be found, as limp as a rag doll, and no one will know what happened to you."

Balfour attempted to keep his eyes open.

"But," I added brightly, "I really do not believe such a thing would ever be necessary. Do you know what I believe? That the most you would be able to stand would be one broken finger. Shall we put this theory of mine to the test, or will you tell me what I wish to know?"

Balfour remained silent for what seemed an interminable period. I understood what went on in his head. He searched for a way, some other way, than his giving me information, that he might avoid any repercussions from the man he would have to betray. I suppose he mulled it over from every angle, but in the end he could only think of how to avoid a torment now—the torment to come would be dealt with later.

"I was paid to engage your services," he said at last, "by a man who could not have known that I had sent my father's stocks to Rochester. He hired me because it would seem very plausible that I should have an interest in the inquiry. And it was he, not I, who wished to put you upon this course. I merely stood to profit from it. I again thought that if I could make some small money from my father in his death, why should I refuse? I never believed you should learn of my involvement."

"Who is this man that hired you?" I asked.

I know not what name he might have given that would have surprised me. Had he said the King of Prussia, the Archbishop of Canterbury, or the Nabob of Bengal I would have thought these as likely villains as anyone else. But the name he gave me was perhaps less surprising.

Jonathan Wild had paid Balfour to set me upon my inquiry.

I stood up, and looked down at Balfour, who could not decide if he should attempt supplication or righteous indignation. "Did Rochester give you the remainder of what he promised?"

Balfour shook his head. "He never did send it."

"Good." I hit him hard in the face. I wanted that he should bear a mark of our encounter, for every time he was asked of its origins, his lie would remind him of his villainy and his cowardice.

THIRTY-TWO

THE NEXT TWO DAYS were very grim ones for me. I had learned so much—I had unearthed the great conspiracy that Elias had predicted, and I had done so largely with the aid of philosophy, something I would never have believed. I knew who had killed my father, why he had done so, and how he had done so. But Rochester had hidden himself too well. He had known from the outset that to cross the South Sea Company was a dangerous business, and he had taken care that an enemy should never find him out.

I had exhausted every possibility, but I could not crack the edifice that Martin Rochester had erected to protect himself. I thought of pursuing his three henchmen once again, but I could not convince myself that it would be worth my while. Rochester had gone to such great lengths to conceal himself that he would hardly divulge his true name to a group of murderers-for-hire who might sell it at the first opportunity. In addition, Rochester's villains were aware that I knew who they were, and it struck me as probable that they would make themselves hard to find, at least for a few weeks.

I wished heartily to talk to Elias, but he could spare me little time as he made the final preparations for his play. There was a great deal of rewriting to be done, but he assured me that Rochester was going nowhere. Once the play was successfully launched I could count on him for assistance.

With little else to occupy my time, I spent my days in Jonathan's, drinking far too much coffee and hoping to overhear conversations of note. I saw no more of Mr. Sarmento, and my uncle mentioned in passing that he was most concerned that the clerk had not been to the warehouse for two days. I did not think it my place to tell him of what I knew.

Miriam and I had been almost entirely estranged since our brief kiss, and her efforts to mend our breach, as she had done in the hall, had been courageous, but no single gesture of goodwill—no matter how daring—could hope to set aside so monstrous a discomfort as that which now lay between us.

The afternoon before the premiere of Elias's play she and I sat in my uncle's drawing room. It was the first time we had spent together since we shared that particular intimacy in the inn, and I found I could tolerate her presence only by attempting to put that incident out of my mind. She, on the other hand, sat as though entirely comfortable as she devoured a romance entitled *Love in Excess.* When not casting secret glances upon her, I pored over pamphlets on the Bank and the companies and anything else I could find. I understood almost none of what I read, and I suppose the effort was fruitless. I wished to find some reference to Rochester, but I knew there could be none.

I watched Miriam read, studying her look of enjoyment as her eyes passed over this foolishness. "Miriam," I said after some time, "is it truly your intention not to marry me?"

She looked up at me, her face taut with horror, I suppose, but there must have been something upon my face—something impish rather than desperate—that made her burst out laughing. Not laughing in a mocking way, you understand, but laughing at the absurdity of all that had passed between the two of us. It was most infectious, and I too fell to laughing. And so we remained, laughing together, each encouraging the other, until both of our stomachs ached.

"You are ridiculously direct," she said at last, through gasps of air.

"I suppose I am," I agreed, as the last of the laughter departed. "And so I shall be direct with you," I said formally. "What are your plans now? What will you do with your money?"

She blushed a little, as though talking about money embarrassed her. Perhaps it was only *this* money. "I shall need to find someone to help me—someone I can trust. But I shall then invest it, I suppose. If I do so carefully, I may yield 5 percent on it, and with that money, along with my jointure, I should be able to afford a place that I find satisfactory."

I felt myself awash with disappointment and shame. I was disappointed that Miriam would now move out, establish her own household, and become independent. While she had been subject to my uncle, she had seemed somehow more accessible; now she would be truly beyond me and my selfishness in this matter left me ashamed.

I opened my mouth to begin a speech that I know not how I might have composed, and I still know not, for fate intervened. I heard the door open, and Isaac entered the room with a card resting upon a silver tray.

"For you, Mr. Weaver," Isaac said. "A lady."

I examined the card, on which the name *Sarah Decker* was printed in a handsome type.

"Did she state anything of her business?"

"I believe she's looking to employ your services," Isaac answered.

I was in no mood to take on new charges, but my inquiries had cost me a great deal of money, and I could see the value in giving myself some new task or other. Besides, the name Sarah Decker sounded familiar to me. I could not quite place it, but I knew that I had heard of it sometime in recent weeks.

Miriam excused herself, and Isaac sent in the lady. I immediately felt gratified that I had not sent her away, for she was an astonishingly beautiful woman of shining yellow hair, ample eyebrows, and a round, delicate face. She wore a dress of ivory with a blue petticoat and a matching bonnet. Her demeanor was genteel, but I could see she was ill at ease, calling upon a man such as myself in a neighborhood such as Dukes Place. I bade her sit and asked if I could offer her a refreshment, but she would have none.

"I come upon a difficult matter," she said. "I have long thought that there was nothing I could do to better my state, but it has grown worse, and when your name was mentioned to me, Mr. Weaver, I thought of you as my last hope."

I bowed. "If I may be of any assistance, it shall be my honor to serve you."

She smiled at me, and for such a smile, I believed, I would serve her in any way I could. "It is awkward to discuss, sir. I hope you will not grow impatient with me."

I would soon need to leave for the theater, but I nevertheless assured her she might take as long as she required.

"It is about Sir Owen Nettleton. I believe you know him."

I nodded. "Yes, I expect to see him at the theatre this very night."

"Do you believe him to be a man of honor?"

It was a delicate question, and one that I had to answer cautiously. "I believe Sir Owen to be a gentleman," I said.

"You performed a service for him, did you not? Did he mention my name to you?"

I now knew how I recalled her name, for Sir Owen had told me of his plans to marry Sarah Decker.

"Sir Owen mentioned you in only the most laudatory terms," I said. "May I ask why you inquire?"

She shook her head. "I hardly know how I can explain it," she said. "It is my hope that you might be able to speak with him, to make him see reason. I know not what else to do. I have discussed the matter with a man of law, but there is no crime he has committed. My brother has told me he will duel, but I know Sir Owen to be my brother's superior with the sword, and I could not stand that something should happen to him on my account."

"Madam," I said, "you must tell me the nature of your difficulty. Have you and Sir Owen had some sort of rupture?"

"That is the very thing," Miss Decker said. "We have never had anything that might be ruptured. I have met him on some social occasions, shared some words with him, but he and I are no more than distant acquaintances. Yet he tells the world that we are to be married. I know not why he does it. Everyone who is acquainted with him believes him to be sound of mind in all other respects."

"Does he attempt to visit you? To see you socially?"

"No. He merely speaks publicly of his engagement to me."

I regretted most sincerely that Miss Decker had declined refreshment, for I found myself in want of something of more than the usual strength.

"I do not understand," I told the lady. "He spoke of you to me in the highest terms. I should have had no reason to doubt that his engagement to you was genuine. Indeed, when he spoke of it, he framed it as though it might cast him in a bad light because of the recent death of his wife. I wonder if this fancy of his that he will marry you is some sort of delusion brought upon by grief."

"But Sir Owen was never married at all. He speaks of his late wife, and none of his friends know how to respond, for Sir Owen has never had a wife."

"Gad," I breathed. *What, then, had I retrieved for him?* I nearly said aloud. "Why should Sir Owen recount these fables? Have you any idea?"

Miss Decker shook her head. "You must understand, Mr. Weaver, that I neither know nor any longer care. These lies of his damage my reputation. They drive off gentlemen my father might think appropriate suitors, though he refuses to act on the problem, and my brother can think of no solution but violence. I hoped that the cooler head of a woman might find some alternative course—an intermediary such as yourself. If only this would end, for it is in no way fitting, I think, for me to be associated with a man like Sir Owen, hardly more than a common stock-jobber."

"Hardly more than *what?*" I rose from my chair.

Miss Decker shrank back, recoiling in horror from my advance.

I lowered myself to my seat. "I did not mean to frighten you, but I have never heard—that is to say, I was unaware that Sir Owen had the reputation of dealing in the funds."

She nodded. "He does it quietly, for fear that it might injure his reputation, but it is known all the same. I think I have heard that when he deals in the funds he uses a false name, as though he could shield his reputation from the taint of stock-jobbery."

I barely dared to breathe. "What is this false name?"

"I hardly know," she told me. "But surely you can see, can you not, why I should wish to have nothing to do with this man. Can you offer me some assistance?"

I rang the bell and rose to my feet. I began to pace about the room. "I shall offer you every assistance, madam. Let me assure you of that."

Isaac entered, and I bade him fetch my outerwear, for I should be leaving the house immediately.

Miss Decker was all confusion. She had removed a fan and was waving it vigorously before her face. "Have I somehow offended you, Mr. Weaver?"

"Madam, do not allow my agitation to distress you. I believe you have provided me with an important piece of information for another matter in which I am deeply concerned."

"I do not understand," she sputtered. "Will you not talk to Sir Owen?"

"I shall." Isaac arrived and helped me into my coat. "I shall see to it that he never mentions your name again. You have my word upon it."

I asked Isaac to show Miss Decker out while I headed toward the theatre where I knew Sir Owen would be seeking his evening's entertainment.

Thirty-three

I T OCCURRED TO ME as I approached the theatre at Drury Lane that I had no evidence with which to call in a constable, but I could wait no longer to confront this man. He had killed Kate Cole because she was able to identify him, and it was likely that he would kill again to keep his secret. After all, he had little to lose. Were he caught, he could be hanged but once, regardless of the numbers of dead attributed to his wickedness.

My heart hammered within my chest, and I found it difficult to think clearly. In my mind I had a vision of Sir Owen at my mercy as I beat him and beat him again until he confessed to the villainy of his actions, until he begged my forgiveness for all he had done. I knew I had to guard against my impulse to act out this dangerous fancy, for I should not find the consequences pleasant were I to attack a baronet, without clear provocation, before a crowded theatre. But what other choices did I have? I could bring him before South Sea House and ask them to tend to their counterfeiter. I could not be sure they would punish him, however. They might be content to send him out of the country with a promise never to speak of what he knew. There were certainly other options. I could ruin Sir Owen's reputation, publish a pamphlet exposing him as a murderer and a stock-jobber. And if that approach did not prove sufficient, I knew no small number of blackguards who would gladly do far more permanent damage in exchange for a kind word, a few shillings, and a promise of a full purse to be found upon Sir Owen's body.

I was pleased to see that the theatre was quite full, in part, no doubt, because the opening piece of German jugglers and ropedancers was a significant attraction in the city—certain unruly elements enjoyed spending their time hooting and throwing refuse at Germans, and the rest of the audience enjoyed watching the assault. For Elias's sake I hoped that the crowd would give the evening's comedy a warmer reception than they gave our King's countrymen. By the time I arrived, the opening performers had completed their act, and the audience engaged itself in the pleasantries of the social world while awaiting *The Unsuspecting Lover.*

The lower level of the theatre was crowded with the sort who frequented the pit upon such occasions. There were, of course, many of London's lower orders who could afford only the mean price of a pit ticket, and intermingled amongst them were the young sparks who approved of the freedom the pit gave them to make merry and to generate confusion.

Sir Owen, I knew, was of the temperament of these fellows, but hardly of an age where such diversions are acceptable. A man of his standing would no doubt seek higher ground, and I therefore sought him upon the upper levels. Rather rudely, I think, I made my way to the balconies, shoving aside all who stood in my path. Without concern for propriety, I stuck my head in many a box, looking for my man. The aisles were thick with gentlemen and beaux and ladies and coquettes who had little or no concern for what happened upon the stage, caring only for the latest gossip or the opportunity to take note of one another. The theatre was, as it remains today, a fashionable place of making and improving acquaintance. That there are men and women below who perform for their entertainment is merely an added delight—or, for some, a distraction.

I should have behaved in a subtle manner to make my approach invisible, but my frenzy and expression must have betrayed me, for the object of my search saw me at the precise moment I saw him. He was in a box across the way with another gentleman and two ladies of fashion. Our eyes locked for a moment, and I was sure at that instant that he knew what I knew, and he knew that I was in no mood to let the wheels of ineffectual justice grind over this matter.

I dashed through the hall outside the balconies—as much as the crowd would permit dashing—and boldly entered Sir Owen's box. I must have cut a dreadful figure, my clothes somewhat disheveled, my hair awry, my face flushed from heavy breathing. The baronet's companions stared at me with utter disbelief—as though a tiger had suddenly wandered into their box. One of the ladies, a pretty woman of copper hair in a gold-and-black gown, placed a hand to her mouth.

"How unexpected," Sir Owen stammered. He stood up and dusted himself off awkwardly. "Did we have an appointment?" he asked in a low tone. "I must have erred terribly. I do apologize. Perhaps we can meet on another occasion."

"We shall meet now," I said, unimpressed by his efforts to salvage the situation from social ruin. "It is best if your friends know what you are."

I knew I had frightened the woman in the gold-and-black gown, for she now placed two of her gloved fingers in her mouth and began to chew upon them. The other gentleman, a gouty older fellow—far too old for the young woman he held in attendance—proved no less fearful than his companions of the other sex. He pretended to look out into the audience for an acquaintance, muttering to himself that the rascal was not to be seen.

"Good God, Weaver." Sir Owen cast twitchy glances between me and the people in his party. "We may discuss of this matter later, I say. I shall come pay you a visit in the morning."

"Yes," said the gouty man, emboldened by Sir Owen's restraint. "Run along, I say."

I ignored this man. "Sir Owen," I hissed, barely able to contain my rage, "you will come with me now."

"Go with you?" he asked incredulously. "Are you mad, Weaver, to think you may order me about? Where would I go with you?"

"To South Sea House," I said. I had no intention of taking him there, but I wished to let him know that I knew of his connection to that place.

He laughed aloud. "I think not. I find it wisest never to go to such places, I assure you."

"Nevertheless," I told him, "you will attend me there."

Sir Owen was trapped. He knew it. He wanted desperately to talk his way out of this confrontation, and he could not think how. "You have quite forgotten yourself. I am a gentleman, in the company of a gentleman and ladies. You may have business with me, but I assure you there is an appropriate time and place. I have no patience for any hot-tempered Jews just now, so get you gone and I shall call on you should I see fit."

I felt nothing at that moment but a murderous rage. I confess, reader, that I was an eye-blink away from grabbing this pompous villain by the neck and strangling him upon the spot. For him to affront me in this way when he had committed so terrible a crime against me and my family was more than I could endure. I think that this rage I felt must have indeed shown itself upon my face, for Sir Owen saw it. He saw what was in my heart and he knew he was seconds away from feeling my wrath.

In a word, he ran.

It was well that Sir Owen was no young or sprightly man, for while my leg ached terribly, I was able to keep pace with him. He dove quite suddenly into the crowd and rudely shoved several gentlemen and ladies aside, and I suspect the moment he behaved so abominably in public he knew there was no turning back, for how could he account for this behavior? This realization only made him desperate, and he knocked patrons out of the way with increasing determination, rushing for the exit as if it were the gateway to safety itself. I, for my part, attempted to play the courteous pursuer, but there can be no doubt that I was guilty of my share of bruises and bumps.

The Unsuspecting Lover began upon the stage, but the scuffle in the balcony had already attracted the notice of the patrons in the pit. In Elias's opening scene, his protagonist and his friend projected their voices loudly, complaining of their distresses in love, but even in my pursuit I could hear an unmistakable note of desperation as the actors sensed that something entirely unrelated to their performances had arrested the audience's attention.

I knew not where Sir Owen hoped to go, and in truth I suspect he knew not either, for soon he found himself at the end of the balcony, no stairs in sight, and nowhere to go but toward me or thirty feet down to the stage. Panicked, he reached into his waistcoat and revealed an ornately decorated pistol of gold and pearl. I too had my pistol upon me, but I was not reckless enough as to fire it in so crowded a venue.

Seeing him remove his weapon, the ladies in our immediate vicinity let out a series of horrified and shrill cries, and this sound sent a wave of panic that spread throughout the theatre. I heard the rumble of footsteps below as half the crowd looked upward and the other half scrambled for a better vantage from which to view the commotion. Understanding the precariousness of his position, Sir Owen attempted a narrative that would shield him from the censure of others.

"Weaver," he shouted, "why do you pursue me?" He turned to the crowd, which had begun to settle. Sir Owen placed one hand on his hip and thrust his chest outward—as now he found himself the central attraction in the theatre, perhaps he thought he should conduct himself like a tragedian. "This man is mad. It is in Bedlam he belongs, not at the playhouse."

"Surely it is you who do not belong here," I said calmly, "for such a poor performance would put even Drury Lane to shame."

This quip drew a few laughs from the audience, but only unsettled Sir Owen even more. "Perhaps you should give some thought to who I am," he said, waving his pistol about, "and what courtesies belong to me."

Having reached an impasse, I thought it best to lay my cards on the table and see what came of it. "As you have surmised," I shouted, for during my time as a pugilist I had learned a thing or two about projecting my voice, "I have discovered that you are indeed the same person as Martin Rochester, the most notorious and unscrupulous stock-jobber ever to live. Consequently, I know you to be responsible for several murders: those of Michael Balfour, Kate Cole the whore, very likely Christopher Hodge, the bookseller, and, of course, my father, Samuel Lienzo."

A murmur went up in our surroundings. "What? Sir Owen is Martin Rochester?" Below I saw young men pointing upward. Women of his acquaintance gasped in shock. The words *murder* and *stock-jobber* circulated like handbills.

Sir Owen responded to this accusation about as badly as he could have. He was trapped. He could think of nothing. I had exposed him before all of London. Perhaps if what I had said was untrue and he had laughed off the accusations he might have preserved his name and his reputation, at least for that evening. Rather than countering my claims, however, he acted the part of a desperate man. He fired his pistol at me.

The crack of the pistol forged a momentary pocket of silence in the excited theatre, and the smell of burning powder hung in the air. Everyone, even the desperate players upon the stage, paused to inspect their persons for signs of penetration. It was my good fortune that Sir Owen possessed no good aim, and he missed my person, but a liveried footman who stood some ten feet behind me, gawking at my confrontation with the baronet, fared not so well. The ball of lead struck him squarely in the chest, and he staggered backward and dropped to the floor. He gaped with utter surprise at the red stain that spread across his livery. It was as though someone had tipped over a bottle of wine upon a tablecloth and no one could think of what to do. He looked upon his injury for a quarter of a minute, and then, without letting out a groan, he toppled over and expired.

I could hear nothing in the theatre but the actors haplessly intoning their lines below. This quiet passed in but an instant, however, and the panic rose from a light simmer to a boil as the patrons rushed to the exits to escape Sir Owen's murderous rampage. Unwilling to let him pass me by in the mayhem, I plunged forward, intending I know not what—perhaps to pummel him into unconsciousness and drag him before the magistrate. The truth is that I had no plan and I knew not what to do beyond the instant.

Madly, Sir Owen arose and attempted to strike me upon the face with his hot pistol, but I dodged his blow easily and responded with a calmly executed punch to his ample belly. As I expected, he doubled over and dropped his now-useless firearm. But he did not quit. He was desperate, and he would fight until he escaped me or until he could fight no more.

The baronet took a step backward and reached for his hangar. I therefore reached for mine, and had it out and at the ready before he had even drawn his. I made the mistake of believing that I should have the clear advantage in this arena. I stepped forward, ready to drive my sword through his body.

Sir Owen took his first pass at me, a nimble and well-executed thrust aimed for my upper chest. A scoundrel like Sir Owen did not live to be his age by being a mean swordsman, and I confess I felt a tinge of fear as I hastily parried the thrust and attempted to conceive of a strategy. I had been overconfident, for I was not the master of all the arts of self-defense, and saw at once that Sir Owen could prove to be a match for me.

Despite his frenzy, Sir Owen held his blade with a kind of instinctive aplomb, and he moved it gracefully as he slashed back and forth with a few strikes meant merely to disorder me. I should like to say that the sword seemed an extension of his arm, but if that had been the case the sword should have been fat and ungainly—it was more as though the arm became an extension of his light and delicate weapon, and Sir Owen, under its spell, moved with equal parts grace and violence.

These were not conditions under which I relished taking on a skilled opponent with murderous intent. Let me assure you, reader, a strategy is a difficult matter to formulate when parrying blades with a villain in a theatre crowded with hundreds of panicked patrons screaming and fleeing for the doors.

Sir Owen launched another attack, aimed again for my chest, but at the last moment he shifted targets downward, thinking thereby to slash my leg and impair my ability to maneuver. I only narrowly blocked his thrust and then countered with a passionate jab toward his side, under his right arm, hoping he would have trouble blocking this blow. For a man his size, he maneuvered with stunning quickness, effectively avoiding my advance.

Although I was forced to concede that he was a man of exceptional swordsmanship, when I looked at his face I saw none of the pleasure that a man takes at exercising his talents—only murderous passion. I thought Sir Owen's passions would surely provide me with a considerable advantage, but there was none to be had. He made another pass, this time at my sword arm. I blocked it, but I felt our blades lock. In my efforts to regain control of my sword, I applied far too much pressure to my weak leg, and the pain, shooting through my body, distracted me for an instant. It was an instant too long, for Sir Owen took advantage of my confusion, and spinning his hangar deftly, he deprived me of mine, which arose in a high arc and clattered to the ground some fifteen feet from where I stood.

I thought that he would now surely flee, but his own rage and terror clouded his judgment. I have rarely in my life seen anything so horrific and yet comical as his face, now deep red—almost purple—in color, except for his lips, pressed together so hard as to be ghastly white. He stared at me, holding his blade outward. "You have ruined me," he said in a low growl, barely audible over the noise of the terrified crowd.

He intended to run me through. I was sure of it. I could have escaped, I suppose. I might have gotten away unscathed, but I could not bear the thought of fleeing, of running from this villain whom I had labored so hard to find. So I did what he no doubt never imagined an unarmed sane man would do to a sword-bearing adversary; I rushed him.

I lunged forward, ignoring the sting that made me feel as if my limb should snap in two. Surprised at first by my dash toward him, Sir Owen held forth his sword in the hopes of running me through, but I was on no self-destructive course. Instead, using a trick I had learned fighting upon the streets, I dropped downward and tackled his legs, hoping to topple him as one does pins upon the bowling green.

Sir Owen dropped his sword and, propelled by his efforts to flee, fell backward. He escaped my grip and scurried back upon his legs like a crab, reaching his feet again at the time I did. Now, against the rail of the balcony, he stepped up, I suppose to gain greater leverage, and aimed a blow at me. We had been reduced to two men, deprived of rank and station, matching our strength in a contest of rage. And it is no idle boast, reader, that, in a contest of this order—of fist and brawn and willingness to take punishment—a lazy, well-fed baronet stood not a chance against me.

Sir Owen swung and missed.

Unbalanced by the exertion of the blow, he propped himself up against the railing of the balcony. He swung again—recklessly and aimlessly. He knew not what he did, and he flailed about wildly. In the confusion caused by this mad offense, and the further force of the impressive blow with which I responded, the baronet lost his balance, and with a fearful yelp, fell backward, thirty feet down, onto the stage where the actors had been intrepidly continuing with Elias's play. Their efforts had been valiant, but I suppose even those most disciplined of players could not ignore the arrival of a large baronet flung from the heavens.

I remained still, breathing heavily, my heart pounding and, indeed, my limbs shaking. I could not think of what to do next. I think but a moment passed, though it felt to me an endless expanse of time, before it occurred to me to determine if Sir Owen still lived.

I leaned over the rail to see if Sir Owen was dead, merely unconscious, or perhaps unharmed and ready to flee. But before I could gather a look, I was grabbed by countless hands who forced me to the ground and held me immobile. I was no longer Sir Owen's accuser. I was no longer the man who stood between a deranged fool with a pistol and the innocent theatre-goers. I was now a Jew who had attacked, perhaps killed, a baronet.

Two stout-looking gentlemen held me in place. They struck me as capable-enough bucks, but I could probably have evaded them if I chose. But I did not so choose. I should have to face the law sooner or later, and I had no desire to risk an injury in an attempt to escape.

Around me the crowd swarmed violently. Some ran to view the form of Sir Owen on the stage below. Others milled about, looking as dazed as cattle. The copper-haired woman in gold and black who had sat in Sir Owen's box screamed violently while a young gentleman attempted to comfort her. She cried out for some minutes and then she began to sob more gently. The young gentleman wisely began to move her closer to the stairway that he might deliver her of the theatre.

"You must be calm, Miss Decker," he said. "You must not agitate yourself."

I stared. I knew not what to think. "Decker," I said aloud. "Sarah Decker?"

One of the men who held me looked at me quizzically. He surely found my curiosity as unaccountable as it was inappropriate. "What of it?"

"Do you know her?" I asked him. "Do you know that woman?"

"Yes," he said, his face wrinkled with confusion.

"That is Sarah Decker?" I asked. I began to feel disoriented, even a little dizzy.

"Yes," he repeated, somewhat irritably. "She is to marry the very man you have tried to murder."

I could do nothing but let the men lead me away.

THIRTY-FOUR

I THOUGHT THAT I should be brought before the magistrate that night, but this proved not to be the case. Perhaps there were far too many witnesses to call on—witnesses of degree and rank—and the hour was too late to begin such an affair. In any case, the gentlemen who held me turned me over to the constables, who locked me in the Poultry Compter for the night. I fortunately had enough silver on me to procure a private closet on the Master's Side that I might avoid the horrors of that jail, for the Common Side is among the most foul and wretched of places upon this earth.

My closet was small, smelling of mold and perspiration, and furnished with naught but a broken wooden chair and a hard straw bed, which, had I used, I would have been forced to share with a colony of gregarious lice. I sat down on the chair and attempted to think of some course of action. It was hard to know what to think or how to proceed, for I knew not with what I would be charged come morning. Much would depend not only on Sir Owen's condition but also on the nature of the witnesses the constables brought forward.

My case was dire, and I concluded that I had few options other than to impose on my uncle, and ask of him to offer something to the magistrate that I might not be bound over for trial. I could in no way be sure that a bribe would work. If Sir Owen was dead, I should certainly be charged with manslaughter, if not murder—no bribe could hope to convince him to alter his ruling if it was a clear attack against a man of Sir Owen's breeding. But if the baronet was only injured, I flattered myself that I might hope to escape a trial.

I called for the turnkey and told him I wished to procure of him some paper and a pen, and then I wished to send a message. I was not certain I would have enough silver upon me for the exorbitantly priced goods, but as it turned out the prices mattered little. "I can sell you paper and pen," the short, greasy-skinned fellow told me as he tried to keep his stringy hair from his eyes, "but I can't have nothing delivered for you."

"I don't understand," I said, still in something of a stupor. "For what reason?"

"Orders," he explained, as if that one word clarified everything.

"Whose orders?" I had never heard of a prison refusing to allow its inmate to send messages. I had never heard of a turnkey refusing to earn a little silver by doing so.

"I can't say," he replied stoically. He began to pick at some loose skin about his neck.

I believe my voice betrayed my inability to believe what I heard. "Does this apply to all the men you hold here?"

He laughed. "Oh, no. The other gentlemen are free to send such messages as they like. How else could I buy my bread? This is only for you, Mr. Weaver. We can't let *you* send any messages. That's what we been told."

"I should like to speak to the master of the prison," I told him in a stern voice.

"Certainly." He continued to pick away. "He'll be in sometime tomorrow afternoon. I don't think you'll still be here, but if you are, you can speak with him then."

I considered my options for a moment. Breaking this fellow's neck struck me as a pleasant enough method to get what I wanted, but not a very wise one. I thought on a less violent plan. "I shall make your arranging for a message to be delivered well worth your while."

He only smiled. "It's already been made worth my while to see otherwise. Shall I fetch you that paper and pen?"

"Who has paid you to prevent me from sending messages?" I demanded.

He shrugged. "I can't tell you that, sir."

He hardly needed to, for I had my suspicions. "Do you really wish to commit yourself to dealing with a man such as Wild?" I asked the guard.

He merely smiled. "Well, I reckon that in certain kinds of trade, one cannot but deal with Mr. Wild, don't you think?"

I thought on my uncle's words: *Mr. Mendes likes to say that in certain kinds of trade, one cannot but deal with Wild.* "Give my regards to Mr. Mendes," I muttered.

He showed me a rotted grin. "You're a clever one, aren't you? I'm almost sorry I tangled with you, sir, but that Wild's a mite cleverer, I suppose."

I sent the impudent blackguard away. I could not believe my ill-fortune. My lines of communication had surely been severed in order to make it impossible to send precisely the sort of message I wished to send. If I should be prevented from reaching my uncle, it was almost certain that whoever plotted against me would also see to it that I stood trial. I could not imagine the South Sea Company would relish such a thing—indeed, if I were bound over for trial I should consider my life at risk at every moment, for the South Sea Company had much to lose from a trial. The Bank of England had a great deal to gain, however, and I could only assume that Bloathwait was behind this plot to isolate me.

I slept not at all that night, but neither did I think much on what had happened to me nor of what I had seen. I sat in my uncomfortable, broken wooden chair and tried to banish it all from my mind. But I could not quite dismiss the sight of pretty Sarah Decker. If she *was* Sarah Decker, who had I met earlier that day, and what could that meeting mean? I found myself, as Adelman had said, in a labyrinth in which I could not see what lay ahead or even behind. I only knew where I was—and I was trapped.

THE NEXT MORNING I was brought to the magistrate. Justice Duncombe faced me in his house on Great Hart Street. "I am astonished," he said, and clearly he was so. "Mr. Weaver, once again, and a matter of murder, once again. Really, sir, I see I must lock you up forthwith before you depopulate the entire metropolis."

I swallowed hard at the word *murder.* I must confess that the situation terrified me, for it boded ill to say the least. "Am I to understand that Sir Owen is indeed dead, your honor?"

"No," Duncombe explained. "The physician has explained that Sir Owen's wounds are superficial and that he is expected to make a full recovery. There is the matter of this other fellow, the footman, Dudley

Roach, who is indeed quite dead. Tell me, Mr. Weaver, are you pleased or displeased about the expectation of Sir Owen's recovery?"

"I must confess I am of mixed emotions," I said boldly, "but in truth I should prefer him to be alive that he might be forced to confess of his crimes. I hope he will be well guarded that he might not escape."

"It is your crimes that we are here to discuss," the magistrate sneered, "not those of a baronet."

I held myself straight and spoke with confidence. "I am convinced the witnesses of the event will testify that Sir Owen fired a gun at me and attacked me. It was he who shot this footman, who was but an unfortunate witness to Sir Owen's rampage. I wished only to defend myself and to apprehend a man whose crimes should be notorious. That I injured him was an accident—no more."

"From what I hear of the constables," he replied, "that is not the case. It appears you attacked Sir Owen, and if he was zealous in his defense, the outcome of the conflict may justify his concern. If you incited him with an attack, and he felt the need to defend himself, the charge of manslaughter must be brought against you, not Sir Owen. Do you not agree?"

I did not agree, and I told him as much.

Duncombe asked me an endless series of questions about what had happened, and I answered as best I could without revealing anything of the forged South Sea issues. I said only that I had come to learn that Martin Rochester had committed several murders and that Sir Owen was indeed Martin Rochester. As it had the night before in the theatre, this information elicited no small surprise. Duncombe stared at me with astonishment, while the crowd in the courtroom erupted in a loud murmur. The magistrate banged his gavel and restored a respectful quiet.

"If you knew this man to be what you say," he asked me, "why did you not seek a warrant for his arrest?"

This question surprised me, and I had no answer. I feared Duncombe believed my confusion a sign that he had caught me in a lie.

He questioned me for what felt like hours, though I believe it was not nearly so long. Duncombe then began the task of questioning the witnesses. I shall not ask my reader to endure what I endured, listening to the endless details of my conflict with Sir Owen. It is enough to say that more than a dozen witnesses offered testimony, and none of them sought to exonerate me.

Faced with the arbitrary nature of our legal system, I had cause to worry, for if someone in power wished me bound over for trial, then I could see no way to avoid that fate. And it was not without some self-condemnation that I considered the death of this innocent footman. While he had fallen victim of Sir Owen's somewhat changeable humor, it was a humor I had provoked, and I now knew that I had provoked Sir Owen based on a deception. Someone had gone to a great deal of difficulty to make certain that I believed Sir Owen had lied to me. Someone had arranged for an impersonator to expose me to lies that could only make me believe Sir Owen a rascal. I no longer knew what to believe.

Duncombe's questioning of the witnesses lasted more than four hours, and I was too exhausted by its conclusion even to guess how the judge would rule. I could see no reason why he would not bind me over for trial, and this prospect terrified me. At last, having heard all the witnesses, the judge announced that he was ready to make his decision.

I sought for signs in the way he held himself, wishing to know my fate before he could pronounce it, but I could divine nothing from the judge's stern and unflinching countenance.

"Mr. Weaver, you are without doubt a dangerous and excitable man, and you clearly agitated Sir Owen, but you never obligated him to produce a weapon nor to discharge it so recklessly. I suspect you may give me cause to wish, in future times, that Sir Owen had been a better aim, but that is not our concern here today. I find no reason to charge you with man-slaughter. If Sir Owen wishes to prosecute you for assault, then I fear I shall see you before this court shortly. I heartily wish you may work things out amongst yourselves. You may go."

I realized later that I should have felt myself awash with relief, but per-haps I was too disordered. I knew not how to understand his decision. I could only presume that Duncombe had been bribed on my behalf, but who had interceded for me? Had my uncle been informed of my danger in time to intervene? If so, why was he not in the court?

I made my way through the crowd, wanting only to remove myself from that horrid building—before the magistrate changed his mind, I thought. Elias later told me that he was there and grabbed my arm as I passed him, but I have no recollection of seeing him. I shoved my way for-ward, moving with the plodding determination of a dull ox until I escaped from the confines of the judge's court and breathed in the foul-smelling and misty air of the London afternoon. As bad an odor as was in the air that day, and as cloudy and unwelcoming was the weather, I basked in it with a satisfaction I cannot describe. It was a moment of relief, and the knowledge that the relief would be but fleeting made it all the more sweet.

My reverie lasted but a minute, and when the world crystallized before me, as it does after one rubs his eyes, I immediately recognized the coach and the East Indian servant boy as belonging to Nathan Adelman. I stared at the chair for a moment until Adelman poked his head out the window and invited me in.

I stared blankly. I felt as though uttering any sound should take more strength than I had.

"We have won the day, I see." He was not quite grinning, but he glowed with satisfaction. "No easy man, that Duncombe, but he saw reason in the end. Climb in, Weaver."

"I am astonished," I said as I stepped up into his coach, "to see you emerge as my ally. I should have thought the Company would be nothing but delighted to witness my ruin." I took a seat across from the great financier, and the coach heaved forward, headed to I knew not where.

Adelman smiled at me, as though we were to go for a charming ride in the country together. Indeed, his plump little form had every appearance of the proper English gentleman. "I believe that before last evening we would have delighted in your ruin, but things have now changed, and I can assure you that you should be grateful that we struck a bargain with the justice here before our friends at the Bank of England. You can be certain they would have seen to it that you stood trial."

"Of course." I nodded. "I would have been forced to explain my actions, and this explanation would involve the public revelation of Sir Owen's involvement in the forging of South Sea issues."

"Precisely. In the end, I am grateful for your involvement, for we have learned the identity of Rochester, and he will no longer cause the Company any difficulties."

I breathed in deeply. "I am no longer convinced that Sir Owen is Martin Rochester, only that someone has gone to great lengths to make me believe it so."

Adelman stared at me. "I have no doubt that Sir Owen is the man. The Company, I can assure you, has no doubt. And it seems that there are others that have no doubt."

"How do you mean?" I inquired.

"Sir Owen," he said slowly, "is dead."

I am not ashamed to own that I grew disoriented, and I grasped at an armrest inside the coach. "I was assured his wounds were superficial." I could not understand what Adelman told me. If Sir Owen was dead, why had I not been charged with murder?

"The wounds he received from his fall were superficial," Adelman explained. His voice was calm, controlled—almost soothing. "But he received other wounds. As he left his physician's house this morning, he was set upon by a ruffian who stabbed him quite mercilessly in the throat. Sir Owen survived this attack by only a few minutes."

I knew not if I felt anger or elation, fear or joy. "Who was this ruffian?" I demanded.

"The villain quite escaped." He flashed me a smile, a look of unrestrained mischief. I should have liked to have seen villainy, but there was something boyish, pranksterish about his look. Adelman wished me to know that the South Sea Company had disposed of Sir Owen. "It's rather shocking he could have gotten away, with all those people there," he said, smirking. "Sir Owen was a man with many enemies, and I suppose we shall never know the truth of it."

"I quite believe it," I said, conveying more to Adelman with my looks than my words. "We shall never know a great deal, I have begun to realize."

"But there were papers found upon Sir Owen's body that suggest unequivocally that he was the man known as Martin Rochester. There was even a draft of a letter, written to one of the South Sea directors." Adelman handed me several folded pieces of paper.

I opened them to find a difficult hand, but I scanned the pages quickly. The letter was as Adelman claimed. "I seek now only to allow the Company to proceed with its plan," it said. "In exchange for the consideration of thirty thousand pounds, I shall quit this isle, never to return nor speak of what has passed here."

I handed him back the letter. "It looks enough like what little of Sir Owen's hand as I have seen," I said. "But then the matter before us *is* forgery."

"You can rest assured that the man who murdered your father has been punished."

I shook my head. "How did you get this letter from his person?"

"We could take no chances."

"I see that," I said dryly.

"Surely you do not believe that the South Sea Company had him murdered," Adelman said with a gregarious smile. He wished to make certain I had no ambiguity in my mind. I think, however, the look upon my face was one of confusion—though of a moral rather than a factual nature. "Weaver," he said in response, "I would have thought you might be happier at having found your justice."

My stomach churned. I knew I should feel that this unpleasant affair had reached a resolution, but I could not quite believe it. "I wish I knew that I had," I said quietly. "I assume, sir, that you still wish to deny any involvement in the attacks on my person?"

Adelman's face flushed a bit. "I shall not lie to you, Mr. Weaver. We took measures that we found distasteful because we believe the good of the nation depends upon it. When the South Sea Company receives approval from Parliament to launch its plan to reduce the national debt, I do not doubt but that we shall be applauded throughout the Kingdom for our ingenuity in aiding the nation and our investors."

"And yourselves, I am certain."

He smiled. "We are public servants, but we wish to enrich ourselves as well. And if we can do all these things, I cannot see why we should not. In any event, the exigencies of the moment forced us to behave in ways that we wished avoidable. The attacks upon you on the street and at Heidegger's masquerade were regrettable, but I can assure you we never wished you any real harm—only to convince you that the cost of looking into this nasty business would prove too dear. I see now that these attacks only drove you on. In my defense I must tell you that I argued against any efforts to intimidate you with violence, but in the Company I am but one voice."

I was speechless for a moment, but I found my voice soon enough, though my teeth gritted together. My mouth grew suddenly dry. "In those attacks I was set upon by the very man who ran down my father. Surely you cannot expect me to believe—"

"We can only imagine," Adelman interrupted, "that Sir Owen exerted his influence with the desperate fellows we employed—for how can men of that order be aught but desperate, and therefore infinitely corruptible—to insert his element within the gang. The blackguard you killed—the man who killed Samuel—was none of our hiring, I can assure you. As for the rest, I presume that Sir Owen swayed the ruffians in our employ that he might have use of them on occasions such as these. Nevertheless, for the small harm we intended, I must apologize to you. I believe we owe you much, and you, indeed, owe us much. For as you have relieved us from the threat of a pernicious forger, we have rescued you from the consequences of your actions and from the clutches of those who would have forced a trial that I need not tell you could easily have concluded with your hanging. Is it not time for us to reach a rapprochement?"

"A rapprochement," I observed, "that I am certain will involve a promise on my part of silence."

"Indeed, and I do not think it much to ask. You have, after all, uncovered the identity of your father's murderer, which is what you desired, and this fiend has surely paid the ultimate price for his crimes. I cannot think but that your reputation will grow of this. Further, we shall pay you one thousand pounds in company stock. I think this a most amicable offer."

I shook my head. "How can I trust what you say, Mr. Adelman? Did you not, in the South Sea House, look me in the eye and tell me things you knew to be utterly false—that the Bank had deceived me, that you knew of no connection between Rochester and my father's death?"

Adelman's jowly face quivered as he sighed. "Alas, lying to you then was necessary. It is no longer so."

"So you say. But how am I to know that? Your word is meaningless. You have rendered it so. Now you tell me to believe you, but there is no basis for that belief."

He smiled. "You need only choose to believe, Mr. Weaver. That is your basis."

"Like the new finance," I observed. "It is true only so long as we believe it to be true."

"The world has changed, you know. You can either change with it and prosper or shake your fists at the heavens. I prefer to do the former. What about you, Mr. Weaver? What do you prefer?"

I thought that I should not hold myself indebted to the South Sea Company and that a man of principle would reject their bargain, but I needed the money. Part of me wished to ask for more, for what was the harm in asking for more of something that could be printed for the mere cost of paper yet exchanged for real money, assuming there existed such a thing. In the end I accepted this offer and I kept silent of their secret for as long as it mattered, and perhaps even longer. I suppose it no longer matters who knows of these things, and in light of the disaster that the South Sea Company was yet to face, I think hardly anyone would care now that once false stock circulated among murderers and their victims.

Thirty-five

T HE NEXT DAY Elias affected an unwillingness to talk to me, blaming me for the failure of his play, which the management of the Drury Lane Theatre indicated would not continue for a second night. Elias was not to have even one benefit performance. His play had not earned him a single penny.

After some grueling hours of explanation, supplication, and promise of silver, Elias agreed that I had probably not shown up at the theatre with the intent of throwing anyone upon the stage, but he demanded the right to retain his foul disposition. He also demanded an immediate loan of five guineas. I had been prepared for a request of this sort, knowing the extent to which Elias had been depending on the proceeds of the benefit night. And as I, too, blamed myself in some small measure for the failure of *The Unsuspecting Lover,* and I wished to make amends as best I could, I handed an envelope to my friend.

He opened it and stared at the contents.

"You suffered no small amount at the hands of this inquiry," I said. "I thought it only fair that you share in the rewards. Adelman has bribed me with a thousand pounds' worth of stock, so now you will have half of it and together we shall share in the fortunes or misfortunes of the South Sea Company."

"I think I hate you considerably less than I did this morning," Elias said, as he examined the issues. "I should never have made half so much had my play lasted to a benefit night. You won't forget that we need to transfer this to my name?"

"I think I have sufficiently familiarized myself with the procedures." I took the stock away from him for a moment that I might get his attention. "However, I do still require your opinion on some unresolved matters. I have been hardly used, I fear, and I know not by whom."

"I would have thought your adventures to be at a finish," Elias said absently, pretending he felt perfectly comfortable while I held his shares. "The villain is dead. What more could you wish?"

"I cannot but have doubts," I told him. I proceeded to explain how I had been visited by a woman claiming to be Sarah Decker, and how she had exposed Sir Owen in a series of lies. "It was at that moment I concluded Sir Owen to be the villain behind all of these crimes."

"And now you are uncertain."

"Uncertain—yes, that is the very word," I said.

"Is it not the best word to describe this age?" Elias asked pointedly.

"I should like if it were not the best word to describe this month, however. That woman told me she was Sarah Decker so that I might become convinced that Sir Owen was Martin Rochester. But if she lied about her identity and her motives, how do I know Sir Owen truly was Rochester?"

"Why would he have been murdered if he had not been guilty? You must surely have concluded that either the South Sea Company or someone else, equally implicit in these crimes, removed him in order to prevent him from speaking of what he knows."

"It is true," I agreed, "but perhaps this murderer made the same mistake I did. Perhaps Sir Owen's assassin was tricked as I was. For if the South Sea Company had known Sir Owen to be Martin Rochester, why would they not have dealt with him long before?"

The puzzle had his attention. He squinted and dug his shoes into the dirt. "If someone wished you to believe that Sir Owen was Martin Rochester, why not simply write you a note telling you so instead of sending you hints from pretty heiresses? Why engage in an elaborate performance in the hope that you will reach the conclusion the schemer wishes?"

I had thought about this question as well. "Had I just received word that Sir Owen was Martin Rochester, I would have certainly looked into the matter, but as things have been set up, I did not *hear* that Sir Owen was the villain, I *discovered* it. You see, it was the discovery that fired my actions. Had I simply looked into an accusation, I should have done so quietly and discreetly. I believe that someone wished to see me turn to violence. The schemer knew Rochester's true name all along but needed for someone else to remove Sir Owen. I just wish I knew who the schemer is."

"You may never *know* who the schemer is," Elias said as he took his stock back from my hand. "But I would bet that you can guess—in all probability, that is."

He was right. I could.

IT TOOK ME some days to work up the will to do so, but I knew I had to understand the events that transpired in these pages, and I knew that there was but one man who could clarify much of what I had seen. I had no desire to seek him out, to engage with him more than I had to, but I would know the truth, and no one else could tell me. I therefore mustered my resolve and paid a visit to Jonathan Wild's home. He had me wait almost not at all, and when he entered his drawing room he greeted me with a smile that might have suggested amusement or anxiety. In truth, he was as uncertain about me as I was about him, and his uncertainty made me feel far more at ease.

"How kind of you to call." He poured me a glass of port and then limped across the room to sit across from me upon his princely throne, utterly confident in his powers. As always, Abraham Mendes stood silent sentry over his master. "I trust you are here on a matter of business." A smile spread across Wild's wide, square face.

I smiled falsely in return. "Of a sort. I wish for you to help make things clear for me, for much that has happened still confuses me. I know that you were to some degree involved with the late baronet, and that you attempted to control my actions from behind the scenes. But I do not entirely understand the scope or the motivation of your involvement."

He took a long drink of his port. "And why should I tell you, sir?"

I thought on this for a moment. "Because I asked," I said, "and because I was treated rudely by your hands, and I feel you owe me. After all, had things gone your way, I would be in Newgate this moment. But despite your efforts to keep me from contacting anyone while inside the Compter, you see I have emerged victorious."

"I know not what you mean," he told me unconvincingly. He did not wish to convince me.

"It could only have been you who prevented me from sending messages during my night of confinement. Had the Bank of England involved itself so early, surely Duncombe would have ruled against me. You would not have so extended yourself as the Bank would, but it would have been no large thing for you to convince the turnkeys at that jail to perform such a small service for you. So, as I say, Mr. Wild—I believe you owe me."

"Perhaps I shall be open with you," he said after a long pause, "because at this point I have nothing to lose by being so. After all, anything I say to you can never be used against me at the law, for you are the only witness of what I shall say." He glanced at Mendes, I suspected for my benefit. He wished to make clear that any friendly exchanges between Jews should serve me not at all. "In any rate," he continued, "as you are so clever, perhaps you might tell me what you suspect."

"I shall tell you what I *know*, sir. I know that you had a personal investment in my inquiry continuing, and I can only presume it is because you wished to see the demise of Sir Owen, whom you knew to be the same as Martin Rochester. Your reason for doing so was that you, at some earlier point, were Mr. Rochester's partner."

The corners of Wild's mouth twitched slightly. "Why do you believe that?"

"Because I can think of no other involvement you might have with Sir Owen, and because if Sir Owen had wished to sell and distribute this counterfeit stock, he must have needed your help. After all, anyone who engages in a certain kind of trade must sooner or later do business with Mr. Wild. Is that not true?"

I looked at Mendes, and I took some satisfaction in his very slight nod.

"It is still conjecture," Wild told me.

"Ah, but it is all so probable. You sent the much-beleaguered Quilt Arnold to watch me when I put my notice in the *Daily Advertiser.* He told me that he had once been more trusted of you, and that you wished for him to see if he recognized anyone who came to meet with me, and if not, to describe them. Is it not probable, then, as Mr. Arnold had been more trusted of you in the past, that he had been more privy to your dealings with this counterfeit stock? Thus he might recognize a purchaser, and even if he did not, you might from Arnold's description. None of these details on their own are condemnatory, but combined I believe there is no other way to interpret them."

Wild nodded. "You are perhaps more impressive than I have given you credit for, Mr. Weaver. And yes, you are quite correct. More than a year ago, Sir Owen approached me because he wished to engage in a scheme to produce false South Sea stock. He had been, in the past, involved with the South Sea's parent organization, the Sword Blade Company, and as a result he had great insight into their inner workings. But he wished to recruit those who knew their way about the underworld, and he needed connections to make his plan work, and so he wisely approached me. He offered me a percentage I thought generous, and soon we reached an agreement. It was a complex operation, you understand. He wished earnestly that no one should know who he was, because he rightly feared the power of the Company. And so he established the identity of Martin Rochester. With the aid of my men upon the street, and an inside operator at the company itself."

"Virgil Cowper," I speculated.

"The same," Wild acknowledged. "And thus, with all these pieces in place, we had business upon our hands."

"But you later wished to be out of that business," I said. "You told Quilt Arnold to keep a watchful eye for South Sea men. You knew enough of their determination to fear them, yes?"

He nodded. "It took some time, but I came to realize the dangers this operation presented to me, for it left me at another man's mercy, a state I was unused to. When I finally understood what the South Sea Company was, I realized it was a dangerous thing to have such an enemy. When I had first entered into the venture, I presumed the directors to be but a bloated collection of lazy gentlemen, but I soon saw that I should be much better off with the Company caring nothing for me, for if they chose to destroy me I had little confidence that I could equal their power. And so I had to find a way to release myself of the connection."

"Yet," I surmised, "Sir Owen knew at this point too much of your operations, and should you turn on him, you need fear his vengeance."

"Precisely." Wild fairly glowed with the pleasure of his own cleverness. "I needed to find a way to remove him without his suspecting my involvement. It was about the time that Sir Owen and I went our separate ways that he learned that your father and Mr. Balfour had discovered the truth about the false stocks. As near as I can determine, Mr. Balfour discovered the false stocks in his possession, and he approached your father for assistance. When Sir Owen learned that your father wished to make this information public, he lashed out venomously—far too venomously for my taste, for in my business, sir, discretion is all. I knew him to have organized the murder of your father, Balfour, and the bookseller. I knew also that Sir Owen kept about his person a document written by your father detailing evidence of this forgery. I cannot say why he kept these letters—perhaps he thought they would give him leverage with the Company should he ever need it. At any rate, I directed Kate Cole to steal this document from him, knowing it would be easy, for his taste in whores was legendary. And then I planted some rumors that would make him believe that I might be behind the theft—*might be*, you understand. I simultaneously planted rumors that I was in no way involved. I could not have him know me to be his enemy. I merely circulated information to make him not quite comfortable trusting me—but not so uncomfortable that he should risk acting against me. Now, Mr. Weaver, should a man have something lost he wished recovered in this city, and he be unable to trust Jonathan Wild to recover it for him, to whom would he turn? It seemed he would have but one choice."

"Good Lord," I sputtered, "the letters he had me recover of Kate Cole were my father's papers?"

"Indeed. He also carried about with him some sentimental letters of his dead wife, but they were far less important to me. Now, with his incriminating document stolen, I forced him into a position where he would need to hire his victim's son to recover the very proof of the crime. I had no reason to believe he knew that you were Samuel Lienzo's son, so he could have no cause for alarm there, and I could not but suspect that in order to obtain your goods you would read what you recovered—but that was not to be the case."

I still did not understand why Wild had made it so difficult for me to learn of Sir Owen's true identity and his responsibility for my father's death. "Why did you not have your people unseal the packet?" I asked. "Why did you make the recovery so devilish complicated?"

"It was necessary that they did not know they acted a part in this matter, for I could hardly bring those villains into my confidence. I could never trust my own prigs not to 'peach me out to Sir Owen should they find themselves in a difficult position. Thus you had some problems retrieving the document. The death of Jemmy was an unfortunate detail, but what can one do? In any event, because I had to confront the possibility you would be so damnably scrupled in your service to Sir Owen, I took a second precaution—I asked that fool Balfour, in exchange for a ridiculously large consideration of fifty pounds, to involve you in this matter. You perhaps wondered why he lost all interest in finding his father's slayer, but it was only because he cared not a fig for his father or his death to begin with. And so, fired by Balfour's insistence that your father's death involved some hideous plan, you at last took the bait. I tried to lead you in the right direction, which was hard indeed, but now you see why I was forced to treat you roughly in so public a forum, for I had to make Sir Owen believe that I sought to dissuade you, not encourage you, and I had to indemnify myself against the possibility that you would someday be forced to recount your steps. I knew you could not but have discovered the connection with the South Sea Company, so there was no danger in my mentioning it to you."

The stratagems that had so long eluded me were now made clear. "It is for the same reason, then," I speculated, "that Sir Owen conducted his business with me in St. James's Park—in order to make a public showing of our dealings. He wished for word to reach you that he had formed some kind of agreement with your principal rival—in the hopes, I suppose, of making you see that he was not to be trifled with."

Wild nodded. "Both Sir Owen and I were compelled to draw you in for more or less the same reasons. Naturally, he made more mistakes than I did, and as you grew too close, he was forced to attempt to remove you from his path."

"And when you learned from Mr. Mendes that I grew despondent, you sent a false Sarah Decker to put me on Sir Owen's trail."

"And how do you know I did such a thing?"

"Who but Jonathan Wild has at the ready a stable of actress whores?"

"Who indeed?" He laughed.

I was silent for some time after this narrative. "It is astonishing," I said at last. "But you have certainly emerged victorious."

"Of course," he added, "there was another possibility, and that was that in your inquiry you would be destroyed by Sir Owen, and while I would not have lost my current enemy, I should have eliminated a future one."

"I wonder if it was you who had Sir Owen killed," I said. "Perhaps you set him up to appear the mastermind behind the forgeries and then had him killed so he could not deny it."

"Surely you have seen too much to believe that I alone could orchestrate that particular villainy. Sir Owen's death looks to me like the style of these companies, who strike boldly yet secretively. Hardly my way at all. I prefer quietly and secretly."

"As you have tried to deal with me," I noted.

"Precisely. You see, Mr. Weaver, to my mind I owe you nothing. And when I said that I believed we could coexist, I was saying that only to lay down your guard. I do not believe we can coexist, and we must come to blows sooner or later. I should like to add one thing, however, because I sense you are overly nice in your notions of justice. The three men of Sir Owen's employ—the ones who killed Michael Balfour—are even as we speak awaiting trial at Newgate. Not for murder, but for other hanging offenses such as I could muster. These men are a danger to our city, I think you'll agree, and while I profit from their destruction, all of London profits as well."

He paused to chuckle lightly. "In the end, I suppose, the South Sea Company and I did work together—if not intentionally so. But we shared the same goals, and each, in our own way, strove for the same ends. I arranged for the exposure of Sir Owen, with you as my instrument. They, in turn, arranged for his destruction. Indeed, I to some degree depended upon their desire to remove him, for neither I nor the Company could risk his revealing the things he knew."

Wild stroked his chin thoughtfully. "Yet I may give the Company too much credit when I say we worked toward the same goal, for I believe I did lead them along rather effectively. Indeed, I manipulated the Company no less skillfully than I manipulated you."

I knew what he said to be true, but I realized that I had, against all evidence, wanted to believe that Wild had done it—to believe that I had misunderstood Adelman's winks and nods. Wild was powerful, but he was only one man, and he could be destroyed in a moment. The South Sea Company was an abstraction—it could kill, but it could not be killed. In its rapacious desire to circulate paper wealth, it was all that Elias had said: merciless, murderous, invisible, and as ubiquitous as banknotes themselves.

I found I did not like to think on this abstract villain, and I had need to concentrate on the flesh-and-blood villain before me. "I think," I said after a moment's reflection, "I shall rejoice upon your hanging day."

I could see that I had shocked Wild. Perhaps he had grown to believe he could predict my every act, my every word. "You are bold, sir. I should think you would have learned not to think so lightly of me. You believe you can somehow outmatch me, Weaver? You are but one man," he said, "and my forces are legion."

"It is true," I said as I left the room, "but they hate you, and they will be your undoing."

THIRTY-SIX

I BEGAN THIS NARRATIVE with the intent of recounting the adventures of my life, but so many pages later I have only told a single story. Perhaps, as Elias would have said, from these particulars some generalities may be drawn.

Some three weeks after that meeting with Wild, I read in the newspapers that the body of Virgil Cowper had been found washed up on the riverbanks, and the coroner had ruled that he had fallen in the waters while drunk. I asked some questions, but everyone believed that his death had been a mishap of indulgence, and so I concluded that the paper conspirators had taken one more life for which they would never answer.

For my own part, my condition as a guest at Broad Court had grown uncomfortable. Adelman had ceased to visit in the capacity of Miriam's suitor, but business brought him by the house not infrequently, and I could hardly meet the eye of this man I knew so deep within a conspiracy that had so nearly destroyed me. My uncle cared little what Adelman or the South Sea Company had done, only that they had in the end acted against my father's murderer. Perhaps I judged too harshly those who would take the life of such a villain. Whatever the circumstances of his death, Sir Owen had murdered four people that I knew of, including my own father. No, my displeasure was not with the South Sea Company's rough justice. It was something else. It was the coldness of their justice. It mattered not to them that Sir Owen was a villain, only that he endangered their business. Their actions were not about the lives Sir Owen had taken, but about the profits he would threaten. What are the probable returns on this death? What interest will ending a man's life yield? It was a kind of bloody speculation; it was stock-jobbery by murder.

EVERY YEAR IN LATE October Elias and I would find our way to an appropriate tavern to celebrate the anniversary of the death of Sir Owen—Martin Rochester Day, we called it. It was our private holiday, and one that would often prove to be as grim as it was drunken. We recollected our adventures as best we could, and often I wrote much of what we said down for fear I should someday forget. These sloppy scribblings served as the first notes to the memoir I have now all but completed.

By the time of our first anniversary, Elias had cast aside his dreams of the theatre, but his pen would not lie still. He wrote volumes of wretched verse, and much later in his life he wrote some well-received novels and a memoir under an assumed name. For her part, Miriam had by then moved into splendid lodgings near Leicester Fields, where she watched her Company stock yield profits. Unlike the rest of us, she sold when the stock had almost reached its pinnacle, and for a time she had all the independence she could have desired. Alas that such things cannot last, and Miriam saw her long-sought-after freedom crushed by an ill-advised marriage that I have neither the space nor the heart to detail here.

Adelman and Bloathwait both survived the upheavals of the South Sea year and continued with their schemes and rivalries for as long as they lived. Of Jonathan Wild, I hardly need mention the inauspicious conclusion of his life, but before he met justice at the end of a Tyburn rope he lived long enough to cause me far more troubles than he did in this little history. I take some comfort at the thought that the troubles I finally caused him were far more permanent and allowed no opportunity for revenge.

As for me, I find that my many exploits are too varied to recount in this volume. I can only say that my inquiry into the forged South Sea stock changed forever the way I would think of and conduct my business.

At my uncle's urgings, I took my new lodgings in Dukes Place, just off Crosby Street. Elias complained that he should risk his foreskin every time he came to pay me a visit, but to the best of my knowledge, he died with it still attached. I continued to live in that neighborhood until this day, and while I never feel that I entirely belong, I suppose I feel less out of place here than any other neighborhood of the metropolis.

It was at an alehouse near my new home that Elias and I always met to remember Martin Rochester's villainy. I often recall that first anniversary because in the autumn of 1720 the disaster of the South Sea Bubble, as it came to be known, was foremost in our and everyone's thoughts, and it seemed as though Elias's rants on the dangers of the new finance turned out to be nothing short of prophecy.

The South Sea scheme had been approved by Parliament shortly after the events of this history, and holders of funded government issues flocked to exchange their certain investments for the vague promise of Company dividends. As each investor converted his holdings, the South Sea stock rose—indeed it rose more than anyone could have imagined, until my five hundred pounds of stock was worth more than five thousand. Throughout the Kingdom, men who had held but small investments were now as rich as lords. It was an era of opulence and excess and wealth—an era in which men who had been middling shopkeepers or modest tradesmen suddenly found themselves transported to their massive town houses in gold equipages drawn by six stout beasts. We ate venison and drank fine old claret and danced to the most expensive Italian musicians we could import.

Then, in the summer of 1720, London awoke and said, "For what reason is this stock worth so much?" and as though a spell had been cast, those who had made money sought to solidify their holdings, to turn their promises into reality; that is to say, they flocked to sell, and when they sold, the stock plummeted. My five hundred pounds of stock was once more worth five hundred pounds, and men who had unimaginable wealth one day were merely comfortable the next. Countless investors who had bought in after the stock had already risen were utterly ruined.

The nation cried out for justice, for revenge, for the heads of the South Sea directors to be set upon stakes along the London road, but what the nation had not yet learned, what it would never learn, was that the spirit of stock-jobbing, once conjured up by the wizards in 'Change Alley, could never again be banished to perdition. As for justice and revenge, those lofty principles for which the South Sea victims clamored—these too are but commodities to be bought and sold upon the 'Change.

HISTORICAL NOTE

THE SOUTH SEA BUBBLE of 1720 was a real event, best remembered as the first stock-market crash in the English-speaking world, but it was also the culmination of years of confusion and abuses within the London financial markets. For Great Britain in the early eighteenth century, stocktrading, government issues, and lotteries were all relatively new, and the uncertainty that comes with newness created an exciting culture within Exchange Alley. Certain thinkers—some as well-known as Daniel Defoe, others anonymous or forgotten—cast the financial markets as either foreboding or wondrous, promising either bounty or doom. This volatile atmosphere yielded a massive body of writings about the new financial order, which has lately generated an intense scholarly interest in the South Sea scheme, the crash, and eighteenth-century British finances in general. Within the past five years, historians, literary critics, and sociologists have shown a markedly increased interest in the fiscal volatility of this period, and this interest suggests something about the economic uncertainty of our own era.

This novel grew out of my work as a doctoral candidate at Columbia University, where my research focused on the ways in which eighteenth-century Britons imagined themselves through their money. After years in the archives, reading pamphlets, poems, plays, periodical essays, and long-forgotten novels, I failed to find the source that told me precisely what I wanted to know about the new finance. So I wrote one. My goal in this novel has been to capture both the unbridled enthusiasm and the pervasive anxiety of the period leading up to the South Sea Bubble.

Most of the characters in this novel are purely fictional, though they are frequently composites of figures who appeared in eighteenth-century writings and in the historical record. No such person as Benjamin Weaver ever lived, but I found inspiration for his character in the story of Daniel Mendoza (1764–1836), who credited himself with inventing what he termed the "scientific method of boxing" and who later became a professional debt-collector. Jonathan Wild and his henchmen Mendes and Arnold, however, were indeed real people, but I have taken numerous liberties with their characters. From the mid-1710s until his execution in 1725, Wild controlled much of the criminal activity around London, and he is generally acknowledged as the first modern crime lord. Until the early part of this century, Jonathan Wild was a household name on both sides of the Atlantic, but the twentieth century has lately produced enough of its own colorful criminals who are well able to take the great thief-taker's place in our cultural imagination.

I have, in the language of this novel, tried to suggest the rhythms of eighteenth-century prose, although I have made many modifications in the interest of readability. My intention was to invoke the feel of contemporaneous speech without burdening readers with idiosyncrasies that often seem inhospitable or circuitous by today's standards.

Finally, I would like to address the matter of money. British money in the eighteenth century broke down this way: twelve pence equaled a shilling, five shillings a crown, twenty shillings a pound, and twenty-one shillings a guinea. Early readers of this novel have often asked what those denominations are worth in today's currency. Unfortunately, there is no direct mathematical formula that would accurately convey value, because the uses of money varied so dramatically within the different social classes. A poor laborer in London might earn twenty pounds a year, with which he would feed his family bread, beer, and occasionally meat, buy inexpensive clothing and cheap lodgings. A fashionable gentleman might spend twice that amount on an evening's entertainment without risk of being called extravagant. Benjamin Weaver talks of earning one hundred to one hundred fifty pounds in a year, which constitutes a solid middle-class income, particularly for a man living alone. For someone who wished to wear fashionable clothing, entertain guests in high style, keep numerous servants, and drive a handsome equipage, five hundred pounds a year could prove a tight squeeze. Money's value, of course, is most visibly constituted by what it can buy, and in eighteenth-century London, what money bought depended on the social position of the spender.

ACKNOWLEDGMENTS

THE ADVICE OF numerous readers enriched and sharpened this novel, and I would like to thank Paul Budnitz, Mary Pat Dunleavey, Matthew Grimm, Sue Laizik, Michael Seidel, Al Silverman, Brian Stokes, and Chloe Wheatley for their fine criticism and attention. I would like to acknowledge in particular Laurie Gwen Shapiro for her advice, encouragement, and generosity of spirit; she has nurtured this project as if it were her own, and without her help this book might never have happened. I would like to thank Joseph Citarella, who provided me with an extraordinary wealth of information on eighteenth-century clothing. I am also indebted to Kelly Washburn and the Partnership for Jewish Life for their avowed support of Jewish fiction.

I owe a considerable debt to the Georgia State University Department of English, which not only introduced me to the field of eighteenth-century studies but also encouraged my work with sincere and bountiful enthusiasm. More recently, I thank the Department of English and Comparative Literature of Columbia University for many years of support, both financial and scholarly.

I cannot sufficiently acknowledge Liz Darhansoff and, indeed, everyone at the Darhansoff and Verrill agency, who believed in this project from Day One and labored long and hard on its behalf. My editor, Jon Karp, has wonderfully steered and fostered this novel, and I am grateful to him for his keen insight, good humor, and strong encouragement. I'd also like to thank Ann Godoff, Jean-Isabel McNutt, and Andy Carpenter of Random House.

Finally, for reasons that cannot, and need not, be enumerated here, I thank my wife, Claudia Stokes; my much-loved friend Godot Liss; and my family.

A Conspiracy
of Paper

DAVID LISS

A Reader's Guide

A Conversation with David Liss

New York novelists David Liss and Sheri Holman met at a literary roundtable break-fast in Toronto while both were out on lengthy book tours. Sick of room service and eating dinner alone too often, they went out that evening—staying up far too late, over far too many bottles of wine, a great friendship was born. Among the many common bonds Holman and Liss share are a love of baseball, spouses in academia, and gourmet cooking. Ballantine Reader's Circle thought it might be fun to have these two friends interview each other about their mutual passion for history and how they put it to work in their novels.

Sheri Holman *is the author of* A Stolen Tongue, *translated into eleven languages worldwide, and* The Dress Lodger, *nominated for an IMPAC Dublin Literary Award. She is currently at work on her third novel,* The Mammoth Cheese. *You can read David Liss's interview of Sheri Holman in the back of the BRC edition of* The Dress Lodger, *due out in Spring 2001.*

SH: I know you wrote *Conspiracy of Paper* while pursuing your doctorate at Columbia. How did the novel grow out of your studies, and how difficult was it to make the switch from academic writing to fiction writing? Would you like to share with your readers your first title for this book?

DL: I originally enrolled in graduate school because I figured that I couldn't make a living writing fiction, and writing about and teaching fiction seemed like the next best thing. I often found myself looking at my research in light of my interest in fiction, however; when I'd come across an interesting event or figure from the historical record, I would often think, Hey, that would be great in a novel. When I decided to try my hand at fiction again, it seemed natural to take the material I'd been researching for my dissertation and attempt to turn that into a narrative of some kind.

In a way, I found it very easy to switch from academic writing to novelistic writing. Writing a novel offered me the freedom to work outside the bounds of what I could actually prove. I loved writing dialogue and constructing characters. In fact, what I found difficult was returning to academic writing once I had begun working on the novel.

Originally, I thought I would be able to switch back and forth between the two projects fairly easily, but that turned out not to be the case. I had no problem getting into a fiction-writing frame of mind, but it took a lot more work for me to get to where I could write academic prose constructively. As a result, I segregated my time so that I worked on the dissertation during the semesters and the novel during breaks.

As for the original title, I originally wanted to call the novel *The Villainy of Stock-Jobbers Detected*, a name I swiped from a hyperbolic pamphlet by Daniel Defoe. I thought it was wonderful and absolutely evocative of the period, but whenever I mentioned it to anyone I would get pretty unfavorable responses—usually mock gagging.

SH: **Can you tell us a little bit about Daniel Mendoza, the Jewish boxer upon whom Weaver is based? How were they alike? What did you change for dramatic purposes?**

DL: I came across Mendoza's memoirs—sadly, now out of print—while doing research on my dissertation, and he turned out to be a great example of someone I thought would be perfect in a novel. He fought toward the end of the eighteenth century, and his career was remarkable for a number of reasons, among which is that he was probably the first national Jewish sports hero. Everyone, from the King on down, knew his name and followed his exploits. And in perfect eighteenth-century fashion, he took something that had been somewhat chaotically arranged—the sport of boxing—and turned it into an organized and structured system. He invented what he called the "scientific method of boxing," in which he worked out a theory of moves and punches and so forth. But unlike athletes today, he did not make much money, despite his success, and when he retired he hired himself out as a debt collector and all-around tough guy.

When I started working on *Conspiracy*, I loved the idea of doing something with Mendoza, but I wanted to set the novel at the beginning of the century, just prior to the South Sea Bubble. So I took a number of elements from Mendoza's biography and altered them—changed the way he would have boxed and thought about boxing, the kinds of opportunities available to Jews at the time, and so forth.

Weaver is certainly not Mendoza simply placed in another time, but he is inspired by Mendoza in many ways.

SH: You've portrayed the insular Jewish world as overbearingly patriarchal. How true to history is Miriam? Would she have been able to control her own money, or would she have stayed a prisoner in her father-in-law's house? What exactly was the role of women inside places like Broad Court?

DL: If anything, I've exaggerated Miriam's freedom, not her lack of freedom. Miriam comes from a Jewish family of Portuguese origin, and the combination of Jewish patriarchy and Iberian patriarchy produced a culture in which women were horribly oppressed. In truth, it would have been very difficult for her to strike out on her own, even if she had money, and only an exceptional woman would have been able to conceive of doing so. In her culture, the far more expedient thing to do would be to find a husband and run his house for him. Her role would have consisted of little more than making certain that the house was maintained according to Jewish ritualistic standards and supervising the servants.

Of course, this kind of oppression existed in British Christian culture as well, though perhaps not quite in so pronounced a way, and in this period many women began articulating their displeasure with oppressive patriarchy and lashing out against it. Women ran salons and placed themselves at the center of social circles, and British Jewish culture, at least in many cases, was not isolated enough to be uninfluenced by these movements.

SH: Elias gives Weaver a wonderful lesson on the nature of new finance using the metaphor of the clipped shilling. He then goes on to say, "These financial institutions are committed to divesting our money of value and replacing it with promises of value. For when they control the promise of value, they control all wealth itself." What parallels do you see between that philosophy of finance and today's Internet frenzy? Did you write with the present always in mind?

DL: Today, as in 1719, we live in a world in which the representation of money is undergoing a major change. In the early eighteenth century, gold, which many imagined to have real, intrinsic value, began to be replaced with paper money, which is much more abstract in nature. Today our paper money, which we casually imagine as actually having value, is being replaced by abstract electronic money, and the same concerns appear: How do we know the banks who own the computers are being honest? How do we know these abstract ideas about money are not being manipulated by the powerful for their own benefit? I certainly had these concerns in mind when I began working on *Conspiracy*, and I was also interested in the stock market.

In recent years, a number of scholars have begun writing about the eighteenth-century financial markets, and the fact that so many people are suddenly drawn to this topic suggests that something in our own cultures makes it relevant. However, in the time between the sale and the publication of the novel the stock market heated up considerably, and in that sense I guess I should say that I just happened to invest wisely in the right topic.

SH: **The time you write of, just before the South Sea Bubble, was a very heady time for the emerging British middle class. Can you tell us a little about what happened after the crash? Did things go back to normal? What opportunities did the new finance make possible?**

DL: The crash of the South Sea stock produced an intense and immediate response. There were parliamentary inquiries, unruly crowds, calls for blood in the newspapers—but in the end, not much came of it. Parliament passed something called the Bubble Act, which prohibited companies from issuing stock unless they were sponsored by the government, but that was about the extent of the official response. None of the South Sea directors suffered in any serious way. Actually, the government considered the South Sea scheme a success—its goal had been all along to get holders of high-interest bonds to trade in their holdings for South Sea stocks. Most of these investors did so and thereby helped to reduce the national debt. The fact that many investors were ruined seemed beside the point. Ultimately, the Bubble did not change that much, because, despite the ruin it caused, it did not change the essential fact that anyone with money had to invest in the government or in corporate funds, since not earning interest on money is pretty much the same thing as losing money. For the rest of the century, Britons continued to have a very uneasy relationship with the concept of investment.

The thing I find most surprising is that the South Sea Bubble does not remain a rallying cry for very long. There are very few references to it in any kind of literature after about 1730, only ten years after the collapse. However, a strong suspicion of the stock market and investment remains firmly in place for the rest of the century. Many novels present stock trading and Exchange Alley in the most critical terms, but they do so without mentioning the Bubble. Nevertheless, it has long been my theory that the Bubble shaped the British novel, which emerged in its modern form around 1740 (this is an arguable point, but I'm sticking to it). These mid-century novels are preoccupied with the sudden loss or the sudden appearance of wealth because the novelists came of age during the period of the Bubble and its aftermath.

SH: **The Jewish community in *Conspiracy of Paper* is isolated within British society, yet at the same time, its members marginalize the Eastern Europeans among them. What was the hierarchy inside this closed community, and what were you trying to say about intolerance by introducing the old Tudesco Jew? What were you trying to say about Weaver's ambivalence?**

DL: I found it fascinating to write about Jewish characters in this period because the kinds of sweeping intellectual changes brought on by the Enlightenment allowed for Jews to think about themselves in entirely new ways. For the first time, someone like Weaver could imagine his Jewishness as linked to an ethnic identity rather than a system of belief or practice. To do so, however, means that he has to make a number of decisions about his Jewish identity, and that is a very modern way of thinking about religion.

The division between the Iberians and the Tudescos—or the Sephardim and Ashkenazim, as we would say today—is a long-standing one. The two traditions are in many ways very different, and in this period the differences were only becoming more pronounced with the rise of the ecstatic movements among Eastern European Jews. Wherever these two populations lived together, there always seemed to be a certain amount of suspicion and hostility, which, sadly, is just human nature.

SH: **London as you portray it was a pretty lawless town. Before the advent of a police force in the nineteenth century, was there anything in place to check the excesses of men like the historic Jonathan Wild? Did his influence really stretch into areas such as high finance? How does Weaver prefigure later detectives?**

DL: In eighteenth-century propaganda, Britons embraced nothing as strongly as they did the somewhat vague notion of liberty, and anything that threatened liberty was intolerable. The British associated a police force with the absolute rule of the oppressive French government—the idea that a policeman could approach a gentleman and arrest him struck many people as an outrageous infringement upon the gentleman's liberty.

Naturally, this kind of environment bred wonderful opportunities for a schemer like Jonathan Wild, who took advantage of both the society's lawlessness and the fundamental desire for some kind of check on that lawlessness. Wild had his fingers in a number of pies, though we don't know as much about his operations as we would like to. He owned smuggling ships, he had spies in major port cities, and he certainly took advantage of the buying frenzy of the South Sea period, though there is no record, which I am aware of, that he actually traded in financial instruments.

I always take great pleasure from the fact that the father of the London police force is the novelist Henry Fielding, who, in addition to famous works like *Tom Jones* and *Joseph Andrews*, also wrote a highly fictionalized account of the life of Wild. While not writing novels, Fielding served as a London magistrate, and he organized a group of men called the Bow Street Runners who would attempt to apprehend criminals and bring them to Fielding's court for processing—and these men are generally acknowledged as London's first protopolicemen.

One of the real challenges for me was to create an early-eighteenth-century detective who thought in early-eighteenth-century ways. The kind of inductive reasoning that we associate with modern detective work, such as the use of clues to draw conclusions, just began to take shape in this time, and, as I try to demonstrate in the novel, this kind of thinking emerges as a result of speculative finance. One kind of speculation leads to another. Weaver could not have instinctively known how to use clues like a modern detective would—he had to use financial theory to figure out how to do so. I enjoyed writing those portions of the novel in which Weaver puzzles out new methods of detection.

SH: **This novel is very suspenseful, but it's also very, very funny. How much did you draw on eighteenth-century novels? How did you tackle the problem of archaic dialogue?**

DL: I had been reading eighteenth-century novels for such a long time that in some ways it was a relief to be able to write in that idiom without looking foolish. You can't really go around in public saying, for example, that you don't care a fig for something, and expect people to treat you like you're not really, really weird. Nevertheless, the language remained a tricky issue. I didn't show anyone any portion of this novel until it was almost finished, and more than anything else I was concerned about the period tone not working.

I tried to strike a balance between a real eighteenth-century prose style and something that would be fun for contemporary readers. I started writing the book in a third person voice, but I found it almost impossible. I then came up with the idea of using Weaver as a narrator, which meant reworking the novel in fairly serious ways, since I had imagined various scenes in which the reader would know more or less than Weaver would, but in the end I found the setback worthwhile. Once I started writing in Weaver's voice, the work went much more easily. It also allowed me to indulge in more humor than I would have thought appropriate.

When I first started writing I had the very silly idea that historical fiction must be serious, and that means that there can be no humor. However, I instinctively gravitate toward characters who want to say funny things, so having a protagonist with a sense of humor turned out to be a good way to solve the problem.

SH: **Conspiracy is obviously a major theme in this book. How much of the intrigue surrounding the South Sea Bubble is based on fact, and how much of it did you create for the novel?**

DL: Almost nothing that happens in the novel actually happened in real life. From the beginning, I wanted to stay away from dramatizing a real historical event because I felt uncomfortable with the kinds of limitations those projects present. I wanted to be able to make plot decisions based on my desire to tell a story rather than on what actually happened, and I didn't want to have to worry about misrepresenting people who really lived. Instead, I chose to take my interest in the origins of the stock market, and the kind of frenzy and paranoia associated with this time, and tell a story that would articulate the mood of early eighteenth-century London.

The conspiracy—the idea that there is something going on that others know about but you don't—is a very modern kind of concern because it assumes that you, the individual person, have a right to know what people in power are doing. This attitude emerges with the rise of literacy and print culture and newspapers, and a place like the British Isles in the eighteenth century with its coffeehouses and other forums for public discussion was ripe to start worrying about conspiracies. Most of the documents written against the South Sea Company, Exchange Alley, and Stock-Jobbers, use conspiratorial language: These bad men are up to something, they're keeping secrets from us so they can take advantage of our ignorance. In the end, I was more interested in capturing that concern than I was in documenting real activity on the Exchange.

SH: **You've said in interviews that you've become more observant in your faith as you've gotten older. Did working on this novel help that along, and if so, what did Weaver's journey teach you about your inner-life?**

DL: I think I found writing about Weaver useful because it helped me to articulate for myself the problems of being Jewish in a secular environment and the difficulties in having to make decisions about how to observe or not observe. I grew up in a very secular household, and only as an adult did I begin to rethink the decisions that my parents had made about Judaism. In many ways, selling the book helped to facilitate this process for me.

Doctoral candidates face pretty intense demands on their time, and the truth is that whenever I read a book that did not advance my research, I felt horribly guilty (this attitude represented a definite improvement over the period in which I would resent showering because it took me away from my research). I often felt that if I had more free time, I would want to pursue more vigorous Jewish studies.

After I sold the novel, I almost immediately enrolled in a class to learn Biblical Hebrew, which has turned out to be one of the most intellectually rewarding projects I've ever engaged in. I think I am at a point in my life where I want to make careful and thoughtful decisions about how I choose to pursue religious practice; the fact that I was not raised to keep kosher or put on tefilin, for example, no longer seems like a sufficiently good reason to not do those things.

SH: **I think you've created a brand-new genre of fiction: the historical financial thriller. What interests you about the history of finance? Are you planning on continuing Weaver's story in any fashion?**

DL: I first became interested in finance in eighteenth-century literature because so many characters in these stories (like the people who wrote them) are obsessed with their own debts—and as a graduate student faced with frightening credit card bills each month, I found myself drawn to these narratives. To understand the social function of debt in literature, I wanted to link private debt to concerns about public debt, and so I began to learn about finance.

When I decided I wanted to try writing a novel, I thought it natural to take the material I already knew and create a story around it, but it also seemed to me that finance can be the stuff of exciting fiction. Major changes in the way in which people imagine money or do business present opportunities for shifty minds—our own period has demonstrated that repeatedly.

The novel I am working on now is set in the seventeenth century and concerns a plot to corner the market on a newly emerging commodity, and, again, the novelty of the idea—that an individual trader can create a monopoly for himself—makes for lots of exciting possibilities. The protagonist of this novel, by the way, is Weaver's grandfather, but he is a very different sort of person than Weaver. After I finish this book, I think I will most likely write another novel with Weaver at the center, though I will want to do something that is very different, and it will almost certainly not be a story concerning finance.

Reading Questions and Topics for Discussion

1. Do you think Weaver should have constantly bailed Miriam out of trouble? What do think about him not getting the girl in the end? Did you want to see them together or was the book's ending more believable?

2. Did this novel make you change your sentiments about the current stock market? Did it make you want to become more cautious in your own investments? Did you read it as a cautionary tale?

3. For many centuries orthodox Jewish communities have lived inside European societies but also outside of them. In what ways did Lienzo's fear harm his son? In what ways did it protect him? Do you think the Jews of eighteenth-century London did themselves a service or disservice by closing themselves off?

4. The "gentlemen" at Sir Owen's club put Weaver in the uncomfortable position of having to speak for his entire culture. Have you ever been in a situation where you were the only minority (religious, racial, economic, etc.)? How did it feel to have a group looking at you as the spokesperson for your community? Have you ever done it to someone else?

5. Instead of praising his son, Benjamin, for defending the elderly Mrs. Cantas from anti-Semites, Lienzo strikes him? What did you think of Lienzo's behavior? What would it be like to live in constant fear of drawing attention to your community? Can you think of any modern parallels?

6. Who do you think was more honorable in his ways of doing business: the criminal Jonathan Wild, or Nathan Adelman? Why?

7. Near the end of the book, Adelman says to Weaver about the murder of Sir Owen, "You need only to believe, Mr. Weaver." And Benjamin answers, "Like the new finance . . . it is true only so long as we believe it is true." What do you think the author is trying to say about the future of the stock market by letting Weaver believe someone he knows is unreliable?

8. Have you ever been caught up in a mania like the South Sea Bubble? What did it teach you about fads? Would you allow it to happen again?

9. As a child, Benjamin idolized boxers for their ability to fight. Compare his physicality to his relatives' intellectual and financial pursuits. Do you think Weaver's attraction to boxing was a response to the precariousness of his community?

10. At the end of the book the powerful Adelman comes out on top. Yet he is a member of a disempowered group. Do the many conspiracies in this book ultimately benefit the disenfranchised, or the powerful?

11. Discuss the title *A Conspiracy of Paper*. Do you think the author used the word "paper" to evoke written histories and novels as well as money? Do you believe that history is written by those who come out on top? How to you think "paper" will fare in our increasingly electronic age?

About the Author

DAVID LISS was born in 1966 and grew up in South Florida. He is currently a doctoral candidate in the Department of English at Columbia University, where he is completing a dissertation on the intersection of the mid-eighteenth-century British novel with the contemporaneous emergence of the modern idea of personal finance. He has given numerous conference papers on his research and has also published on Henry James. He has received several awards for his work, including the Columbia University President's Fellowship, an A.W. Mellon Research Fellowship, and the Whiting Foundation Dissertation Fellowship. He also holds a Master of Arts from Georgia State University and a Bachelor of Science from Syracuse University. He lives in New York City and can be reached via E-mail at www.davidliss.com